All Chang

Also by Jean Fullerton

No Cure for Love
A Glimpse at Happiness
Perhaps Tomorrow
Hold on to Hope

Call Nurse Millie
Christmas with Nurse Millie (ebook exclusive)

All Change for Nurse Millie

JEAN FULLERTON

First published in Great Britain in 2014 by Orion Books,
an imprint of The Orion Publishing Group Ltd
Orion House, 5 Upper Saint Martin's Lane
London WC2H 9EA

An Hachette UK Company

A CIP catalogue record for this book is available from the British Library.

Typeset by Input Data Services Ltd, Bridgwater, Somerset

Printed and bound by CPI Group (UK) Ltd,
Croydon CR0 4YY

The Orion Publishing Group's policy is to use papers that are natural, renewable and recyclable products and made from wood grown in sustainable forests. The logging and manufacturing processes are expected to conform to the environmental regulations of the country of origin.

www.orionbooks.co.uk

To the men of the family.
My husband and soul-mate Kelvin,
without whose support
none of this would be possible,
and my tremendous sons-in-law
Paul, Andy and Damian.

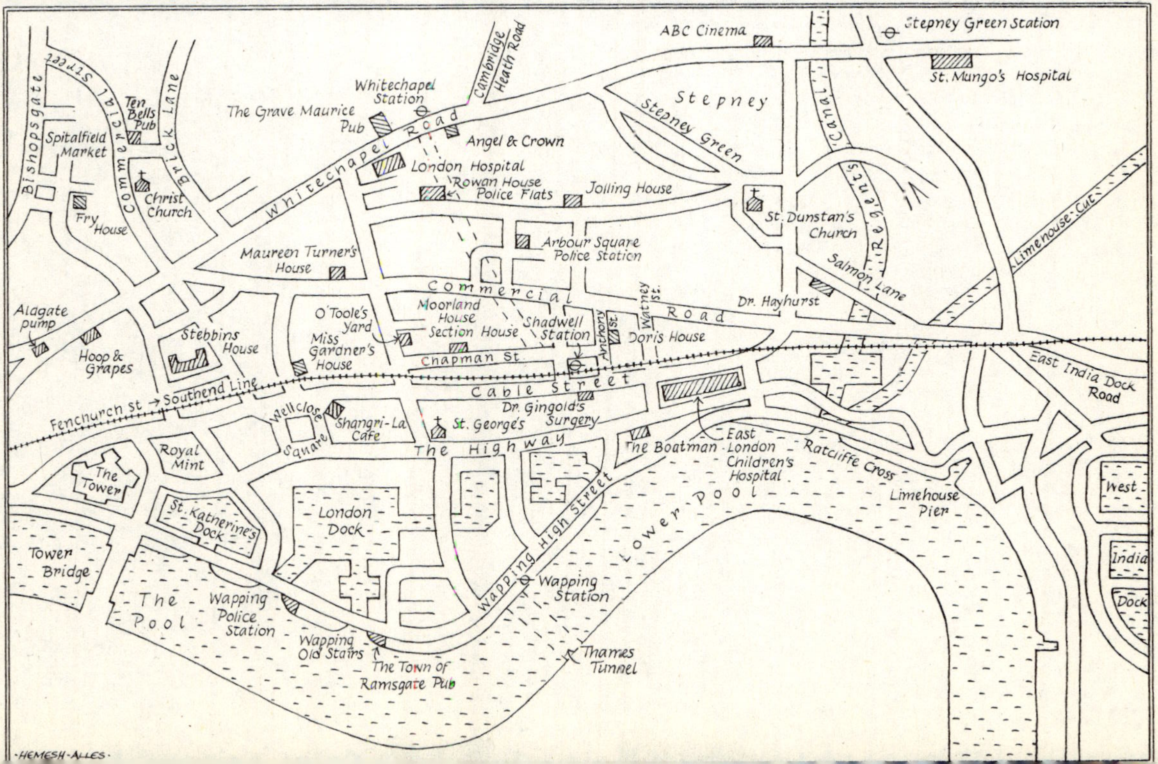
Stepney Green Station
ABC Cinema
St. Mungo's Hospital
Stepney
Stepney Green
Canal
Regent's
Limehouse Cut
Whitechapel Station
Cambridge Heath Road
The Grave Maurice Pub
Whitechapel Road
Angel & Crown
London Hospital
Rowan House Police Flats
Jolling House
St. Dunstan's Church
Salmon Lane
Bishopsgate
Commercial Street
Ten Bells Pub
Brick Lane
Spitalfield Market
Christ Church
Fry House
Maureen Turner's House
Arbour Square Police Station
Commercial Road
Dr. Hayhurst
Alagate pump
Hoop & Grapes
Stebbins House
O'Toole's Yard
Miss Gardner's House
Moorland House
Section House
Shadwell Station
Anthony St.
Watney St.
Doris House
Chapman St.
Cable Street
East India Dock Road
Fenchurch St → Southend Line
Wellclose Square
Shangri-La Cafe
St. George's
Dr. Gingold's Surgery
The Highway
The Boatman
East London Children's Hospital
Ratcliffe Cross
Royal Mint
The Tower
St. Katherine's Dock
London Dock
Wapping High Street
Lower Pool
Limehouse Pier
West
India
Dock
Tower Bridge
The Pool
Wapping Police Station
Wapping Old Stairs
The Town of Ramsgate Pub
Wapping Station
Thames Tunnel
HEMESH-ALLES

Chapter One

Millie Smith, senior sister and midwife at Munroe House, Stepney, picked up her leather nursing bag and set it on the floor under the kitchen table beside her lunchbox. She grasped the hairbrush from the window sill and was just about to drag it through her auburn hair when she sniffed the faint smell of burning.

'Blast,' she muttered under her breath.

Abandoning the never-ending task of keeping her bouncy curls in order, Millie dashed across the kitchen and dragged the grill pan out just as the two slices of bread started to singe. Although Jim, her husband, had insisted that it was the latest thing in home appliances, Millie found her new cooker somewhat fierce after her mother's old enamel stove.

Using her fingertips, she flipped the toast on to the breadboard beside her and then cut the two slices into triangles and set them in the toast rack. She glanced at the clock: six-forty. She'd have to leave by ten-past if she was to avoid the traffic jam on the Bow Bridge and today, of all days, she couldn't be late. Setting the toast rack amongst the condiments and crockery, Millie went through the kitchen door into the hallway.

She rested her hand lightly on the banisters and looked up the stairs. 'Jim, it's almost a quarter to!' she called, trying to keep any irritation out of her voice.

'I'm just coming,' he shouted back from their bedroom at the front of the house. 'Put my eggs on and I'll be with you before they're done, promise.'

Millie sighed and turned to open the front door. Mr Granger, the senior clerk at the Midland Bank in Aldgate, stepped out of the Edwardian terraced house on the opposite side of the street.

'Good morning, Mrs Smith,' he called, raising his hat.

'Morning, Mr Granger,' Millie replied, scooping up the bottle of milk and newspaper on the step. 'Looks like a nice day.'

He nodded. 'And a busy one for you, I'd say.'

Millie smiled and glanced down at the banner headlines across the top of the newspaper.

'YOUR NEW HEALTH SERVICE STARTS TODAY' it said in bold block capitals, with the smaller strapline below 'What will it mean for you?'

Good question, thought Millie, as she tucked the paper under her arm and went back into the house. Returning to the kitchen, she placed the paper beside Jim's place at the table and checked that there was sufficient marmalade in the pot before going back to the cooker. Putting the milk in the stone keep on the kitchen dresser, Millie cut off a knob of lard from the corner of the block and flicked it into the frying pan that she had already set to heat. Using the tea towel to protect her hand, Millie whirled the blob of lard around a couple of times then broke two eggs into the middle. The kettle whistled and she made the tea, then popped the knitted cosy on the pot.

Leaving it to brew, she checked the eggs as heavy footsteps thumped down the stairs. Millie slid the eggs on to her husband's plate just as Jim appeared.

Standing just a shade under six feet tall and wearing his double-breasted navy suit and Royal Air Force tie, the honourable James Percival Woodville Smith, to give him his full but rarely used title, looked every bit the part of a prospective Labour Party candidate.

'Is breakfast ready?' he asked as he straightened his collar.

'Of course,' Millie replied, placing the plate in front of him as he sat down.

He picked up his knife and fork. Millie sat in the chair opposite and poured their tea. She stirred two heaped teaspoons of sugar into her husband's tea and slid his cup towards him.

'So today's the day,' he said, loading his egg on to his fork. 'Excited?'

Millie shrugged. 'Worried out of my mind, more like.'

Jim laughed. 'Oh, Millie, this is one of the greatest days in the history of the working classes' struggle – surely you must be a weeny bit excited?'

She smiled. 'I am, but with the delegation from the local

health board and the Association's committee, along with the mayor and the local press, not to mention half Stepney Council, all descending on Munroe House at eleven o'clock, the superintendent has been chasing everyone from pillar to post for weeks to make sure everything goes to plan.'

Jim plucked a piece of toast from the rack and jabbed his knife in the butter and then spread it thickly across the bread triangle. 'Don't worry, sweetheart. I'm sure you'll be able to handle everything, even a highly strung Miss Dutton.'

'I hope so,' Millie replied in an uncertain tone. 'But I don't know how we're going to run an ante-natal clinic, a dressing clinic and take emergency calls with the world and his wife packed into the building.'

Putting a slice of toast on her plate she reached for the butter.

'Sorry, I've taken the last dollop,' Jim said.

'But that was this week's ration,' she said. 'It's supposed to last until Thursday.'

'Isn't there some marge in the larder?'

Millie dropped the toast on her plate. 'It doesn't matter. I haven't really got time anyway.'

She stood up.

Jim caught her around the waist as she passed and pulled her to him. 'I'm sure with you in charge, the handover to the local health board will go without a hitch, even if that pompous fool Shottington's speech blusters on half the morning.'

Millie laughed. 'That pompous fool, as you call him, is the consultant surgeon in the London Hospital,' she said, enjoying the sensation of her husband's hand on her hip. 'As well as the president of the St George's and St Dunstan's District Nursing Association.'

'Only for a few more hours,' Jim replied as his arm tightened.

Millie slipped her arms around his neck. 'You will be home on time tonight, won't you, Jim?'

He gave her his most charming smile. 'Of course.'

'No, really,' Millie said, holding his gaze.

'Look, I thought we'd been through all this last week,' he said with just a trace of testiness. 'You know what constituency committees are like. It's the same for all the members.'

'You said that about the branch meeting of the stevedores'

union two weeks ago.' Millie traced her finger along his freshly shaven jaw. 'Mrs Woodrow might be thankful that Labour Party business keeps her husband out half the night, but then she's not newly-wed.'

A satisfied look spread across Jim's face. 'I don't know if we can still be called newly-weds after six months but,' his hand moved down to his wife's bottom, prompting a little flutter in Millie's stomach, 'we're certainly well married.'

Millie pressed her lips on his forehead. 'I'll see you later,' she said, unwinding herself from his embrace.

Jim grinned and resumed his breakfast. Millie unhooked her coat from the back door and slipped it on. Taking the silk scarf from her pocket, she secured it over her head to keep her hair in some sort of order for the three-mile scooter journey to work.

Jim unfurled his newspaper. 'I hear Mr Mason, a Labour Party bigwig, is going to be at Munroe House for the handover.'

'Yes, he's representing the Minister, Mr Bevan,' Millie replied, picking up her bag and lunchbox.

'Well, my darling,' he said pleasantly, 'make sure you tell him that you're the wife of Jim Smith, the man destined to take over from the current Leytonstone and Wanstead MP when he retires at the next election, won't you?'

Mercifully, the City-bound traffic was running smoothly over the Victorian cast-iron Bow Bridge, so Millie putter-puttered around the corner on her light-blue Swallow Gadabout into Sutton Street just as St George's clock sounded a quarter to eight. As she bobbed over the cobbles towards Munroe House, Millie had to blink twice to make sure she wasn't seeing things. Starting at the clinic's door and running along the side of the double-fronted brick villa stretched a line of people.

Passing through the rear wooden gates, she rolled to a stop under the bike shelter and parked her scooter amongst the Association's pedal bikes.

Retrieving her nurse's bag from under the seat, Millie walked into the clinic. The acrid smell of bleach tickled her nose as she stepped into the tiled hallway.

Munroe House was once a three-storey family home and it had been handed over to the Association some time ago. Now, what had formerly been the family rooms downstairs were the treatment room, nurses' and superintendent's offices, and the equipment and laundry rooms, along with a nurses' recreation parlour overlooking the handkerchief-size paved garden at the side of the house.

The clinic door opened and Annie Fletcher, Millie's friend who covered the Cambridge Heath Road area further along the Mile End Road, stepped out.

'Thank goodness you've arrived,' she said, her blonde curls bobbing on her shoulder as she hurried over.

'Have you seen the queue outside?' Millie asked, hanging up her coat.

'I know,' said Annie, her blue eyes wide with disbelief. 'And Miss Dutton's in a right two-and-eight, I can tell you. She sent four nurses out at six to cover the morning insulins.'

'What, all of them?' Millie asked, opening the linen cupboard and taking out a fresh uniform from the brown paper parcel with her name scrawled across the top.

Annie nodded. 'She told Sally and three others to scrub the clinic floor, even though we did it last night, and then when the two maids had finished sweeping the whole house Miss Dutton sent them off to do it again.'

'Where are the rest of the girls?' Millie asked.

'Hiding, if they have any sense.'

'Hasn't the baker delivered the cakes yet, Cook?' Miss Dutton's shrill voice demanded from the kitchen at the far end.

'He said he'd 'ave 'em to us by nine-thirty, Superintendent, so don't you fret none,' Mrs Pierce replied.

'He'd better,' the superintendent replied grimly, an octave higher.

'See you later.' Annie shot off into the office just as Miss Dutton strode down the corridor.

Miss Dutton, the Association's Superintendent, was a petite woman in her early forties, with sharp ice-blue eyes and honey-blonde hair scraped off her face under her starched white nurse's cap. It was festooned with gathered lace, as was the collar and puffy cuffs of her navy uniform. Unlike all the other Association's nurses, who wore the Queen's Nursing Institute A-line dress and no hat, Miss Dutton insisted on waltzing about the clinic in a mid-calf-length hospital matron's uniform. It didn't matter, of course, because in the three years she'd been in charge, Miss Dutton had never actually gone out to nurse a patient.

The superintendent's eyes flickered over Millie. 'Good morning, Smith, I was hoping you'd be here by eight.'

'I am. It's just five to,' Millie replied, indicating the grandfather clock at the far end of the hall. 'What do you want me to do?'

'You can check that Nurse Weston and her chums have put the treatment room in order, as I told them to an hour ago, and then you can organise someone to stack the bedpans facing the same way in the rack, and bleach the sluice.'

'I don't think anyone will be inspecting the sluice, Superintendent,' Millie said.

Miss Dutton frowned. 'I can't take that chance. If those pen-pushers from the Ministry of Health find something amiss, I don't know what I shall do.'

'I'm sure everything will be fine,' Millie said soothingly. 'Do you want me to take morning handover while you get on with something else?'

Miss Dutton shook her head. 'I've cancelled the a.m. rounds, as Mr Shottington was most insistent that all the nurses should greet our guests as they arrive.'

'What about the patients?' asked Millie.

'They'll have to wait. It's only for a few hours.' The front doorbell rang and Miss Dutton jumped. 'Off you go, then,' she said with a dismissive wave.

Millie made her way to the small room tucked under the stairs that served as the on-call sleeping and changing room, and went in.

When she'd joined the Association, every nurse was required to live in, but since the end of the war some had moved out, either to live at home or to marry. However, as they were required to work the night rota, a bed had to be provided. Millie swiftly donned her uniform and hung her day clothes up in the single wardrobe at the end of the bed, and then, quickly checking the seams of her stockings, she tidied her hair and, taking her nurse's bag with her, left the room. Ignoring the sound of Miss Dutton berating the poor greengrocer on the telephone in the main office, Millie headed for the door at the end of the corridor.

The magnificent lounge with its block oak flooring was now the treatment room, and it had white enamel cupboards instead of china cabinets around the walls while towards the rear was a boxed-off area where a sluice had been installed.

Inside Gladys Potter and her friend Marge were tidying the last few instruments away while Trudy was cleaning the sterilising unit on the bench. They looked around as Millie walked in.

'Nice of you to drop by,' said Gladys, wiping her ginger hued hair away from her face with the back of her hand.

Millie and Gladys had been students together and although never friends they had rubbed along well enough. That was until the night matron discovered Gladys's American Airman hiding in the linen cupboard. Although Millie hadn't been the tell-tale, Gladys had refused to believe this, and had been harbouring a grudge ever since.

'Yes,' said Trudy in a similarly sour tone, 'some of us have been at it for hours.'

Millie gave her a pleasant smile. 'Have you finished in here?'

'Not that we have to answer to you,' said Gladys, locking the chemical cupboard, 'but yes, we have.'

'Good, then I'll meet you in the office in five minutes for allocation,' Millie said, turning to leave.

Judy gave her a wary look. 'But Miss Dutton cancelled the morning visits.'

'And I'm uncancelling them,' Millie replied firmly. 'Just because there's a bunch of big shots arriving at ten doesn't mean we have to leave our elderly patients in wet beds.'

Millie slipped into the treatment room just as Mrs Harper, the Nursing Association's chairwoman, who was dressed in a Harris tweed suit, with a fox fur, including head and paws, draped around her neck, rose to her feet to start the proceedings. Miss Dutton's eyes fixed on Millie immediately but as Miss Dutton was flanked by the Association's secretary, Mrs Archer, on one side, and a man in a brown suit on the other, the superintendent contented herself with a venomous glare.

The room was packed, as along with dignitaries, a great number of local people had gathered to witness the handing-over of the reins of the hundred-year-old St George's and St Dunstan's Nursing Association to the National Health Service. The Mayor of Stepney, in his long red and black gown, stood beside a mother holding a youngster who kept grabbing for his Corporation chain. The Mayor's wife, on the other hand, was jammed against the wall next to the poster telling you to take syrup of figs for an 'assured bowel motion', while Father Gilbert in his long black cassock was boxed in by two old women in faded wraparound overalls puffing away on roll-ups.

Squeezing herself into a free space next to the dressing cupboard, Millie surveyed the scene.

Mr Shottington, surgical consultant at the London Hospital and president of the St George's and St Dunstan's Nursing Association, was dressed, as always, in an expensive charcoal pinstriped suit with a spotted bow tie at his throat and gold cufflinks. Beside him stood a tall man with such a sallow complexion that, had he been a patient, Millie would have advised him to take a pint of stout each day for iron. In contrast to Mr Shottington's made-to-measure attire, the visitor's off-the-peg navy suit hung loosely from his shoulders. He peered nervously at the sea of faces through thick, horn-rimmed spectacles.

Millie glanced up at the portrait of a young woman in a tartan crinoline above the fireplace and wondered what the Association's founder, Miss Robina Munroe, would have made of it all.

Squeezing herself around a couple of dockers, Annie edged her way over.

'You've cut it fine,' she said.

'Mrs Geary had one of her funny turns so I had to make her a cuppa before I left,' said Millie. She took a quick head count of the nurses in the room. 'Where's Eva?'

'Mrs Brown's. Her husband phoned and said she'd been having pains all night,' Annie replied. 'I see you're second midwife on call today.'

Millie glanced at the blackboard by the door and saw her name chalked up below Eva's.

Blast! After giving Jim an ear-bashing about being home on time, Millie prayed she wouldn't be needed.

Mrs Harper retrieved her notes from her handbag and the murmuring subsided.

'Good morning everyone, and let me say what a pleasure it is to see so many of you gathered for such a historic day and to thank a few people in particular for giving up their precious time. Firstly, Mayor Tucker ...' The chairwoman worked her way through the list of dignitaries, then looked at the man beside her with a coy smile. 'And last, but by no means least, Mr Shottington, who is not only a surgeon of world renown, but he has presided over the St George's and St Dunstan's Nursing Association with both wisdom and consideration for the last twenty years.' There was a flutter of stubby eyelashes and shy clapping from the half-dozen ladies of the committee fussing around him.

'And now,' continued Mrs Harper. 'I would like to call upon him formally to hand over the reins of the Association to Mr Griffiths, who is here today representing the Minister of Health, Mr Bevan.'

The consultant stepped forward. 'Thank you, dear lady.' He smiled benevolently around at the assembled company and drew a thick wodge of notes from his inside breast pocket. 'The St George's and St Dunstan's Nursing Association was founded in 1856 by Miss Robina Munroe, daughter of that great Victorian public-health campaigner and member of my own profession, Sir Robert Munroe, and at that time ...'

As Mr Shottington worked his way at length through the history of the Association and his audience stifled their yawns, Millie's mind wandered to putting the bed sheet in to soak, her planned trip on Saturday to Stratford to meet her mother and aunt Ruby, and then on to making Jim something special for tea before they settled in for a cosy night listening to the radio together.

Mr Shottington turned over the last of the five sheets of paper in his hand. 'And so now I call upon Mr Griffiths to take up on behalf of the new National Health Service the district nursing baton carried for so many years with such care, compassion and selfless devotion by the Association's nurses.'

Mrs Harper handed the consultant a large envelope with a red seal on it. Mr Shottington then offered it to the sallow young man in the ill-fitting navy suit.

'Thank you, Mr Shottington,' Mr Griffiths said quietly,

taking the Association's deeds and raising the corners of his mouth in what could have been a smile.

The crowd clapped and a photographer from the local paper jumped forward. Mr Shottington grasped Mr Griffiths' hand.

'This is a momentous day for all of us,' said Mr Shottington as he adopted a theatrical pose. 'And I'm sure Mr Griffiths will tell Mr Bevan of our unwavering support for his marvellous health reforms,' Mr Shottington was beaming at the camera and almost shaking Mr Griffiths' arm free of its socket. 'And that's Mr Aneurin Bevan, B-e-v-a-n, not Ernest,' he added sharply to the reporters scribbling down his words. 'We wouldn't want any misspelling with the Minister of Health's name, would we?'

The photographer's flashlight blinded them all a few more times and then Mrs Harper clapped her hands. 'Thank you, Mr Shottington, Mr Griffiths, and now the formalities are over, tea and cakes will be served in the nurses' refectory.'

Millie was just about to finish her last mouthful of tea when Miss Dutton's face hoved into view. Tight-lipped and her blue eyes sharp with fury, the superintendent made her way over to Millie.

'How dare you send all the nurses out on their rounds after I expressly told you they were cancelled?' she said as she stopped in front of Millie.

'I only sent half the girls out to deal with the urgent cases,' Millie replied coolly. 'After all, it is supposed to be these patients' health service, isn't it?'

'Don't try to be clever, Smith,' Miss Dutton replied. 'I've a good mind to make a formal complaint to Mr Shottington about you flouting my authority yet again.'

'Mr Shottington isn't in charge anymore, Superintendent,' said Millie smiling innocently. 'And I don't think the Community Health Board would be pleased to hear that you instructed nurses to leave patients unattended.'

Miss Dutton's neck flushed. 'I'm warning you, Smith. The Board might be paying your wages now, but I'm still in charge.'

The superintendent glared at her for a couple of seconds longer, then turned and made a beeline for Mr Shottington, who was standing by the refreshment table. They exchanged a few words and then, glancing nervously around the room, he ushered Miss Dutton out into the hall.

At last the mayor and his entourage said their goodbyes, and the crowds in the treatment room started to leave. Millie finished her tea and put her cup on the tray for the dirty crockery.

'Millie. Millie Smith!' said a man's voice.

She turned and smiled at her husband's old friend, Tim Braithwaite.

Tim topped Millie's five-foot-three by six inches, his understated fawn suit sitting well on his lean frame. He and Jim had met at Oxford before the War and had flown Spitfires together in 74 Squadron. He too had been converted to socialism in the Oxford Union bar and was now climbing steadily up the ranks of the Labour government.

'Tim! How lovely to see you,' Millie said, embracing her husband's old friend. 'But what are you doing here?'

'You too; and I'm here to look after Griffiths,' he said, indicating the junior minister on the far side of the room. 'He's one of the big brains behind the health system, but unfortunately, he's a bit short of what you might call common sense, and so I'm here to make sure he makes it back to Whitehall in one piece.'

'I can see there's a danger he won't,' replied Millie, watching Mr Griffith's near panic as dockers, housewives and children crowded around him.

Tim's attention returned to Millie. 'But more to the point, what on earth are you doing here?'

'Where else would I be, with a new health service just starting and every district nursing service in the capital crying out for qualified nurses?' Millie laughed.

'That's true,' replied Tim uncertainly. 'I know old Woodrow hasn't stepped down yet but I wouldn't have thought an MP with a working wife would have gone down too well with the constituency party. I'm surprised Jim hasn't insisted that you become the little woman at home.'

'He tried,' said Millie, remembering their first marital tiff. 'But I told him I was doing my bit in building the welfare state and that he should be thankful I wasn't a coal miner like some of the women in Russia.'

Tim laughed.

'You must come and see our little house in the country,' said Millie.

Tim pulled a face. 'The country? I wouldn't exactly call Leytonstone a rural idyll.'

'It is compared with the London docks.' Millie slipped her arm through his. 'You and Kay must come to supper. What about next Saturday, the seventeenth?'

'I think we're free. I'll telephone and confirm tomorrow.' Tim grinned. 'I bet Jim's put on a bit of weight with all your home cooking. It's months since I've seen him.'

Millie looked puzzled. 'But you saw him a few weeks ago in the Strangers' Bar in the House of Commons.'

The telephone in the hall rang.

'Goodness, is that the time?' asked Tim, glancing at his watch.

'Sister Smith!' Gladys was standing in the door with her hand clasped over the telephone receiver. 'It's Mr Frazer.'

Millie nodded and looked back at Tim. 'It was the night the Housing Act debate went on to an all-night sitting. He couldn't get a taxi home so you let him sleep on your—'

'He says his wife's having pains every three minutes,' cut in Gladys.

Tim gave her a peck on the cheek. 'You'd better go. Lovely to see you, Millie.'

He turned and threaded his way through the last few people.

Millie walked out of the treatment room and into the hall. Gladys was waiting by the hall desk, waving the receiver at her.

'Thank you, Sister Potter,' she said, taking it from her and covering the mouthpiece with her hand.

Gladys disappeared back into the treatment room.

Millie put the receiver to her ear. 'Good afternoon, Mr Frazer. It's Sister Smith.' She opened her pad on the desk and took her pen from her top pocket. 'Now just calm down and tell me exactly what's happened.'

It was just half-past seven when Millie turned into her road. Relief swept over her. Jim's car wasn't there. Thank goodness!

She'd got back from visiting Jane Frazer, whom, it seemed, had eaten a dodgy plate of eels and hadn't gone into labour, at three o'clock only to find the clinic even now packed with people waiting. Somehow, Millie had managed to remove three splinters, clean grit from several pairs of eyes, extract half-a-dozen beads from a child's right nostril, and still leave Munroe House at six-thirty.

Bringing her scooter to a halt outside her front gate, Millie turned the ignition off and then walked it down the side of the house to the little lean-to at the back. She removed the chops and her nursing bag from the storage compartment under her seat and, as Jim wasn't there to mutter about it being bad manners, Millie let herself through the back door.

Jim's breakfast plate, complete with half-eaten toast, was where she'd set it that morning and the top of the marmalade was sticky-side down on the tablecloth. The butter knife lay beside it and there was a fatty smear under the blade. Plonking her nursing case under the table and the chops on the top, Millie turned on the radio and quickly gathered the crockery into the sink and then lit the oven.

Swaying to the Latin rhythm of 'Begin the Beguine', Millie fetched a basin of dripping from the larder and popped a knob in a small roasting tray, which she shoved into the oven. She rinsed the breakfast dishes and set them to drain in the plate rack above the sink.

Millie took the tray from the oven and, setting the chops in the sizzling fat, returned it to the top shelf. She prepared the potatoes and carrots then, throwing a pinch of salt in both pots, put them to boil and then dashed upstairs to the bedroom.

The BBC Concert Orchestra struck up the next tune and the strains of 'Slow Boat to China' drifted up the stairs.

'All to myself alone,' Millie sang as she scooped Jim's pyjamas from the bedroom floor.

She set his comb and brush straight on the tallboy and then, with a flourish of sheets and blankets, remade their rumpled bed. She picked up her husband's pyjama top and poked her finger through the buttonhole.

The carriage clock in the front parlour chimed quarter to. Blast! Jim would be in any moment and she hadn't even changed.

Millie folded the striped flannelette garment and tucked it under the pillow next to her nightdress. Stripping off her dress and dumping it in the linen basket, she dashed along the landing to the bathroom.

Their house had been built at the end of the previous century. It must have been a real luxury to have a purpose-built bathroom in those days. It wasn't exactly commonplace now, but Jim had been brought up in a country house with running hot water and so he'd been most insistent their own home should have such amenities.

After a quick wash, Millie rushed back to the bedroom and, pulling her yellow-flowered dress from the wardrobe, slipped it on. Checking that her stocking seams were straight, she brushed out her slightly windswept curls, reapplied her lipstick and powdered her nose.

Running back down to the kitchen and, after satisfying herself that the vegetables were almost done, Millie removed the chops from the oven. She allocated Jim the one with the slice of kidney and then arranged the strained potatoes and carrots alongside. After swirling some Bisto powder into the meat juices, Millie poured it over the portions of meat then surveyed the two plates as she removed her apron.

A sense of satisfaction spread through her. Jim would be in at any second and, just for once, she would have his supper on the table just as a loving wife should. Millie opened the oven and put their meals back to keep warm.

An image of the newly made bed upstairs flitted through Millie's mind and a smile spread across her face. And after supper?

The ring of the telephone jolted Millie out of her daydream.

She walked into the hall and picked up the receiver. 'Leytonstone seven, seven, three, nine.'

'Hello, darling.'

'Jim?'

'Yes, I'm afraid it is,' Jim replied. 'Look, sweetheart. I'm really sorry, but something's cropped up.'

'What?'

'Some boring old Dock Labour business,' he explained in a weary tone. 'You know what these shop stewards are like when they start talking.'

'No, I don't,' Millie replied flatly.

He gave a short laugh. 'Well, I wish I didn't. Damn windbags!'

There was a pause. 'But I'm afraid the negotiations are going to run on for hours yet.'

'You promised you'd be home on time,' Millie said in a strained voice.

'I know and I was just on my way out when I got called back. You do understand, don't you, sweetheart?'

Millie didn't answer.

'I am sorry, my pet,' he said in a voice heavy with regret. 'Will you forgive me?'

'Don't I always?' Millie answered after a brief pause.

Down the phone Millie heard some muttering in the background.

'Look, we're reconvening, so I'd better go,' Jim said. 'I'll try not to disturb you when I get in.'

There was a click and the line went dead. Millie replaced the receiver and stood looking at the sunset twinkling through the stained-glass panel in the front door for a moment, then returned to the kitchen.

Taking their plates from the oven, she covered Jim's meal with an upturned dish and put it in the pantry to cool. She couldn't afford to throw away part of their weekly meat ration and so, although it wouldn't be very appetising, she'd have to stretch his meal to tomorrow night's supper.

Millie put hers on the table and sat down to listen to the eight o'clock news. She speared a potato and popped it in her mouth. She cut off a piece of meat.

'And finally,' said the radio announcer. 'Today Lord Burghley announced that the King and Queen will be opening the 1948 Olympic Games in Wembley Stadium at two o'clock precisely. It is expected that—'

Millie reached across and turned off the radio. She put down her knife and fork and stood up. Covering her supper with a plate, she walked across the room and put it in the larder alongside Jim's. She set the pots and pans to soak in the sink and then, without going into the living room across the hall, wearily she made her way upstairs to bed.

Chapter Two

Aunt Ruby eyed the selection of cakes on the trolley and her Fiesta Pink lips pulled a little tighter.

'Is that all you have?' she asked the young woman wearing a black uniform and frilly apron who was standing next to the trolley.

Behind the thick, round-rimmed glasses, the assistant's right eye flickered. 'Yes, Madam,' she said. 'This is our full range of pastries.'

'Surely there must be something to tempt you, Ruby,' Millie's mother Doris said, stirring the teapot in the middle of the table. 'Perhaps a jam puff or cream doughnut?'

'I might if they were made with real cream instead of the powdered stuff,' Ruby replied, regarding the collection of cakes sourly.

Millie was sitting, as she did on most Saturday afternoons, in the ABC tea shop on Stratford Broadway with her mother, Doris, and her aunt Ruby. They had met at the station at one and after almost three hours browsing the shops, felt they could reward themselves with afternoon tea. Although Ruby was the older of the two, now, in their middle fifties, the two sisters could have been taken for twins. Well, in their facial features at least, because whereas Doris had been content to let her hair turn from gold to silver, Ruby had a monthly appointment at the hairdresser to touch up her roots. Their taste in clothing also set them apart, as Doris opted for classic styles while Ruby, who hadn't been blessed with children, retained some of her youthful firmness and always sported the latest fashion. Ruby was, as the saying goes, well preserved.

'I'll have a slice of cherry madeira,' Millie said.

'Me too,' Doris said.

Millie and her mother exchanged a fond smile across the table.

The waitress manoeuvred the slices of cake on to two plates and then stood, cake slice poised, waiting for further instructions.

Ruby sighed. 'Very well, I must have something to soak up the tea, so I'll have some of the lemon meringue.'

The waitress fulfilled the order and left, the wheels of her cake trolley squeaking as she moved on to the two women sitting at the next table.

'So,' said Ruby, popping a forkful of lemon meringue into her mouth, 'have you been very busy this week?'

'Busy!' Millie replied. 'There's been a queue of people stretching halfway down the street almost every morning and then, just when we think we've seen the last of them, the afternoon lot arrive. And it's the same at the surgery. There was almost a riot at Doctor Gingold's yesterday, with people trying to jump the queue.'

Her mother tutted. 'Disgraceful.'

'What do you expect?' asked Ruby, noisily stirring in her sugar. 'This is what happens when you put monkeys in charge of the zoo. It would never have happened if dear Winnie was still Prime Minister. My Tony said, how can Stafford Cripps tell us the country's got no money one day, only to have that Edith Summerskill tell us the next day that no mother need worry if they don't have sixpence for the doctor any more? Tony says his firm would soon go under if he started giving away bricks instead of building houses with them.'

'Well, I for one am pleased that someone's paying for my services. I hated collecting the fees every Monday,' Millie replied. 'And I'm thrilled that I won't have to stand on street corners any more selling flags on Nursing Association Day to raise funds, either. I know people are demanding at the moment, but I'm sure things will settle down when they understand the health service properly.'

Ruby snorted. 'It doesn't take much understanding to know that under this ridiculous new system everything's free.'

Doris nudged Millie's tea towards her. 'You look a little tired, darling.'

'I'm not surprised,' replied Millie. 'I've been up at six each morning and I haven't been home before seven all week.'

'I don't suppose James is very happy about that,' Ruby replied.

She took out a cigarette and lit it. 'A man likes to have his wife and his dinner waiting for him after a day's work.' She forked up another piece of pie. 'And it's not much fun sitting around waiting for your other half to come home.'

'I know,' replied Millie, hearing the tightness in her voice.

Her mother gave her a sympathetic look. 'Was Jim annoyed that you were late? Have you quarrelled?'

Millie shook her head. 'In fact, Jim's been late himself most of the week. And twice I didn't even hear him come to bed.' She forced a smile. 'I shouldn't be cross, really. He's got a very demanding job.'

Doris put her hand over Millie's. 'It takes time.' Softness crept into her eyes. 'I remember me and your Dad, God rest his soul, used to argue like cat and dog when we first wed.'

'Did you?' asked Millie, somewhat surprised, as she couldn't actually remember her parents raising their voices, let alone squabbling.

'Cat and dog.' Her mother winked. 'But then he always made it up to me.'

Millie felt her colour rise again. 'Jim did buy me a huge bunch of flowers,' she said, trying not to let the memory of their heated lovemaking that followed show on her face.

'There you are then, Amelia,' Ruby said, as she blew a stream of smoke out of the corner of her mouth. 'The best way to handle a man is to fuss around them and act helpless with any sort of mechanical thing, and they'll be as happy as larks. Although you might want to get James to spend his money on something more lasting next time, like a bit of jewellery. And remember, men hate to come home to a nagging wife.'

'I know, and I try not to go on at him, but,' Millie looked down at her wedding ring, 'the house seems very quiet without him.'

'Well, the house won't be quiet once you have a baby to fill it,' said Ruby, looking pointedly at Millie.

'Ruby!' Doris said, giving her sister a firm look.

Millie's aunt was unabashed. 'They've been married over six months.'

Although they'd never actually discussed the matter before their wedding, Millie had assumed – as she was almost twenty-eight and Jim was thirty – that they would be starting a family straight away, and she had been more than a little surprised to discover that Jim wasn't as eager as she was to have children.

'Mr Woodrow is retiring at the next election, and so we've decided to wait until Jim is certain he'll step into old Woodrow's shoes.' Millie smiled. 'And of course it means we can enjoy ourselves for a while before all those sleepless nights.'

Ruby looked confused. 'I don't see how having a family will interfere with James's plans. After all, you're the one who'll be looking after the baby, not him. And surely his mother must be keen for him to—'

'Mind your collar,' Millie interrupted, pointing at the stack of fine ash hanging off the end of her aunt's cigarette.

Ruby jumped and the ash fluttered down on to her olive jacket. She grabbed a serviette from the metal fan in the middle of the table and dabbed at the residue.

Millie took a sip of tea, thankful that her aunt's spent cigarette had rescued her from having to think about the joys of having Lady Tollshunt as her mother-in-law.

Millie yawned as she scootered down Cable Street toward Dr Gingold's surgery. The street, which ran east to west and parallel to the Highway, took its name from the shipbuilding heritage of the area, but the rope makers who would have twisted their hemp between empty fields two hundred years before had now been replaced by dilapidated houses offering cheap lodgings.

It was in the centre of Millie's patch and if the east end of the street was bad, the west end was dreadful. Here the three-storey Georgian houses housed seedy cafés at street level, with brothels above, and seemed to be exclusively run by Maltese criminals with shifty eyes and flashy suits. Even in the middle of the day, no respectable women could walk along that end of the thoroughfare without being accosted by drunks. Wellclose Square, with its scruffy central park to the south, was little more than an open-air knocking shop.

Weaving her way between the lorries from the docks and avoiding a pack of dogs let out for the day while their owners were at work, Millie pulled up outside Dr Gingold's surgery and chained her scooter to the railings.

As she lifted her bag out, Ada Parkin, whose children were always in the clinic for something or another, and Kitty West standing alongside, spotted her.

'Oi, oi, Sister Smith,' laughed Ada as she repositioned the toddler on her hip. 'You'd better get your skates on. The surgery started an hour ago.'

Millie looked amazed. 'What, at seven o'clock?'

'That's right,' said Kitty, handing her one-year-old sitting in the pram another portion of sticky bun. 'Doc couldn't see everyone yesterday and so she opened early this morning.'

'But why are you here at this time?' Millie asked.

'I 'ad to be here at the crack of dawn to have me ears unblocked in case all those bloody sick buggers used up all the stuff,' replied Ada.

'And I want to see the doc about, you know, my little problem *down below*,' Kitty mouthed silently.

'I did tell you last week that it was perfectly natural and would right itself in time,' Millie replied, trying not to sound annoyed.

'I know, but now that it won't cost I thought I'd get Doctor to take a butcher's. No disrespect to you, Sister,' Kitty said, looking apologetically at Millie.

Ada took a roll-up from behind her ear. 'And then we're off to the dentist, ain't we, Kit?'

'Yes,' agreed Kitty. 'My Steve ain't got no more than three teeth in 'is head and needs some gnashers.'

'I think he has to go to the dentist himself to be fitted for dentures,' Millie said.

Kitty looked surprised. 'Does he?'

'Never mind, ducks,' said Ada, nudging her friend playfully. 'We'll pop in at the eye doc's instead. I want to get myself some specs.'

'I didn't know you had a problem with your eyes, Mrs Parkin,' said Millie.

'I ain't, but I thought I'd get myself a pair just in case,' she said cheerily.

An old couple stepped out of the surgery door and the queue shuffled forwards.

Millie smiled politely. 'If you'd excuse me, ladies, I need to push on.'

Ada blew out a stream of cigarette smoke by way of reply and Millie walked into the two-up two-down house that was both Dr Gingold's workplace and home. Quickly passing the packed waiting room to her left, Millie headed towards what had once been the back parlour and scullery and was now Dr Gingold's consulting room. She knocked lightly on the door.

'Come!'

Millie entered the room.

With wiry grey hair scooped into a loose bun on top of her head and a very individual way of wearing sweaters and tweed, Rachel Gingold looked every bit the eccentric philanthropist she was. The only surviving member of a Polish-Jewish family who counted philosophers, scientists and statisticians amongst their number, she had opened her practice in Cable Street on almost the same day as the Luftwaffe first came calling. Having just been chased out of one country by Hitler's storm troopers, she was in no mood to be moved on again, and immediately she set about organising the area's doctors and nurses.

The doctor, who was a shade under five feet, was standing in front of a lanky man who seemed to be in danger of having his forehead burnt by the light bulb hanging just above. On his upper body he was wearing the rough clothes of a dock labourer, but his trousers were bundled around his ankles. He looked acutely embarrassed as he spotted Millie, as well he might, as Dr Gingold had hooked her index finger into the waistband of his baggy grey underpants.

'Mmm,' she said, in a thoughtful tone as she peered down at his genitals. 'The last time I saw anything like that was in Singapore in thirty-two.'

The colossus looming over her went white. Dr Gingold let go of the elastic and it snapped back against his hairy stomach.

'Thankfully we have ointment to treat it now.' She sat down at her desk and rummaged around for a sheet of headed notepaper. 'Rub this in morning and night for a week and it should go. But no you-know-what until a month after it's completely gone. Do you understand?'

She scribbled across the bottom of the paper and offered it to the man.

He took the prescription. 'Thank you, Doctor.' He grabbed his trousers, yanked them up and stumbled out of the consulting room.

'My goodness,' said Millie as the door clicked shut. 'What on earth did he have?'

'Heat rash,' replied the doctor. 'But he's got a taste for the oriental ladies in Limehouse, so I thought I'd add a bit of celibacy to his medication.' The doctor ran her careworn hands over her face. 'And now, Sister Smith, tell me what you want of me.'

Millie perched on the edge of the chair. 'I popped in to pick up any new patients and wondered if you'd given any more thought to setting up a child health clinic?'

'*Oy vey*!' Dr Gingold threw her hands up. 'With people banging on my door day and night demanding this and that, I have time to think of clinics?' she asked the central lampshade.

'I just thought—'

'Fifty people,' Dr Gingold continued, clutching her hands together on her bosom in supplication, 'and not one of them with anything more dangerous than a septic boil. And if that's not enough, the health committee promised me a dozen prescription pads, none of which have arrived, and now that old *idiota* Marcavitz, in the chemist's, is querying if the government will pay him for dispensing medication on headed notepaper.'

Millie stood up. 'Perhaps I'll come back when you're not so busy.'

'No, no,' said Dr Gingold with a heavy sigh. 'Sit, sit.' She waved Millie back into the chair and searched amongst the papers on her desk again, and then handed Millie a list. 'I'm afraid there are over a dozen new referrals.'

'That's all right,' replied Millie, praying they weren't all daily bed-baths.

The doctor patted Millie's hand. 'And I have rung Father McMahon about using his church hall every other Tuesday. If he agrees, I thought we could start the clinic the day after August bank holiday, on the third.'

'I'll sort out a rota of nurses.' Millie said. A yawn escaped her.

'Excuse me,' she said, quickly covering her mouth with her hand.

Dr Gingold's wrinkled face lifted in a smile. 'I can see I'm not the only one run off my feet.'

Millie smiled but decided to not mention that it was her husband coming in at gone midnight again, and not the new health service that was the reason for her tiredness.

Having waved goodbye to her last morning patient, and dropped off the weekly small-dressing order to Letterman's the chemist in Commercial Road, Millie arrived back at Munroe House just after twelve-thirty.

The meaty aroma of lamb stew wafted out of the kitchen and through the open door. Of course, as each nurse living in Munroe handed over her food ration book each week, the midday meal was only for the resident nurses, and this meant Millie had to bring her own sandwiches.

Ignoring her rumbling stomach, Millie made her way to the treatment room where Annie and Sally were tidying up equipment after the morning dressing clinic before setting the chairs out in readiness for the afternoon's ante-natal session. They looked up as Millie walked in.

'Have you just finished?' Annie asked, rolling the two screens out from the corner and setting up the two nurses' stations.

Millie nodded. 'It took me over an hour to wash Mrs Jobson,' she replied, plonking her bag on the work surface. 'Her legs just won't take her weight any more and my back won't either. I'm going to have to make her a two-person visit in future. What have you two been up to?'

'The usual,' replied Annie. 'Boils, burns and blisters, although one chap came in with the biggest carbuncle I've ever seen on the back of his neck. It took a good while to staunch the oozing after I lanced it, I can tell you.'

Millie wrinkled her nose and pulled her dirty equipment out of her bag. She took it to the deep butler sink in the corner and turned on the taps.

'There was a phone call from Miss Robertson's secretary at the health board confirming that our six new QN students will be arriving next Monday as planned, but they are going to meet the health director first and then come on after,' Annie said, as she set out the urine-testing equipment on the stainless-steel dressing trolley.

'Six! We were only expecting four,' Millie said, running her used equipment through the water. 'I bet that news pleased Miss Dutton no end.'

'We haven't told her,' said Sally.

'But—'

'She was in a right mood after she found out we've got through our monthly supply of dressings in just ten days,' said Annie. 'And if that wasn't enough to start her frothing at the mouth, the chap from the equipment department at the Bancroft telephoned, telling her she'd sent in the wrong form and that she'd have to resend it in triplicate before they can issue us any more.'

'And so we thought it best not to disturb her, didn't we, Annie?' said Sally.

'We did,' agreed Annie, tucking a stray tendril of hair back behind her ear.

'And as you're deputy superintendent, we thought you'd like to tell her the good news yourself,' Sally said.

Millie raised an eyebrow. 'Thank you very much, I'm sure.'

Her friends grinned.

'Leave your bits, Millie, and I'll clean them along with this lot,' Anne said, indicating the bowls, ear syringes and enamel pots from the morning's dressing clinic.

Millie dried her hands and, making sure her apron was straight, made her way to Miss Dutton's office at the end of the hall.

Millie knocked at the door. She heard a noise and walked in.

'I'm sorry to disturb you, Miss Dutton.' Millie stopped dead.

Instead of sitting, head bent, rewriting the dressing requisition, Miss Dutton was standing beside her desk with a flushed face and her frilly matron's hat slightly askew.

Casually lounging in the antique armchair just to her right sat Mr Shottington. He was dressed in his usual sartorial way in a morning suit, striped waistcoat and sporting a club bow tie at his throat. He, too, was slightly red in the face and, although he regarded Millie calmly, the cigar sticking out of the side of his mouth was unlit and the wrong way around.

'Oh, Mr Shottington,' said Millie, feeling her own cheeks glow. 'I didn't realise.'

'You're supposed to wait for me to say "come" before you barge in, Sister Smith,' Miss Dutton barked, glaring at Millie.

'I'm sorry,' Millie replied, noting the button of the superintendent's frilly white collar was undone. 'I thought you did.'

'Well, I never,' snapped the superintendent. 'Mr Shottington and I were in the middle of an important discussion.'

'I can see,' replied Millie.

Miss Dutton's eyes flickered to the surgeon. 'He was just—'

'Making sure the pen-pushers on the health committee are giving our valued superintendent all she needs,' cut in Mr Shottington, surreptitiously removing a blonde hair from his sleeve.

Millie smiled pleasantly. 'I'm sure Miss Dutton is very pleased to have your continued support.'

A splash of colour flared on Miss Dutton's throat, but Mr Shottington smiled urbanely.

'There's nothing official yet, but I have indicated to the health authority that I would be willing to chair the management committee.' His self-satisfied smile widened. 'I'm certain their grateful acceptance letter is already in the post.'

'I hope so,' said Miss Dutton, fluttering her pale eyelashes at the portly surgeon.

They exchanged a look and then Mr Shottington rose to his feet. 'Well, dear ladies, as much as I would like to continue in your company, I have an assortment of appendixes, hernias and peptic ulcers waiting for me in theatre.' He picked up his bowler from Miss Dutton's desk. 'Good day, Superintendent, Sister Smith.'

'Oh, do call by again soon, Mr Shottington,' Miss Dutton twittered.

He touched the brim of his hat and strolled out.

The superintendent stared at the closed door for a moment and then returned to her chair behind the desk. She looked coolly up at Millie.

'Well? What was so urgent that you had to burst into my office?'

Millie told her about the student Queen's nurses.

'Would you like me to allocate them and set out their training programme as I did with the last group?' Millie asked.

Miss Dutton nodded. 'But make sure they know to keep out from under my feet.'

'Also, Doctor Gingold is going to be setting up a child health clinic at St Aiden's in August, and I said I'd do a rota of nurses to help if you're happy for me to oversee it,' Millie said.

'As long as it doesn't land on my plate, you can go ahead.' Miss Dutton picked up her pen and jabbed it in the inkwell. 'Is there anything else?'

'Not at present,' replied Millie.

Miss Dutton looked down at her work.

'Would you mind if I asked you something?' said Millie.

The superintendent looked up.

'Why haven't you told Mr Shottington that I know about you and him?'

The flush returned to Miss Dutton's face, but there was also trepidation in her clear blue eyes. 'He would be very annoyed with me for being indiscreet.'

Millie looked puzzled. 'It was hardly your fault. It was pure chance that I saw you together.'

'Perhaps, but Mr Shottington has his reputation to think of. He's held in very high esteem by the Royal College, and there's a whisper that he might be offered a knighthood, and so he can't afford even a hint of scandal.' Miss Dutton looked sharply at Millie. 'And I hope you'll respect that.'

Millie regarded her levelly. 'If I'd wanted to make trouble I'd have done so before now. But perhaps if his reputation is so precious to him he should have thought twice about having an affair.'

Miss Dutton's eyes flashed. 'It's not like that. Mr Shottington is a model husband who has given his wife everything she could wish for, but she doesn't appreciate him.'

'Oh, I see,' said Millie, not even trying to hide her amusement.

Pain flickered across Miss Dutton's face. 'Once his children are older he is going to divorce his wife and we'll be married.' Her expression tightened. 'Now, if there's nothing else, Smith, I have this order to rewrite.' She turned back to her task.

Millie studied the lace fluting on the top of Miss Dutton's

nurse's cap for a moment, then walked to the door. As she grasped the handle, Miss Dutton spoke again.

'I suppose you think I'm some sort of Mata Hari for stealing another woman's husband,' she said bitterly.

Millie turned and looked at the superintendent's pinched white face. 'No, Miss Dutton, I think you're a fool for believing that you have.'

As the jazz quartet, who were squashed on the small stage against the back wall, played the opening bars of the next number and couples filled the floor to jitterbug, Millie gazed through the noisy, smoke-filled Feldman Club at 100 Oxford Street to where Jim leant casually against the bar. Wearing a tailored black suit and with his hair swept back he looked every inch the sophisticated Man About Town.

As if sensing her eyes on him, Jim turned and the familiar self-assured smile spread across his face. He sauntered back.

'One martini for the lady,' he said, placing it in front of her and slipping into the seat beside her.

He raised his glass. 'Here's to us.'

'Cheers.' Millie removed the olive and took a sip. 'This is nice.'

Jim nodded approvingly. 'Just the right mix of lemon and vermouth.'

'No, I mean us being out together,' Millie said.

A warm look she'd not seen very often recently stole into his eyes. 'Yes it is, but,' his expression became grave, 'my dear, I have a terrible confession to make.'

'Confession?' said Millie, feeling an icy lump in her chest.

He took her hand. 'I confess,' he said in a solemn tone, 'that I am the worst husband in the world.'

'Oh, Jim,' she laughed. 'Don't be silly, you're not the worst husband in the world.'

'No, don't be kind, Millie. I am.' He kissed her hand. 'I have the most beautiful wife waiting for me at home and yet I spend most evenings with crusty old men.'

Millie giggled. 'But it's your job and you said yourself how much the minister relies on you to keep the unions on side.'

Jim slipped his arm around her. 'But that's no excuse for neglecting my lovely wife.'

He pressed his lips on hers.

Millie slipped her arm around his neck. 'I'm sorry I'm a grouch about it but it's lonely at home without you.'

'I know.' Jim kissed her again then picked up his drink. 'Now, bottoms up. It's Saturday night and neither of us have to get up for work in the morning.' He winked. 'And who knows, we might stay in bed all day.'

A warm feeling spread through Millie. She took another sip of her martini and suddenly felt rather giggly.

'You know, Jim, you gave me a fright,' she said. 'For a moment there I thought you were going to tell me that on your last trip to Russia you'd married some female steel worker and had half-a-dozen children living on a commune in the Ukraine.'

Jim laughed. 'Oh, Millie, have you ever seen a woman steel worker?' He flexed his bicep. 'They've got bigger muscles than me and bushier moustaches.'

Millie giggled again. 'That's a terrible thing to—'

'Hello, James,' a woman's voice interrupted. 'Fancy seeing you here.'

Still bubbling with laughter, Millie turned and found herself looking at a slightly built young woman with a sharp elfin-like face and blonde hair caught back into a crocheted snood glaring down at them.

'Eddy!' Jim said, looking slightly flustered.

'It's Edwina now,' she replied. Her gaze flickered over Millie and her crimson lips pulled into a tight smile.

'How lovely to see you, Edwina,' Jim said, smoothly. 'This is my wife, Millie. Millie, this is Edwina Winkworth. We were at Oxford together.'

Edwina gave a condescending smile. 'Charmed, I'm sure,' she said, offering Millie a gloved hand.

'Nice to meet you,' Millie said, shaking the hand and knowing this woman with pearls around her neck could tell her outfit was a makeover. 'So you and my husband were friends at university?'

'Yes, dear James and I were friends, good friends,' Edwina's eyes slipped towards Jim. 'Weren't we, James?'

'It was a long time ago, Edwina,' Jim replied flatly.

Amusement warmed Edwina's icy expression a little. 'And

now you're married to this gorgeous creature. I bet your mother was beside herself with joy.'

Jim smiled and put his arm around Millie's shoulder. 'My mother was delighted.'

Annoyance flickered over Edwina's face but then her lively smile returned. 'I suppose he's just dragged you to see some dreadful modern play about oppressed peasants in the Urals,' she said to Millie.

'No,' replied Millie, snuggling closer to her husband. 'We've just been to the Empire Leicester Square to see *Easter Parade* with Judy Garland and Fred Astaire.'

'It's been good to see you again, Eddy, but we shouldn't keep you any longer.' Jim turned towards Millie. 'Give my regards to your brother.'

Edwina's red lips pulled into an ugly line for a second and then she tottered back to the bar.

'I'm sorry about that, Millie.' Jim said, his amiable expression returning. 'Edwina was always one for the dramatic.'

'So you knew each other at Oxford,' Millie said.

'Yes,' he replied, taking a mouthful of martini. 'She was at Somerville, studying something or another. A whole crowd of us used to hang around together in the university's Communist League and we were quite close at one time.'

'How close?'

Jim looked down and took a sip of drink. 'Oh, you know.'

'No, I'm not sure I do, Jim.'

He raised his eyes. 'All right, we were lovers, but—'

'You were engaged to her!' Millie chipped in.

He laughed. 'Good God, no. It was 1939. Everyone believed the Nazis would take over Europe and we were swept up in the moment; we weren't the only ones.'

'I'm sure you weren't, but she must have thought you were going to marry her, or why else would she?' Millie asked.

'Let me have my wicked way?' Jim joked.

'I was going to say give up her good name,' Millie replied evenly.

'That went long before I met her,' he replied in a matter-of-fact tone. 'With one of her father's gamekeepers, according to her brother.' Jim threw back the last of his drink. 'It was just a fling like you and that Alex chap who disappeared abroad.'

'That wasn't a fling! We were engaged. We'd even booked the wedding,' she said, uncomfortably. 'And you promised you'd never mention it.'

He slipped his arm around her waist. 'I'm sorry, Millie, sweetheart.' Jim kissed her lightly on the lips. 'Forget about Edwina and let's enjoy our evening together.' He took her glass. 'I'll get us a top-up.'

He stood up and headed to the bar. As she watched her husband order their drinks, Millie tried to force her thoughts from the image of the tall, dark and mesmerizingly handsome man she'd so nearly married and back on to having a pleasant night out with her husband.

Chapter Three

'It's been just the same here, Millie,' Connie Byrne said, rolling her green eyes. 'We've had patients queuing halfway down Middlesex Street every day.'

Millie was sitting on her friend's bed, propped up against the headboard with her legs stretched out. Connie sat at the opposite end of the bed, supported by the footboard and with her toes resting on the pillow beside Millie. They had sat in this comfortable and informal way for as long as they had been friends, some eight years or more.

As Jim wouldn't be home until seven, Millie had hopped on a bus to Aldgate to catch up with a bit of welcome gossip.

Unlike St George's and St Dunstan's Association, which was brought into being by a founder, Miss Robina Munroe, and which had right from the start a charter of clearly set rules, the Spitalfields and Shoreditch Association was obviously a much more rough and ready affair. But perhaps it needed to be, as the alleyways around Whitechapel High Street were notorious.

Unless there was actual trouble, such as a knife fight or murder, the police turned a blind eye to the goings-on in the decaying, bug-infested tenements, and even in broad daylight skimpily clad young women hung around on corners to ply their trade.

Of course, the problem wasn't so much the young women themselves, but the illegal abortions, sexual diseases and the violence they could face, not to mention the regular discovery of new-borns with plastic bags tied over their heads.

Instead of the tight-knit family communities of the docks Millie was familiar with, the clinic where Connie worked dealt mainly with those who were newly arrived in London or who had been displaced, and everyone was squashed into the gloomy old Victorian tenements, trying to avoid the meths drinkers loitering about in Itchy Park (or Christchurch graveyard, to give it its correct name) or who congregated amongst the bombed-out ruins of the old St Mary's Church.

The Spitalfields and Shoreditch Nursing Association had restored Fry House in Dorset Street four years ago, installing hot water and baths on each of the floors, but the new mod cons couldn't disguise the house's eighteenth-century origins. However, with lace curtains at the window, china knick-knacks on the old fireplace and geraniums dancing merrily in the window box outside, Connie's room was straight out of the pages of *Woman & Home*.

Millie laughed. 'I suppose I can't blame them. And I'm sure things will soon settle down.'

Connie didn't look convinced. 'You've been saying that for a month and it's still no better. You've got too much faith in human nature.'

'No,' replied Millie. 'I like to give people the benefit of the doubt.' She raised an eyebrow. 'Which is just as well, isn't it?'

Connie laughed as she played with a curl close to her ear. 'Will you never let off about that pair of stockings? I told you before I thought they were mine or I'd never have taken them off the radiator.'

'And I gave you the benefit of the doubt,' replied Millie, giving her friend an indulgent look. 'And yes, I'll have another cuppa please.'

Connie swung her legs off the bed and poured them both another tea.

'So, how's Jim?' she asked, resuming her position.

'Busy, as always,' Millie replied.

'On the newly-married front, I hope,' said Connie, lowering her eyes on to Millie's stomach and letting them linger for a moment.

'Honestly, Connie, you're as bad as aunt Ruby,' replied Millie, shifting and making the spring beneath boing in protest. 'I thought I told you the last time you started with your not-so-subtle hints that we've decided to wait a little while.'

Connie gave her a sympathetic look 'You did, but I thought it was only because you hadn't talked Jim around yet.'

'It not just Jim, it's me too,' said Millie, ignoring the little pang of longing in her chest. 'The dock unions and the Port Authority are constantly at each other's throats and Jim puts in long hours at the Ministry trying to keep the peace, as well as working with the Leytonstone and Wanstead Labour Party committee, and so it's not really the right time to start a family just now.'

Connie looked dismayed. 'But you could be waiting another two years.'

'There's no hurry,' replied Millie. 'And even if it is that long, I'll only just be thirty, and lots of women have their first one at that age.'

Connie sat forward, and changed the subject. 'Now, come on, you've been here an hour or so – spill the beans and tell me the latest gossip at the old place.'

Millie gave her friend a crafty smile. 'Well.' She then ran through the various dramas at Munroe House, from Annie finding a mouse in her underwear drawer to Mrs Pierce's latest attempt to make Spam more appealing. 'And of course, Sally must have told you last week that Joyce is leaving.'

'Is she really emigrating to Canada?' Connie asked, incredulously.

'As soon as their papers come through apparently,' Millie replied. 'Her husband got a job with the railways over there somewhere near Toronto. Oh, and Gladys has got a new fellow.'

'I don't call that news, Millie,' Connie scoffed. 'She changes her men more often than her knickers.'

'Apparently this chap is different,' Millie said. 'He's some spiv with a flash car and lots of money to throw around.'

'Just Gladys's type then,' replied Connie. 'Perhaps we'll hear wedding bells for her soon, although I hope she doesn't have the gall to stroll down the aisle in white.'

Millie laughed. 'How's Malcolm?'

A coy smiled spread across Connie's pretty face. 'Oh, same as ever,' she replied, happily. 'Monday we sit in, Wednesday it's the pictures, Saturday at the Rose and Punch Bowl for a quiet drink, and then Sunday lunch at his mother's one week and mine the other.'

'Oh, that's nice,' said Millie.

'Of course, Malcolm goes to his model railway club on

Tuesday and I go shopping with mum on Saturday while he's train-spotting at Stratford,' Connie added.

'What do you do on Thursday?'

'Wash my hair.'

Millie took another mouthful of tea and so did Connie.

'And how long have you been walking out?' asked Millie.

'Two years, three months next week, since the St Andrew Hospital funding dance at Poplar Town Hall. You couldn't come because you were still recovering from being knocked off your bike, do you remember?'

Millie didn't, but she smiled. 'Has he mentioned anything about getting engaged, yet?'

Connie's happy expression slipped a little. 'We've discussed it a couple of times but we don't want to rush things. And neither does his mother. And actually, with all the things going on at the moment, I'm quite pleased he's not rushing to settle down. Did I tell you that we're setting up a special health programme for the prostitutes in the area?'

'Goodness,' said Millie. 'It's about time, but I can't see any of the local GPs being very keen to take it on.'

'Neither can the super, and so she asked the committee to employ a doctor,' Connie explained. 'She wants me to be the lead nurse for the project, so you see,' she gave a little shrug, 'even if Malcolm proposed tomorrow, I haven't got time to sort out a wedding and set up a home. Now, have you got time for another?'

Millie glanced at her watch.

The under-secretary was on a fact-finding mission to Liverpool, and so Jim should be home on time. Of course, that was supposing some other crisis didn't blow up before he got out of the door.

'Oh, all right,' said Millie. 'But I have to be on the train by five if I don't want Jim walking into an empty house.'

Connie stood up. 'You put your feet up while I go and make another pot.' She picked up the tray and went out.

Millie settled back against the headboard and glanced over at the picture propped up on Connie's bedside cabinet. With a sensible-looking pipe jutting from his mouth and his hair Brylcreemed firmly to his square-shaped head, Malcolm Henstock stared back at her. He was wearing his regular combination of tweeds and knitwear and he stood proudly holding a model steam train in one hand and a rosette in the other.

Millie gave a heavy sigh. Connie's young man might be as dull as dishwater with the spontaneity of a bath sponge, but if he did ever get around to making an honest woman of Connie she'd never have to wonder if he was coming home each night.

Millie scootered along Commercial Road with the late-afternoon traffic heading west until she reached the second turning after Watney Street and then she swung into her mother's street. Although there was an autumnal nip to the air, there was still a group of boys kicking a football about in the middle of the road and a handful of girls jumping in and out of a hopscotch grid chalked on the pavement. Bringing her scooter to a halt, Millie hopped off, pulled it on to its stand and then chained it securely to the iron boot-scraper fixed into the brickwork.

Pulling the string with the key attached through the letter-box, she let herself in.

'Yoo-hoo! Only me, Mum!' she called, putting her case on the floor and removing her nurse's mac.

'I'm just putting the dinner in,' her mother responded from the kitchen. Millie hooked up her coat and, moving her mother's knitting off the seat, flopped into the fireside chair. The kindling in the hearth had burnt through and the coals were just beginning to glow. As the front room of her mother's two-up two-down was no more than fifteen feet by fifteen feet, it wouldn't take long for the room to warm up.

Millie rested her head back and closed her eyes, enjoying the feeling of well-being her old home always gave her.

Her mother walked in. 'Don't get up.'

'Too late,' Millie replied, rising to her feet and kissing her mother on the cheek.

'I've only just got in as I was late leaving work,' Doris said.

'Aren't you always,' replied Millie, taking the poker from the stand and loosening a couple of coals so they tumbled in the flames.

'I had to get a paint order ready for the morning delivery,' her mother continued. 'With the council throwing up houses left, right and centre, the demand for decorating supplies has gone through the roof. And now that Mavis has gone, me and Rose are rushed off our feet all day. But never mind about me; how's your day been?'

'Oh, you know, bed baths and dressings,' Millie said, with a sigh.

The kettle whistled from the kitchen. Doris shoved her feet into her slippers and pulled herself out of the chair.

'You stay where you are,' she said firmly and this time Millie didn't argue.

Doris switched on the radio and went through to the scullery. Millie closed her eyes again as the soft strains of the BBC Concert Orchestra filled the room. By the time Millie had hummed her way through the 'Blue Danube' and a mellow version of 'When You Wish Upon a Star' her mother had returned, carrying a tray groaning with crockery and cake.

'I don't suppose you've eaten since dinnertime,' Doris said, putting the tray on the coffee table between them.

'No, I didn't have time.'

'You have to eat properly, Millie,' Doris said, looking anxiously at her. 'Or you'll be ill yourself.'

Millie smiled. 'Yes, Mum.'

Her mother tutted. 'Sometimes I think that Miss Dutton forgets there are other nurses in Munroe House besides you. How was Connie yesterday?'

Millie picked up her cup and cradled it. 'Fine, and she sends her love.'

'Any sign of wedding bells yet?'

Millie shook her head. 'I don't think you could ever accuse Malcolm of being impulsive.'

Doris rolled her eyes. 'Silly boy. Connie's a pretty girl and if he's not careful some chap with a bit of fire in his belly will whisk her off her feet while he is still umming and aahing.'

Millie took a sip of tea.

'That's right, love. You get that cuppa and a bit of cake down you before you dash off home,' Doris said, putting a slice of seed cake on a plate and placing it in front of her.

Millie blew across the top of her drink. 'I'm in no rush, Mum, as Jim's not home until late.'

'Again?' Doris replied.

'I know, but he can't leave while the House is sitting.' Millie picked up her spoon and made a play of stirring her drink. 'Hopefully it won't be for much longer. Don Wethersfield, one of the bigwigs from Party headquarters, is coming to the constituency dinner and dance in November, and if Jim can make a good impression then, it will almost guarantee he'll be adopted as the constituency candidate when Bill Woodrow retires.' She sighed. 'Of course, as Jim pointed out, I've got to make a good impression too. I just hope my clothing coupons will stretch to something sophisticated and glamorous.'

'I'm sure that whatever you wear you'll look lovely and Jim will be very proud of you,' her mother said.

Millie bit her lip. 'I hope so. I don't want to let him down. Not after he's worked so hard.'

Doris regarded her thoughtfully for a moment and then spoke. 'Millie, are you happy?'

Millie gave a hollow laugh. 'What sort of daft question is that?'

'Are you?'

'Of course,' replied Millie, shifting under her mother's intense gaze. 'I admit it's not much fun eating supper alone, but I know Jim would much rather be home than hanging around in the Strangers' Bar in the House for hours on end.'

Doris sighed. 'I know things were different when I was your age, but from the day we were wed your father was home at six on the dot every night.'

Something unsettling gathered in Millie's mind, but she shoved it away.

'I'm fine, Mum. Really I am.' She reached across to squeeze her mother's hand. 'And once Jim's the Labour candidate for Leytonstone and Wanstead, we'll be sitting at home drinking our cocoa and listening to the radio every night like a regular old Darby and Joan.'

Mrs Pierce bustled out of the kitchen pushing the afternoon tea trolley towards the nurses' refectory just as Millie got to the treatment room. She went in and joined Eva and Sally who were setting out the rack of test tubes and chemicals for the afternoon clinic. Millie unlocked the filing cabinet and pulled out the box containing the patients' notes.

'Aren't you going out on your rounds, Millie?' Sally asked.

'I will when Annie gets back,' Millie replied, unhooking the blackboard and scrawling down the addresses of her afternoon visits. 'She was called out a couple of hours ago to Mrs Cohen in Hessel Street. It's a fifth child and so she shouldn't be too long. I don't want to trek all the way to Ratcliffe Cross only to be called back to deliver a baby in Dock Street. In fact, if the truth was told, I'd prefer to leave delivering babies to someone else today, as I've promised Jim faithfully I'll be home on time.'

Sally winked. 'Oh, that sounds like he's desperate for something.'

'He is,' replied Millie. 'Not to be late for the party's annual bun-fight tonight.'

'Ooo-errr,' said Eve, putting half-a-dozen thermometers in a jar of disinfectant. 'Have you got something posh to wear?'

Millie nodded. 'I have. It's a fitted pink and dove grey candy-striped sateen evening gown with a nipped-in waist and a full circle skirt.'

Eve's jaws dropped. 'But that must have taken yards of fabric.'

'Eight and a half, to be precise,' said Millie. 'Plus another five of poplin and net for the petticoats.'

'How on earth did you get all that material?' Sally asked.

'My aunt Ruby knows someone in the rag trade who got it at cost,' Millie replied. 'But it still took every clothing coupon I had, plus some of Mum's and Ruby's too.' A smile spread across her face. 'I might not be able to buy myself a pair of knickers until Easter, but, if I say it myself who shouldn't, it does look a proper treat.'

'Well, I wish you well to wear it,' Sally said, spreading a draw-sheet on the examination couch ready for the first patient.

Leaving her two friends to begin the clinic, Millie put a couple of extra dressing packs in her case. As Mrs Lemmin, who was twenty stone if she was an ounce and took a full hour to bed bath, had been admitted to hospital, Millie had managed to squeeze in two of her Friday-afternoon calls before midday, and so was hopeful that she'd be motoring through the back gates of Munroe House on time for once.

Smiling at the first few pregnant mothers waiting in the corridor, Millie headed towards the back door. Just as she reached for the brass handle the phone rang. Her stomach lurched uncomfortably.

She retraced her steps back to the hall table. Of course, it might be a doctor or the hospital ringing to refer a patient or the equipment store checking an order.

Millie lifted the receiver from the cradle.

'Good afternoon, Munroe House, Sister Smith speaking,' she said.

'Fank Gawd,' said the man's voice at the other end. The pips went and then the line connected again. 'Stan Fry 'ere. Me missus's waters have just gone.'

Chapter Four

Jim paid the taxi driver and, without waiting for Millie, marched up the steps to Snaresbrook Golf Club. Millie hooked her handbag over her arm and trotted after him.

They had travelled the mile-long journey from their house in stony silence, and now Millie wondered if she'd have to sit through the whole meal with Jim fuming beside her.

Snaresbrook Golf Club was about a hundred years old and had once been a country house. Although some of the downstairs internal walls had been removed to create a huge dining room, this didn't detract from the building's classic proportions. The black-and-white tiled lobby was filled now with couples chatting, drinks in hand. Like Jim, all the men were wearing dinner suits while their womenfolk broke up this panorama of unremitting black with an array of brightly coloured evening gowns, sparkling jewellery and fur stoles. Ruby had offered Millie the use of her fox wrap, but as she didn't fancy the idea of eating her supper with a tail and paws hanging from her shoulder, Millie had tactfully declined.

As they entered through the double doors Ted Kirby, the chairman of the local party, spotted them and hurried over, the gold chain strung across his paunch bouncing as he came toward them.

'For God's sake, Jim, where the pigging hell have you been?' he said in a stage whisper, grabbing Jim by the arm and propelling him towards the bar. 'Wethersfield's been downing double whiskies for twenty minutes waiting to meet you. It's costing me a small fortune as the man can drink like a ruddy fish, and he won't remember anything after a couple more.'

'I'm sorry, Ted,' Jim replied, giving Millie a baleful look. 'I'll square up with you later.'

Ted's belligerence lifted a little. 'Well, thankfully old

Woodrow's not here yet either, and so we've put dinner back for a bit, which leaves you a good half-hour to get on Don's right side.'

He led Jim forward.

Millie reached out to catch her husband's arm, but he snatched it away and moved off abruptly, and so she followed a few paces behind, pushing through the crowds and smoke in Jim's wake. They came to a halt in front of a large man with a ruddy face and several chins, who was clutching a cut-glass tumbler three-quarter's full of scotch.

'There you are, Kirby,' he said, clenching his teeth around the cigar wedged in his mouth. 'By 'eck, I were about to send out a search party.'

'Sorry, Mr Wethersfield, but you know what it's like at these things,' Ted replied, with a sycophantic smile. 'But I hope the bar staff have been looking after you.'

Mr Wethersfield grunted by way of an answer, and then his bloodshot eyes turned to Jim. 'This 'im then?'

Jim offered his hand. 'Jim Smith. I'm honoured to meet you, sir. I read your piece on the future of the coal industry in the *Herald* last week, and found it gave a most valuable insight into the issues.'

Mr Wethersfield raised a scraggly eyebrow. 'You're a bit on the posh side for a Labour man.'

'We're all one in the cause, comrade,' Jim replied affably.

Mr Wethersfield studied him for a second or two longer, and then grasped his hand. 'Aye, we are. And I hear that you are keen to take the baton from Woodrow at the next election.'

'I don't think it will be easy to fill Bill's shoes,' Jim replied in a sincere voice. 'But I'll do my best if the local party members judge me worthy.'

Ted slapped Jim heartily on the back. 'He's the committee's choice,' he said, beaming benevolently up at him.

'Not all of them.' Mr Wethersfield drew on his cigar and puffed a couple of circles upwards. 'While you were out searching for your lad I had a right interesting chat with your treasurer, Elwin Topping. He was waxing on about some train driver called Guthrie.'

Ted sucked on his lips. 'Len Guthrie's a good party man, right enough, but he's a bit of a hot-head and rabble-rouser. What you need in an MP is someone who can see a question from every angle and who knows the ropes in the House. Did I mention that Jim is the Under-secretary for Trade and National Service's number-one assistant?'

'Once or twice,' Mr Wethersfield replied. His eyes slid on to Millie. 'And is this the little woman?'

Without glancing at her, Jim put his arm stiffly around Millie. 'May I introduce my wife, Millie?'

Mr Wethersfield took her hand in his hot and damp one. 'How do, Mrs Smith.'

'Good evening, Mr Wethersfield,' Millie replied, smiling sweetly.

He released her hand. Millie fought the urge to take out her handkerchief and wipe it.

'Mrs Smith was born and bred in the area,' Ted chipped in. 'Father was a union man all his life.' He forced a jolly laugh. 'You know what they say, Mr Wethersfield: behind every successful man is a good woman at home.'

Mr Wethersfield's thin mouth pulled tighter. 'Except I hear as like that Mrs Smith isn't. Elwin tells me, Smith, that your missus is a nurse or some such thing.'

Millie felt Jim stiffen beside her but she held the politician's gaze. 'I work for the new health service as a senior sister and midwife in Stepney,' she said in a deliberately pleasant tone.

A sour expression settled on Mr Wethersfield's fleshy features. 'To my mind a woman's place is in the home.' He took hold of his lapels. 'My wife hasn't done a day's work since the day we wed and has contented herself with caring for me and our nine children. I'll have no truck with these new-fangled notions of women having a career.' He grinned at Jim and Ted. 'I mean, if you go down that road this year, they'll be asking for the same money next.'

Millie raised an eyebrow. 'You've got nine children!'

'Aye,' Mr Wethersfield replied, swelling his chest and stretching the buttonholes on his waistcoat. 'And six boys amongst them.'

'Well, with that number to cook and clean for, your wife probably works harder than any man I know,' Millie said, giving the politician an ingenuous look.

Irritation flickered over Wethersfield's face and his attention returned to Jim. 'I take it you've no young 'uns.'

'Give 'em a chance,' said Ted jovially, signalling for the bar man to replenish Wethersfield's glass. 'They've only been wed less than a year.'

'You know the Party is looking for candidates who set an example to the nation by their own family life, Smith,' said Mr Wethersfield.

'I do,' Jim replied. 'And my wife will be leaving work in the New Year, sir.'

Millie's jaw clenched as she stared at her husband.

'Oh, there you are, Ted.'

Millie looked around to see Ted's wife, Bessie, pushing her way through the crowd. Bessie Kirby had spent most of her working life as a garment presser in a Whitechapel sweatshop, as her brawny arms testified. Her square-shouldered figure was squeezed into a lilac chiffon evening gown that was supposed to be mid-calf in length but on Bessie hovered around her ankles.

'Thank goodness I've found you,' she said, putting her hand on her considerable bosom to steady her breathing. 'The chef says if he doesn't serve the dinner in the next ten minutes it will be ruined. But there's still no sign of Bill and Lena. I rang their house but there's no reply, so I imagine they're on their way. What should I do?'

Wethersfield drained his glass. 'Well, as my stomach thinks me throat's been cut, I'd suggest we start dinner, and Bill and his missus can catch up with us when they get here.'

Millie popped the last of her dessert into her mouth and put her fork and spoon together on the dish.

She and Jim were sitting two tables away from the main one where Mr Wethersfield and the important members of the local committee were ensconced. The golf club had pulled out all the stops in its efforts to satisfy the constituency committee's yearly visitation, and so along with a pristine white damask tablecloth there were pretty bouquets of winter foliage and berries in the centre of each table. More significantly, now that rationing had eased up a little, the menu had improved too and the all too familiar dried-egg puddings had at long last given way to light pastries.

As the couple sharing their table were chatting to people on the table behind, Millie's eyes drifted up to the evening's honoured guest.

Mr Wethersfield had just finished his second helping of dessert and sat, cigar in one hand and a double Scotch in the other, like some medieval despot presiding over his court. To one side of him sat Ted Kirby, and on the other, stretching across Bill Woodrow's still empty chair, was Elwin Topping. Bessie Kirby and Marge Topping had been relegated to either end of the table and looked none too pleased about the arrangement.

Millie glanced at Jim. 'Where do you think Bill and Lena have got to?'

He shrugged and continued to stare glumly at the top table.

'I hope they haven't been in an accident,' Millie persisted.

Jim didn't reply.

Millie put her hand on his arm. 'I'm sure Mr Wethersfield will give you his endorsement.'

Jim's head snapped around. 'I'm bloody not.' His blue eyes regarded her icily. 'Not after that fiasco earlier. If it wasn't bad enough that you made me late, you had to mention your bloody job.'

'We were only a few moments later than everyone else,' Millie replied, smiling at the people who'd looked around at Jim's heated voice.

'We were late enough to allow that bastard Elwin to put in his five-pennyworth on behalf of his cousin,' he continued, heedless of the attention he was attracting.

'Who?'

'Len Guthrie is Elwin's cousin,' Jim replied, sounding now as if he were talking to a two-year-old.

Millie looked puzzled. 'Wasn't it him who was made deputy chairman of Poplar council two months ago?'

'It was.'

'Well, then, he's not serious competition for the party's nomination,' Millie said in a light tone.

'He wouldn't be if there was an election in the next few months,' Jim replied in a lower tone. 'But as Attlee intends to stay for the full term, Guthrie'll have plenty of bloody time to step down from the council.'

'That still doesn't mean he'll get the nomination,' Millie said.

Jim's eyes narrowed. 'But he's got a better chance now, thanks to you.'

'Me!'

'I told you not to tell him about your job.'

'But he already knew,' replied Millie.

'Yes, because Elwin told him,' Jim snapped back. 'But he wouldn't have been able to do that if we'd bloody well arrived on time. And then you go and make fun of his wife.'

'I did not.'

Jim regarded her coldly. 'What was all that about her working harder than any man you knew, then?'

'For goodness sake, Jim.' She rolled her eyes. 'It was just a light-hearted comment. This is a social occasion after all.'

'Well, he didn't bloody well take it that way,' Jim replied. 'And keep it down, will you?' he said out of the corner of his mouth. 'I don't want everyone knowing our business.'

They exchanged a hostile glare and then Jim raised his glass to one of the party officials who was looking questioningly at them.

Millie leant towards her husband. 'You're the one raising your voice,' she said under her breath. 'And while we're on the subject of who said what, who said I was leaving work after Christmas?'

'I've tried to be reasonable about this, hoping that you would see where your duty lies,' he said in a wounded voice. 'But it seems I'm going to have to put my foot down. I want you to put your resignation in.'

'But ...'

Jim raised his hand. 'I won't be moved, Millie. And after the way you've wrecked my prospects tonight, I'm surprised you even have the gall to argue.'

The main door burst open and one of the minor members of the local committee dashed in. Without pausing he headed for the top table and bent over to speak to Ted. Ted turned to Mr Wethersfield and whispered in his ear and then stood up. Taking his spoon, he rapped it on the table. The room fell silent.

'Comrades, if I could have your attention.' The hubbub

subsided and Ted continued. 'I'm afraid I've just received some unexpected and,' Ted put his hand over his heart, 'very sad news. It seems earlier this evening, as he was getting ready to join us for this convivial occasion, Bill Woodrow collapsed.' There were shocked gasps. Ted raised his hand and the room fell silent again. 'He was rushed to Whipps Cross Hospital, where the doctors did their best to revive him. But I'm afraid it's my unhappy duty to inform you that our dear and esteemed comrade and Member of Parliament passed away this evening at half-past seven.'

The assembled company looked at each other in utter disbelief. A couple of the wives of long-standing constituency members started to cry, while several men in the room, including Ted, took a steadying drink. For a split second jubilation flitted across Jim's face, then he grabbed his pint of beer and stood up.

'I'd like to raise a toast to Comrade Bill, the best Member of Parliament any constituency could hope to have,' Jim said in a voice that quelled any whispering. 'He was a man whose work and dedication to his fellow men is a shining example to us all. He will be greatly missed by everyone who knew him and, for those of us privileged to call him friend, he,' Jim paused as if trying to master his emotions, 'will be deeply mourned.'

There were nods of agreement.

Jim raised his glass. 'Comrade Bill,' he said, with a tiny croak in his voice.

There was a scraping of chairs as the assembled company stood up.

'Comrade Bill,' fifty-plus voices echoed.

Ted took out his handkerchief and blew his nose noisily.

Mr Wethersfield sat motionless for a moment, and then stubbed out his half-smoked cigar and stood up. 'Nicely said, lad,' he said, raising his glass and regarding Jim with a wry smile.

'Yes,' agreed Ted. 'I know he and Lena thought of you as the son they never had, Jim.'

Jim cast his gaze around the shocked faces. 'I'm sure I can speak for everyone here,' he reached down and took Millie's hand, 'when I ask you to assure Lena that she and the girls will be in everyone prayers.'

Ted nodded. He and Jim exchanged a look and then both men resumed their seats.

The room broke into chattering again and a number of the men went to the bar to replenish their drinks.

Jim let go of Millie and picked up his pint. He took a large mouthful of beer and then sat staring at the glass.

Millie closed her hand over Jim's. 'What terrible news.'

Jim turned and a crafty look spread across his face. 'Yes, it is; for Len Guthrie.'

Jim fell against the door and closed one eye as he tried to locate the lock with the end of the door key.

'I know it was here when we left,' he said, jabbing the key into the wood.

It was probably half-eleven by now and although they'd heard of Len's demise just after nine, Jim and Ted, along with the rest of the committee, had spent the following hour and a half consoling each other in the bar. In a true spirit of fraternity, Mr Wethersfield had joined them in their sadness, and Ted had finally poured him into a taxi back to Westminster twenty minutes ago. Thankfully, another taxi had arrived just afterwards, and Jim hailed it much to Millie's relief.

'Shhh, you'll wake up the neighbours,' Millie whispered, guiding Jim's hand towards the keyhole.

'So what?' he slurred. 'I have to start my campaign somewhere.'

He stepped out from the doorway. 'Comrades,' he shouted, flinging his arms wide and swaying towards the hedge. 'Behold your new Member of Parliament for Leystead and Wanstone.' He gave Millie a baffled little-boy look.

'You mean Leytonstone and Wanstead,' she laughed, leading him back to the front door. 'And don't you think your campaign could wait until after Bill's buried?'

He nodded sagely and slipped off the step. 'You're right. The voters wouldn't like it.'

Millie took the keys from his hand and opened the door. 'And we should visit Lena in a day or two to give our condolences.'

Jim looked sad. 'Poor Lena.' Then his sober expression changed and he wrapped his arm around Millie. 'But let's not worry about her now. There's something more pressing.'

He pulled her into the shadow of the weather porch. Grasping her bottom, he pressed her against his erection.

Millie laughed softly. 'Jim Smith, behave yourself.'

He backed her on to the door and nuzzled her neck. 'How can I, with a pretty little wifey like you?'

He pressed his lips on hers and the taste of whisky filled Millie's mouth. She wriggled out from under him and guided him through the door. As she closed it behind them, Jim grabbed her and pulled her to him again.

'You looked good tonight,' he said, grabbing the straps of her new gown and pulling them down. A shiver went through her as his fingers slid over her skin.

Millie stretched up and kissed his chin. 'Let's go upstairs.'

'You took the words right out of my mouth.'

He kissed her again and tightened the knot of excitement in the pit of her stomach.

Millie led him up the stairs.

As they reached their bedroom Jim let go of her hand and shrugged off his dinner jacket. He let it fall and drew Millie to him again.

'Come here, woman.' Jim's arm slipped around her as he drew her close. Millie's hand went to his chest. He kissed her again, but as Millie tried to kiss him, he pulled back. He grabbed her shoulder strap and then buried his teeth into her bare neck.

'Ouch!'

'You taste sweet,' he murmured, as he fumbled with the fastening at the back of her dress.

'Not too hard or you'll leave a mark,' Millie said, pulling away from him.

He gave a low laugh. Jim's mouth closed over hers as he tugged frantically at the mother-of-pearl buttons running down the length of the fitted bodice.

'Careful, you'll rip it,' she said, pushing him away. 'I'll do it,'

He released her and, swaying slightly, stepped back.

Millie, twisting her arms up her back, undid her dress and let it fall to the floor.

Jim's eyes grew flint-hard. He tore off his bow-tie, shirt and vest, discarding them in a crumpled heap on top of her clothes. He grabbed her and his mouth closed on hers in a harsh kiss; he shoved her on the bed.

Millie fell with her arms and legs outstretched. He stepped up to the edge of the bed. 'Take it off. All of it.'

Millie unhooked her brassiere and slipped it off.

Jim's eyes remained on her face as he unbuttoned his flies and lowered his trousers and pants. Caressing his freed penis with one hand, he reached out and spread her legs with the other. Kneeling between her thighs, he let his gaze run over her for a second or two and reached across to his bedside cabinet. His weight pressed down on her, driving the breath from her lungs as he retrieved the packet of Durex. He flipped it open.

'Damn.'

Jim's gaze ran slowly over her. And then he tossed aside the empty packet. 'What the hell?'

Chapter Five

As Millie palpated Iris Webb's swollen stomach a little foot or hand pushed back. She straightened up and pulled the mother-to-be's dress down.

It was Wednesday afternoon ante-natal clinic at Munroe House, and as the rain was lashing down outside, many of the mothers had brought their deep-bodied prams inside. They were lined up under the window, which meant that the room filled with chairs, toddlers and equipment was even more cramped than usual. It was her half-day really, but Jim was attending Len Woodrow's funeral that afternoon and would no doubt go to the Wanstead Working Men's Club for afters, and so Millie had volunteered to cover Eva's rota that day so that Eva could take her mother to a hospital appointment.

'Well,' Millie said, smiling at the heavily pregnant woman lying on the couch. 'I'd say that the newest member of the Webb family is almost ready to make an appearance.'

Iris, a thick-set mother of three young children, struggled on to her elbows. 'You're telling me. Some days it feels like he's trying to punch his way out.'

Millie helped her patient sit up, then turned her attention to the two little girls perched, with their feet dangling, on the chair beside the bench.

'Are you going to help Mummy when the new baby arrives?' she asked.

The children nodded solemnly.

Iris gave her daughters a soft look. 'Liz and May are as good as gold. It's Harry who's giving me grey hairs.' She crossed herself. 'But I shouldn't say so. Not after nearly losing him to the polio last summer.'

'How is he?'

'Dashing around the same as ever, now he's had his callipers fitted,' Iris replied. 'God bless Bevan for this new health service. If it wasn't for that, me and Pete would never have been able to get him proper ones.'

She swung her legs over the side of the couch and stood up. Moving the ear-trumpet and tape measure aside, Millie leant on the stainless-steel trolley and signed Iris's notes.

'Well, provided you don't call one of us out before, I'll see you next week, Mrs Webb,' she said, tucking the notes in their manila envelope.

'Thanks, Sister.' Iris took her coat from the back of the chair and shrugged it on. 'Come on, girls,' she said, taking a packet of cigarettes from her pocket. 'Let's get ourselves a bit of something for tea before the market shuts up.'

The two little girls jumped off the chair and, holding each other's hands, followed their mother to the door.

Millie dusted down the draw-sheet ready for the next patient and pulled back the screen. Taking Iris's notes, she headed across the room.

'Sister Smith.'

Millie turned and saw Annie's head poking around the sluice door.

'Can you spare me a moment?'

Millie filed the record in the wooden box on the nurses' desk and went to join her friend.

'What is it?' she asked, when they were out of earshot.

'I'm a bit concerned about a new patient,' Annie replied. 'I've put her at almost five months pregnant, but she's very large. She was an infant-school teacher so I don't think she's got her dates wrong and I doubt it's twins because there isn't any on either side of the family.'

'There's always a first time,' Millie replied.

'I know but her stomach is full of baby and there's something else,' Annie indicated the test-tube propped up in the wooden rack on the draining board.

'Goodness,' Millie said, staring at the quarter an inch of brick-red-coloured fluid in the bottom of the glass tube.

'I thought at first the Benedict fluid had gone off, so I did it again and got the same result,' Annie said. 'Have you ever seen so much sugar in a pregnant woman's urine before?'

'I have and it wasn't a happy turnout,' Millie said. 'Who's her doctor?'

'She hasn't got one. They only moved here three weeks ago when her husband started as headmaster at Hessel Street School, and,' Annie looked worried, 'she's forty-three, and this is her first baby. Would you mind taking a look at her before I tell her what I suspect? I don't want to alarm her and her husband unnecessarily if I'm mistaken.'

Millie gave her friend a questioning look. 'Husband?'

'Yes, he's here, too.'

Millie opened the screen shielding the examination bench in the corner and walked in. An elegant woman with short hair lay recumbent on the couch. Unlike most of the Wednesday-afternoon customers, who made do in the later stages of their pregnancy by pinning their ordinary clothes across their bellies, Mrs Joliffe was wearing a navy maternity dress with a wide white collar and matching cuffs, and seed-pearl earrings. Beside her and holding her hand was a tall man dressed in a dark suit with a club tie at his throat. They turned and smiled at Millie and Annie as they walked in.

'Sorry to keep you waiting,' Annie said, pulling the screen closed behind them. 'As you seem further on than your dates, I've asked Sister Smith to take a look. I hope you don't mind.'

'Not at all,' replied Mrs Joliffe.

Mr Joliffe, a round-faced man with a receding hairline and lively grey eyes shook his head. 'The more the merrier.'

In Millie's experience, having played their part in propagating the next generation, men usually took a back seat in the proceedings until it was time to wet the baby's head. It was therefore somewhat disconcerting to have one taking an interest in the intervening stage.

Millie picked up the patient notes with 'Dorothy Joliffe' written across the top. 'If I could just ...' She ran through the questions Annie had already asked, and Mr and Mrs Joliffe repeated their previous answers.

'And how long have you been married?'

'Twenty-two years,' Mrs Joliffe replied.

'And four months,' her husband added, squeezing her hand.

'As soon as we could without our parents' consent.'

The husband and wife exchanged a tender look.

'And this is your first child?' continued Millie.

'Yes,' replied Mr Joliffe, without taking his eyes from his wife.

A little lump stared to form in Millie's throat so she looked down at her notes again.

'Forgive me asking, Mrs Joliffe, but there have been no other pregnancies or miscarriages in all that time?'

'No,' said Mrs Joliffe. 'Not so much as a missed monthly.'

Mr Joliffe smiled at his wife. 'We'd resigned ourselves, years ago, that we weren't going to be blessed with the large family we wanted, didn't we, Dorothy?'

'We did, but here we are,' laughed his wife. 'On the wrong side of forty, going grey and about to be parents.'

Her husband put his arm around her shoulders. 'And I can't wait.'

The middle-aged couple giggled like a pair of schoolchildren.

'Sister Fletcher was a little concerned by your size, Mrs Joliffe.'

Her husband put his hand on his wife's stomach. 'Perhaps it's going to be a strapping rugby player.'

'Not if it's a girl,' replied his wife.

'Would you mind if I examined you?' Millie asked, in as light a tone as she could muster.

Mr Joliffe's expression became serious. 'There's nothing wrong is there, Sister?'

'I'm sure everything fine,' Millie replied, with a professional smile. 'We just want to be certain everything is as it should be.'

Mrs Joliffe lifted her dress. Millie moved closer to the bench and placed her hands either side of the woman's stomach, just above her pubic bone. Staring at the faded screen opposite, Millie explored gently with her fingertips, trying to make out the shapes beneath. She found the head without any trouble, but it was more the size of a baby at full-term than one with twelve or so weeks to go. The infant's bottom was also too high for a foetus at the supposed stage.

'The head's down,' Millie told the anxious couple.

They looked relieved and Millie felt a twinge of sadness for them. Being breech would be the least of the baby's problems.

She picked up the foetal stethoscope, breathed on the broad

end and placed it over where she calculated the baby's spine should be. Pressing her ear to the flat end, she immediately heard the infant's heart. Glancing down at her watch she counted for half a minute and then straightened up.

'That's fine, too,' she said.

Mr and Mrs Joliffe let out an audible sigh of relief.

'But there are two things I'm not happy about.' Mr Joliffe put a protective arm around his wife and Millie felt the lump in her throat return. 'You firstly, your blood pressure is a hundred and forty over ninety, which wouldn't be a too much of a concern if we hadn't found sugar in your urine. Are any of your family diabetics?'

Mrs Joliffe nodded. 'But only on my father's side. His mother and sister had sugar diabetes.'

'But it won't affect our baby, will it?' asked Mr Joliffe.

Millie looked at the anxious parents-to-be and her heart went out to them.

'Now it's by no means certain that you have got diabetes, as you'll have to have a test at the hospital for us to be sure. But if you have, then there might be complications as you get nearer to your delivery date.' She put her hand over Mrs Joliffe's. 'I know it's difficult not to worry, but medical science has come a long way since the war and I promise we will do everything we can to help.' Millie forced a cheery smile. 'I know you've only just moved into the area, but it is important that you see a doctor as soon as possible.'

Mrs Joliffe looked helplessly at her husband. 'Who's our nearest doctor?'

Annie spoke. 'Doctor—'

'Doctor Gingold,' Millie said quickly.

Annie looked as if she were about to reply, but Millie gave her a meaningful look and her friend closed her mouth.

Millie turned her attention back to the Joliffes.

'Her surgery is around the corner from Watney Market in Cable Street. Evening surgery starts at four-thirty and I'd take your wife along there tonight, Mr Joliffe. I'll write a letter for you to give her so the doctor knows we've seen you at the clinic. Either me or Sister Fletcher will pop around to the surgery in the morning to get further instructions.' Millie squeezed Mrs

Joliffe's hand again. 'Doctor Gingold is very good and my own mother is her patient.'

'That's recommendation enough for me,' said Mr Joliffe as he helped his wife off the couch.

'If you take a seat outside for a moment, I'll write you a letter,' Millie said.

Mr Joliffe gave Millie and Annie a heartbreakingly grateful smile. 'Thank you, Sisters.'

He tucked his wife's arm in his and guided her through the screen.

Annie closed it behind the couple and then turned to Millie. 'Why didn't you tell them Doctor Gillespie's surgery was around the corner from them in Senrab Street?'

Millie rolled her eyes. 'If you were Mrs Joliffe would you, honestly, want Doctor Gillespie as your doctor, Annie?'

'Oh, I see what you mean,' Annie replied. 'But you'll be in trouble from Miss Dutton and the health board if it gets out that you sent a patient in Gillespie's area to another doctor.'

'Well, I'd rather take my chance with Doctor Gillespie than force Baby Joliffe to.' Millie tucked the record card back in to Mrs Joliffe's notes. 'Now, as I'm sure you want to get home sometime before midnight, I'll go and write that letter if you wheel in the next customer.'

Trying not to think that it was already half-past five and she still had to pick up her meat from the butcher before heading home, Millie pointed to the list of nurses in the open book.

'I think if you allocate Nurse Flaherty to work with Nurse Haycock on the Ben Jonson Road patch, and Nurse Lynch to the Sydney Street one with Nurse Pattison, we'll have a much better complement of staff in place.'

Miss Dutton, sitting behind her large oak desk, pursed her lips. 'Until another one of them runs off and gets married.' Her mouth pulled tight. 'In my day, nursing was a vocation and when we trained we put aside hopes of marriage and a family.'

Millie was sitting as she always did on a Thursday afternoon in the superintendent's office to discuss the problems and changes to the next week's clinic rota. They were usually finished by now but unfortunately the monthly meeting of the local health committee earlier had over-run quite considerably. Thankfully, Miss Dutton approved now the various clinic schedules with a cursory nod, and so they were almost done.

'Well, there's been a world war since we trained.' Millie pointed out, with a smile at the woman seated on the other side of the desk.

Miss Dutton glanced over Millie's staff configuration again. 'Well, I suppose it will have to do, but I'm not happy about the health board agreeing to take on this new-fangled enrolled nurse assistance.'

'Right now I'm glad they did,' Millie replied. 'As even with the trainee Queenies who arrive next month, we'll still be three bodies down.'

'It's going to cause trouble once the patients find out they're being cared for by untrained nurses.'

'They aren't untrained, Miss Dutton,' replied Millie, with just a hint of exasperation.

Miss Dutton sneered. 'Surely you don't consider a couple of months working in a hospital equivalent to the three years of slog we went through to get our State registration?'

'No. But neither does the board,' Millie answered, 'which is why they will be allocated to a Queen's Nurse for three months to assess their capabilities and then, as their title states, they will assist a nurse. And so instead of two nurses going to do a bed bath, the enrolled assistant will assist by doing the bed bath, leaving the nurse to dress a wound or give an injection. I think it should be a more efficient system.'

Miss Dutton sighed heavily. 'Well, some might regard having barely trained young women tending the sick the modern way of doing things, but I'm not one of them.'

'Time will tell.' Millie tucked her pen in the spine of her notebook. 'Will that be all, Superintendent?'

'For now, Sister Smith, but there is something you might be interested to know.' A little self-satisfied smile lifted the corners of the superintendent's mouth. 'The council has agreed to fund a purpose-built clinic as part of the new Jamaica Street development. It won't be for a year or so as they have to rehouse the tenants from the old house, but when it's ready, Munroe House will just be a nurses' home.'

Millie's face lit up. 'That's fantastic news.'

'And the health board,' the superintendent continued, 'has decided to separate the district nursing service from midwifery. They intend to put the hospital in charge of the home maternity services. By January 1950 all midwives working in the community will work out of either the hospital maternity wards or the East London Lying-in Hospital.'

Millie looked aghast. 'What, all of them?'

'Except the nuns at St John's in Poplar. Apparently, they're a special case.' Miss Dutton shrugged. 'The Association only had midwives because Miss Munroe insisted it be part of the founding charter. It's a blessing, as far as I'm concerned. Without the maternity cases we won't have nurses dashing off at all times of the day and night, and dozens of snotty, screaming brats in the clinic every Tuesday and Thursday.' Miss Dutton snapped closed the clinic diary. 'So, Smith, by the end of next year you and the other midwives in Munroe House will have to decide whether you're a midwife or a district nurse.'

Feeling a little as if the air had been sucked out of her, Millie stared dumbly ahead.

'Smith.'

Millie jumped.

Miss Dutton waved a well-manicured hand at her. 'That will be all.'

Millie stood up. 'Goodnight, Superintendent.'

With feet feeling as if they'd suddenly turned to lead, Millie left the office. Closing the door, she took her coat from the hat stand in the hall and was just about to put it on when the telephone rang. She picked up the receiver. The pips went and then the line clicked as it connected.

'Is dat the nurses' house?'

'Yes, this is Munroe House,' Millie replied, forcing her mind to the here and now.

'Tank the Mercies for dat. And is dat there young Annie with the golden locks I'd be speaking to?' a male voice said with a soft rolling lilt.

'No, it's not. It's Sister Smith. How can I help you?' Millie asked, glancing at her watch.

'It's Seamus O'Toole and it's about me mammy.'

Millie's grip tightened on the receiver. 'What about your mother?'

'She says she's terrible sick right enough,' Seamus replied. 'And would you do her a kindness and stop by tomorrow?'

'Didn't Sister Scott see her yesterday? And Sister Muir the day before that?'

Seamus gave a soft laugh. 'As you say, Sister, and although both were the very angels from heaven, me mammy wasn't sure they understood the full particulars of her afflictions.'

'Mr O'Toole, to my certain knowledge your mother has seen almost every nurse in Munroe House in the last four weeks and none of them have found anything wrong with her.'

'So I'll be telling mammy that you'll be calling at the yard tomorrow then, Sister,' Seamus said.

'I really don't think—'

The pips cut across her words.

'But be sure and come before she goes to the bookies at noon,' Seamus said before the line went dead.

Millie stared at the handset for a moment just as the tall clock in the hall struck six o'clock. She replaced the receiver and wearily picked up her coat again. The butcher's would probably be closed when she got there, and that would just round off a perfect afternoon.

The O'Tooles' scrap-metal yard occupied the space on the corner of Chapman Street, and enclosed three old Victorian brick-built railway arches. It had once been surrounded by grand merchants' houses, but thanks to the Luftwaffe only the odd one or two remained, shored up by beams and standing amongst the rubble like old teeth. The finest example in the street of the area's previous affluence was enclosed by the upended broken bottles fixed to the top of the walls of the scrap yard, and it housed the huge extended O'Toole family.

Coasting through the gates with 'O'Toole & Sons, Scrap Metal Dealers' scrawled on the battered sign, Millie came to a halt. Pulling her Gadabout on to its stand she stepped off. Three shaggy dogs of indeterminate parentage sprang into life and dashed forward snapping and snarling, only to be yanked back abruptly as they reached the end of their chains. Although

O'Toole's yard did contain buckled cartwheels, stoved-in car panels and mangled iron fences in abundance, it was also home to a metal bin of smashed glass, stacked paint pots with drips of dried colour around the sides, and disembodied chair arms and legs.

To provide some sort of office area for the business, the O'Tooles had boarded up one of the arches with a peculiar assortment of wood, shoved a door in the middle and added mismatched windows either side. As the dogs settled back to gnawing their bones, the door opened and Seamus and his younger brother Michael stepped out.

There were five O'Toole brothers in all, ranging from Seamus in his early forties, through to Pat the Lad in his late twenties. From their father they'd inherited their bull-like physique and flaming hair in a variety of hues from Dougan's carrot-orange to the less garish rusty brown of Brendan's, but their ability to turn threepence into sixpence came straight from their mother.

The two brothers spotted Millie and ambled over.

'Good day to ya, Sister,' Seamus shouted, wiping his hands down the front of his grimy dungarees. 'You know our Mickey, don't you?'

Millie smiled at the younger brother. 'I do, and how's Breda?'

A broad grin creased Mickey's ruddy face. 'Grand, and growing by the day.'

'I know it's her sixth, but she should come to the clinic so I can check her over,' Millie said, regarding the tall Irishman levelly.

Mickey touched his knitted hat with his finger. 'And so she will, Sister,' he said earnestly. 'I'll tell her to go to the very next one.'

Millie raised an eyebrow and decided not to hold her breath.

'And how is your mother today?' Millie asked, retrieving her case from beneath her seat.

A mournful expression spread across Seamus's face. 'Aw, she's been up half the night with the agony of it.'

'And where exactly did you say—'

'Let me carry that for you, Sister,' Mickey said taking her bag. 'Sure, you must be fair worn to the bone with all the fetching and carrying you do all day.'

Seamus hooked his finger and thumb under his tongue and sent out two sharp blasts. The office door opened again and his sons Peter and Paul, all gangly legs and puberty spots, stepped out.

'Shift the fencing ready for when your Uncle Pat gets back with the wagon while we see the Sister into the house,' he called across.

The boys nodded, hitched up their baggy overalls and headed for the haphazard pile of metal in the corner.

Seamus smiled at Millie. 'Mammy's waiting for you.'

Moving her coat aside to avoid the rusty spool of barbed wire to her left, Millie followed the two brothers towards the waist-high fence that separated the yard from the house at the far end.

The family area had been the old tack-yard and it still retained its flagstones and the drainage channel down the middle. Strung across it from the house to the fence were half-a-dozen washing lines all packed with nappies and children's clothes flapping in the late November breeze. Beneath the drying laundry were three prams of various vintages with a dummy-sucking infant at each end; and there were a handful of toddlers stamping about in the mud, and a huddle of bigger girls playing a clapping game while their brothers and cousins kicked a half-inflated leather football around.

The last time Millie had done a head count of the O'Toole children she'd got to twenty-four. But as at any given time at least one of the sister-in-laws was pregnant, there could be at least two or three more babies by now.

Millie headed for the front door. Mickey got there before her and opened it with a flourish. Millie stepped inside.

The house was a domesticated reflection of the main yard and it was cluttered with all sorts of bric-a-brac. Faded prints and photographs lined one wall while an old Victorian mirror with an advert for London Gin etched into it was fixed to the other. There was even a stuffed stag's head complete with antlers nailed above the parlour door.

'Ma's in the kitchen, Sister,' Mickey said, leading Millie down the hall to the back of the house.

'It's the nurse come to see to you, Mammy,' he said as he opened the door.

*

Ma O'Toole was sprawled in a threadbare armchair beside the old-fashioned cooking range, with her arms hanging limply at her sides.

She was sixty if she was a day and although a shade under five feet, she probably tipped the scales at something approaching sixteen stone. Today, as always, she wore a shapeless dress of an indistinguishable colour and without supportive underwear. Her thin steel grey hair was scraped back into a conker-sized bun and her pixie-like face was etched with lines. But while her outward appearance gave the impression of age and infirmity, Mrs O'Toole's sharp, coal-black eyes gave a clue to the woman within. As Millie walked in, the old woman raised her short arms above her head.

'Oh, tank the blessed Virgin for her mercy,' she wailed.

Millie put her bag on the table. 'Good morning, Mrs O'Toole. I understand you're not very well again.'

'Unwell, you're saying! Breathing me last, more like,' Mrs O'Toole looked forlornly at her. 'Sure, wasn't I expecting the call from St Peter himself with the pain of it?' Her nose crinkled in an oddly girlish smile. 'But I'm in safe hands now I have the best nurse to tend me.'

Millie slipped off her coat. 'And where exactly is the pain?' she asked, folding her mac and sliding it into the paper bag she carried for the purpose.

'All over.' She crossed herself. 'It's like the very deevils from Hell jabbing me with hot pincers.'

'But where is it worse?'

'Me old pins.' Mrs O'Toole ran her hands down her thighs. 'Just crumbling away, they are, just like my poor old mother's, and her mother's before, and her mother's before that.'

'So bad legs run in your family, do they, Mrs O'Toole?' Millie said, with just a hint of amusement.

The old woman's innocent expression didn't waver. 'For as far back as can be remembered.'

Millie pulled out a set of notes from her bag and glanced at them. 'When Sister Fletcher came the day before yesterday, it was your back.'

'It's that as well.'

'And two days before that it was your—'

'Poor old arm joints.' Mrs O'Toole grabbed Millie's shoulders. 'I'll tell this and tell you no more, Sister; it's no fun getting old.'

'So I understand.' Millie took the old woman's hand and pressed her fingers lightly on the pulse.

'It's so weak it's a miracle that it ain't stopped altogether before now,' Mrs O'Toole said in a faltering little voice.

Taking a grubby cushion from one of the chairs, Millie knelt on the floor and released the elastic garters just above the old woman's knees. As Millie rolled the old woman's stockings down to her ankles, Mrs O'Toole ground her teeth, sucked in her lips and drew a sharp breath in quick succession.

Millie surveyed the old woman's legs. They looked like a pair of fat white sausages but, considering she'd had five children, there was hardly a swollen vein on them and her ankles weren't puffy.

Millie rocked back on her heels. 'Can you stand for me, Mrs O'Toole?'

Mrs O'Toole nodded. 'I'll try. But don't take no mind if I scream out.' She gripped the arms of the chair with a tortured expression worthy of Frankenstein's monster in its death throes, and struggled forward for a couple of seconds before falling back to her chair.

'I'm sorry, Sister.' Mrs O'Toole put her hand on her chest and took a couple of deep breaths. 'I've barely been able to get out of this chair for days.'

'That's funny,' Millie said, deliberately looking puzzled. 'I could have sworn I saw you in Watney Market on Friday.'

The old woman looked amazed. 'It must have been someone with the look of me.'

Millie smiled. 'So what would you like me to do, Mrs O'Toole?'

'Well, I could do with a wheelchair so one of me boys can wheel me to Mass.'

'I thought, after your falling-out with Father Sebastian last year, you'd stopped going to church,' Millie said.

Mrs O'Toole heaved a sighed. 'Ha! Well now, I had, but as I'm not long for this world I can't afford to have me soul in such peril.' She looked heavenward briefly and then her lively eyes returned to Millie's face. 'So, can you put in for a wheelchair for me?'

Millie packed her patient's notes back in her case and stood up. 'I'm afraid it's not that simple. I'll have to ask Doctor to send you for a full assessment. And not only is there a six-month waiting list, but wounded servicemen take priority over everyone. So even if the panel agree to you having one it's likely to be a long wait.'

'But it says in this here,' Mrs O'Toole dragged a grubby, dog-eared leaflet from the side of her chair and waved it at Millie, 'dat I'm entitled to everything free.'

Millie took it from her. 'But if you look closely, it also says *if* you need it.'

Mrs O'Toole snatched the pamphlet from her. 'It's 'cause I'm Irish you won't give me one.'

Millie gave an exasperated look. 'And why would that be, Mrs O'Toole, when I'm a Sullivan myself?'

The old woman sucked her gums for a second. 'Then it's because you don't think my Pat's good enough to be walking out with that Nurse Annie of yours.'

'I didn't know they were, Mrs O'Toole. But thanks for telling me.' Millie stood up and retrieved her coat from the bag. 'I'll get the doctor to call and give you some stronger pain killers but as to a wheelchair I don't think it will be possible.'

The door burst open and a lad of about nine or ten with ginger hair like a sweep's brush and with dirt smudges across his nose dashed in. Without pausing, he ran to the kitchen range and snatched a caddy from the mantelshelf above.

'Da said to fetch the scrap money.'

As if shot through with electricity, Mrs O'Toole leapt from her chair and crossed the kitchen in three swift steps.

'Joseph Dermot O'Toole, will you get your mitts off me bookie's fund!' she yelled, swiping it out her grandson's hand. 'It's the other one your father's wanting.'

'Sorry, Gran,' Joseph replied, bobbing up to retrieve the second tin on the shelf.

He sped off back the way he came, banging the door behind him.

There was a long moment of silence. Then Mrs O'Toole's eyes opened wide, and a look of wonderment spread across her face. 'Did you see that, nurse?' She fumbled around her neck and pulled out an old rosary. 'It was a blessed miracle sent straight from the Queen of Heaven herself.' The old woman kissed the crucifix and gazed heavenward.

The corners of Millie's lips twitched. 'It was indeed, Mrs O'Toole, and I'll wish you a good day.'

Chapter Six

Putting her hand on the teapot lid to stop it toppling off, Millie poured herself and Connie a cup of tea. 'And you should have seen the relish in old Dutton's eyes when she told me about us losing midwifery,' she said.

'I can imagine, but everything's going to be based at the hospital now,' Connie replied, taking her cup from Millie.

They were squashed in the corner of Bourne and Hollingsworth's fourth-floor restaurant behind a spindly potted palm with several paper shopping bags around their feet. After four hours of Christmas shopping in Oxford Street, Millie and Connie felt they'd earned an early-afternoon cream tea.

'So what will you do?' Connie asked, taking a dollop of jam. 'About the maternity, I mean?'

Millie took a scone from the cake stand and put it on her plate. 'As I'll be at home doing housework and cooking by then, it won't affect me,' Millie replied, hearing the resentful tone in her voice.

Connie looked sympathetic. 'I thought Jim would have cooled down by now.'

Millie shook her head. 'Every time I mention the subject he just flies off the handle. The last time he stormed out of the house and didn't come home all night.'

Connie looked shocked. 'Where did he go?'

'A hotel somewhere, I expect.' Millie stirred her tea briskly. 'I thought it best to let the matter lie.'

Connie looked as if she were about to add something, so Millie delved in the Liberty's shopping bag and pulled out a paisley silk scarf.

'I'm still not sure,' she said, turning it back and forth in her hand.

'But it's so pretty,' Connie said, looking at the coloured silk that had cost Millie as much as her mother's and aunt Ruby's presents combined.

'It is, but Jim's mother will hate it nonetheless.'

Connie smiled. 'What makes you think that?'

'Because she hates me,' Millie replied.

'I'm sure that's not true.'

'I'm certain it is.' Millie shoved the scarf back in the bag.

Connie gave her a sympathetic smile. 'I take it you're not looking forward to Christmas at the manor house then.'

'No, I'm not.' Millie sighed. 'It will be exactly the same as it is every time we visit. His mother will watch me with a face like she's been sucking lemons, Jim and his father will argue about politics over dinner until one of them storms off swearing. And if that weren't enough, I have to suffer his brother Lionel and his snide remarks about chirpy Cockneys. Even the servants look down their noses at me.'

'Poor you,' Connie said with feeling. 'Still, it's only for a couple of days.'

'Thank goodness,' Millie replied, trying to push away the feeling of foreboding a visit to her in-laws always provoked. 'And at least we'll see the New Year in with my family. Where are you going?'

'My mum's for Christmas Day and Malcolm's on Boxing Day.' Connie's eyes lit up. 'I've had a bit of luck with Malcolm's present. Mum was in the market a couple of weeks back and one of the stalls was selling off skeins of wool, so she got me four and I've knitted a pullover for him.'

'What colour?'

'Grey,' Connie replied. 'The council's highways department frowns on its employees looking too flamboyant. What are you giving Jim?'

'I'm not sure yet,' Millie replied, taking another sip of tea.

If her monthly didn't arrive by the end of next week she might be giving him a bolt from the blue for Christmas.

'Changing the subject, did Annie say anything to you about having a new fellow when you saw her last week?' asked Millie.

Connie leant forward conspiratorially. 'No, but has she?'

'According to Mrs O'Toole, she's courting her youngest, Patrick.'

Connie gave a knowing smile. 'I can understand why. He's very easy on the eyes.'

'He might be,' said Millie. 'But there's something about Patrick that unsettles me.'

Connie laughed. 'I'm not surprised. Patrick O'Toole is cast out of the same mould as Alex Nolan.'

Before Millie could stop it, her mind summoned up an image of Alex Nolan: tall, dark and with eyes so green you could see your soul in them. She forced a light laugh. 'Nonsense.'

'I grant you, he's not as broad and hasn't got the mass of wavy black hair. But Pat O'Toole has the same effortless way of carrying himself and the same easy confidence as Alex had,' Connie replied, biting into her Bakewell tart.

The memory of Alex holding her close in a slow waltz joined the image of him in his police uniform in Millie's head.

'You're not upset I mentioned him, are you?' Connie asked anxiously.

Millie gave her friend a jolly smile. 'Don't be daft. It was so long ago I've almost forgotten what he looked like.' She glanced at her watch. 'I ought to be off. It's our anniversary and I'm making something special for Jim.'

Connie looked mortified. 'I'm so sorry, Millie, what with Christmas and everything I'd forgotten.'

'Don't worry. We're not making a big thing of it.'

Millie finished her tea and put her cup back in the saucer. Connie stretched across and put her hand on Millie's arm.

'Before you go Millie, I've got something to tell you.' Connie looked strangely bashful. 'Malcolm proposed.'

'Why didn't you say something when I met you at Aldgate?' Millie asked, looking incredulously at her friend.

'I was waiting for the right moment.' Connie said excitedly.

Millie rolled her eyes. 'Oh, Connie. You are the end!'

Connie poked her tongue out and Millie pulled a face.

'We're going up to Hatton Garden next Saturday to choose a ring,' continued Connie. 'Isn't it wonderful?'

'Yes,' replied Millie, trying to muster some enthusiasm. 'I'm delighted for you, of course I am.'

Connie's joyful smile returned. 'And you must, must, must be my matron of honour.'

'I'd never speak to you again if I wasn't,' laughed Millie. 'I bet your mum's pleased.'

Connie rolled her eyes. 'She's beside herself. She's now referring to me as her engaged rather than her unmarried daughter, and even before I've got the ring on my finger my sisters are arguing as to who's doing what for the big day.'

'When is the wedding going to be?'

Connie's joyful expression faltered a little. 'October 1950, probably the 7th, although if Malcolm's mother has her way it will be October 1960.' Connie brightened up again. 'But it will definitely be in St Martha and St Mungo's – whatever his mother says – and I thought perhaps pink for the bridesmaids and, as there'll be so many of us, a three-tiered cake. What do you think?'

'It all sounds lovely,' said Millie.

'And by then the clothes rationing will be over and I can have yards of fabric for my wedding dress,' bubbled Connie. 'You'll come with me to choose it, won't you?'

'Of course, I will. But …' Millie ground to a halt.

'But what?'

'Are you sure Malcolm's the right man for you?' she asked.

Connie laughed. 'Oh, Millie, you are silly. Of course he is. He's no Clark Gable, I grant you, and with his trainspotting and miniature modelling he can seem a bit on the dull side. But I'm certain he'll be a wonderful husband. Just like Jim.'

Something hard pinged in Millie's chest, but she forced it away. 'I'm so glad to hear it,' she said to her dear friend, putting on her brightest smile. 'I don't want you marrying the wrong man, now do I?'

Millie glanced at the silver-domed clock Jim's mother had given them as a wedding gift and her lips pulled into a straight line.

Five past ten! Anger and hurt pinched the corners of her eyes.

Grabbing the armrest of her chair, she stood up and, switching the wireless off, marched into the kitchen. The tightness in her eyes returned as she surveyed the neatly laid out table. Striding to the oven she pulled the door open and stared balefully at the dry chops, discoloured potatoes and shrivelled carrots on the two plates.

Turning off the low heat, she snatched the tea towel, wrapped it around her hands and pulled her and Jim's dinners out of the oven. Slamming the door shut with her hip, she set one plate on top of the other and strode to the back door. Tearing it open, Millie stepped out into the icy December night. With seasonal smells of snow and coal smoke drifting around in the still air, Millie lifted the dustbin lid and threw the ruined food away. She banged the lid back in place.

Returning to the house, she turned the key in the back door and switched off the light. She had to be up at six and so, without bothering to go back into the front room, Millie made her way upstairs, unbuttoning angrily as she went the lustrous and figure-hugging gown she'd put on so excitedly four hours ago.

Someone banging furiously on the front door woke Millie, her heart all but bursting from her chest as she sat bolt upright and fumbled for the bedside lamp switch. The stark light of the forty-watt bulb illuminated the bedroom and Millie shielded her eyes against the glare. Blinking, she peered at the alarm clock. Two-thirty!

Throwing back the blankets and candlewick bedspread, Millie swung her legs out of bed and shoved her feet in her slippers. The chill air set the skin on her bare legs tingling, driving the last remnants of sleep from her mind. She shrugged on her dressing-gown, flicked the switch of the upstairs light and ran downstairs. Through the frosty glass of the door Millie saw the bulky figure of a man silhouetted in the street lamp.

'Is that you, Jim?' Millie called through the door.

There was no reply.

Fear gripped her once more. She glanced at the telephone. Maybe she should ring Mr Granger across the road or even the police.

The knocker rapped again.

Millie grabbed the chrome-plated vase from the hall table and, holding it upside down, slowly opened the door until the safety chain caught.

She could have cried with relief when she saw the distinct oval-shaped London taxi badge pinned to the thick-set man's ex-Navy duffel coat.

'Sorry Miss,' the cabbie said. 'But is this one yours?'

With a grunt he grabbed something at the side of the doorway and heaved. Jim stumbled forward into the beam of the outside light. He was tie-less and the top two buttons of his shirt were missing and his trousers were splashed with mud. Jim stared at his wife with unfocused red-rimmed eyes for a moment, and then he fumbled towards some sort of consciousness.

'Darrrling,' he slurred, reaching out toward her but hugging air instead.

Millie's mouth pulled into a tight line. 'Unfortunately he is.'

'Well, thank Gawd,' said the cabbie with obvious relief.

Millie released the chain and opened the front door.

'Where do you want 'im?'

'In the parlour,' Millie replied. 'On the left.'

The taxi driver hooked Jim's arm around his neck and, wedging his shoulder under him, manhandled him over the threshold and into the front room. Millie returned the vase to its spot and closed the door. The driver was just lowering Jim on to the sofa as she joined them in the parlour. Jim made a half-hearted attempt to right himself but he soon gave up and just sprawled. He belched and the sharp smell of Scotch wafted up. His head lolled back and he started snoring softly.

'Where did you pick him up?' Millie asked as she watched Jim's top lip move back and forth as he breathed.

'Whitehall,' the cabbie replied. 'Just down from where the 'orses stand.'

Millie reached for her handbag on the sideboard. 'How much do I owe you?'

'It's all right, luv, your husband's chums stumped up when they poured him in,' The cabbie touched his cap peak. 'I'll see myself out.'

He left, closing the front door behind him.

As Millie studied her unconscious husband, an image of Jim's favourite lemon pudding lying at the bottom of the dustbin flashed into her mind. How could he do this? And on their first wedding anniversary too!

Jim opened his eyes and leered at her. 'There you are, my very own sweet little wifey,' he slurred.

Millie regarded him coolly and didn't reply.

A sullen expression spread across his face. 'Don't look like that, darling, I didn't … It's not …' Laboriously he pulled himself to his feet, and blinked as he struggled to focus.

Millie pulled her dressing-gown tightly across herself.

'Sssswwwweetie!' Jim lunged up at her but, inevitably, lost his balance and pitched forward. He tried to right himself but his legs gave way and he crumpled to the floor. His head slid under the coffee table. He farted and then started snoring again.

Millie regarded Jim for a moment and then she grabbed the shawl she'd wound around her legs while she had sat patiently waiting for him to come home, and threw it over him.

Stepping over her comatose husband, Millie switched off the light and went back upstairs to bed.

Taking the stainless steel syringe firmly in one hand Millie drew up the warm soapy water.

'If you could just hold this nice and tight to your neck, Mr Moore, I'll make a start,' she said.

Bill Moore, a labourer who lived with his wife and eleven children in one of the old houses at the back of the market, tucked the horn-shaped receptacle under his ear. Millie grasped his large and hairy lobe.

'Now this may feel a little strange,' said Millie. 'But try to keep still or you might end up with a wet collar.'

'Right you are, Sister,' he replied, tilting his head.

Millie inserted the nozzle in the central cavity and slowly depressed the plunger.

The secret of shifting earwax was to shoot the water in with sufficient force to dislodge the secretions but not so hard as to damage the drum. Of course the patient had to do their bit and put warm olive oil in their ears for a week before presenting themselves.

It wasn't the most enjoyable way to spend a Tuesday afternoon, but as the headache she'd woken up with hadn't budged, despite two doses of aspirin, Millie had volunteered to man the clinic. Dealing with the routine dressings and procedures didn't tax her powers of concentration, which was just as well, as she'd only managed to snatch a few hours of fitful sleep before the alarm went off at six. And she needn't have worried about what to say to Jim over the breakfast table because when she went downstairs he was more or less where she'd left him. He still hadn't roused by the time she'd had her breakfast and cleared away, and so she'd left a note on the table telling him where his clean shirts were and left.

Having emptied the syringe, Millie extracted the spout and threw the dirty water in the zinc bucket under the chair. She was just about to refill the syringe when there was a light knock on the treatment room door.

'Come,' called Millie.

Annie appeared around the door holding a dozen red roses. 'These have just arrived.'

'Would you mind putting them in the sluice, Annie?' Millie said.

'I'll try.' Annie gave her a pointed look. 'I only just about squeezed the last lot in.'

'Well, could you leave them on the draining board if you can't,' Millie said.

'All right,' said Annie. 'But I don't know how you're going to get them all home on your scooter.'

'Thanks.'

'Don't mention it.' Her friend winked and shut the door.

'Your old man in the dog-house, is he?' asked Bill.

'No,' said Millie, forcing a carefree laugh that did nothing to fool Bill. 'It's our anniversary, that's all.'

She dried her patient's ear and then changed sides, putting the towel over his other shoulder and repositioning the collection cup.

As she drew up another full syringe and Bill twisted his head as far as he could to look at her. 'So how many bunches has he sent?'

'Four,' Millie replied.

Bill chuckled. 'Blimey, what did he do? Get caught with 'is hand on a barmaid's knee?'

'No,' replied Millie firmly with the sweetest smile. 'My husband's just very affectionate.'

Bill gave her a sceptical look. ''Course, Sister,' he said.

Millie inserted the nozzle in Bill's right ear and continued with her task.

Just under an hour later, after she'd seen Bill on his way, then lanced a boil, and carefully trimmed three sets of diabetic toenails. Millie finally turned the sign outside the clinic door to 'closed'.

Gathering together in an enamel basin the equipment she had used, she took it to the butler sink. Taking a scoopful of carbolic soap flakes from the box under the basin, Millie threw some soap in and then turned on the Ascot. The scalding water from the wall-mounted gas boiler splashed over the collection of pots, surgical scissors and hypodermics, causing the soap to lather.

Leaving the dirty equipment to soak, Millie took a large bottle of Dettol from the cupboard below, mixed it in a stainless steel dish with water to get it ready for the cleaned surgical instruments to be dunked for their overnight sterilisation.

As she ran the enamel kidney bowl under the tap, there was a knock on the door. Millie glanced at the clock.

As the bouquet of red roses had arrived on the hour and every hour since one, she guessed this was someone telling her about the five o'clock delivery.

'Come.'

The door opened.

'Just put it with the others,' Millie called over her shoulder without turning around. 'And no. I don't know how I'm going to get them all home, either.'

'Well, perhaps I can help you carry them.'

Millie spun around.

Jim stood in the doorway wearing a contrite look on his face and clutching a bunch of roses. He was dressed in his black chalk-line suit with a crisp white shirt beneath and his Royal Air Force tie knotted at his throat. He'd been for a haircut and a close shave and, despite her displeasure, Millie couldn't help but notice how good he looked. But she shoved the thought aside as the hurt and humiliation of the night before welled up strongly.

Millie sighed. 'You're not supposed to be in here.'

'I know, but . . .' he stepped into the treatment room and closed the door behind him. 'I'm so sorry for last night, sweetheart.'

'Are you?'

'I am. Truly, I am,' Jim said, looked appealingly at her. 'I shouldn't have gone for a drink after the Tin-plate and Welders' Union meeting.'

'No, you shouldn't,' replied Millie.

Jim took a step closer. 'I'm a terrible husband.'

'You are,' agreed Millie, feeling her defences start to falter.

'I don't know why you put up with me,' he said in a low tone, smiling disarmingly down at her.

The fresh smell of the aftershave she particularly liked on him drifted over to her and, despite herself, Millie smiled. 'Neither do I.'

'It's unforgivable.'

'It is,' Millie agreed. 'And on our first anniversary, too.'

'I know.' Jim offered the flowers.

Millie regarded them for a second and then took them from him. Their fingers touched and Jim caught her hand.

'Will you forgive me?' he asked, running his thumb over her knuckles gently.

'I suppose I'll have to,' Millie replied, lifting the roses higher and breathing in their sweet fragrance.

Jim's arm encircled her and he drew her closer. 'Oh, Millie, I'll make it up to you, darling. I promise.'

He pressed his mouth on hers in a deep kiss. Millie's free hand ran up his chest and wove around his neck. After a few heady moments Jim released her lips.

'And I'm going to start right now, my sweet darling,' he said lifting her off her feet and whirling her around.

He tried to capture her lips again but Millie held him off.

'Stop it,' she said, laughing. 'I'm not finished up here yet.'

Jim gave her a brief peck and then released her.

'Well then.' He pulled out the chair from behind the nurses' desk and sat down. 'I'm going to sit right here until you do. And then I'm going to make amends for last night's spoiled dinner by taking you for a champagne supper in the West End.'

Millie laughed. 'Well you can wait until I've finished if you like, but I don't think I'll be eating anywhere but Tubby Isaac's whelk stall dressed like this,' she said, brushing her hand down her navy uniform.

Jim raised an eyebrow and gave her that pulse-racing smile of his. 'Didn't I mention, Millie, my very own little sweetheart, that we're stopping off at Bond Street on the way as I've persuaded a very exclusive gown shop to stay open a little later just for us?'

Weaving her way between two Jewish men in their long grey coats and wide-brimmed hats gesticulating at each other, Millie chained her scooter against the rusty railings outside number seven Cannon Street Road. She supressed a yawn.

Supper had actually turned out to be a swanky dinner followed by a late night jazz club in Soho, and so she and Jim, along with a half-dozen bunches of roses and the same number of Bond Street shopping bags, had finally arrived home just before one in the morning.

Stretching her eyes and taking a deep breath Millie looked up at the door of her next visit.

The house must have once been a grand affair, as the ornately carved canopy over the front door testified. But its glory days had long gone. Although the old shutters still remained on most of the upstairs windows, they were almost bare of paint and looked as if they'd been closed for half a century. The house's outside rendering had fallen away in places, exposing the brickwork, while buddleia hanging over the top parapet indicated that the guttering on the roof might need attention. The house, once the home of a merchant or port official, was now sandwiched between a wholesale haberdasher's shop with a sweatshop above on one side and a cardboard-box manufacturer's on the other.

Millie made her way up the steps to the front door and as there wasn't a knocker she rapped with her knuckles. There was no answer and so she pushed on the door until it creaked open.

Millie stepped in and looked around. As her gaze ran over the faded flock wallpaper, gas mantles jutting out from the walls and the threadbare rug on the scuffed floorboards, she wondered if she'd slipped back a hundred years.

'Yoo-hoo, district nurse!' she called.

The door at the far end of the hall was opened and Millie expected a woman in a crinoline to emerge, but instead a little bird of a woman wearing a wraparound apron, down-at-heel slippers and carrying a broom stepped out.

Millie closed the front door. 'The doctor asked me to call, as I understand Miss Gardener hasn't been well.'

'Naw, she hasn't. Poor old darling's been coughing like a steam tug all Tuesday. She's in the front room, through there.' She indicated the room to her right then shuffled off back to the scullery. Millie walked into the parlour.

The sparse furniture in the room was of some quality but had definitely seen better days. Although the window faced full west, the thick net curtains and fringed chenille drapes kept the sunlight at bay. On the marble fireplace that dominated the room, sepia photographs of upright soldiers and plump children stared out from silver frames.

On a chaise longue at the far side of the room lay an elderly woman. She looked up as Millie entered.

'Good afternoon, Miss Gardener. I'm Sister Smith,' Millie said, taking in her patient's too-bright eyes, transparent skin and shallow breathing in one sweep. 'Doctor Masterson asked me to call.'

'That's kind of you, nurse.' Miss Gardener replied. Her blue-tinged lips lifted at the corners. 'But I don't want to be any trouble to you.'

Millie put her bag down and smiled. 'It's no trouble at all. May I sit down?'

Miss Gardener nodded. 'Why don't you …' A chest-ripping cough seized her and she put her handkerchief over her mouth. 'Water,' she gasped, waving towards the jug of water on the table.

As Millie went to give it to her the door burst open.

A woman, who must have been six foot if she was an inch, strode in. She had fine-boned features that age had refined, and short silver-grey hair cut straight around just above her ears and clipped close to her neck. She wore a man's pair of trousers and shirt with dabs of colour around the cuffs. Without glancing at Millie, she marched across the room and knelt beside the woman on the chaise longue.

'I'm here, Dodo' she said, moving a stray lock of damp hair gently from the sick woman's forehead.

Miss Gardener opened her eyes and smiled.

The tall woman looked up. 'Why are you just standing there?' she barked at Millie.

'Good afternoon,' Millie said holding her temper in check. 'I'm Sister Smith and—'

'I don't give a damn if you're Florence Nightingale,' the woman replied, glaring at Millie. 'Shouldn't you do something instead of just watch her choke to death?'

'It's all right, Harry,' Miss Gardener said quietly, having got her breath back.

Harry raked her fingers through her hair. 'But I could hear you from upstairs.'

'I'm fine,' said Miss Gardener, curling her bony fingers around the other woman's wrist.

She looked at Millie. 'Please forgive Miss Moncrieff's hasty words,' she said, wiping moisture from her mouth again.

'Of course,' Millie replied, giving the companion a chilly smile.

Miss Moncrieff sat down, brusquely crossed one long leg over the other and glared.

Millie perched on the armchair next to the chaise longue and set her bag beside her. 'Doctor Masterson asked me to call because he thinks you should have regular nursing care.'

'Nursing care! What we need is a damn doctor who knows what he's doing, that's what,' Miss Moncrieff burst out. She picked up a bottle of white tablets from the small table and threw them on Millie's lap. 'Old fool gave us these a few months ago. But they're no good. Can't he see that poor Dodo is getting worse, not better?'

'I'm sure Doctor Masterson knows best,' Millie said glancing at the label and putting the bottle back on the table. 'Now, if you don't mind. I need to ask you some questions.' Millie established Miss Gardner's daily routine. 'And you wash and dress Miss Gardener every day, Miss Moncrieff?'

'Of course I do.'

Millie noted it on the card. 'And what about her other needs, during the day?' She indicated an old cabinet commode in the corner.

'Harry pops down every hour or so. She has a studio in the top of the house, where the light is better.' Miss Gardener gazed fondly up at her companion. 'She is a gifted artist.'

A surprisingly warm expression crept into Miss Moncrieff's eye. 'You're the only one who ever thought so, Dodo.'

Millie tucked her notes back in her bag. 'I feel that a visit every other day should suffice at present.'

'Thank you, Sister,' said Miss Gardener, just before a wet cough gripped her again and turned her cheeks red and her lips blue.

Miss Moncrieff jumped up. 'Dodo!'

Millie stood up, grabbed the pillow from behind her patient, put it across her lap and then patted the breathless woman's back firmly. Grabbing the Japanese willow bowl on the table, Millie managed to get it under her chin just seconds before she coughed up a huge quantity of frothy fluid.

'For the love of God!' shouted Miss Moncrieff, catching Millie's arm. 'You're making her sick!'

'It's not vomit,' replied Millie, pulling herself free and rubbing her arm. 'It's the fluid from her heart leaking back into her lungs. Didn't Doctor Masterson explain?'

Miss Moncrieff's cool, finely chiselled features distorted into an expression of fury. 'I don't care what you and that quack say, Dodo's going to get better, do you hear?'

She tore out of the room, slamming the door behind her. Millie stared after her for a moment and then turned back to her patient.

'Don't mind Harry, Sister,' Miss Gardener whispered, with a ghost of a smile. 'She's artistic.'

Millie smiled noncommittally and then repositioned the pillow before handing Miss Gardener a fresh handkerchief.

'Thank you,' Miss Gardener said, dabbing the last traces of spit from her lips. 'And I hope you have a Merry Christmas, and I look forward to seeing you again after.'

Heavy footsteps thumped overhead. Millie raised her eyes to the ceiling and wished she could have said the same.

Chapter Seven

As Jim swung the car through the wrought-iron gate and up the gravel drive towards Tollshunt Manor, Millie's heart did its usual impersonation of a stone floating on water. Even with the ice sparkling winsomely on the shrubs and the light dusting of snow on the mock-Medieval turrets and stone window sills, the squarely built country house looked less than inviting.

Jim's ancestral home had been built by his grandfather some eighty years earlier, on top of the foundations of the original sixteenth-century hall. The rebuild had been inspired by the grand houses of the seventeenth century, such as Blenheim and Chatsworth, but Tollshunt Manor lacked somehow the elegant proportions of the buildings it was emulating and so it sat instead like an indolent toad on a lumpy hillock overlooking the village. But in truth it wasn't so much the vista that caused Millie's spirits to plummet, but the prospect of three whole days with Jim's family.

'Here we are then, sweetheart,' Jim said, stamping on the brake and sending stone chips flying in all directions. 'All safe and sound.'

'Yes.'

Jim slipped his arm around the back of Millie's seat and hugged her. 'Come on, sweetheart, cheer up. I know you don't relish three days cooped up in the family pile with Lionel, but you just have to learn to ignore him like I do.'

'Ignore him!' Millie said, looking incredulously at her husband. 'The last time you were both in the same room together at Easter you nearly came to blows.'

'You don't expect me to let him rattle on about the rights of the landed gentry without telling him where to get off, do you?'

'No, but neither do I expect to see two grown men shoving

each other in the chest as if they were arguing over who's got the best conkers,' Millie commented.

Jim looked indignant. 'He started it. At least this time we won't have to suffer him alone. My aunts and cousin Evadne are joining us for the festivities.'

Millie tried to look pleased at the prospect of spending time with still more of Jim's relatives.

He jumped out of the car and came around to Millie's side to open the door. Millie swung her legs out and then, grabbing her skirt and all three lace petticoats with both hands, shook them out.

Jim raised an eyebrow. 'Don't do that too often unless you want to give everyone an eyeful.'

Millie laughed. 'I can't get used to all this fabric.' She smoothed the folds of her skirt and the hem skimmed her ankle bone. 'And it's so long.'

Jim had made good his promise to atone for his appalling behaviour on the night of their anniversary by taking her on yet another shopping spree last week. Of course, because of clothes rationing, he couldn't have bought her something as extravagant if it had been new, so he took her to the shops in Bond Street that imported second-hand clothes from the French couture houses. Their definition of second-hand was that it had once been on a model's back for a couple of hours in a show. The dress she wore now was a beautiful apricot, with a nipped-in waist, full skirt and broad belt but, even as Jim paid the cashier, Millie wondered how long she would actually be able to enjoy it.

Her period was now a full four weeks late. Although she'd missed the odd one or two in her early teens, for the past dozen years she'd been as regular as clockwork. Her next monthly was due in ten days but Millie knew in her heart of hearts that it wasn't going to arrive either.

The front door of the house opened and Paget, the old butler, stepped out.

'Good afternoon, Master James,' he said, making his way unsteadily down the marble steps.

'And to you, Paget,' Jim said, putting his hands in the small of his back and stretching. 'The old place looks the same as ever.'

'Thankfully so,' the old man replied. 'And good afternoon, Mrs Woodville Smith.'

'Good afternoon, Mr Paget,' she replied, smiling warmly. 'You're looking well.'

'It's kind of madam to say so.'

'Are the three sisters gathered around the cauldron?' asked Jim, rubbing his hands together.

'Her Ladyship is taking tea in the drawing room with Lady Pegrum and Miss Augusta,' the butler responded.

'Splendid,' said Jim. 'Our bags are in the boot, and so if you could get one of the lads to carry them up pronto, I'd be obliged.'

The old man shuffled off to fetch a groundsman.

'I thought you didn't go in for all this servant-master stuff,' said Millie as Jim guided her up the steps.

'I don't,' said Jim in a pained tone, 'but I can't embarrass Mummy in front of her sisters, can I?'

Mrs Littlechild, the housekeeper, greeted them as they entered the house. The Mrs was a courtesy title, as the middle-aged woman had been in service to Jim's family since she was twelve. Beside her stood a slender young girl of about fourteen who had bright red hair and a sprinkle of freckles across her nose, and who was wearing a maid's uniform at least two sizes too big. She stepped forward and bobbed a curtsy.

'Good afternoon, sir, madam. Can I take your coats?' she said, with a strong country burr.

'We know you *can,* Eliza,' boomed the housekeeper. 'But the correct way of addressing guests is, "*May* I take your coats?"'

'I'm sorry, Mrs Littlechild,' said Eliza, her oversized white cap wobbling ever so slightly as she looked up at the older woman.

Mrs Littlechild gave a sharp nod.

Eliza curtsied again. 'Good afternoon, sir, madam. May I take your coats?'

'You may,' Jim replied.

He helped Millie out of her new full-length emerald-green coat before taking off his gabardine mac.

'Thank you, Eliza,' he said, handing them to her.

She dipped another curtsy and fled towards the kitchen.

The housekeeper rolled her eyes. 'I'm sorry, Master James.'

Jim smiled. 'That's all right Mrs L. We all have to learn.'

'It's so hard to get staff nowadays,' continued Mrs Littlechild with a sigh, 'but I'm sure that when I've drummed some manners into her, Eliza Reacher will pass muster.'

'She's one of the Reacher girls?' Jim asked.

'Yes, sir.' Mrs Littlechild's lips pulled into a tight bud. 'I'm sure you remember her sister Tillie who used to be the under-housemaid.'

Jim smiled. 'Indeed I do, Mrs Littlechild.' He slipped his arm around Millie's waist. 'Shall we join Mama?'

'James, thank goodness you've arrived,' a voice shrilled from behind them. 'I've been positively out of my mind with worry thinking of you driving in such dreadful conditions.'

Millie turned to see Jim's mother, Lady Wilhelmina Tollshunt, hurrying down the hall towards them.

She was dressed in a drop-waisted dove-grey day dress that highlighted her neatly crimped white hair. As it was the afternoon, she'd limited herself to one string of pearls and clip-on earrings.

'The main roads were fine,' Jim said, hugging his mother and kissing her on the cheek.

Lady Tollshunt's gaze shifted to Millie. 'Amelia, my lamb, how lovely to see you.' She hugged her stiffly and kissed the air next to her cheek.

'And it's lovely to see you, too, Lady Tollshunt,' Millie replied.

Jim's mother had never invited her to address her in any way other than her title, as it was clear from their first meeting that their relationship would never be anything but formal.

'Where's Pater?' Jim asked.

'He's gone up to Three Elm Wood with Jackson,' Lady Tollshunt replied. 'There's been a spate of poaching and your father is not convinced the men have been keeping the fences properly maintained. He'll be back for dinner. Evadne's gone with him to give her boys a bit of fresh air.'

'That's nice,' said Millie. 'I don't think it's really Christmas without children around.'

'Mother means Evadne's three pointers, Millie,' said Jim. 'Wellington, Monty and Nelson.' His eyes narrowed. 'And talking of dogs, where is Lionel lurking? In the dungeons, tearing the wings off ladybirds and the legs off spiders to pass the time?'

'Don't be tiresome, dear,' his mother replied. 'You know Tollshunt Manor hasn't got dungeons. Actually, Lionel isn't able to join us this Christmas.'

Jim frowned deeply. 'Oh dear, what a shame. I'm so disappointed.'

His mother gave him the sort of glacial look that could send a chambermaid into a flood of tears at fifty yards. 'For your information, James, his good friend Cuthbert Merricote – you know, Lord Selwyn's son who owns the art gallery just off Dover Street—'

'The one who wanted to be a ballet dancer?'

Lady Tollshunt nodded. 'He came off the slopes at St Moritz, hurt his back and can't be moved. Naturally, Lionel had to stay with him.'

'Naturally,' replied Jim, smiling urbanely. 'They are very close.'

His mother gave him a sharp look.

'Never mind,' said Millie, trying not to look too pleased that she didn't have to suffer Lionel's acid tongue for three days. 'Hopefully we'll see him at Easter.'

'We will just have to do the best we can without him,' said Jim, taking Millie's arm. 'Let's go into the drawing room, sweetheart, and I'll introduce you to my aunts.'

The drawing room was much larger than the whole downstairs of her mother's cottage in Jane Street and it had grand French windows overlooking the garden. There were high ceilings, a huge moulded rose in the centre with a brass five-armed light-fitting with a miniature chandelier on each arm. There was old-fashioned pink and green flowery wallpaper covering the walls, and an assortment of rugs scattered about the floor.

Jim guided Millie past the unmatched chairs to the two saggy leather sofas facing each other in front of the fire that had an elderly woman sitting on each. As they saw Jim approaching, they started wriggling around on their seats like a couple of excited schoolgirls.

'Is it James?' one squealed.

'Yes, dear,' answered the other.

As they cooed over him, Jim hugged them in turn.

'My sisters are very fond of James,' Lady Tollshunt explained to Millie.

'I can see that,' Millie replied.

Jim finally escaped the two old ladies' attempts to smother him, and he drew Millie forward.

'This is my aunt Georgina,' he said, turning towards the one hunched up on the right sofa.

Lady Georgina Pegrum was Lady Tollshunt's senior by at least a dozen years, which put her somewhere in her late seventies. Like Jim's mother, she had a mass of white hair, but hers was haphazardly gathered up into a topknot and secured with half-a-dozen tortoiseshell combs. She was dressed in a fussy lace and satin gown which harped back to the roaring twenties, as did her thick silk stockings and button-up shoes.

Millie bent forward. 'Good afternoon, Lady Pegrum. It's so nice to meet you at last.'

The old woman jumped. 'What?'

'Porgie, darling,' Lady Tollshunt bellowed from behind. 'This is James's wife, Amelia.'

Lady Pegrum's wrinkled face screwed up in confusion. She groped around beside her and pulled out an ancient brass ear trumpet.

She stuck the narrow end in her ear. 'Who?'

'My wife,' shouted Jim.

'They married last year,' Lady Tollshunt added, enunciating her words very clearly. 'She's a nurse and looks after poor people.'

'How very charitable of her,' replied the old woman.

Millie stepped closer and caught a whiff of a familiar odour that the old woman's lavender water couldn't quite mask.

'It's nice to meet you,' she said again, with a friendly smile.

Lady Pegrum gave Millie a perfunctory once-over and then looked back at Jim's mother. 'Is there more tea coming?'

Lady Tollshunt nodded. 'I've told Judy to fetch a fresh tray.'

Jim turned Millie towards the other sofa. 'Aunt Augusta,' he said, tapping the other old lady on the shoulder, 'this is my wife Millie.'

In contrast to her elder sister, Miss Augusta Horncastle's steel-grey hair was scraped back from her face and secured in a tight bun at the back of her head. She wore a baggy green and brown tweed suit with an unadorned shirt and printed scarf around her neck. The pleated skirt finished at her knees, which was unfortunate, as her flesh-coloured bloomers gathered just under. Cable-knitted beige stockings and a pair of lace-up brogues completed the ensemble.

James's maiden aunt, who had just celebrated her seventy-third birthday, screwed up her eyes and looked around.

'Over here, Gussy,' said Lady Tollshunt, waving directly in front of her middle sister's face.

Miss Horncastle patted her chest until she found the metal-rimmed spectacles suspended on a chain around her neck and then jammed them on the bridge of her nose.

'Is she a dancer?' Miss Horncastle asked, her grey eyes unnervingly large through the thick lenses. 'Your grandfather tried to marry a dancer from the Moulin Rouge in ninety-eight, James, but your great-great grandmother soon put a stop to that, I can tell you.'

Millie and Jim exchanged a puzzled look.

'It's her eyes, poor darling.' explained Lady Tollshunt. 'No, Gussy, she's not wearing a dancing skirt – it's the New Look. Dior! There was a four-page spread about it in last month's *Lady*.'

Miss Horncastle sniffed. 'They didn't mention it in *Country Women*.'

The door opened and the maid staggered in carrying a huge tray on which was a teapot, two hot-water jugs, at least a dozen cups and saucers plus a three-tier cake stand. She put it on the Chinese lacquered coffee table between them.

'Thank you, Judy,' Lady Tollshunt said as she sat down at its end.

Jim nestled next to his aunt Georgina while Millie took the space beside Miss Horncastle.

'James's wife is a pretty little thing, don't you think, Gussy?' Georgina hollered across at her sister.

The old woman sitting next to her regarded Millie through the distorting lenses of her spectacles. 'I suppose so. But she's a little on the thin side for breeding.'

Millie felt the colour rise in her cheeks and without thinking her hands went to her stomach.

Lady Tollshunt rattled the spoon around inside her Royal

Doulton teapot to help the tealeaves release their flavour, then replaced the lid. 'Shall I be mother?'

The organ blasted out the final note of 'Hark the Herald Angel', and Millie sent a silent prayer of thanks to the ornate cross standing in the middle of the altar. After having almost an hour and a half of Jim's aunts untunefully hooting out the hymns immediately behind her, Millie was convinced another carol would start her ears bleeding. And if that wasn't bad enough, both sisters had strong views about how a service should and shouldn't be conducted and were not afraid to say as much, regardless of the irritated looks from the congregation or the embarrassment of the vicar.

St Helen's, which had seen generations of the Woodville Smith family both into and out of the world, was a pretty standard country church, with oak-hewn pews that were too narrow and guaranteed to cause cramp within ten minutes of resting one's rear on them. Shields and memorials to Jim's ancient ancestors covered the whitewashed walls and in the chancel on the left-hand side was a canopied tomb with an effigy of a couple wearing sumptuous robes, disk-shaped ruffs and their hands pressed together in perpetual prayer. This was the final resting place of the first Lord Woodville, who had been granted the manor by King Charles II for services rendered to him by Lady Woodville. The Smith in their name came generations later, when an over-fondness for the roulette table forced Jim's great-great grandfather into the arms of an American heiress.

Millie was sitting in the family pews in the east transept – the west housing the lady chapel – and it had three tiers of individual seats, which were carved versions of wing-back armchairs. They sat higher and well apart from the rest of the worshippers, and they had comforts such as cushions, tartan blankets and an old paraffin stove at the back to keep the lord of the manor's party warm.

On Millie's left was Jim, and on her right Lady Tollshunt, with Lord Tollshunt next to her. Jim's father, a red-faced man of few words and even fewer manners, had slept through the whole service. Behind them sat Lady Pegrum and Miss Horncastle, and Jim's cousin Evadne, who was a strident, horsey woman with bobbed hair and a downy top lip. She'd brought her dogs into the church and they had fussed and fidgeted under Millie's pew throughout the service.

As Reverend Barclay gave the final notices, Millie shifted her weight on to her other hip and glanced around. As her eyes cast over the congregation, she spotted the familiar face of someone she'd met at last year's summer fête.

Although her rich auburn hair was tucked under her narrow-brimmed felt hat, and her pretty face was half hidden by her turned-up collar, Millie knew it was Beth Scarrop, the pretty young mother who had made a point of calling her four-year-old son over to meet her and Jim.

Millie smiled. After a moment, Beth smiled back warily, afraid no doubt of incurring Lady Tollshunt's wrath for appearing to be too familiar with her betters.

The choirboys took up their places and the vicar and servers processed out. The organist started to play again and the congregation knelt for a last swift prayer, and then rose to their feet. They stood respectfully, looking at the Woodville Smith family.

Jim's father snorted, shook himself awake like a tweed-coated dog and stood up.

'I'm off for a walk,' he announced and marched off.

'Don't forget lunch is at two, dear,' Lady Tollshunt called after him.

The congregation bowed and curtsied as he passed down the aisle and then they turned back to look at Jim's mother.

Lady Tollshunt rose to her feet, as did everyone else, including Millie. Black spots suddenly popped in the corners of her vision and she swayed.

'You've gone very white, darling,' Jim asked, looking anxiously at her. 'Are you unwell?'

Millie shook her head and wished she hadn't, as the floor suddenly rose up to meet her. She gripped the rail in front of the pew to steady herself.

'I think you had better wait here in the warm, sweetheart, while Mother and I do the necessary outside,' he said, sitting her back in the pew.

Millie looked questioningly at her husband.

'It's customary for myself or Lord Tollshunt to give the village and estate workers festive good wishes after the Christmas morning service,' Jim's mother explained. 'And as my husband has pressing business elsewhere and Lionel isn't here, I thought James could do the honours with me at the door. You don't mind do you, Amelia?'

'Of course not, Lady Tollshunt,' Millie said, meekly.

Lady Tollshunt stepped out of the pew and her sisters in the row behind heaved themselves to their feet and, gripping their walking sticks in their gnarled hands, hobbled out after her. Evadne stood up behind Millie and stretched. The three dogs, sensing some fun in the offing, started winding themselves around their mistress's legs expectantly.

Jim gathered a couple of cushions and a blanket and tucked them around Millie. 'I'm sorry about this lord-of-the-manor nonsense.'

'It's fine,' said Millie, quite enjoying being fussed over.

Jim covered her legs with the tartan blanket. 'You know, if I had my way I'd scrap the whole blooming lot but,' he shrugged, 'old habits die hard.'

'James!' his mother summoned.

Millie smiled up at him. 'Go on. Do your duty.'

Jim gave her a peck on the cheek and then joined the rest of his family at the chancel steps, and the congregation began to file out.

As the church emptied, Millie snuggled into her improvised nest, shut her eyes and rested her head back into the winged pew. She was just dozing off when the oily smell of burning paraffin drifted into her nose. A wave of nausea swept over her and she retched. Her stomach churned and bile burned the back of her throat. Throwing off the blanket and clamping her hand over her mouth, Millie jumped up and dashed for a small door opposite.

Passing through what had once been the leper entrance and out into the graveyard, Millie gulped in a deep breath of air and the nausea faded a little. She leant back and rested her head on the rough flint and mortar of the wall for a moment. Tucked away behind one of the buttresses, she wasn't visible to anyone still milling around at the front of the church, for which she was grateful. She really didn't want Jim's mother to see her looking sickly and to start putting two and two together, coming up with the inevitable four. And it was inevitable. Only that morning Millie had noticed her brassiere cups were a little tight and her waistband was definitely pinching.

Millie smiled. Her hands slipped down protectively on to her stomach. A happy glow spread through her as she thought about the little life tucked inside. Of course, as the doctor wouldn't be able to confirm for another few weeks yet, she couldn't tell anyone, not even Jim. And despite him wanting to wait until he was a little further on in his career, she was sure he'd be as pleased as punch when he found out he was going to be a father.

Feeling a little better, Millie stood away from the buttresses and started to pick her way through the graves towards the church entrance. There was still a considerable crowd of people milling around outside, and so Millie expected her husband still to be standing with his mother and aunts at the front door, but as she turned the corner of the church, Lady Tollshunt and her sisters were chatting to their tenants and Jim was nowhere to be seen. Thinking he'd probably gone back inside to find her, Millie turned and retraced her steps back to the side door.

She was just about to re-enter the church when something moving behind the holly bush that grew up between some of the older tombs caught Millie's eye. She turned to see Jim half-hidden through the foliage and she could hear him talking to someone. He had his back to Millie so she couldn't see who it was. She was just about to call his name when he moved aside and she saw Beth Scarrop.

Smiling, Millie started towards them but then, when she caught sight of Beth, she stopped dead, unsure what to do. It was clear from the look on Beth's face that she was upset about something. Knowing how the locals looked to the Woodville Smith family to sort out everything from a sick cow to a smoking chimney, Millie guessed Beth had caught Jim at the church door about some landlord-tenant matter.

She was just about to tiptoe away to save the woman's embarrassment, when Beth placed her hand on Jim's arm and looked lovingly up at him.

Stepping carefully over the leaf mulch, Millie felt compelled to see what happen next. She tucked herself out of sight behind one of the taller headstones and strained her ears.

'Please, Master James,' Beth's voice pleaded.

'You'll have to speak to my mother,' Jim replied. 'She deals with such things.'

'I have three times now, but she refuses to help.'

'Well then, there's nothing I can do.'

'All I'm asking for is that you get him a place at the cathedral school at Chelmsford,' Beth cut in.

'It's not that simple.'

'Why not?' Beth retorted angrily. 'He's yours, after all! Surely you can do something.'

'Keep your voice down,' said Jim sharply.

A clanging sound started in Millie's head.

Beth hung her head. 'I'm sorry, Master James, but I just want the best for him. After all, Joe's all I have left of what we had.'

Jim took the handkerchief from his top pocket and handed it to her. 'Grabbing me in front of my family won't help you do that, will it, Beth?'

'No, Master James.'

'It was fortunate for you that my wife wasn't there,' Jim added.

'Yes, Master James.'

There was a long pause and then Jim spoke again. 'Well, all right. I'll have a word with Lady Tollshunt. But you note that I won't be happy if you accost me again like this.'

'Yes, Master James, and I'm very sorry,' said Beth in a soft voice.

'Very well, and now run along before your husband wonders where you are.'

A twig snapped followed by the sound of light footsteps crunching away over gravel. There was quiet for a moment before Millie heard Jim's much heavier tread as he walked away.

Millie stood there looking bleakly ahead for a moment, then she turned and threw up her breakfast on to a small cluster of early snowdrop buds sprouting between two moss-covered tomb slabs.

Although there was a small fire in the hearth warming the room, Millie shivered as she lay under the eiderdown cover with her hands folded on her chest. Their room was on the first floor, where all of the family rooms were and, like them all, it was the same size as a place a family of seven would call home around the London docks. Its high walls were papered with blue Chinese-style wallpaper and ornate plaster cornices. There was a central light with a white glass shade suspended from the ceiling by a long chain, along with a marble topped wash-stand in the bay window and sofa at the end of the four-poster bed.

It had been Jim's room since he was a boy and Millie wondered in passing if Beth Scarrop had also once stared up at the same heavy velvet canopy.

There was a faint knock and the door opened. Millie turned her head as Jim appeared around it.

'There you are, sweetheart,' he said, coming into the room and closing the door behind him.

Millie didn't reply.

He crossed the floor and sat on the bed beside her. 'I wondered where you'd disappeared to.'

'Did you?'

'Of course,' he said taking her hand. 'I worry about you, and Mother said you were unwell again outside the church. Are you better now?'

Millie regarded him steadily. 'Why didn't you tell me you are the father of Beth Scarrop's son, Jim?'

His mouth dropped open. 'How do—'

'I heard you talking together outside the church.'

'You were spying on me?' Jim tried to shift the feeling of blame as he sprung to his feet.

'Don't you dare try to make this my fault, James Smith,' Millie replied, struggling on to her elbows.

'Well, what were you doing in the bloody graveyard?'

'And I'd thank you not to swear at me either,' Millie said, glaring at him. 'The paraffin fumes made me feel sick and as I didn't want to throw up on the chancel carpet, I made a dash for the nearest exit, which happened to be the side door into the graveyard, close to where you and Beth were having a tryst.'

'We were not having a tryst,' he replied, raking his fingers through his hair. 'She just wanted—'

'I heard what she wanted,' Millie shouted. 'What I asked was why didn't you tell me?' Tears sprang into her eyes. 'You should have told me.'

She covered her face with her hands and sobbed as the scene in the churchyard replayed in her mind.

For a long moment the only movement in the room was Millie's trembling shoulders and then the mattress dipped as Jim sat back on the bed. He gently peeled her hands from her face and held them gently.

'I'm sorry, my love,' he said, trying to kiss her palms. Millie snatched her hands away.

Jim sighed and his shoulders sagged. 'You're right. I was wrong not to tell you about Beth. But in all honesty, I'd practically forgotten about her and the boy until last year when we met them at the summer fête. After all, it happened almost six years ago in the middle of a war. I'd just come home on leave after the operation over Normandy. I was tired from flying sortie after sortie and I was living on adrenaline and strong coffee. Beth had worked in the house as the upstairs maid and had a bit of a soft spot for me and one thing led to another.' He shrugged. 'I was mustering at Dover ready for D-Day when I got the letter from Mother telling me that Beth was in the family way. I couldn't get back and so Mother dealt with everything, from the lying-in hospital to her marriage to Tom Scarrop.'

'Does her husband know about this?'

'Of course,' Jim replied, looking surprised at the question. 'Mother let him have the lease on Three Tree Field on the estate at a peppercorn rent by way of compensation.'

Millie rolled her eyes. 'This is like something from the Dark Ages.'

'Well, what was I supposed to do?' Jim asked angrily. 'Marry her?'

'That's what usually happens when you get a girl in trouble.'

'Things are done differently in the shires,' Jim replied. 'Look, Millie, I know I should have told you, but it's in the past. And I couldn't marry her because—'

'She was a servant?' Millie cut in as she felt tears sting the corners of her eyes.

'No. Because I didn't love her.' Jim took his wife's hands again. This time Millie didn't take them back. 'Beth only did what thousands of other women did for men going off to face death in defence of their country, and I don't think she should be made to suffer for that.'

'Neither do I.'

'Surely you'd agree it's better that she be provided with a husband and home rather than being forced to give up her baby for adoption because she has no way of supporting herself?'

An image of a hollow-eyed unmarried girl waving goodbye to the infant for ever at Prescott Street Mothers' Home flashed into Millie's mind.

'That's true.'

'And,' Jim pressed his advantage home by taking Millie's fingers to his lips and kissing each in turn, 'if I had married Beth then I would never have met you, my darling.' He slipped his arm around her shoulders and tried to gather her to him but Millie held him off.

'I want you to promise me that you'll get Joc into the school she wanted,' Millie insisted.

His eyes, the same colour as Beth's son's, looked deep into Millie's. 'I promise. Now say you'll forgive me. Please.'

Millie's rigid posture yielded a little. 'How can I not?'

Jim gathered her into his arms and laid her back on the bed. Taking his weight on his elbows, he covered her with his body, pressing his mouth on hers in a demanding kiss. Millie kissed him back, running her fingers through his hair to hold him to her. His hand smoothed over her still flat stomach and then up to cup her breast. He grabbed her skirt and pulled it up in a flurry of netting and lace, but as his hand reached her stocking-tops, Millie pulled away.

'And you must promise me too that you'll tell me everything in future.'

Jim smiled down at Millie and scraped his fingers back and forth across his breastbone. 'I promise, sweetheart. Cross my heart.'

The costermonger leaning on the piano raised his full glass in one hand and swung it as a signal for the rest of the pub to join in. As the woman at the keyboard stretched her chubby fingers and struck up the chorus of 'My Old Man', Ruby put her hand on Millie's arm.

'That's beautiful, Amelia,' she said, indicating the initials J and A entwined together.

Millie touched the custom-made sapphire broach pinned just below her left shoulder. 'Thank you. It was a late Christmas present from Jim.'

'And she's got earrings to match,' added Doris.

They were sitting in the corner of the Two Puddings pub on Stratford Broadway. The pub was a well-known hostelry just west of the grand Victorian town hall. It was an up-and-coming place with live music and dancing at weekends in the room upstairs. Usually, Ruby wouldn't have been seen dead in a public house in East London on New Year's Eve, but the landlord was a good friend and business partner of her husband Tony, and so this time she had made an exception. Also, as they were invited for 'afters', when they could continue drinking after closing time, the whole family had gathered to see in 1949.

Ruby wrinkled up her nose in an oddly girly fashion. 'You're so lucky to have such a thoughtful husband.'

Millie gave a wan smile.

'Did you have a nice time at Jim's mother's?' Doris asked.

'It wasn't as bad as it could have been,' replied Millie. 'And I got to meet his aunts Porgie and Gussy, and cousin Evadne, although she spent most of the three days galloping across the county with her dogs and shooting things.'

'What about his brother?' asked Doris. 'Did they come to blows like the last time?'

'Thankfully, Lionel wasn't there,' Millie said. 'He had to look after one of his chums who had hurt himself skiing.'

'I'd have thought Lionel would have been married by now,' said Ruby.

Millie gave a wry smile. 'I think Jim's mother would agree, but as far as I can tell he and a group of old school friends spend one half of the year on the Riviera and the other up a Swiss mountain.'

Ruby raised her eyebrows. 'Well, it seems a very a queer way for a grown man to behave, if you ask me.'

'Well, there was an upside, as at least we didn't have the usual fireworks when Jim and his brother are in the house together,' said Millie.

'And Doris tells me that old maid Miss Dutton rang you and told you to come back to work early,' said Ruby.

Millie nodded. 'The phone was ringing when we walked in the door on Monday.'

Ruby looked affronted. 'Blooming cheek.'

'She didn't have much choice,' said Millie. 'She's got four nurses laid up with the flu, and Annie's sprained her ankle slipping down an icy step, which means that they are really short. Plus there's at least a dozen women due to deliver in the next week, and you can bet your bottom dollar if we're short of midwives then at least half of them will go into labour early.'

'Well, it won't be your problem for much longer,' said Ruby. 'When are you leaving?'

'I haven't put my notice in yet, but I suppose if I give it to Miss Dutton on Monday, I'll finish at the end of the month,' said Millie miserably.

Her mother put her hand over hers. 'Cheer up. Think of all that time you'll have when you're at home for making the house look nice, and cooking.'

'And,' chipped in Ruby, 'I'm sure after a long day at the office, Jim will be very glad to find you at home waiting for him.'

'I'm sure he will,' replied Millie, her gaze moving past her aunt and on to her husband propping up the bar alongside Tony.

Jim said something and those standing close by roared with laughter. He picked up a tray of drinks and made his way back to Millie, Doris and Ruby.

'There you are, ladies,' he said, setting it in the middle of the table they were sitting around. 'Now it was a martini for you, Ruby. A G&T for you, Doris,' he said, handing them their glasses. 'And a lemonade for my darling wife.'

'Is that all you're having, Amelia?' asked Ruby taking a sip of her drink.

'I've had a bit of a delicate stomach for the last couple of days,' said Millie.

'You didn't say, dear,' said her mother, looking enquiringly at her.

'It was hardly worth mentioning, that's why,' replied Millie nonchalantly.

'It's nothing to worry about, Mrs S,' said Jim pulling his chair closer to Millie and sitting down. 'It was the paraffin heater in Tollshunt church on Christmas Day that upset her. I've told the churchwarden straight that before they start splashing out on new cassocks for the choir or a replacement vestry window, the PCC needs to fix the heater in the family's pews.'

'As I said, so thoughtful,' said Ruby, looking meaningfully at Millie.

Jim patted Millie's knee. 'My darling is always my first consideration. Plus I need her fit and well to help me win the by-election in ten weeks.'

'Goodness, is it that soon?' said Doris.

Jim supped the froth off his pint and nodded. 'It's set for the 7th of March and so we got the leaflets printed before Christmas; but now we're going for a really big push to get a good turnout on the day.' He turned and looked adoringly at Millie. 'And with Millie beside me, it will be an easy job in persuading them.'

'Well, it never did any man harm to have a pretty wife on his arm,' Ruby pointed out.

'And when she's given up work she'll be able to help you even more,' chipped in Doris. 'You know, at conferences, and she can go with you when you travel around the country.' She beamed at her son-in-law. 'All those dismal hotel rooms you're always telling us about won't be so unwelcoming if you've got Millie with you, will they?'

An odd expression flitted briefly across Jim's face 'No,' he said thoughtfully. 'I suppose they won't.'

The barman banged on the bar with a wooden ashtray. 'You lot, listen up,' he bellowed over the noise.

His wife, standing behind the bar next to him, twiddled the knob on the antiquated wireless next to the tiles and, after a few whistles and squeaks, the distinctive sound of Big Ben's bells resounded around the pub.

'Everyone up,' shouted Tony, hurrying back from the bar. 'Quick, before the last one.'

Putting down their drinks, Doris and Ruby got out of their

seats and Jim helped Millie up. He slipped his arm around her waist as the whole pub started clapping in time with the chimes. 'Eight, seven,' they screamed as the last few seconds of 1948 ticked by, and then there was the final heavy bong as Big Ben struck twelve.

The pub went wild as everyone hugged their nearest and dearest, and complete strangers. Tony hugged Ruby, Millie hugged Jim and then her mother. Jim hugged Doris and Ruby together, planting a noisy kiss on both their cheeks while Tony clasped Millie in a good-hearted bear hug.

'Quick,' yelled Ruby, grabbing Doris's hand and signalling for Millie to take the other. Millie and Jim crossed their arms, clasped hands and then they all joined the rest of the pub in a rowdy version of 'Auld Lang Syne' before someone struck up on the piano again and the landlord and his wife led their customers in a conga out of the pub and into the street. Jim put his hands on Millie's waist and she grabbed on to her mother as they high-kicked out in a line.

In the street the scene was much the same, with people embracing each other and dancing over the cobbles. The trams passing along the Broadway hooted, as did the cars. Someone started singing 'Knees Up, Mother Brown', and soon all the women in the street were swinging their legs in the air like Tiller Girls.

Jim caught Millie around the waist. 'Happy New Year, darling.' He kissed her lightly.

Millie smiled up at him. 'And to you.'

He kissed her again and then a frown creased his forehead. 'You know, I can't help feeling I'm being terribly selfish.'

'Selfish? How?'

'By taking an experienced nurse like you away from the people who need you most,' Jim replied, seriously.

'Really?' replied Millie, trying to keep a sudden surge of hope in check.

He nodded. 'It just doesn't seem right. Not with you being so short of staff just now at the clinic.'

'Well, perhaps I could stay until the worst of the winter is over, say until Easter,' said Millie, holding her breath as he mulled it over.

'It means I won't be able to take you to the Transport and General Union's dinner dance in February but,' Jim gave a resigned sigh, 'we'll still be able to turn heads at the Party Conference in May.'

'We certainly will,' Millie laughed, imagining the looks she'd get swirling around a dancefloor at seven months pregnant.

'And it would be the right thing to do,' said Jim.

'It's only for a few months,' said Millie.

By her own calculations she was almost three months pregnant and would have to give up work at Easter anyway.

Jim drew Millie back into his arms and smiled lovingly down. 'Well, I suppose I can put up with having a working wife for a bit longer.' He pressed his lips on to hers in a long lingering kiss that set her pulse racing. And then he whispered close to her ear, 'Do you think anyone would mind if we sneaked off home?'

Chapter Eight

Turning into Cannon Street Road, Millie tramped with Annie along the icy pavement towards Miss Gardener's crumbling house. With the road conditions being as they were, Millie had left her scooter at home and caught the early train to work. Although this meant she had to walk everywhere, it didn't matter, because a combination of daily deposits of snow, a daytime thaw and nights of below-zero temperatures meant that it was virtually impossible to get anywhere that wasn't a main road except by foot.

Even though it was only the early afternoon, the overcast sky and gathering fog from the river meant that the lights were already on in most of the houses, casting a pale yellow light into the streets below that added to a general feeling of gloom. But after the visit to her GP last Tuesday confirmed what she'd suspected since the middle of December, Millie was completely immune to the mid-January blues.

Of course, what with Jim campaigning from dawn to dusk and her covering for sick nurses, Millie hadn't actually found time to tell him the good news yet. But on Saturday she was going with Jim to meet voters in Leyton Market, and so she planned to look for an opportunity then.

A little niggle of doubt started to gather itself together in her chest but Millie stamped it down firmly. Jim would be surprised, stunned even, which would be only natural. But she was certain that once the initial shock wore off, he'd be as thrilled as she was.

Putting all thought of Jim and his impending fatherhood aside, Millie knocked on Miss Gardener's front door and then pushed it open.

'Only me,' she called, stepping into the hall.

'Only me who?' a man's voice echoed back.

Millie shut the door after Annie, and went into the front room.

Miss Moncrieff had got a single iron-framed bed from somewhere and had put it by the French door at the far end of the room so that, despite the chill from the draughty frame, her friend could look out on to the garden.

Miss Gardener lay as usual, with her fringed shawl over the counterpane, barely making a dent in the mattress. Millie was surprised to see that warming the backs of his legs in front of the fire was a young man dressed like a trackside bookie in a bold checked jacket and flannel trousers that were at least one size too small.

'Ah, "only me" is a pretty little nurse,' he said, without taking the cigar from the corner of his mouth.

Millie turned to her patient. 'I'm sorry I'm a bit late, Miss Gardener, But I had an extra home visit to squeeze in this morning.'

The flash young man grinned lasciviously. 'I wouldn't mind you squeezing me in one morning, Sister. I could do with a bed bath.'

'Freddie, please,' said Miss Gardener, struggling to sit up but setting off a coughing fit in the process.

Millie handed the elderly lady a clean handkerchief from the pile on the arm of the chair. She then plopped her bag on the table and opened it.

'This is my cousin Winifred's son, Freddie Kite,' Miss Gardener explained.

Millie forced a smile. 'Nice to meet you, but if you don't mind, Mr Kite, I have to get on,' she said, unpacking her equipment.

'Righty O, I'll go upstairs to 'ave a gander at Henrietta's latest scribble.'

Miss Gardener looked alarmed. 'Please leave Harry alone, Freddie. You know how much you upset her last time.'

Freddie's piggy eyes opened wide. 'Did I?' He flicked his cigar butt into the fire and then strolled out, banging the door behind him. 'Well then, I'll go and see if I can do it again.'

Miss Gardener flopped back. 'I'm sorry, Sister. He just comes and goes as he pleases.'

'But surely you don't have to let him into the house?' Millie said, as she spread the towels out ready.

'I do. It's his house. Or at least it will be when I'm gone.' The old woman started coughing again. 'Which I don't think will be very long, do you?'

Millie smoothed a lank strand of hair off her clammy brow. 'Are you in pain?'

The old woman nodded. 'Across my chest.'

'I'll give you your medicine before I start to move you,' Millie said.

She took the bottle of morphine syrup prescribed by Dr Masterson, measured out a teaspoon and gave it to the old woman.

'Now, while that's taking effect, I'll boil a kettle.'

Miss Gardener looked more relaxed when Millie returned and didn't flinch or groan as Millie removed her nightdress. Then, keeping her wasted body covered with towels, Millie washed and dried the old woman thoroughly, before putting on fresh bedclothes. Then she helped her on to the commode.

Swiftly, Millie and Annie changed the top sheet to the bottom, repositioned the oblong mackintosh across the middle of the bed and placed newspaper to absorb any accidents, and then covered it with a draw-sheet before helping Miss Gardener back into bed.

'Annie, will you brush Miss Gardener's hair and tidy around?'

Miss Gardener lay with her eyes closed while Annie brushed her hair with a soft-bristle brush.

Leaving her patient to rest Millie went back into the kitchen. Unfortunately, Freddie was there, rummaging around in the cupboards.

'How is she?' he asked, turning the old silver coffee pot he was holding and glancing at the hallmark on the bottom.

'As well as can be expected,' replied Millie, pouring the water down the sink. She went to walk past, but Freddie stepped in her path.

'How long do you think before ...?' He rolled his eyes upwards.

'I really couldn't say,' Millie replied in a professional tone.

'Because I wouldn't want her to suffer, I mean.' He leaned forward, wafting an overpowering smell of cheap cologne over her. 'I hope you'll do something to help her.'

'I'll do my best to keep her comfortable,' replied Millie neutrally.

'Good, good. And give her perhaps a bit more,' he winked, 'you know, at the end. After all, you wouldn't let a dog suffer like that.'

Before Millie could reply, the door opened and Miss Moncrieff walked in dressed in her usual shirt and trousers, with an oversized, paint-splattered artist's gown covering them.

Her eyes flicked towards Freddie. 'I thought you'd gone.'

'You wished I had, you mean.' He put the coffee pot back in the cupboard and closed the door firmly. 'I suppose you've come down to keep an eye on me.'

'I've come down to clean my brushes.' She pushed past him and went to the sink.

She thrust the three brushes she had in her hand under the tap and turned it on then glanced at Millie. 'How is Dodo?'

'Comfortable,' replied Millie. 'I've given her a dose of her medication so she should settle.'

Freddie walked to the sink. 'She won't last much longer, you know, and then you and your junk upstairs will be out on the street.'

Miss Moncrieff looked at him coolly. 'Do you really think I care?'

Freddie's face turned purple. 'You bloody will when I make a bonfire with all your poxy paintings.'

Miss Moncrieff turned away from him.

'Don't you turn your back on me, you fucking bull,' he shouted, his colour deepening considerably. His eyes ran over Millie. ''As dear Harry offered to paint you in the buff yet, Sister? Like she did my aunt.'

Millie looked away. 'I really should get on.'

'How do you think your family would take to it, Sister, having all your goodies displayed in a bloody gallery for anyone to gawp at?' Freddie said spitefully. ''As she offered to show you her etchings?'

Miss Moncrieff flicked the water off her brushes. 'I'll see you tomorrow, Sister.' She walked slowly out of the kitchen. Freddie crashed out after her and ran to the bottom of the stairs.

'That's it. Scurry up to your fucking studio. You can play the man, but you can't best one,' he bellowed up after her. 'Just you wait, you unnatural cuss. When I torch your fucking artworks it'll make the Blitz look like a pissing sparkler!'

Millie wriggled her toes inside her new court shoes in an attempt to get some warmth back in them. In truth, with the temperature just a degree above freezing, it would have been more sensible to have worn her fleece-lined boots, but after almost three hours traipsing up and down Leytonstone High Street, her feet weren't the only part of her feeling numb.

It wouldn't have been so bad if it had just been her and Jim handing out campaign leaflets and talking to people, but instead there was a whole entourage of people, including Ted Kirby, a couple of fresh-faced university students cutting their political teeth, and a reporter and photographer from the *Leytonstone Bugle*.

Millie refreshed her pleasant smile and tried to look more like a prospective MP's wife.

'So,' said the smartly turned-out woman whom Jim had collared outside Bearman's department store, 'just how many Jerries did you shoot down?'

'I'm afraid that's still classified,' Jim said, with an affable laugh, 'but what I can tell you is, Mrs ...?'

'Mrs Hill,' the woman said, adjusting the handbag on her arm.

Jim's expression became grave. 'What I can tell you, Mrs Hill, is the thing that helped me get into my Spitfire day after day and night after night was knowing that when we crushed Hitler and his Nazi thugs we'd be able to build a better England for all its people.' Jim grasped her hand and he looked earnestly at her. 'Can I count on your vote?'

The stout matron giggled under his intense gaze. 'Of course you can, young man.'

'Thank you, Mrs Hill.'

Jim disentangled his hand and Mrs Hill walked on to continue her shopping. Millie stamped her feet and tucked her hands under her arms.

'Couldn't we have lunch?' she asked, as her stomach rumbled.

'We just had a cup of tea,' Jim replied, scanning the High Street for the next vote to secure.

'That was almost two hours ago,' Millie replied. 'And then Ted dragged us out of the ABC before we'd finished.'

'Well, we've got to catch the morning rush,' Jim replied. 'We'll have lunch in a while.'

'But Jim, I'm cold and—'

'Look, darling,' he said, taking her hands. 'I know it's hard work pounding the streets, but the Liberal's a local man, so I'm chasing every single vote.' Jim gave her a dazzling smile. 'Just one more shopper and then I promise we'll stop for a bite.'

Millie nodded. 'But only if—'

'Oi! Jim! Over 'ere.'

They looked around to see Ted Kirby huffing and puffing towards them.

'What is it?' asked Jim, as his campaign manager came to a halt in front to them.

Ted grabbed Jim's arm and dragged him towards the church. 'Quick, I've found a woman with twins.'

'That's nice,' said Millie, picking up her pace to keep up with them.

'Too right it is,' said Ted over his shoulder. 'A picture like that might even make the front page.'

The quick walk to Station Road brought the blood back into Millie's toes but as she came to a halt by the library steps she felt suddenly dizzy. She leant against the 1930s entrance to steady herself.

The nausea and tiredness she'd experienced since Christmas had largely disappeared, but she still hadn't yet found the right moment to tell Jim. But she was almost four months pregnant, and if she didn't tell him soon, she wouldn't need to, as he'd see for himself.

'Darling, can I have your expert assistance, please?' Jim called.

Taking a deep breath to clear her head, Millie walked over to where her husband was trying to manoeuvre a couple of disgruntled-looking infants into his arms.

'Let me.'

Millie took the larger twin and tucked it into the crook of Jim's arm then did the same with the other. The babies stopped crying and studied Jim solemnly.

'See,' she said, to her awkward-looking husband, 'babies like to feel a firm hand holding them.'

'We'll want Mum in the shot, too,' called the photographer, waving at the anxious-looking young woman standing with Ted.

She came forward and took up her position next to Jim to get St John's Church in shot too. Millie stepped back out of the way while the photographer checked the light and then took half-a-dozen photos, using a hand-held flash to illuminate the subject.

The flash-lights popped in Millie's vision and her head spun for a couple of seconds and then righted itself. Jim handed back the children and started talking to Ted.

Millie went to join them.

'Ted was just saying we ought to stroll down to the station and catch shoppers coming back from the West End,' Jim said.

'I'd love to,' said Millie. 'But I'd like something to eat first.'

'What do you think, Ted?' Jim asked. 'Have we got time?'

Ted sucked on his lips for a moment or two and then nodded. 'We'll go to the pie and mash shop and take a couple of shots of you in there. You know, to show you've got the common touch.'

Jim pulled a face. 'As long as you don't want me to eat eels.'

'Pie and mash it is then,' said Millie.

They set off up the hill back to the High Street but as Millie turned the corner by the church gates her head swam. She put her hand out to steady herself but fell against the low wall.

'Are you all right?' Jim asked from what seemed to be a long way away.

'I'm fine,' said Millie, focusing on a lamp-post on the other side of the street to get her balance. 'I'm just very hungry.'

Jim offered his arm. Millie took it and they started off again but after only a few steps red spots started to appear at the edge of Millie's vision. She staggered and her legs gave way. She felt Jim's arm around her, but it was too late. The black clouds filling her mind closed in and Millie tumbled on to the icy pavement.

Sneezing as the smelling salts bore up her nose brought Millie back to consciousness. She opened her eyes to find herself lying on a bed with Jim and Ted Kirby sitting either side of her. Behind them were ranged the young activists and a handful of spectators, all staring at her.

'Thank goodness,' said Jim, taking her hand.

Millie looked around. 'What happened?'

'You fainted, sweetheart,' said Jim.

'You hit the floor like a Frenchman threatened by a popgun,' added Ted.

The two activists standing behind him laughed.

'And your husband,' Ted cast his gaze around the audience and raised his voice, 'the local Labour candidate and war hero, carried you in here.'

One of the young university students appeared with a cup of tea and handed it to Millie. Ted gave him and his friend a sharp nod and the two party workers drifted away with the crowd.

'Here?' asked Millie

'The furniture department of Bearman's,' Jim told her.

'And I hope you're enjoying our very finest Dreamtime bed, Mrs Smith,' said a thin chap standing at her feet.

'Er, yes. Thank you,' muttered Millie.

'And as I've just told your husband, should you take a fancy to the stylish yet affordable luxury of the Dreamtime Galaxy I'm sure we could—'

'Thank you, Mr Wells,' Jim stopped the sales spiel. 'You and your staff have been most kind.'

The salesman's thin face lifted in an ingratiating smile. 'Not at all.' He returned to his duties.

Millie drank her tea and the sugar in it steadied her head a little, but she was in no hurry to move.

'Are you all right?' asked Jim. 'I mean, you still look very pale. Are you ill?'

Millie shook her head. 'But I must have something to eat.'

'Right you are, love,' said Ted. He glanced at his watch. 'But we'll have to make it quick, Jim. We're meeting with the chamber of commerce at the town hall in an hour and a half and we haven't touched the Kirkland Road yet.'

'Well, you'll have to do without me because after dinner I'm going home,' Millie said.

'Now, Millie,' said Ted, screwing his heavy features into what Millie took to be an appeasing expression. 'You know how the punters like to see the candidate's wife with him on the road.'

'I'd like to have a private word with my husband, Ted,' said Millie.

'Surely it can wait till you get home?' said Ted.

'If you don't mind.' She smiled sweetly.

Ted rolled his eyes and then stomped off, muttering under his breath.

Jim waited until Ted was out of earshot and then spoke. 'Look, Millie, I want to eat too, but—'

'I'm pregnant,' Millie said.

Jim stared at her. 'How? I mean when?'

'I think it was the night of the dinner dance, you know when you'd run out of … things,' she said, willing him to look just a little pleased.

'Are you sure?'

Millie nodded. 'I was pretty certain when I was sick in church at Christmas.'

They hadn't spoken of Beth and her son since Christmas morning, and Millie certainly didn't want to now.

'Doctor Fallow confirmed it a few weeks ago. And the baby's due at the end of May,' she said quickly. A knot of anxiety tightened in her stomach. 'I know we'd planned to wait.'

'Oh Millie,' Jim laughed. 'That's fantastic!'

Millie stared at him for a second and then laughed, too. Jim took her in his arms and hugged her.

'Oh, Jim,' she said, as the weight she'd been carrying for weeks suddenly lifted from her shoulders. 'I'm so happy.'

'Me too,' he said brushing his lips on hers. 'It's absolutely perfect.' He kissed her again. 'We'll call him James.'

'It might be a girl,' Millie said, swinging her legs off the bed and sitting up.

'Are you sure you're all right to stand, darling?' he asked anxiously.

Millie laughed. 'I'm pregnant, not ill.'

Jim cupped his hands around his mouth. 'Ted! Come here.'

Ted, who had been eyeing up a glass-fronted drinks cabinet, lumbered over.

Jim put his arm around Millie's shoulder. 'Millie's having a baby,' he said, grinning happily at his campaign manager.

Ted's hard-bitten face dissolved into a sentimental expression. 'That's wonderful.'

'That's what I thought,' said Jim.

'Congratulations, Millie, love,' said Ted, patting Millie on the shoulder.

'Thank you, Ted,' replied Millie, wondering if she'd perhaps misjudged him a little.

'In fact,' Ted turned and scanned the showroom. 'Oi, Tom,' he said, waving frantically at one of the students who was chatting to a pretty red-haired shop assistant.

Pushing his black-framed glasses back on his nose, Tom slouched over.

'Shoot down to the Walnut Tree, lad,' barked Ted. 'And fetch that reporter and his mate back here right away.'

Tom hurried off and Ted grasped Jim's hand. 'Good on you, lad,' he said, pumping it vigorously. 'If we pitch it right, a story about your preggers wife campaigning alongside you will capture the petticoat vote, and swing the election. Well done!'

Closing the treatment-room door behind her, Millie stepped into the hall. The sound of someone singing and bathwater being run drifted down. Putting her hand in her pocket, Millie felt the envelope containing her resignation letter.

The telephone on the table next to her rang. Millie picked it up but before she could speak, she heard Miss Dutton's voice.

'Munroe House. How can I help you?'

'It's me, Lilly,' said Mr Shottington.

'Oh, Algie.'

Millie gently replaced the receiver and hoped the lovers wouldn't hear the click as the line cut off. She looked toward the superintendent's office and turned her letter over in her hand. She'd had it there since Monday and if she didn't give it to Miss Dutton today, it would be so crumpled she'd have to rewrite it.

Millie thrust it back in her pocket and continued down the hallway to Miss Dutton's office. As the superintendent's high-pitched voice could be heard through the door, Millie waited for a couple of moments then knocked.

There was a long pause before Miss Dutton called, 'Come.'

Millie walked in. 'I'm sorry to disturb you.'

Instead of wearing her old-fashioned matron's uniform, Miss Dutton was dressed in a chocolate-coloured two-piece suit, a tiny veiled hat and lipstick, and there were tears in her eyes.

She blinked them away. 'What is it?'

'I'll come back on Monday,' said Millie.

'No, I'm not busy,' said Miss Dutton bitterly. 'In fact, I've got nothing to do all weekend now.' She glared hatefully at the telephone. 'What do you want?'

'To give you this.' Millie took the letter out of her pocket and offered it her. 'I'm having a baby and will be leaving at Easter.'

Miss Dutton's thin face twisted with disapproval. 'You'll have to carry out all your duties, you know. I can't give you special consideration just because of your condition.'

'I'm not asking for any,' Millie replied.

They stared at each other for a moment, and then Miss Dutton took Millie's letter. 'Well, I suppose I should congratulate you.'

'Thank you, Miss Dutton,' Millie replied with the sweetest of smiles. 'And have a nice weekend.'

With a satisfied smile on her lips Millie closed Miss Dutton's door and headed for the nurses' changing room at the end of the corridor. Within minutes she'd stripped off her uniform and donned her civvies. Putting her navy dress into the laundry hopper she buttoned her three-quarter-length coat and secured her scarf over her hair for the journey home.

With her handbag in the crook of her arm and thought of the weekend in front of her Millie remerged into the hall just as Sally picked up the on-call telephone.

'Good afternoon. Munroe House,' she said, rolling her eyes.

Millie waved at her as she past.

Sally held up her hand. 'Just a moment and I'll see if she's still around.' She clamped her hand over the mouthpiece. 'It's for you.'

'Who is it?' Millie asked.

Sally shrugged. 'It must be one of your old patients, as he asked for Sister Sullivan.'

Millie glanced at the grandfather clock at the bottom of the stairs and nodded. Sally removed her hand. 'I've just found her, and so if you'd just hold on a moment.'

Sally handed her the telephone, waved goodbye and went back into the treatment room.

Millie put the receiver to her ear. 'Hello, Sister S—'

'Millie, is that you?'

The floor under Millie's feet shifted a little and she grabbed the table to steady herself.

'Are you there, Millie?'

'Alex?'

A laugh rumbled down the telephone. 'I'm glad you remembered.'

Something akin to ice water washed over her, and her knees buckled. Clutching the phone she slid on to the chair next to her as jumbled memories of the man at the other end of the phone swirled around her head.

'Is it really you?'

'Yes it is,' he replied. 'In the flesh.'

'Are you all right? I mean, you're not injured?'

'Injured?'

'By the Zionists.'

'No.' Alex laughed again. 'I've been sitting around in Cypress since they kicked us out.'

'Oh.'

'Look, I'm sorry to spring it on you and I know this is a bit sudden, but could we meet up say for a coffee or a bite to eat or—'

'I don't think that would be a good idea.'

There was a pause. 'Look, I know things weren't right between us when we parted.'

'It's not that,' Millie said, feeling her wedding ring pressing on the Bakelite phone. 'I mean, there's been a lot of water under the bridge since then.'

'I know, but I just want a chance to talk to you, that's all, Millie. No strings or anything. Honest. Just for old time's sake,' pleaded Alex.

A long-forgotten ache welled up in Millie's chest and she closed her eyes.

'Millie, are you still there?' he asked anxiously.

'Yes, I'm still here.'

'Please.'

Millie took a long deep breath. 'All right, but just for a quick coffee.'

'Thank you.' He let out an audible sigh. 'Are you free tomorrow? I'll pick you up and we could go anywhere you—'

'I'm busy.'

'Sunday then, after lunch perhaps?'

'I can meet you Monday,' Millie said firmly. 'But it'll have to be in my morning break at Kate's café as we're two nurses down.'

'Yes, yes. That's fine. Wherever you like,' Alex replied.

'About eleven,' said Millie.

'I'll be waiting for you. Until Monday then.'

The line went dead.

Millie held the receiver to her chest for a moment and then slowly pressed her finger on the disconnect bar.

Almost unable to put her finger in the correct number Millie turned the dial. The call connected and it rang four or five times before it was picked up.

'Good evening. Fry House,' said a woman's voice at the other end. 'How can I help?'

'I need to speak to Sister Byrne urgently. Is she there?'

Millie had just glanced at her watch for the fourth time when the Grape and Hoop's saloon bar door swung open and Connie stepped inside.

Millie breathed a sigh of relief. Although the narrow-fronted public house just opposite Aldgate Station wasn't a dockside alehouse, it was still uncomfortable to be a woman alone in a bar surrounded by self-important City types giving her the eye.

Peering through the whirls of smoke Connie spotted Millie and hurried over.

'Thanks for coming so quickly,' Millie said, embracing her friend.

Connie untied her rain hood and shook it out. 'Don't be silly. Now let me get a G&T, and then you can tell me everything.' She unclipped her handbag and pulled out her purse. 'What do you want?'

Millie nodded. 'I suppose another brandy won't hurt.'

Connie looked surprised. 'Another? How many have you had?'

'Two.' Millie replied.

Connie's fair eyebrows almost disappeared under her fringe but she went to the bar and ordered their drinks. Millie resumed her seat.

'There you go,' said Connie, after a few moments, putting a glass on the cork coaster in front of her.

'Thanks.' Millie took a large mouthful, pulling a face as it burnt the back of her throat.

'Where've you parked your scooter?' asked Connie, taking a small sip of her own drink.

'I left it at the clinic,' said Millie. 'I thought it best.'

Connie raised an eyebrow. 'I'm glad to hear it. I don't fancy your chances navigating around Stratford Broadway with three brandies inside you.

Millie gave a sheepish grin and took another sip.

'Now,' said Connie, putting on her best matron expression. 'What's happened?'

'Alex phoned.'

'Alex?' Connie put her hand over her mouth. 'No!'

'Yes,' said Millie. 'An hour ago.'

'No wonder you're throwing back brandies,' said Connie. 'What did he say?'

'Nothing much,' Millie replied, replaying the two-minute conversation with her ex-fiancé in her mind yet again.

Her friend gave her a questioning look. 'You did tell him you were married?'

Millie looked down as she swilled the drink in her hand. 'Not as such.'

'Millie!'

Her head snapped up. 'Well, it's not the sort of thing you can say easily over the phone. Is it?'

Connie's eyes stretched wide like two cornflower-blue saucers. 'You're not going to meet him?'

'Just for a quick cuppa, that's all. On Monday,' Millie cut in. 'What else could I say?'

'"I'm sorry Alex, I'm married and so I can't meet you" might have done it.'

'For goodness sake, Connie. We're having a mid-morning coffee in Kate's Café, not a weekend in Brighton.' Millie frowned. 'We were close once but a lot has happened since then.'

'Yes, like you being in the family way for a start,' said Connie, her gaze drifting down to Millie's still-flat middle.

Millie's hands closed protectively over her stomach as memories of the children she and Alex had planned to have flitted through her mind.

'So you'll tell Jim, then,' Connie's voice said, cutting across these thoughts.

Millie looked up. 'Naturally. And I'm sure Alex will tell his wife.'

'Ah, yes. I forgot,' said Connie.

Millie hadn't, especially as he must have walked down the aisle in Cyprus around the same time she did in St George's.

'He's probably got a baby, too, I shouldn't wonder,' Millie added. 'He always was mad keen to start a family.'

Connie carefully scrutinised her friend's face for a couple of seconds, and then spoke again. 'Are you sure it's wise to open up old wounds?'

Millie shoved aside all the unsettling memories Alex's phone call had stirred up, and forced a brittle laugh. 'Don't be silly, Connie. After all this time of course there aren't any wounds left to open. And I'm sure Alex is just as happily married as I am.'

Chapter Nine

'It sounds as if, for once, you've had a pretty uneventful week at work, Millie,' said Doris, lifting the flowery china teapot to pour three cups of tea.

After an afternoon of walking up and down Kensington High Street, Millie, her mother and aunt Ruby were now sitting in Pontins restaurant on the third floor, with a loaded tea tray and a tempting plate of cakes in front of them.

Of course, Millie's summary of the week's news hadn't included the phone call from Alex. As, aside from the fact she didn't feel in the mood to listen to Ruby recount the many things she loathed about Millie's ex-fiancé, Millie couldn't very well say what had occurred until she had actually told Jim about Alex getting in touch. And she was determined to do that, just as soon as a good moment presented itself.

Doris picked up the *Leytonstone Bugle* sitting next to her elbow that Millie had brought to show them. 'That's certainly a lovely picture of you and Jim, isn't it, Ruby?'

'It certainly is,' replied Ruby, blowing a stream of cigarette smoke towards the ceiling. 'And such a pretty dress. Where did you get it?'

'Selfridges,' replied Millie.

Ruby looked impressed.

'Jim's mother came to London last week and we met her in the hotel where she was staying. They had some family business to attend to, and so I did a bit of shopping while they were with their solicitor,' Millie said. 'It's part of their new maternity range, but it was still eleven coupons.'

'Well, I wouldn't worry too much,' said Ruby. 'I heard that the government's ending clothes rationing in a few weeks.'

'That's what Jim said, and just my luck, too.' Millie ran her hand over her still smooth stomach. 'While everyone's rushing out to get the latest fashion, I'll be wearing maternity frocks.'

'Well, at least you'll be able to buy ones with lace, pleats and pin-tucks,' said Doris.

'And that's one thing you can't complain about. Jim's very good at letting you have money to spend on yourself,' said Ruby.

'No, I can't; he's very generous and he does like to see me looking nice,' said Millie, thinking of the handful of white five-pound notes in her purse.

'Where has he gone this weekend?' asked Ruby.

'Oxford, for some university reunion or another,' Millie replied.

'I'm surprised you didn't go too,' Doris said.

A little wave of annoyance flared in Millie's chest.

As much as she hadn't relished the thought of spending the weekend with Jim's old university chums, it would have been nice if actually he'd asked her if she'd like to come, rather than simply assuming she wouldn't.

Millie gave a hollow laugh. 'What, and spend two days listening to them retelling their undergraduate pranks and scrapes?'

'I expect Jim's mother was as pleased as Punch when you told her about the baby,' said Ruby.

'I bet she spoke of nothing else,' said Doris. 'I know I haven't since they told me.'

'Me neither,' said Ruby, exchanging an excited look with her sister.

Doris had already knitted two matinée jackets and matching booties since Millie had told her the previous week, while each week Ruby was putting away small items like cotton wool, zinc and castor oil, and baby soap to help Millie stock up.

'No, she didn't,' fibbed Millie.

In fact, other than a chilly kiss on the cheek and perfunctorily enquiring after Millie's health, the entire conversation over the afternoon tea when Jim had broken their happy news was about people Millie had never heard of and farming issues she didn't have a clue about. Other than saying please and thank you to the uniformed waiter who served them, Millie hardly said a word during the two hours of their visit.

'So what is she buying for the baby?' asked Ruby.

Millie shrugged. 'It didn't come up in the conversation.'

Ruby stubbed out one cigarette and took another from her case. 'I expect she'll just set up a trust fund and then order something from one of those fancy Bond Street shops. Or maybe she's planning to give you some crib or highchair that's been passed down through Jim's family for centuries.'

'Perhaps,' said Millie.

'Well, make sure you tell her I'm buying the pram,' said Doris emphatically. 'I liked that Silver Cross one we saw in Selfridges.'

'I thought the Pedigree Luxury was just as good,' Millie said, thinking of the nine-guinea price difference.

'Nonsense,' her mother replied. 'If a Silver Cross is good enough for the king's grandchild, then it's good enough for mine. And it's not as if it won't be used again, is it?'

Millie rolled her eyes. 'Will you let me have this one first, Mum?'

Doris put the strainer over her cup and poured herself another tea. 'I'm just saying. And who knows, it might be twins.'

'Have you thought of any names?' asked Ruby.

'James if it's a boy.'

'Naturally,' said Ruby approvingly.

'And if it's a girl I wanted to call her Patricia, after Little Nan, but Jim doesn't like it.'

'What's wrong with our mother's name?' asked Doris, looking slightly affronted.

'Nothing, as far as I'm concerned. But I expect it's too Irish.'

'What name does Jim like?'

'Wilhelmina. After his mother.'

Ruby flicked her cigarette into the ashtray in the middle of the table. 'Well, let's hope it's a boy.'

Millie laughed. 'I don't mind, as long as it's healthy.'

'And you know what they say,' said Doris, covering Millie's hand with her own. 'A son's a son until he takes a wife but a daughter's a daughter all your life.'

Millie and her mother exchanged an affectionate look.

'It really is a very good picture of the two of you.' Ruby held up the newspaper again.

Millie studied the photo filling a full quarter of the front page. It had been taken in front of the Leytonstone and Wanstead Labour Party offices in Wanstead High Street and at Ted's insistence Jim's campaign banners were displayed prominently in the background. She was standing on Jim's left, holding his arm, and they were smiling at the camera. Although there was only the slightest rounding out below her navel, Jim had wanted her to wear the navy maternity smock with a white Peter Pan collar and neck tie that made her look further on than she was. It was a good picture, Millie could see, although it made her uncomfortable to look at it.

'You should ask the paper if you could have a print of it,' continued Ruby.

'They already offered,' said Millie. 'But I said I didn't want one.'

Doris looked puzzled. 'Why ever not?'

'To be honest, Mum,' Millie said, 'I'm a little embarrassed to see myself splashed all over the front page.'

Ruby refolded the newspaper. 'Well, you'd better get used to it, Amelia. Because Jim's an ambitious man, and once he's an MP I wouldn't be surprised if this time next year you're not plastered across the front of the national papers on a weekly basis.'

Millie woke with a start to the sound of the telephone ringing. She was sitting in her easy chair by the hearth with her feet up on a footstool and a blanket over her legs. She'd drawn the curtains against the February gloom when she'd got home from her mother's at six.

Apart from the soft red glow of the fire the only other light in the parlour was from the standard lamp behind her. She remembered listening to the ten o'clock news and the shipping forecast, but she must have fallen asleep just after.

Millie switched off the cracking wireless on the cabinet beside her and peered at the clock on the mantle shelf. Eleven-thirty!

Shoving her feet into her slippers Millie stepped into the chilly hallway and picked up the receiver. 'Leytonstone seven, seven, three, nine.'

The pips sounded and then the line connected.

'Hello, darling, it's me,' said Jim's voice. 'I'm really sorry to get you out of bed about this but I'm afraid I won't be able to get back tonight.'

'Are you all right?' asked Millie.

'Yes, yes, I'm fine. It's Richie.'

'What's happened?' asked Millie.

'It's too tiresome to go into over the phone but it means I've had to drive him to his parents' place just outside Huntingdon.'

'Is that where you are now?' she asked.

'Yes,' Jim replied. 'It's thick fog up here and I can hardly see my hand in front of my face and so I'm going to bed down for the night, and then head into the office at first light.'

'I suppose that's sensible, but why are you in a call box?' Millie said, hearing the rumble of voices around him. 'And who's with you?'

There was a pause. 'What do you mean?'

'Who's talking in the background?'

'Oh that. The Lodge's telephone isn't working, so I've walked down to the pub in the village to call you. It's just the customers at the bar, that's all. And, oh my darling, I'm really sorry to have got you out of bed, especially as you're up at six.'

'Actually I wasn't in bed, I was sitting in the parlour waiting for you,' Millie said.

'I'm sorry, sweetheart, I really am,' said Jim, his voice heavy with regret.

Millie sighed. 'Well, these things happen, I suppose. As long as you're all right.'

'I am,' Jim said in a brighter tone. 'Did you have a nice time with your mum?'

'Yes, and I've decided on a pram, although Mum wants to buy—'

The pips started again.

'Look, I'm out of pennies but I'll see you tomorrow at six. Bye.'

'Bye, Jim, I'll—'

But the phone line was already dead.

Millie put it back on the cradle and then, switching off the light, made her way up to bed.

Millie waited for the brightly painted front door with a lion's-head knocker to open. A bolt slid back, the door opened and Derrick Joliffe stood in the hall.

'Sister Smith, how nice to see you,' he said, smiling at her.

'Good morning, Mr Joliffe,' Millie said. 'I thought I'd pop by and see how your wife is getting on. Is it convenient?'

His smile widened. 'Of course. She's in the lounge.'

Millie stepped in and he closed the door behind her.

The Joliffes lived in one of the Georgian terraced houses on the south side of Arbour Square. Unlike many of the old houses, which had been stripped out and modernised, the Joliffes' house retained many of its original features. Although recently they had decorated the room in what would be considered by many to be old-fashioned wallpaper and colours, it blended exactly with the house's olde-worlde feel.

Dorothy Joliffe was sitting with her feet up on the sofa beside a glowing fire. She was, as always, immaculately dressed in a green candy-striped maternity smock that was tented over her considerable stomach. As usual she had a little piece of knitting on her needles and the sound of the orchestra on the Home Service playing quietly in the background.

She looked up as Millie walked in and smiled.

'Sister Smith, what a pleasure,' she said, putting aside her knitting and attempting to stand.

Mr Joliffe was immediately beside her. 'Where do you think you're off to, Mummy?' he asked, giving her a comically serious look.

'I was going to make Sister a cup of tea,' Dorothy replied.

'No you're not,' her husband laughed. 'Didn't I say you were to keep your feet up?'

'Yes.'

Derrick raised his hand.

Dorothy giggled and saluted. 'Yes, sir – Daddy.'

The couple smiled at each other and then Mr Joliffe turned to Millie. 'Sugar?'

'One, please.'

He left the room.

At the homes of some of the patients Millie visited, you wouldn't want to wash your hands in their sink let alone drink out of one of their cups, so as a general rule the usual reply to an offer of tea was that you had had one in the last house; but in the Joliffes' house that decree didn't apply.

Millie put her bag on the floor and sat on the chair to the side of Mrs Joliffe. 'What are you knitting?'

'A matinée jacket,' Dorothy replied, holding up the tiny piece of knitting on her needles.

'It's a lovely colour,' Millie said, feeling the lavender-coloured sleeve of three-ply.

'I thought so,' Dorothy replied, smiling fondly at her work. 'And it will do for a boy or a girl.'

'Have you any preference?' asked Millie, noting the puffiness around her patient's ankles.

Dorothy shook her head. 'As long as it's got ten fingers and toes, I don't mind. Although I suspect Derrick secretly wants a girl.'

'To sit on his knee and adore him,' Millie laughed.

'Exactly.' Dorothy gazed down and smoothed her hand over her stomach.

'Have you got any names yet?'

'William if it's a boy and Margaret, after my mother, if it's a girl,' Dorothy replied.

The door opened and Mr Joliffe walked in carrying a tray. 'Tea is served, ladies,' he said, putting it on to the coffee table.

'There you go, Sister.' He handed a bone china cup and saucer to her. 'And what's a cup of tea without a bit of cake to soak it up?'

'That's very kind,' Millie said,

She opened her case. She took out her sphygmomanometer and thermometer, and her ordinary and foetal stethoscopes. Removing the thermometer from the antiseptic, Millie popped it under Dorothy's tongue.

'I'm sorry about the taste,' she said, opening her sphygmomanometer.

Wrapping the blood-pressure cuff around Dorothy's right arm, Millie hooked the ends of the stethoscope in her ears, placed the percussion end in the crook of Dorothy's elbow and pumped up the cuff until the pulse ceased. She glanced at the upright black and gold gauge and pressed her lips together: 160.

Millie released the valve and listened carefully for the blood to pump again, willing it to be in double figures. At 115 it started again.

Millie deflated the cuff and took the thermometer out of her patient's mouth.

'I can see from your face it's still high,' said Dorothy.

'It's the same as last week,' Millie replied, folding away her equipment.

'What was this morning's urine result?' she asked.

Mr Joliffe beamed at her. 'I can show you.'

He went to the small bureau in the chimney alcove and pulled down the front flap.

'Derrick tests every morning,' Dorothy explained as her husband sorted through the internal shelves. 'And writes it all down.'

'Here it is,' he said, flourishing a dull green exercise book. 'I also put down what Dorothy eats and drinks.' He handed it to Millie.

She opened it and scanned down the fastidiously written columns. 'I wish some of my fellow nurses would write as neatly.'

Mrs Joliffe smiled tenderly at her husband. 'I couldn't ask for a better nurse.'

'I see your wife's early-morning sugar has risen slowly over a couple of weeks,' Millie said.

'I gave Dorothy an extra couple of units of insulin as Doctor Gingold told us,' Derrick explained.

'When are you back to the hospital?'

'Friday,' said Dorothy.

Millie scanned the column of neatly written numbers again then handed the book back to Mr Joliffe. 'If it's 2% tomorrow morning I want you to ask Doctor Gingold to visit, and you must tell her that I said you should.'

Anxiety flashed across Derrick's face. 'Is there something wrong?'

Millie snapped the top back on her pen. 'I won't lie to you. Mrs Joliffe's blood pressure is high, as is her blood sugar. I'm also concerned, as Dr Gingold is too, about your wife's swollen legs, especially as the hospital found a trace of albumin in your wife's urine last week. What we have to do is just keep everything stable for at least another two weeks, until you're fully eight months gone and it's safe to deliver the baby.'

'I can't say I'm looking forward to having a caesarean,' said Dorothy.

'I know, darling,' said Derrick, kneeling beside his wife and taking her hand. 'But it is best for both of you.' He kissed her fingers. 'And you know it will all be worth it when we have our little baby.'

Dorothy gave her husband a brave little smile and a lump formed in Millie's throat.

Derrick was right, of course. When she'd trained as a midwife ten years before, the chances of an older mother with diabetes being able to carry a child to anything close to full term, let alone deliver it alive, were next to zero. And many of these mothers and babies died in the attempt. Now, however, women like Dorothy could not only survive childbirth, but also had the real hope of leaving the delivery room with a child in their arms.

However, with still a few weeks to go before Dorothy's baby's organs would be fully developed, Millie wouldn't rest easy until she saw little William or Margaret lying peacefully in their crib.

'Tell me, which door was it you fell against?' asked Millie, dabbing the gash on the young woman's brow.

'The kitchen,' mumbled Maureen Turner through her swollen lip. She wouldn't meet Millie's gaze.

Dr Robinson had asked Millie to visit Maureen when she'd popped into the surgery to pick up a couple of prescriptions that morning. He'd asked Millie to 'see what she could do', which meant that the problem was social rather than medical. In Maureen's case that problem came in the form of husband Mickey Turner.

The Turners lived, with their two children – Susan, a bright ten-year-old, and Sidney, a cheeky tearaway aged six – in the flat above the newsagent's at the corner of Watney Street Market. Maureen was a machinist and took in piece-work from a local trouser factory to pay the rent and put food on the table. Mickey was known throughout the area as having a hair-trigger temper and for doing a bit of this and that, mostly on the wrong side of the law.

In contrast to her barrel-chested husband, Maureen was a pale, stick-thin woman who was probably only a year or two older than Millie herself. But her mid-brown hair already had grey streaking through it, and constant anxiety had etched deep lines around her colourless mouth.

Millie took out a bottle of iodine and poured a small amount on to a piece of gauze. 'I thought you said it was the bedroom.'

Maureen's weary blue eyes looked up at Millie. 'Did I?'

'Yes,' Millie replied. 'And last week you tripped and hit yourself on the pantry shelf.'

Maureen sighed. 'He don't mean it, Sister, honest, he don't.' Her battered face took on a soft expression. 'And 'e's the best of husbands really. But when the drink gets 'old of 'im, well ...' Maureen winced as Millie dabbed the antiseptic on her broken skin.

'But this is the fourth time in as many weeks, Mrs Turner,' Millie said, dropping the dirty gauze into the makeshift newspaper bag at her feet. 'The cut on your forehead's still raw from before, and now you're going to have a lovely shiner to go with it.'

Maureen's shoulders slumped. 'I know, but this time it was really my fault. I knew that my Mickey had a run-in with the foreman at Walfords, and so I shouldn't have started on at him about the rent.'

'But surely that's no excuse,' Millie said, putting the cork stopper in the iodine bottle and slipping it back inside her case. 'And what about the children?'

'They've learnt to keep out of their dad's way when he's been on the bottle.'

Millie frowned. 'It's not good for them to see what he does to you.'

'I try and keep it from them, but it's hard, especially when he starts shouting and swearing like he does.' Maureen smiled, showing a missing front tooth. 'Susie's good, though. She gets her brother away as soon as she sees her father's getting himself worked up.'

'Is Sidney still wetting the bed?'

Maureen nodded. 'But 'e's getting better. I know you think Mickey's a wrong 'un, Sister, but he loves me, really he does, and 'e's right sorry when he sobers up. And he's no worse than the rest of them around here,' Maureen concluded, slicing through Millie's unsettling thoughts.

'Except that most men only lash out at their wives after closing time on a Saturday night,' Millie pointed out.

The image of Jim lying unconscious on the lounge floor and his rough handling after sinking a dozen Scotches with Ted and Don Wethersfield were slow to leave Millie's mind but she pushed these troubling thoughts aside.

'But what can I do, Sister?' Maureen asked. 'He's my 'usband, after all's said and done.'

'That doesn't mean he can treat you like a punchbag,' replied Millie. 'Couldn't you go to the police?'

Maureen shook her head. 'I tried that last year when he busted my nose, but they said it was a domestic and they couldn't interfere.' Maureen forced a lopsided smile. 'Don't you fret yourself, Sister. I'll mend.'

Millie regarded her patient sadly and snapped her case closed. 'Well, I can patch you up again this time. But I'm afraid, Mrs Turner, that what really ails you needs a bit more than gauze and bandages.'

After deciding it was too cold to walk past Kate's café for the third time on the other side of the road, Millie steeled herself and marched across the road. She grasped the handle and with her heart thundering in her chest, she opened the door. In contrast to the chilly March morning the small interior was a warm fug of fried food, stewed tea and muttered voices against the melodious background of *Music While You Work*.

The working-man's eating house on the Highway had been dishing up fried eggs and bacon each morning and filling pies and potatoes at midday for as long as Millie could remember, and there was always a steaming urn of tea on the brew. It was Pearl the landlady's proud boast that even when the incendiary bomb landed on St George's church and blew out all the café's windows, they'd still opened for breakfast the following day.

As it was almost eleven-fifteen, the mid-morning rush was over although there were still a handful of men huddled around the scrubbed wooden tables. Millie gazed around, to find the ground shifting under her feet when she caught sight of Alex Nolan, the man she'd once loved with every beat of her heart.

Millie took in his tall and muscular frame in one sweeping

glance. He still had the full head of thick black hair that used to slip through her fingers like silk. The memories of them entwined in each other arms making love flashed through Millie's mind, and then gave way to her last image of him, furious and storming from the nurses' small sitting-room in Munroe House, clutching the engagement ring she'd just thrust back at him.

They stared wordlessly at each other for a moment, and then Alex smiled at Millie. And the last twenty months of her life simply vanished.

'Millie,' he said, standing up and striding towards her.

He stopped just an arm's reach away. Millie looked up and noted that although the scar on his chin had faded, there was a fresh one on his right cheek.

'Hello, Alex,' she said, gripping her nurse's bag tightly. 'I'm sorry I'm late.'

His smile widened. 'Don't worry. I've got us a spot in the corner,' he indicated the table with two empty cups on it where he'd been sitting. 'Is that all right?'

'I can't be too long,' Millie replied.

'Of course.'

Millie stared up at him for a moment and then Pearl's voice cut between them.

'What can I do you for, Sister?'

Millie dragged her gaze away from Alex. 'The usual, thanks Pearl. And no sugar,' she said to Pearl, who was making up sandwiches behind the counter.

'And I'll have another,' Alex said rummaging in his trouser pocket before putting a shilling on the marble counter.

As he stretched across her Millie caught the faint smell of fresh aftershave, and her heart thumped all over again.

Alex stood back to let her pass, and Millie weaved her way between the customers to the table by the far wall. He collected their teas and followed her.

'How's your Mum?' he asked, putting her tea in front of her.

'Fully recovered thank you,' Millie replied, tucking her nurse's bag under the chair and sitting down.

'I'm pleased to hear that,' Alex said. 'And your aunt Ruby?'

Millie smiled 'Exactly the same.'

Alex swung himself into the chair but as he did his fawn

trench coat opened. Millie caught the flash of silver buttons with MP stamped on them and a whistle chain strung across his chest.

'But aren't you still in the Palestine police force?' Millie said, wondering if she was thinking right.

Alex shook his head and the rebel curl over his left eyebrow broke free, just as Millie remembered it doing so many times before. 'I finished my contract just as the Zionists kicked us out a few months back, and so I re-joined the Met.'

'How long have you been back?'

'A month,' Alex replied. 'I had a few days with my sister in Benfleet before being sworn in again by the Assistant Commissioner, after which I'm spending a mind-numbing two weeks at Peel House on a course for officers joining the Met.'

'Officers?'

Alex pulled back his coat collar to show a single pip on his epaulette, and grinned. 'I'm the new Inspector for B relief at Arbour Square.'

Millie stared across the table at him.

'I wanted to contact you as soon as I got back, Millie.' Alex lent forward on his elbows and wrapped his well-formed fingers around his mug of tea. 'Well, the truth is that I didn't know if you would want to see me after all that happened.'

Millie forced a genial smile. 'Don't be silly.'

A wry smile lifted the corner of his mouth. 'Can't tell you how pleased I am to hear you say that.'

Millie waved the notion away. 'And I'm glad to see you're all in one piece still. Although I see you've got a new war wound.'

Alex's hand rose to his right cheek and he grinned. 'Just a misunderstanding with a matelot in Ashdod.' his expression grew sombre. 'I wasn't sure you'd come.'

'I almost didn't.'

The expression in his eyes softened. 'Oh, Millie, I'm so —'

'I came because I wanted to tell you myself that I'm married.' Millie uncurled her left hand from around her tea and laid it flat on the table.

Alex stared at the small band of gold on the third finger of her left hand for a long moment. And then a smile spread across his face, although Millie wasn't quite sure it reached his eyes.

'That's terrific news,' he said in a low voice that, for a moment, almost convinced Millie. 'I'm so very happy for you. Truly, I am. Congratulations.'

'Thank you.'

Alex leant back and stretched out a long leg. 'Who's the lucky fellow?'

'His name's Jim … Jim Smith,' Millie replied, her husband's name sounding odd between them.

'Local chap, is he?'

Millie shook her head. 'From Essex. We met when he was down here on business.'

Alex's smile widened. 'So, when did you and lucky old Jim get spliced?'

'December 1947,' Millie replied. 'The week before Christmas, in fact. It was a small affair, you know, just family and a few friends.'

'Marvellous.'

Millie put her cup down and let her hand rest lightly on her stomach. 'Not only that, but—'

'Is that the time?' Alex glanced at his watch as he interrupted. 'Sorry, Millie, but I have to see the Chief at twelve.'

He stood up abruptly.

'But what about you?' asked Millie.

Alex shrugged. 'Dodged a few bullets, had a few laughs but nothing much else to tell really.'

'Nothing to tell?' said Millie incredulously. 'But from what I heard, you must have walked down the aisle about the same time I did.'

'I'm not married,' he said distantly.

Millie looked puzzled. 'But when I met Georgie Tugman, he said you were.'

An odd emotion flitted across Alex's face, sending a faint tremor of a long-forgotten excitement through her.

'There was someone, but it didn't work out.' He threw back the last mouthful of tea. 'It's been really great seeing you again, Millie, and do please give my best to your mum.'

'Yes, of course I will,' Millie replied quietly.

Alex gave a quick nod and then spun around and marched to the door with Millie's eyes riveted to his every step.

Chapter Ten

The eight o'clock pips sounded and the radio announcer started reading the morning news.

Millie tucked her dressing-gown around her and wriggled her toes in her slippers, feeling ridiculously guilty at still being in her nightclothes at this time, even though it was her day off.

'I'm only going to show my face at the Party office to say hello to the volunteers, and so I'll try and get back for lunch,' said Jim, as he popped the last piece of toast and marmalade into his mouth.

'That would be nice. It seems as if we've barely seen each other since Christmas,' Millie said, hearing a little catch of emotion in her voice.

Jim reached across the table and patted her hand. 'I know, darling. And I'm sorry, truly I am. But this is the last week of the campaigning and I have to give it all I have, especially with the weather being so dreadful for the last three days.'

'I do understand,' said Millie with a sigh. 'I just wish we could spend more time like a normal married couple. You know, going to the cinema or for a meal together, or even sitting by the fire listening to the radio would be nice for a change.'

'And we will do very soon, I promise,' said Jim, 'Ted says there's a very good chance that I'll increase Woodrow's majority in votes, so after next week I won't have to spend every blooming hour God sends me addressing meetings and attending committees.' Jim smiled and glanced at his empty cup. 'A splash more milk this time, if you please, my love.'

Millie poured him another tea.

'Of course, it doesn't help with you having to cover for every sick nurse in Munroe House,' he added, spooning in two sugars.

'I know,' said Millie. 'And I have to admit that with having to find cover for at least one shift every week since the New Year because of sickness, I'm beginning to wish I had left Munroe House at Christmas.'

Jim swallowed the last of his tea and stood up. 'Leave now, then. I don't mind.'

'I couldn't do that,' said Millie, feeling suddenly hollow at the thought. 'Not with half the population coughing and spluttering with bronchitis because of the smog.'

He shrugged on his jacket hanging over the back of his chair and then went to check himself in the small mirror that was hanging above the sink. 'Well, they'll have to do without you in two months.'

Jim took a dab of Brylcreem from the tub on the window sill and ran it through his fair hair. An image of Alex's jet-black curls flashed unbidden through Millie's mind.

'Jim, I've been meaning to tell you something,' she said, as she watched him straighten his tie.

Jim pulled a grave face at her in the reflection. 'That sounds terribly serious.'

'No, not really, just something that happened the other day at work,' Millie replied with a little laugh. 'It's nothing, really, in fact.'

'I'm already running late so can it wait?' asked Jim, slipping his comb into his breast pocket.

'Yes, of course.' Millie took another sip of tea. 'It's not important.'

Jim turned and walked over to her. 'Well, you must do what you feel is right, darling,' he said, kissing her on the forehead. His eyes flickered down to the gold and enamel locket sitting just above her dressing-gown and smiled. 'Have you taken that off since Monday?'

'Only at work,' Millie replied closing her hand over it, feeling the warmth against her skin. 'When your husband gives you such a wonderful present you want to make sure he knows you appreciate it.'

Jim's lips pressed on hers again and this time they lingered. 'It's just my way of saying sorry for Sunday night.'

He gave her a heart-stopping smile, and a fizz of excitement ran through Millie.

He stood up and took his loose change and keys from the

dresser. 'I've got to get myself a haircut and run a couple of errands this afternoon, but why don't we pop up to Woodford and have dinner? Save you cooking.'

Millie smiled at him. 'That would be lovely and it will give me a chance to show off my unexpected present,' she said, fingering the gold oval at her throat again.

'That's a date. And make sure you put your feet up while you can today,' he said.

Millie kicked out the spare chair next to her and put her feet up on it. 'Don't worry, I will.'

Jim laughed. 'But could you remember to pick up my navy suit from the cleaner's?'

Millie nodded. 'I've got to get a couple of postal orders for my cousin's kids' birthdays and so I'll collect it on the way back from the Post Office.'

Jim picked up his briefcase, blew her a kiss and left.

Stretching over, Millie twiddled the dial on the wireless away from the ponderous tones of the Home Service and on to the cheerier Light Programme and, tapping her feet in time to the Ink Spots, she buttered the last slice of toast and bit into it.

By the time Millie walked out of the butcher's at eleven o'clock, Leytonstone High Street was filling up with midday shoppers. She'd started at the Post Office and had worked her way back home via the Home and Colonial Food Shop for eggs and tea, Stolls the baker for two crusty rolls for lunch, and Sainsbury's in Church Lane for corned beef and butter to go in them. Now, with a full basket over her arm, she was heading for her last call of the morning – to collect Jim's clean suit.

As she pushed open the laundry door the starchy smell filled Millie's nose, bringing back childhood memories of washdays. The bell jingling above her head drew Mr Irvine from the back of the shop. He was a small, tightly made man and, although he was nudging fifty, he had attempted to retain his youthful appearance by rather misguidedly dyeing his hair.

'Mrs Smith,' he said, the pencil moustache that hugged his top lip lifting as he smiled. 'I have your husband's suit all ready for you.'

He unhooked it from the rack behind him. Millie gave him

the collection ticket and he stuck it on the spike next to the till.

'And I've given it a double pressing because I know it's for his special night,' he said, as if Jim was going to be acclaimed king rather than, hopefully, a Member of Parliament.

He folded Jim's trousers up and then carefully slipped the suit into a large paper bag with the shop's name on the side.

He handed it to her. 'Take care now that you don't catch yourself on the pins,' he said, indicating the two colour-headed pins securing the bottom.

'I will.' Millie placed Jim's suit on top of her shopping. 'How much do I owe you?'

'Three and six.'

Millie handed over the money and picked up the basket at her feet.

'Oh, and there were a couple of things I rescued from his pockets.' He rummaged around under the counter and pulled out a brown envelope. 'Just a few scraps of paper and receipts, but I don't like to throw customers' personal items away in case they are important.'

Millie took the envelope and slipped it in her pocket. 'Thank you.'

Hooking the basket in the crook of her arm Millie left, and twenty minutes later was walking through her back door. Taking Jim's suit out of the basket, she left her shopping on the table and, without taking off her coat, Millie went straight upstairs and hung his suit up on the wardrobe door to let any cleaning fumes disperse, and then went back to the kitchen.

She lit the gas under the kettle and switched on the wireless to catch the last half an hour of *Music While You Work* before the midday news. Humming along to a lively tune, Millie slipped off her coat and was about to take it into the hall when she remembered the envelope in her pocket.

She took it out and dropped it on the table, and then went back into the hall to hang up her coat. She scooped up the midday post from the front-door mat and returned to the kitchen just as the kettle started whistling. While the tea was brewing, Millie quickly packed the food away before pouring herself a cup.

Sitting down at the kitchen table, she sifted through the post, set the half-a-dozen letters addressed to Jim aside, and opened hers, which were a long letter from her cousin May with a photograph of her and her husband at some national Scouts gathering, and an appointment from Whipps Cross Hospital to see the obstetrician in charge of her delivery.

Millie put the appointment in her handbag and May's letter aside to read properly later, and picked up her tea. Taking a sip, her gaze fell on the brown envelope. Mr Irvine had only tucked the flap inside and the half-hour journey in her pocket had crumpled it so that now the envelope gaped open. Now Millie could see a bill poking out with an Oxford address on the heading. Thinking it might be a petrol receipt that Jim needed to save in order to submit it for reimbursement, Millie pulled it out and placed it on his letters, but as her eyes ran over it, she snatched it up.

It was a bill for two nights at a hotel in Oxford dated the previous weekend, and beside the sum of £6 7s 6d was Jim's florid signature.

Millie stared at the paper in her hand for a few more moments then she stood up and went into the hall. Her heart thumped uncomfortably in her chest as she lifted the telephone receiver and dialled the number at the top of the bill. There was a pause and then someone picked up at the other end.

'Castle Hotel. How can I help you?' a woman's voice said.

'Good afternoon, I'm Mrs Smith,' Millie said. 'My husband—'

'Mrs James Smith?'

'Yes.'

'Oh, what a coincidence,' said the woman in a chirpy voice. 'I've just left a message with your husband's secretary. The maid found the earring you lost under the pillow after you left on Monday. I've put them in the post to you not an hour ago.'

Something akin to cold water ran over Millie. 'Which address did you send them too?'

'Your country house in Tollshunt.'

'Thank you,' Millie forced out.

'Good day, Mrs Smith.' The phone went dead.

Millie dropped the receiver in the cradle and slumped back against the wall as a wave of nausea washed over her. She locked her knees to stop them trembling wildly and then took a deep breath to steady her pulse. As her sickness receded, Millie opened her eyes and studied her reflection in the old octagonal mirror opposite for a second or two then, grabbing the gold and enamel locket around her neck, she tore it off and flung it across the floor.

Millie lifted her head from her hands and looked up as the front door slammed shut. She glanced at the clock on the wall.

'Sweetheart?' Jim called from the hall.

Millie didn't answer. After sobbing for a solid hour face-down on the bed, she'd made herself get up and have something to eat. Having forced down a bread roll, she went back upstairs, washed her face and put on some lipstick. Coming back down, she'd made herself another pot of tea and it was the second cup of that brew that sat half-drunk on the table in front of her along with the hotel bill.

With her eyes fixed on the door, Millie waited. The sound of Jim's footsteps grew nearer and then the handle rattled as he opened the kitchen door.

'There you are,' he said, sauntering in with his hands in his pockets.

Millie regarded him steadily and didn't answer.

He gave her his stock apologetic smile. 'Sorry about not getting back earlier, but old Peter Wilson, the Party vice-chairman's secretary, collared me and I couldn't get away. Any chance of a cuppa?'

'In the pot,' replied Millie flatly.

Jim looked taken aback but then he smiled again. 'That's right, my love, you take it easy.'

He crossed the kitchen to the stove.

'I picked up your suit as you asked,' Millie said.

'Thanks.' He spooned in two sugars. 'I booked a table at the Warren for eight. It a bit stylish so I thought you might wear that new blue dress I bought you.' He grinned and patted his stomach. 'You might as well wear it while you can.'

'The dry cleaner found a couple of bits and pieces in your suit pocket, including this.' Millie picked up the receipt. 'It's a bill for Saturday and Sunday nights' stay in Oxford last weekend with your signature on the bottom,' Millie said in a conversational tone, turning it so he could see it.

Jim smiled nonchalantly and glanced over it. 'Oh, yes, so it is. It looks like they've charged me double for Saturday. It's obviously a mistake.'

Millie smiled. 'I thought it must be.'

Jim's stance relaxed. 'Don't worry, darling, I'll ring them in the morning and set it right.'

'You needn't bother because I already have.' Millie's mouth pulled into a tight line. 'And they kindly informed me that they found *my* earring in the bed after *we* left on Monday.'

Alarm flashed across Jim's face.

'I can explain,' he said in a contrite voice after a long moment.

Millie jumped to her feet. 'How could you, Jim?'

'Calm down, sweetheart,' Jim said, taking a step towards her. 'It's not good for the baby if you get yourself too het up.'

'Is that what you were thinking of when you were rolling about under the covers with another woman, Jim? Our baby?' she asked sharply.

Jim came around the table toward her, but Millie side-stepped, keeping it between them.

'Was it that slut Edwina?' she asked as tears of humiliation stung her eyes. 'Or perhaps some other old tart you had a bit of a fling with in your undergraduate days, or perhaps some poor young girl like Beth?'

'It's not like that.' Jim stretched his arms out in front of him. 'If you'd just let me explain, darling.'

'Don't you dare "darling" me, you liar,' Millie shouted.

'If you'd just let me get a word—'

'Do you know what?' Millie cried, raising the flat of her hand. 'I don't care who the bloody earring belonged to. What matters is that after only just over a year of marriage and when I'm carrying your child, you betrayed me and then lied to cover your shabby behaviour.'

The words caught in her throat as searing pain cut through Millie again. Knocking over a chair, she stumbled around the table and headed for the door.

Jim reached out to touch her as she passed, but she slapped his hand away.

'Don't you dare touch me, you bastard!' she screamed, shoving him aside and dashing out of the kitchen.

Jim ran after her into the hall.

'I'm so sorry, Millie,' he called up the stairs after her.

'Go to hell,' she yelled back.

She slammed the bedroom door as hard as she could, and then threw herself on the bed again to sob scalding tears.

Millie lay staring up at the fringes of the central bedroom light and guessed, as the light was going, it was probably early evening, but she didn't care. She wasn't hungry and even if she were, Millie didn't have the energy to get off the bed. Her ribs ached and her eyes stung from an hour of futile crying. She was utterly exhausted, both physically and emotionally.

She rolled her head and caught sight of their wedding photo on the dressing-table. As the streetlight outside the window bathed the picture frame in a soft yellow glow, Millie stared at the laughing couple sprinkled with confetti. Jim was smiling lovingly down at her and she was holding tightly on to his arm and gazing adoringly up at him. Tears bunched at the corner of her eyes again but Millie blinked them away.

There was a faint knock on the door and then it creaked open.

'Millie, darling,' Jim said, coming into the room and closing the door.

She didn't answer.

'Sweetheart, I want to explain what happened,' he said, crossing the floor and perching on the edge of the bed.

Millie shuffled across the bed away from him.

Jim sighed. 'Look, Millie, I know you're hurt and angry. But you must believe I didn't plan this.'

'That's not how it looks to me,' replied Millie. 'You made it quite clear you didn't want me along, and then you tell me that you had to look after a friend and stay at his house, and now I find you'd had the gall to book an extra night in the hotel. The only truthful thing you've told me is you were in Oxford. From where I'm sitting it looks like you were planning to have a dirty weekend all along.'

Jim raked his hands through his hair. 'Look, I did go to the debate and then the old gang went for dinner and we had a few drinks. As always with these things, we got talking about our undergrad days and the pranks we used to get up to, and we started fooling around in the hotel bar.'

Millie raised an eyebrow.

'It was just a bit of high spirits, that's all,' Jim replied, plaintively. 'Then we ran into a party of girls who were in town for a teaching convention or something. We asked them to join us and, well,' he shrugged, 'things got a bit out of hand.'

Millie looked incredulously at him. 'Out of hand! You slept with another woman, Jim!'

'I know,' he said, shaking his head. 'But I've been under such a lot of stress with the election campaign.'

'Don't try that old one,' shouted Millie. 'It wasn't as if you just tumbled together in a moment of weakness, was it? After all, you did stay with her for a second night, and rang me with some cock-and-bull story in order that you could. And even when I challenged you about the hotel bill, you tried to brazen it out.'

Jim hung his head. 'You're right, Millie. I've got no justification. I was stupid and I've let you down badly. But I am sorry. Truly, I am.' He took her hand and fell to his knees beside the bed. 'I love you, Millie, and so I'm begging you. Please, please, my darling,' he closed his eyes and pressed his lips to her fingers twice, 'try and find it in your heart to forgive me.'

Jim risked an imploring look up at her.

Millie regarded her husband for a few moments, and then spoke again. 'I suppose anyone can make a mistake.'

'Thank you,' he said, kissing her forehead repeatedly. 'I pledge that I'll never do it again.'

Millie pushed him away. 'You'd better not. I'll not forgive you a second time.'

Jim got back on the bed and slid closer. 'Thank you, my love. I promise I'll make it up to you.' He gave the impish smile Millie found so irresistible. 'And I'm starting right away by taking you, my adorable wife, to dinner, and then I think perhaps a shopping trip up town might be in order sometime next week, don't you think?'

He tried to gather her into his arms, but Millie held him off. 'It's going to take more than a shopping trip to make me forget how badly you've behaved and how very much you have hurt me.'

'I know.' He drew her to him. 'But let me try.' Jim kissed Millie's forehead as he held her close. 'Please, my darling.'

After a moment, Millie put her arms around him. Jim relaxed his head on to her shoulder and just as he did, Millie felt the small bubbling sensation of their baby moving for the very first time.

Chapter Eleven

Dodging to avoid being slapped by the flapping washing on the line, Millie marched across the O'Tooles' front garden towards the house.

Although it was still bitterly cold, thankfully in the last few days the thaw had set in and the temperature had risen above freezing during the day at least. With the clocks going forward on Sunday, here at last was the promise of warmer weather. The sun was out today and doing its best to brighten up the afternoon, although it wasn't doing much to raise Millie's spirits.

Without pausing, she shoved open the door and strode in to the O'Tooles' house.

The hall was empty but there was a domestic hum of people talking and children playing drifting down from upstairs.

A door opened and Millie looked up.

The top half of Kitty, Brendan's wife, appeared over the upstairs banister holding her youngest, six-month-old Aiden, on her hip. Although still in her early twenties, Kitty was already a mother of three and, if the records from last week's booking-in clinic were anything to go by, already carrying another.

'Oh, it's yourself, is it, Sister,' she called down. 'How are you?'

Millie put on her professional smile. 'I'm fine.'

'And your own man, is he keeping well?'

'He's in good health, too,' replied Millie.

It wasn't a lie; five nights of sleeping in the spare room had done him no harm at all.

'And is it right that you're in the family way yourself, Sister?' Kitty asked.

'I ... I ... how did you know?' asked Millie.

Kitty shrugged. 'Word gets around. How far gone are you?'

'Almost five months,' Millie replied.

'And you still have your waist,' said Kitty, admiringly. 'Sure, didn't I look like a barrage balloon at three?' Kitty laughed. 'Well, God love you, Sister. And may he send you a little darling such as me own.'

She gave the child in her arms a noisy kiss.

'Thank you, Kitty,' Millie said, feeling her bitter core melt a little at the thought of her baby. 'Now, if I can get on.'

'Of course, Sister, you've probably a hundred patients waiting on you, so you have, and his mammy's waiting for you in her chair in the back,' she said before disappearing.

Millie walked down the corridor, pushed open the door and walked in.

'Good morning, Mrs O'Toole,' she said, banging her bag down on a spare chair. 'What seems to be the problem this time?'

The old woman's wrinkly face was screwed up in agony. 'It's me belly,' she said, gripping the rolls of fat around her middle. 'I tell you, Sister, me vitals are clawing at me something terrible, so they are.'

'And when is this?' Millie asked, perching on the edge of the only uncluttered chair in the room.

'Day and night, there's no rest from it. And when I have a shite!' Mrs O'Toole put her face through another series of contortions. 'And I can't stop it when it's upon me. That's why I've had to have this close.' She tapped the zinc bucket beside her chair.

'Really?'

'Oh, yes, it's like Limehouse Mudchute after a storm.' Mrs O'Toole smiled ingratiatingly. 'So I was wondering if you could see it in your way of letting me have one of them chairs with the gazunder beneath.'

'You mean a commode?'

'That's the fella. It would save me from staining the carpet.' She indicated the colourless, threadbare rug under her chair.

'Before I consider that, I'd need to run through a few things with you first, Mrs O'Toole,' said Millie in a pleasant tone.

'Right you are, Sister.'

Millie pulled out Munroe House's loan book from her bag and opened it on her lap.

'Our records show that you've already borrowed several items from us.' Millie scanned down the page. 'So many, in fact, that there is probably more of our equipment in your house than in our own loan cupboard.'

'Is there?'

'There is.'

'Well, if I have it's because I need it, all of it,' Mrs O'Toole banged her chest and coughed. 'As you know, I'm not a well woman.'

Millie's gaze returned to the inventory. 'You have three of our six full-size mackintoshes, Mrs O'Toole.'

'Haven't I just been telling you I'm squirting through the eye of a needle?' the old woman asked crossly.

'What about the other two?'

'One's on the twins' mattress to save it,' explained Mrs O'Toole. 'They're only three and haven't yet got the hang of the potty, and the other's on the coal-hole roof. There's a slate missing and the rain pours in fit to baptise you.'

Millie raised an eyebrow. 'Two air rings?'

'Well, you know yourself that our Seamus's Francine just delivered and she can hardly sit for the soreness.'

'Francine's baby is four months old,' said Millie.

'After six it takes its own time to heal.'

'And the other one?'

'Mitesy's took a fancy to it and is nesting down in it ready for her kittens,' Mrs O'Toole replied without a trace of embarrassment.

'And the bedpan?'

Mrs O'Toole looked confused. 'I can't rightly recall a—'

'I think it might be over there, with the aspidistra inside it,' Millie said, as her eyes drifted pointedly towards the window sill.

'Oh, that,' Mrs O'Toole said, following her gaze. 'I'm using it until I get another pot.'

Millie shut the book and shoved it back in her bag.

'I'm afraid, as you're complaining of being ill, I will have to ask your GP to call yet again to make sure there's nothing untoward going on,' Millie said, not relishing yet another conversation with Dr Willis about Mrs O'Toole. 'And before I can issue any more equipment, I must insist you return the items you're not using.'

Mrs O'Toole heaved the heaviest of sighs. 'Very well, Sister, I'll have the boys deliver them back to you in a day or two.'

'I believe you told Sister Scott the same when she raised the issue two weeks ago, and the items still haven't arrived back with us,' said Millie. 'So I'm afraid I'll have to take the things you're not using with me now, as there are people who need them.'

Millie rose to her feet and went to the window; although it had been sunny just a few minutes ago, now the sky was overcast and there was a sharp squall. Grabbing the plant, Millie lifted it out of the china bedpan and set it on the sill. She tucked the bedpan under her arm and, collecting her bag from the floor as she passed, Millie opened the kitchen door and marched back through the house.

'Where are you going?' shouted Mrs O'Toole, lumbering down the hallway after her.

Millie continued across the garden and into the yard. Brendan and Dougan, who were manhandling an old boiler on to the back of a wagon, stared open-mouthed at her and their mother as the two women dashed between the scrap metal towards the coal shed.

Raising her arm above her head, Millie grabbed the fluttering edge of the waterproof sheet and tugged it free. 'Now, where's the cat?'

'In the stable,' replied Mrs O'Toole.

Millie crossed back to the stable and went inside with the old woman still hot on her heels.

In contrast to the chilly atmosphere in the yard, the stable was warmed by the bales of hay stacked inside. Two of the three O'Toole horses were in their byres, softly munching at their hay at the far end. They regarded Millie with mild interest for a second or two and then turned back to their supper. Millie marched on until she spotted the cat curled up in the centre of the tan-coloured doughnut that by rights should be under the rear end of one of Munroe House's patients to prevent a pressure sore.

The tabby looked at Millie with gold-green eyes; unlike many of the yard and factory cats Millie would see out and about, this one was well fed with a glossy coat. As she bent down and stroked the cat's soft fur, she felt movement beneath. The cat purred and rolled over to reveal her swollen belly. Crouching in the peaceful outbuilding, Millie's own roundness pressed on to the tops of her thighs. Millie tickled the cat behind the ear and then she stood up. She turned to find Mrs O'Toole behind her.

'Well, the rubber ring's ruined and so I'll have to bill you for that,' Millie said, nodding at the tabby who was now cleaning her front paws. 'And as I can't carry any more, I'll take the mackintosh and the bedpan for now, but I'll be back on Friday for the rest of the equipment.'

'Right you are,' said Mrs O'Toole, looking suitably chastened.

Millie tucked the folded rubber sheet under her arm and marched past the old woman back into the yard, pleased to have liberated at least two pieces of Munroe House equipment.

'Will it be yourself coming back on Friday?' Mrs O'Toole called after her.

Millie turned and allowed herself a little triumphal smile. 'Yes it will, Mrs O'Toole, at about three o'clock.'

The old woman clasped one hand over the other in front of her. 'Then I'll be happy to see you, but tell me, will you be bringing the commode with you or should I send one of me boys to fetch it?'

Still arguing with the old woman in her head Millie put on her wet-weather gear and marched between the oily puddles, rusty screws and the shards of glass twinkling in the mud towards the main gates.

Just as she reached halfway there, the double gates swung back and a horse wearing blinkers and an antique harness plodded into the yard with Patrick O'Toole strolling alongside.

Although he had the odd freckle dappled across his nose and forehead, Mrs O'Toole's youngest had fewer ginger tones, as his hair was more auburn than red and his eyebrows and whiskers were even darker. Standing taller than his brothers at just under six foot, and with broad shoulders, a barrel chest and hands like shovels, he could have been mistaken for a prize-fighter until, that is, you looked at his straight nose, which clearly had never been broken.

Although Millie was muffled up now in a long mac with a rainhood over her hat and had donned galoshes, Patrick O'Toole was dressed as if for a spring day in May and his only concession to the weather was an ex-army camouflage jacket, which wasn't even done up.

'Afternoon, Sister Smith,' he said. 'And how are you this fine day?'

'I'm very well, but if you ask me, you're looking to catch your death dressed like that,' Millie said, indicating his partly unbuttoned shirt with her eyes.

Patrick looked at the leaden sky. 'It's no more than a bit of soft weather, so it is.' He turned the horse so the rear of the cart sat alongside the back wall. 'How's me Mammy?'

'The same as ever,' replied Millie, in a matter-of-fact tone.

'That's the truth of it?' he said, releasing the horse from the shafts.

He slapped it lightly on the rump and it ambled off into the stable. Patrick sauntered around to the back of the wagon and effortlessly heaved an old radiator off the back.

'And what about you, Patrick?' Millie asked. 'How are you keeping?'

'Oh, you know.'

'I suppose now the shortages are easing up, the yard's picked up.'

'That it has.'

Patrick slung an old mangle on top of a pile of treadle sewing-machine frames and the ring of metal on metal echoed around.

Millie shifted her weight on to the other foot. 'I'm surprised you haven't settled down like your brothers by now.'

A hint of a smile lifted the corners of Patrick's mouth. 'Truth be told, Sister, I'd never given it much mind until a few months ago. But recently I've been turning the matter over in my head something powerful-like.'

'Have you?' said Millie, annoyed that she had to tilt her head to keep eye contact.

'That I have.' He pulled a weather-beaten zinc bath off the cart and deposited it alongside his other finds. 'And having meself some young 'uns.'

Despite being able to see her breath in the icy air, Millie felt suddenly warm. She lowered her eyes and tucked her woolly scarf in place.

'Well, I must get on,' she said, in a voice reminiscent of the old training matron at the London. 'After all, no rest for the wicked.'

'Not when the devil drives,' he replied. He continued to look down at her for a couple of seconds, then stepped out of her path and returned to the task of unloading the scrap wagon.

Tightening her grip on her bag, Millie continued on until she reached the gate, but as she put her hand on the iron ring-handle of the main gate, Patrick called after her.

'Sister Smith!'

She turned.

Patrick slung another piece of metal aside and then, shoving his hands in his snugly fitting canvas trouser pockets, he sauntered over. He stopped just a little too close.

'Will you do me a kindness?' he asked, in a lilting, musical tone. 'Will you tell Annie I'll be picking her up at the usual time on Friday?'

Millie forced herself to hold his gaze. 'Yes, of course.'

'I'm obliged to you, Sister.' Patrick pointed a grubby finger to his forehead making a cheery salute to her.

Millie watched him as he went back to the wagon whistling a lively ditty to himself.

Pat the Lad had had a well-earned reputation for being a local Casanova. Millie had always wondered about that, but standing in the shadow of his powerful frame, she had suddenly understood why the women of the area ignored their mother's warnings and fought each other for Patrick's attention. But as she watched his rolling gait, Millie's eyes narrowed.

How on earth could Connie say that Patrick O'Toole, with his sea-green eyes, roguish good looks and devil-may-care swagger resembled her ex-fiancé Alex Nolan in any way whatsoever?

Half an hour later and with her nose half frozen and her fingers numb with cold, thanks in no small way to having to waste her time on the unnecessary visit to Mrs O'Toole, Millie finally walked through Munroe House's back door. She hooked her hat and coat up on the hall stand and then headed for the treatment room.

Dumping her bag on the cabinet, she put the earth-soiled commode and dirty mackintosh in the sink and then turned on the Ascot. Tossing in a handful of grated carbolic soap, Millie rested her hands on the edge as she waited for the water to cover them.

The grey clouds outside must have moved aside because as Millie watched the water rise, a shaft of sunlight shone through the window on to her left hand. Her wedding ring glinted in the pale light just as tears gathered in her eyes. She tried to hold them back, but instead they escaped and joined the frothing water in the sink.

The treatment-room door behind her opened. Millie dabbed her eyes with the back of her hand and squared her shoulders.

She glanced over and saw Annie.

'That bloody O'Toole woman,' Millie spat out as she scrubbed the bedpan furiously. 'I see her at least three times a week trotting down the market and she had the barefaced cheek to ask me today for a commode.'

'Did you give her one?' Annie asked, taking out her dirty instruments.

Millie's head snapped around. 'No, I jolly well didn't. She's already got half our equipment around there.'

Annie studied her face. 'Have you been crying, Millie?'

'I got a bit of carbolic in my eye, that's all. It must have caught under my fingernail and I rubbed it in.' She looked down into the sink and worked on the china pan again. 'That old woman's hoodwinked half the nurses in the place into giving her stuff. Still, at least you weren't one of them.'

'Just because I'm walking out with Patrick O'Toole doesn't mean I'd give his mother anything she asked for,' Annie replied.

'Well, I wouldn't have been surprised if you did,' Millie said. 'Men like Patrick O'Toole have a way of getting what they want.'

Annie frowned. 'What do you mean, "men like Patrick"?'

'You know, the sort of an Irish rogue, Jack-the-lad type,' Millie replied. 'And I would have thought you could have found someone a bit better than a rag-and-bone man.'

'Don't you dare talk about Patrick like that,' snapped Annie, with a tight look on her face.

Millie felt the blood rise to her cheeks. 'There's no cause to take that tone. I'm only trying to stop you making a mistake. I've told you before, Patrick has women from the length of

Knockfergus chasing him, and the O'Tooles are banned from more pubs than they're welcomed in. Plus there's not a week goes by without the police searching that yard. Men like Patrick are all charm and sweet words until they've got a ring on your finger, and then you find out what they're really like.'

'Is that so?' replied Annie, glaring at her.

'Yes it is.'

'Well, let me tell you something, Sister Smith,' Annie said, thrusting her face into Millie's. 'Patrick may have had women making eyes at him all the time, but since we've been walking out he's never so much as looked at another woman. Added to which he hasn't taken one single liberty with me. His brothers might be banned from every pub from Aldgate to Bow Bridge, but Patrick's welcome in any of them, and I've never seen him any the worse for wear. And if the police want to waste their time searching the yard they can, because, even though you might believe otherwise, everything the O'Tooles trade, they've come by honestly. And I don't know what's got into you lately,' she continued. 'You're like a bear with a sore head most mornings, and you snap at everyone.'

'No, that's not true,' protested Millie.

'Yes it is,' Annie insisted. 'You chewed Veronica out two days ago just because she spilt tea over her notebook and you had poor Doreen in tears last week because she lost her stethoscope.' Tears sprang into Annie's eyes. 'I know people call Patrick's family tinkers and crooks, but I thought you were different and better than that.'

'I never call them that!' said Millie, taken aback.

'Not in so many words. But that's what you mean,' Annie replied. 'I know Patrick's mother's always on the lookout for something for nothing, but have you thought that maybe she's had to be like that? From the way the boys talk about their father, it's clear she got no money or help from him to raise them. Sean told me once that when they were younger she had to buy cat's meat to feed the family and sometimes they had boiled potatoes for breakfast, lunch and supper because there was nothing else.'

Millie was shocked. Her mother and Ruby had their fair share of 'when we were kids' stories of hardship and poverty, but none featured horse-meat.

Annie regarded Millie coolly. 'But I think the real reason you don't like Patrick is because he reminds you too much of Alex Nolan.'

From nowhere, an image of Alex flashed into Millie's mind. 'Did Connie tell you that?'

'She didn't have to,' Annie replied. 'You did when you called Patrick "an Irish rogue". Wasn't that what you used to call Alex?'

'Don't be ridiculous,' said Millie, waving the notion away dismissively. 'That was years ago, and I'm married now.'

'Surely you mean happily married?'

Millie didn't reply.

Annie smiled coolly. 'You know, not all of us can marry a man with money and live in a house with more rooms than people, but I'll tell you this, I'd rather have Patrick O'Toole and his family than a man who buys me roses one week and makes me weep into a sink the next.' Annie snapped her bag shut and thumped it on to the table. 'I'll clean my instruments later, when you're done.' She marched, head held high, towards the door.

Remorse flooded through Millie. 'Annie, I'm sorry. I didn't mean it to sound like that.'

But the door slammed and Annie was gone.

Millie looked at her watch. 'They should be going in soon.'

'I hope so,' replied Connie shifting her weight on to the other foot. 'These new shoes are pinching my toes.'

She and Connie were standing two abreast down the side of the ABC cinema along with at least fifty other women on a damp March evening. Under the mute yellow glow from the street lamps the last few city workers were getting off the seven o'clock buses and making their way home. As the working day drew to a close the evening activities were just gearing up in the pubs and cafes along the Mile End Road.

'I'm glad you got away from work on time for once, Connie,' said Millie.

'What with Dr McEwan's new clinic in the Thrawl Street and child inoculations in his surgery, we've been rushed off our feet in Fry House,' Connie replied.

Millie looked impressed. 'A new broom; just what the area has needed for years.'

Connie nodded enthusiastically. 'He's very dedicated and although he's only been there a few weeks the locals are already beginning to warm to him.'

'You make him sound something special,' Millie nudged her friend playfully. 'You'd better be careful in case Malcolm gets jealous.'

Connie's cheeks flamed. 'I'm just helping out, that's all. There's no ... nothing more to it than that. Honest, there isn't.'

'I was only pulling your leg, Connie.'

Connie smiled self-consciously and looked at the floor. 'Are you all right with all this standing?'

'Fine,' Millie laughed. 'Never felt fitter.'

Connie ran an experienced eye over her. 'Well, you're certainly blooming. But it won't be long before you'll have trouble buttoning your coat across.'

Millie smiled. Almost half way through her pregnancy there was a decided roundness to her stomach now, but her ankles were as slim as ever even at the end of the day. And at the moment, with plenty of room for the baby to move about in, there wasn't an hour when Millie didn't feel a little fluttering movement.

'So what are you going to do about Annie?' asked Connie as another half a dozen people walked past to join the end of the queue.

Millie shrugged. 'Every time I try to apologise, she walks out. It's my fault, I know. I was upset about something else and I spoke without thinking. And the moment the words left my mouth I realised I'd let my temper get the better of me, but it was too late.'

'Well, I suppose you touched a raw nerve,' Connie replied. 'Did you know her mother's not been talking to her since she started walking out with Patrick seriously?'

A further twinge of guilt caught in Millie's chest. 'No, I didn't. But I'll try to talk to her again tomorrow.'

Connie gave her friend a sympathetic smile. 'I'm sure she'll come around eventually.'

'I hope so,' said Millie glumly. 'I can't bear us to be at odds with each other.'

Connie slipped her arm through Millie's and squeezed. 'Come on, cheer up. We're supposed to be enjoying ourselves.'

Millie forced a smile. 'It's just like old times, isn't it?'

'Yes, and it's the only way I'll get to see *Little Women*,' Connie added. 'I tell you the way Malcolm fidgeted all the way through the *Red Shoes* you'd think he had ants in his pants.'

'I'm sure Jim would have been the same,' Millie replied. 'Although I can't remember the last time we went to the flicks.'

Connie gave her a querying look. 'I thought you went up to the West End a few weeks back.'

'We did, but it was to see some opera,' replied Millie. 'And I must say, I was the one shuffling in my seat that night.'

Although Jim had appeared engrossed by the dozen or so beefy men and women singing at each other in Italian, Millie had been much less impressed. Had she been asked what she'd like to see, she would have plumped for *On the Town*.

The line shuffled forward.

'At last,' Connie said.

As they turned the corner of the building a number 25 bus drew up at the bus stop and several people got off. Millie's heart thumped in her chest as a tall familiar figure hopped off the back. In a tailored suit that fitted his athletic figure like a glove, a long military-style trench coat and fedora tipped over one eye, he looked mighty good, and a pang of longing caught hold of Millie before she could stop it.

'Is that Alex?' Connie asked.

'I'm not sure,' replied Millie vaguely while watching his every move.

'It is,' Connie said, interrupting her disturbing thoughts. 'And who's that with him?'

Millie's eyes fixed on to a petite blonde he was helping down from the running board. 'I've no idea.'

As she stepped off, the girl wobbled on her heels and Alex caught her around the waist. She giggled and he gave the young woman in his arms what looked to be a warm smile.

Millie's heart lurched as she remembered him smiling at her.

He guided the young woman on to the pavement and then, tucking her arm in his, they walked off.

Connie stared over at him for a moment and then nudged her friend playfully. 'You're a right old fibber, Millie Smith.'

'What?'

'When I asked what Alex looked like after all this time you said "all right".' Connie grinned. 'But from where I'm standing he looks more than just all right. If you asked me I'd say "temptation on legs" would be closer to the mark. I tell you, Millie, I bet that woman in Palestine must be kicking herself at letting Alex Nolan slip through her fingers.'

Millie's gaze followed that of her friend. 'Yes, I'm sure she is,' she replied, softly.

Chapter Twelve

Putting the QN students' skills books she was taking home to mark on the shelf of the coat stand, Millie unhooked her mac and shrugged it on, thankful that for once she was finishing work on time.

The phone rang. The door on the first-floor landing opened and Joyce Pattison, the nurse from the Ben Jonson Road patch, ran down the stairs. Acknowledging Millie with a quick smile, she snatched it up.

'Good evening. Munroe House. How can I help you?' she said, picking up the pen next to the message book.

'What name and address is it?' Joyce scribbled the caller's particulars across the page. 'And what's happened?' She wrote the answer. 'I see. That doesn't sound too serious.'

Joyce rolled her eyes at Millie and mouthed first baby. Millie smiled and nodded.

'But I'll leave a note for the on-call midwife to pop round when she gets back,' continued Joyce. 'And if anything else happens in the meantime, please call back, Mr Joliffe.' She put the phone down.

An uneasy feeling prickled between Millie's shoulder-blades. 'What's wrong with Mrs Joliffe?'

'It seems she had a few abdominal cramps since lunchtime,' replied Joyce. 'Probably just some practice contractions. I'll put her on the list for Mary's evening calls.'

'Don't worry,' Millie said, 'I'll nip around there now. Could you drop these into the office for me?'

Millie handed Joyce the nurses' workbooks and then went back into the treatment room to get her midwifery bag, just in case.

Ten minutes later Millie rolled to a halt outside the Joliffes' front door. Quickly chaining her scooter to the railings, she climbed the three front steps. But before she could knock, Derrick opened the door. He looked relived to see her.

'Sister Smith. I didn't think you were on call this evening,' he said, as she stepped into the house.

'I'm not,' replied Millie. 'But I thought I'd just drop in on my way home. What's happened?'

'I've probably got you out on a fool's errand, Sister.'

'Derrick!' Dorothy screamed from upstairs.

He took the stairs two at a time, with Millie hot on his heels. They found Dorothy slumped against the bedroom doorframe, clutching her stomach. The front of her ankle-length nightdress was soaking wet and there was a pool of liquid gathering around her feet. Derrick dashed forward and caught his wife as her knees folded.

'It's all right, my love,' he said, taking her weight.

Millie took the other side and between them they manoeuvred Dorothy through the door and lowered her back on to the bed. Millie dumped her bag on the floor and stripped off her coat.

'Call an ambulance,' she said clearing the side table and opening her bag. 'Tell them you wife's waters have gone a month early and she's a diabetic.'

Derrick dashed downstairs and out of the house. Millie ripped a clean apron out of her bag, hooked it over her head and tied it in the small of her back. She pulled out the delivery pack and put it on the side table.

'Now, Mrs Joliffe, the ambulance will be here in about ten minutes but until then you have to do everything I say. I'm just going to wash my hands quickly, but I'll be right back.'

Dorothy nodded sharply and a bead of perspiration dripped from her nose.

Millie dashed along to the bathroom at the end of the hall then, after drying her hands, snatched the two hand towels from the washstand and hurried back to the bedroom.

Taking up position between Dorothy's legs, Millie started to tuck a towel under Dorothy's bottom, but as she did, the expectant mother curled forward and, grunting, strained downwards.

'Try and hold back, Mrs Joliffe. You've got a large baby there and I need to make sure he's in the right position before you start pushing,' said Millie, trying not to contemplate a big baby stuck in the birth canal.

Dorothy gripped the bedclothes and tried to do what Millie wanted, the veins standing out on her neck as she struggled to resist the overwhelming urge to bear down.

Millie waited for the wave to pass, then anchoring the baby with one hand she palpated Dorothy's bulge with the other. She quickly found the curve of the baby's back, and moving down, she stretched her hand across the top of Dorothy's pubic bone and rocked gently to gauge where the head was in the pelvic cavity. Thankfully it was just where it should be.

'He's in the right place,' Millie said, with a sigh of relief.

'Thank God,' gasped Dorothy.

Whipping out the foetal stethoscope from her bag, Millie placed the trumpet end on Dorothy's stomach and put her ear on the other, counted the baby's heartbeats against the second hand of her watch and bit her lower lip. One hundred beats per minute was much too slow.

'Is everything all right?' Dorothy asked.

'So far so good,' Millie said, trying not to sound alarmed.

The door flew open and Derrick rushed in.

'The ambulance should be here any minute. What's happening?' he yelled, dashing to his wife's side.

'The baby's not going to wait,' Millie said, fumbling to tie her mask in place.

She positioned the stethoscope again. The baby's heart rate had slowed to ninety and now, equally worryingly, was the fact that Dorothy's gaze was wavering.

'We need to get your wife's blood glucose up,' Millie said, straightening up and looking at Derrick. 'Dilute a tablespoon of sugar in half a cup of water and then put the door on the latch so the ambulance men can get in without you having to go down.'

Derrick dashed out the room.

Dorothy's eyelids were fluttering down and her gaze was obviously unfocused.

'Mrs Joliffe,' Millie shouted, shaking her awake. 'I need to deliver your baby as soon as possible, but you have to help me.'

Millie unpacked her instruments. They'd been sterilised at the clinic and should have been boiled again, but just now this was the least of Millie's problems. She shoved on her rubber gloves and put her forearms on Dorothy's knees.

'Open your legs, Mrs Joliffe,' Millie shouted.

Dorothy did so, just as another contraction swept over her.

'Now, push down into your bottom and breathe with it,' said Millie firmly.

Dorothy nodded, curled forward again and bore down, going red in the face as she tried to push her baby out. The pregnant woman's stretched vulva spread aside as a damp patch of hair pushed its way forward. Millie placed her hand on the taut perineum, trying to help it stretch. The baby's head crowned a little further before the contraction subsided and the patch of hair retracted.

Dorothy vomited on the floor and then slumped back on the bed, moaning just as Derrick rushed in carrying a cup.

'Oh, God!' he screamed, seeing the scene in the room. 'Where's that bloody ambulance?'

'Why don't you give your wife the sugar water?' Millie said much more calmly than she felt.

Derrick pulled himself together and put and arm around his wife's shoulders.

'You're doing marvellously, my love, and so drink this for me,' he said, helping her hold the cup. 'Not long now and we'll have our baby.'

The couple exchanged a fond look, which brought a lump to Millie's throat. She picked up the stethoscope and positioned it just below Dorothy's navel. As her second hand returned to the number twelve, alarm flared in Millie again. Only eighty!

Millie picked up her scissors. 'Mrs Joliffe.' Dorothy looked up, her eyes a little more alert. 'When the next one starts you must hold back until I tell you, and you must then bear down with everything you've got. Do you understand?'

Dorothy nodded feebly, and then her stomach tightened causing her to gasp.

'Remember! Wait until I say so; and then push as hard as you can,' Millie instructed.

Dorothy gritted her teeth. As the baby's head pushed through again Millie slipped her two fingers in and, with a firm stroke, snipped with the scissors to widen the aperture.

'Push NOW, Mrs Joliffe,' Millie cried, throwing the scissors on the floor and easing the almost transparent edges of the vulva back over the baby's head.

'Keep pushing,' Millie yelled as she felt the tension receding.

Dorothy dragged in a breath, strained again and at last the baby's head popped out just as his mother collapsed back on the pillows.

Millie tucked her index finger under the baby's chin and panic seized her. The umbilical cord was entangled around the baby's neck and trapped between its shoulders and Dorothy's pelvis. Desperately, Millie tried to slip it over the head to release it, but it remained stuck.

Millie wiped the sweat off her brow with her forearm. 'You need to do the same again with the next contraction, Mrs Joliffe.'

Dorothy muttered something and then sat up as the next contraction took hold.

As the pressure built, Millie grasped the baby's head firmly and eased one shoulder free and then the other. All at once the baby slithered out into Millie's awaiting hands. He was blue and had clearly been in some distress in the birth canal, as he'd released his bowels on the way out.

With trembling hands Millie clamped off the cord and laid the limp baby on the towel.

'What is it?' asked Derrick.

'A boy,' Millie replied, rubbing him vigorously. 'I'm just taking him nearer to the window so I can see better.' Clambering off the bed, she carried the inert infant to the dressing-table. She cleared the mucus from his mouth with her little finger but still he didn't move.

'Oi, oi, ambulance,' a gruff voice shouted outside the room.

'Up here,' called Derrick.

'Bring the oxygen!' yelled Millie.

Heavy feet tramped up the stairs and a bluff-faced ambulance man brought the cylinder over, turned on the valve, and laid the rubber mask next to the new-born's face. He gave Millie a sympathetic look.

'Can you get your mate and the stretcher?' she said.

The ambulance man nodded and walked to the door. 'Bring the stretcher, Ron.'

'Right you are, Bill,' his pal shouted from below.

Millie turned her attention back to the child lying motionless on the towel and tears stung her eyes. Like every midwife, she'd delivered her fair share of stillborn babies. Each one was remembered with deep sadness, but whether it was because she was carrying her own child or because she knew that the Joliffes had so desperately wanted a baby for almost twenty years, the sight of this tiny child lying so still on the towel cut through Millie to the marrow.

Her mouth pulled into a determined line. 'Come on, come on little chap,' she whispered, frantically massaging his small chest.

Suddenly, the child twitched, opened his mouth and gave a little cry.

Millie could have wept with relief.

'Is he all right?' asked Derrick from behind her.

'Yes,' Millie called over her shoulder as she rubbed the baby's legs and arms to encourage the circulation. 'He's just getting used to the world.'

Millie flicked the bottoms of his feet. The baby jumped and then cried much more vigorously, filling his lungs and changing his colour from grey to pink in a couple of breaths. Millie rested her hands either side of him and closed her eyes, sending up a silent prayer of thanks.

The sound of footsteps on the stairs sounded behind Millie, along with the hushed voices of Dorothy and Derrick congratulating each other. There was a crash as the two ambulance men manhandled the stretcher clumsily through the door and then the bed springs boinged as they moved Dorothy.

'Can I see him?' asked Dorothy.

'Of course you can,' laughed Millie, wrapping the birth-smeared infant in the towel.

She tucked him into the crook of her arm and turned around. One of the ambulance men came over and carried the oxygen cylinder as Millie, holding the mask close to the child's face, carried him over to his mother.

Dorothy, who was already strapped on to the stretcher with a red blanket over her legs, took him.

'Look, Derrick,' she said, cradling her son.

'I know,' croaked Derrick, with tears welling in his eyes. 'Hello, William,' he said lovingly to his son.

Millie looked at the baby in his mother's arms and alarm bells clanged again. Although his chest was rising, the blue tinge had returned to his lips.

She went over to the new parents. 'He's had a bit of a rough ride, Mrs Joliffe, and we need to get him and you to hospital as quickly as we can,' she said, taking the baby back.

She looked at the ambulance men.

'Right, love,' said Bill with understanding, as he and Ron took up position at either end. 'You 'eard the Sister, so off we go. All speed ahead.'

They lifted the stretcher and walked towards the door. Dorothy twisted around and looked anxiously at her son.

'We're right behind you, Mrs Joliffe,' Millie said, holding the oxygen mask close to the child's face. 'And, Mr Joliffe, can you carry the oxygen cylinder?'

Millie closed the door to the nurses' office and crossed to the desk. Switching on the table lamp she sat down, picked up the telephone receiver and dialled her own number.

She heard the tickety-tick of the number being connected and then it rang at the other end. Millie glanced down the next morning's list and waited.

As the tenth unanswered *briiiing briiiing* echoed down the line, Millie's shoulders slumped as a feeling of emptiness hovered over her.

After the business of the hotel receipt the week before, Jim had been attentive, considerate and home on the dot at seven each night. Until Tuesday, that is, when he'd walked in the front door just as the late-night shipping forecast was concluding at ten-thirty. And last night she hadn't heard him come in at all and this morning over breakfast he'd muttered something about an urgent meeting being called.

Millie reached out to replace the handset back in the cradle when there was a click and the call connected. She snatched it back.

'Leytonstone seven, seven, three, nine,' Jim's well-spoken voice said down the phone.

'Oh, Jim, thank goodness,' Millie said, clutching the handset. 'I'm so sorry, Jim, I've been caught at work.'

'Poor you,' he said in a sympathetic tone.

'Yes,' replied Millie. 'Mr Joliffe phoned just as I was—'

'Who?'

'His wife is the diabetic mother I told you about,' Millie said.

'Did you, sweetheart?'

'Don't you remember?' replied Millie.

'Can't say I do.'

'I've been caring for her for months now,' continued Millie, 'and she'd been doing so well, keeping her glucose even and blood pressure down.'

Millie briefly recounted the traumatic events in the Joliffes' house two hours before.

'Oh Jim,' she concluded, with a sob in her voice. 'I really thought their child wasn't going to breathe.' She clutched the phone tighter. 'Even with the mask by his face in the ambulance he was still blue around the lips and—'

'How terrible!' interrupted Jim.

'It was. But what made it worse was that all the way to the hospital the Joliffes kept telling me they were so grateful to me for helping them have their "miracle baby".' Tears sprang into the corners of Millie's eyes. 'And all the while they were thanking me, the poor little mite's chest was labouring up and down as he fought just to draw the next breath.'

'Oh dear.'

Millie blinked her tears away. 'It's silly, really, reacting like this,' she said, trying to swallow the growing lump in her throat. 'After all, it's not as if I haven't delivered a poorly baby or two before.' Millie placed her free hand on her growing bump. 'But all the time I was trying to get him to breathe, I couldn't stop thinking of our baby.'

'Just a minute,' Jim cut in.

He put his hand over the mouthpiece and spoke to someone in a muffled voice.

'Sorry, my love,' he said, coming back on the phone. 'I've got Ted here and we're going over some of the last-minute things for tomorrow.'

'Tomorrow. Of course,' said Millie dully.

'I thought we'd spend most of the day at the Party office with everyone, and then go on to the town hall for the count,' continued Jim. 'What do you think?'

There was a pause.

'Are you still there?' Jim asked.

'That's fine.'

'It's going to be a great day and everyone's sure I'll gain an increased majority,' he said cheerily. 'Will you be home soon, sweetheart?'

'In about fifty minutes,' Millie said tiredly.

'Good,' said Jim. 'Ted and I had fish and chips, and we got you a portion. It's in the oven waiting for you. Drive carefully and, Millie, I am very sorry you had all that bother earlier, but try and stop thinking about it now.'

The line went quiet.

Millie stared at the nurses' rota pinned on the cork board next to the door for a moment, then she replaced the receiver, switched off the desk light and left the office.

Crossing the dark and silent hall, Millie went into the treatment room, retrieved a bottle of Dettol from the store cupboard and took it over to the deep butler sink under the window. After filling the large rectangular stainless-steel container on the draining board, she took the wire wool from the dish and plunged her hands into the soapy water in the sink to clean the dirty equipment she'd left soaking while she phoned Jim.

As she swilled the dirty instruments in the carbolic water, Millie looked out of the window and into the back yard. As the girls doing the put-to-bed rounds hadn't returned yet, the back gate was still open. Her gaze drifted through the gate and on to the lamp-post on the other side of the road, where she saw Patrick O'Toole standing patiently under its beam.

Unlike the last time she'd see him in the scrap yard, Mrs O'Toole's youngest son was smartly dressed in a double-breasted suit and he had a tie knotted at his throat. He leant against the cast-iron lamp-post with his hands in his trouser pockets and his trilby perched on the back of his head.

Munroe House's back door banged shut and Annie, wearing her brick-red coat and new hat, dashed across the yard towards the gates. As he spotted her, Patrick crossed the road and she ran into his waiting arms. Annie tilted her face up to him and, curling his body around her, Patrick pressed his lips on hers.

Without warning an image of Alex Nolan standing under the same lamp-post waiting for her to let him into the nurses' home and into her bed flashed into Millie's mind. She tried to push it out but, instead, memories of passionate embraces and breathless kisses flooded in, too. Something hard and uncomfortable settled on her chest and Millie looked down at her silver nurses' buckle as she fought back tears.

As Millie walked into Leytonstone Town Hall the next evening, the noise and heat inside almost knocked her off her feet.

'It looks like the count's well under way,' said Jim as he followed her in.

'Yes,' said Millie, looking at the benches and tables set out in neat rows the length of the late-Victorian ballroom.

Sitting at them were dozens of election clerks who were pulling paper squares from a mound in front of them and stacking them into distinct piles. Dodging between the tables, with colourful rosettes pinned to their chests, were the officials from the various political parties.

Scanning the sea of faces, Millie saw Ted at the far end with a couple of the Party committee members. He spotted them and excitedly beckoned them over.

Jim took Millie's elbow and guided her through the busy election hall.

'There you are,' said Ted, slapping him heartily on the back. 'I was beginning to think you'd fallen in Eagle Pond.'

'Sorry Ted mate,' Jim replied, smiling affably. 'But I had a frantic phone call from the minister. There's an emergency Cabinet meeting tomorrow afternoon about the balance of payments with the Chancellor, and the minister needs me to attend.'

'Attending a Cabinet meeting, eh!' Ted said, winking at Jim. 'You play your cards right and it'll be you sitting around that polished table before too long.'

'And I'll have you to thank for it when I am,' Jim replied, giving his campaign manager an ingenuous smile.

Ted puffed out his chest. 'Just doing my bit for the cause, comrade.'

'How's it going?' Jim asked.

'There's been a good turnout and by the look of things you're way ahead.' Ted nudged Jim and nodded towards the stage. 'You can tell that by the sour look on the Tory candidate's face.'

Jim eyed the thin man with slicked-back hair who was wearing metal-rimmed glasses and a dinner suit, and he gave a short laugh.

'Over half the wards are completed and the tellers are going well, and so with a bit of luck we'll have a result this side of midnight,' Ted added. His piggy little eyes slid on to Millie. 'Oh, evening, Millie, my love.'

'Good evening, Ted,' Millie said. 'Is Bessie with you?'

'She's about somewhere,' he replied, not bothering to glance around.

As if she'd heard her name mentioned, Ted's wife appeared through the crowd. She spotted them and hurried over, the string of pearls bouncing on the considerable bosom of her twin-set.

'Millie, my dear.' She enveloped Millie in a motherly embrace. 'So nice to see you.'

'You too, Bessie,' Millie replied, hugging the older women. She was, too, as her presence would curb Ted's wandering hands.

Bessie turned her attention to Jim. 'And how's my favourite young man?'

Jim kissed one of Bessie's red cheeks. 'All the better for seeing you, Bessie.'

She gave a girlish giggle.

'Right, Jim,' said Ted. 'Let's leave the ladies to chat while we get down to business.'

'Where's the bar?' Jim asked as a chap walked past carrying a pint.

'In the Leyton and District Working Man's Club opposite,' Ted replied.

Millie raised her eyebrows. 'I didn't think you could drink at the official count.'

'You can't, but the returning officer is a good sort and turns a blind eye,' chuckled Ted.

'Well, then.' Jim rubbed his hands. 'What can I get you?'

'My usual.'

'What about you, Bessie?' Jim asked

Bessie started to speak. 'I'd—'

'Thanks, Jim,' Ted butted in. 'She's had two and we don't want a re-run of the Christmas do. Not with press here. I'm sure the ladies will be happy enough with a fruit juice, ain't that right, Millie?'

'You're too kind, Ted.'

The two men wandered off. Millie and Bessie found themselves seats at the side of the hall out of the way. After a while a young Party worker with lank hair and a scruffy corduroy jacket brought their drinks over. Millie and Bessie thanked him and took their orange juices.

Bessie held out her glass. 'Can you 'old this for me, ducks?'

Millie took it. Bessie plonked her handbag on her knee, opened it and took out a small hip flask.

'Want a splash?' she said, offering it to Millie.

Millie shook her head. 'No, thank you.'

Bessie took her glass back and, shielding it from view behind her handbag, poured gin into her drink.

She raised her glass to Millie and grinned. 'What the eye don't see, the heart don't grieve over.' She slipped the flask back in her bag. 'So, when's the baby due?'

'Mid-May or thereabouts,' replied Millie, smoothing her fingers over her growing bump.

'And Ted tells me you're still working.'

'Just for another month,' Millie replied.

'I don't know,' Bessie sighed, 'you modern girls. In my day you were told to stay at home with your feet up for nine months, not drive about on a scooter.'

There was a flurry of activity and everyone in the hall suddenly looked at the stage as the returning officer, a nervous-looking man in a saggy grey suit, climbed on to the stage.

Jim was standing with his hands in the pockets of his made-to-measure charcoal three-piece suit. A handful of eager young Party workers, all keen to do their bit for the brave new world, clustered around him. They were mostly university types, but in amongst them were two young women. One was had light-brown hair and wore a tweed suit, while the other, a slim blonde, was dressed in slacks and a raspberry-coloured beret.

As the returning officer motioned for the candidates to join him, Jim mounted the stage. He looked across at Millie and smiled. She smiled back.

The four candidates lined up with their managers behind. The returning officer stepped forward to the middle of the stage, raised his hands for quiet then pulled a set of half-rimmed spectacles from his top pocket and put them on.

'I'm Oliver Pugh and, as the returning officer for the Leytonstone and Wanstead constituency, I will now read out the number of votes cast for each candidate,' he said, in a deep voice that was rather at odds with his delicate appearance. 'Mr William Henry Coverdale, Liberal, 9,290.'

There was a smattering of applause.

'Mr Ambrose Rupert Fairchild, Conservative, 11,137.'

Again the audience clapped politely.

'Mr Ronald Edgar Lamb, Communist, 5,241.'

Bessie gripped Millie's hand. 'Isn't it exciting?'

Millie gave a wan smile.

'And finally, Mr James Percival Woodville Smith, Labour, 17,689,' announced Mr Pugh.

The hall exploded as the local Party workers congratulated each other and yelled Jim's name.

'I therefore declare that Mr Smith is the new Member of Parliament for the Leytonstone and Wanstead constituency. I now call upon him to say a few words.'

Jim stepped forward to a burst of wolf-whistles and shouts from the floor. He gazed around, enjoying the acclaim, and then his eyes rested on Millie.

'Before I say anything, I would like my wife to join me.' Jim held his hand out towards Millie. 'Come on, darling.'

Millie tried not to look reluctant as she stood up and made her way to the stage.

Jim met her at the steps and offered her his hand. 'Careful, sweetheart.'

Millie took it. 'Thank you.'

She climbed on to the platform and Jim guided her to the front.

'Firstly, I'd like to thank Ted Kirby, the chairman of the local Party, and my mentor. He's been beside me every step of the way and I wouldn't be here now if not for him.'

People clapped and Ted preened himself like a peacock on a lawn.

'Secondly, I'd like to thank all the many volunteers who have worked tirelessly by putting leaflets into letter-boxes and canvassing people in the street. I'd also like to thank the people of Leytonstone and Wanstead for their trust in voting for me, and I promise to work diligently on their behalf in Parliament.'

There was another enthusiastic round of applause, which Jim acknowledged with a benevolent smile. 'But lastly,' he slipped his arm around Millie's waist and drew her to him. 'I'd like to thank my wife, Millie, who, despite having other things to occupy her at the moment, has been my greatest support through this campaign. Thank you, darling,' he said, smiling adoringly at her.

There was an audible 'ah' from the audience.

Millie forced a smile.

Jim turned back to the people in the hall and waved. A roar went up and Millie stepped back as others crowded on to the stage and around Jim to congratulate him.

Bessie clambered, huffing and puffing, up on to the stage.

'Congratulations, Millie dear,' she said, planting a gin-smelling kiss on each cheek. An indulgent expression settled on her matronly features. 'I hope you know you are a very lucky girl.'

A flicker of red behind Bessie caught Millie's eyes. She looked over the older woman's shoulder.

'Yes, aren't I,' Millie replied, watching her husband, with that all too familiar happy-go-lucky smile on his face, chatting to the blonde in the beret.

Chapter Thirteen

As she reached the second floor of the London Hospital, the mix of antiseptic and floor polish filled Millie's nose, taking her right back to her training. She smiled as she remembered walking down these Victorian corridors. First, as a very nervous student nurse in 1937 and, later, as a staff nurse on Charrington Ward, evacuating casualties to Brentwood during the Blitz. She'd briefly left the old hospital to do her midders at Woolmer Park in Hertfordshire, two weeks after the Japanese attacked Pearl Harbour, and then she had returned to deliver babies as the Allies invaded Italy, leaving, finally, to train as a Queen's Nurse as Monte Cassino fell in May 1944.

Although the nurses bustling past her wore the same distinct lilac pin-striped uniform that Millie had, and no doubt the matrons were still just as fierce, in the past year the London seemed to have moved into the modern age, thought Millie as she spied new equipment to make procedures such as blood transfusions safer, and up-to-date medicines, such as penicillin, that could combat previously fatal diseases.

Putting her memories aside, Millie turned and headed for Colette Ward at the far end of the passageway. The squeak as she pushed open the door brought the ward Sister, a round-faced woman with wiry ginger hair, out from the treatment room. She drew a breath and was about to recount the visiting times when she spotted Millie's navy uniform.

'Good afternoon, Sister Colette,' Millie said, addressing her in the traditional manner.

The Sister glanced down at Millie's stomach pushing out the front of her nurse's dress. 'Aren't you about five months too early for us?'

'Four actually.' Millie laughed. 'But I wonder if I could see Mrs Joliffe for a few minutes.'

The Sister glanced at the ward clock on the wall. 'I'm expecting Doctor Wiltshire in half an hour at twelve, but you can pop in for ten minutes. Is she one of your patients?'

Millie nodded. 'I've been looking after her since before Christmas and I was the midwife who delivered the baby.'

'Were you?' The Sister couldn't help but look impressed. 'I read your notes and it seems it was touch and go.'

'It was. I could have cried myself when he started breathing,' replied Millie. 'I phoned the ward yesterday and they said Baby Joliffe was in an incubator. Is he still there?'

'No, he was transferred back to the nursery yesterday evening,' said the Sister. 'The paediatric team thought he might be able to manage without the extra oxygen.'

'And can he?' said Millie.

'Just about. It's difficult to say with diabetic babies because of their larger size, as you well know, but the doctors think he's nearer to two months early, than according to Mum's dates. In any case his lungs aren't fully functional. Added to which, part of the afterbirth was necrotic, and so it looked as if the poor thing had been on half rations for some time.' The Sister's face clouded. 'I'd say you were very lucky to have got the little chap out alive.'

'Do the parents know the long-term outcome isn't good?'

The Sister shook her head. 'Doctor thought it kinder to let the parents enjoy him while they can.' She sighed. 'Still, I'm sure we've both seen worse who have survived, and so let's not give up hope,' she said in a tone that implied otherwise. 'Mrs Joliffe's on the right, just past the nurses' station.'

Millie thanked her and then walked down the ward between the rows of beds.

As usual, the mothers in the beds nearest the nurses' station were the ones who had delivered most recently. They were all sitting and holding bundles of blue or pink in their arms. When Millie had been a staff midwife on a maternity ward, to ensure the women rested completely during their enforced three-days' post-delivery bed rest, infants were cared for in the nursery and only brought to their mothers for feeding. As this meant that you often had a ward full of crying women, many of the more sensible Sisters disregarded the rule.

Clearly the Sister in charge of Colette Ward was one such.

Millie cast her eyes down the ward and spotted Dorothy surrounded by pillows staring down at the child in her arms. Millie put on a bright smile and walked towards her.

Dorothy looked up. There were dark circles under her eyes and the hair flowing unpinned around her face showed more than a few grey streaks, but the joy in her eyes lit up her face like a young girl's.

She waved at Millie.

'Sister Smith,' she laughed. 'How lovely of you to come.'

'I thought I'd drop by and see how you are before dinner,' said Millie, taking the chair next to the bed and putting her nurse's bag under it.

'Well, we're both doing just fine. Aren't we?' Dorothy kissed her son gently on the forehead and then turned him in her arms. 'Say hello to Sister Smith, William.'

Millie smiled at the infant.

Although he was oversized for a premature baby and was sleeping peacefully enough in his mother's arms, William's narrow chest rose and fell at an alarming rate and he grunted at the end of each breath. His nostrils flared wide, too, as his lungs tried to drag in more air.

'How much did he weigh?' Millie asked.

'Ten two,' Dorothy replied. 'The doctor said it was the sugar in my blood that caused him to weigh so much and that you did a very good job getting him out.'

'I think you were the one who did well,' Millie replied. She tickled William's palm. His fingers curled around hers, but they didn't grip. She grazed her finger along his cheek to see if he would turn towards it. He didn't.

'How's he feeding?' she asked.

Dorothy smiled down at her child. 'I'm not sure either of us have quite got the hang of it, but I'm determined to feed him myself.'

'Good. It will give him the best start,' Millie replied. 'What about you?'

'I'm very sore underneath but,' Dorothy gazed adoringly down at the baby in her arms, 'this precious little boy is worth it.'

'So I'm told.'

'You'll know first-hand soon, Sister,' Dorothy laughed, glancing at Millie's middle. She moved the blanket down from William's puffy face. 'Do you think he looks like Derrick?'

'Well, he has his hairline,' replied Millie.

'That he does.' Dorothy kissed her son's downy head. She looked up at Millie. 'I know it might seem odd, but I can already see him and Derrick going off hand in hand to watch cricket.' She pressed her lips to the baby's forehead again and looked up at Millie. 'How can I ever repay you, Sister, for our beautiful son?'

Millie's throat constricted, but she forced a happy smile. 'By you and Mr Joliffe enjoying every precious minute with him.'

After allowing two porters to push a bed with a man in a full-frame leg traction to go past, Millie made her way down the winding stone stairs to the hospital's main corridor. The Friends of the London Hospital shop was now packed with visitors buying magazines and cigarettes for their nearest and dearest languishing in the wards above.

Mentally running through her afternoon visits, Millie hurried towards the main Whitechapel Road entrance, but as she came level with the double doors leading in to the Accident and Emergency department, she spotted Susan Turner slumped on the front bench in the waiting room.

Rummaging in her handbag Millie retrieved her purse and headed for the Friends' tuck shop. Having handed over her last couple of sweet coupons for two Mars bars, she pushed open the doors to Accident and Emergency and entered.

Although there were a few doctors with stethoscopes slung around their necks and charts in their hands striding back and forth, most of the dozen or so cubicles had their curtains pulled back. She could also see a handful of nurses at the desk writing up their notes, while a couple of others tended to patients but, overall, compared to the mayhem and carnage after chucking-out-time, Casualty was eerily quiet.

'Susan,' Millie said, letting the heavy glass door swing closed behind her.

The young girl looked up. 'Hello, Sister Smith,' she said politely.

Millie slid her case under the chair and sat on the seat next to her. 'Have you had an accident?'

Susan shook her head. 'It's Mum. She's broke her arm. That is,' hurt flared across her young face, '*he* broke it. The pig.'

'Oh my goodness,' said Millie. 'What happened?'

'He came home stinking drunk this morning after visiting one of the early houses near Spitalfields market and started laying into her about summink or another,' Susan replied in a flat tone. 'Anything can set him off when he's had a few. It must have been bad this time because Mr Cohen from the corner shop came over and tried to stop him.' Susan glanced towards a cubicle with a faded curtain. 'He's being stitched up in there. It was when he staggered out of the house bleeding that Mrs Cotton opposite called the police. They arrived in the hurry-up wagon and took him away. Then the ambulance turned up to collect Mum.'

'Where's Sidney now?'

'In number three with the Davisons,' Susan replied. 'They said we could stay with them until the hospital lets Mum out.'

'Is your mum in one of the cubicles?' asked Millie.

'No. They've taken her to surgery to pin the bone back together,' said Susan. 'They said I should go home and come back tomorrow, but I said I wanted to stay until I know she's all right, and so the nurse in charge said I could wait here.'

'But that could be quite a while,' said Millie.

Susan gave Millie a brave look. 'Don't worry, Sister, I'll be all right. The copper who was in charge said he'll come back and take me home once Mum is out of the operating theatre.'

Millie opened her notebook, scribbled down the telephone number of Munroe House and gave the torn-out page with it on to Susan.

'If the policeman doesn't come to fetch you, get the A&E sister to ring the clinic,' she said. 'I'm there until half-past and when I go I'll leave a note for the nurse on call.'

'Here he is.' Susan looked towards the entrance.

Millie turned just in time to see Alex walk into the department.

He halted momentarily as he saw her but then he marched over and, acknowledging Millie with a quick smile, sat on the other side of Susan.

Alex took off his flat cap and raked his fingers through his hair. 'I see you've found someone to keep you company.'

'Yes,' replied Susan, swinging her legs back and forth under the chair.

'I've been visiting Susan's mum off and on for a couple of years,' Millie explained.

Alex nodded and then his attention returned to the child between them. 'So is there any news?'

Susan shook her head as tears welled in her eyes.

Millie slipped her arm around the girl's frail shoulder. 'Don't worry, dear, I'm sure your mum will soon be as right as rain.'

'There you go,' Alex said giving the young girl beside him a warm smile. 'And Sister Smith knows all about these sorts of things.'

Susan's lower lip quivered. 'But what about next time?' She covered her face with her hands and started to cry. Alex looked helplessly at Millie.

Gently, Millie squeezed the child again. 'There, there, sweet. Look you've got Inspector Nolan, the top policeman in Arbour Square, on the case and on your side.'

Susan lifted her head and Alex shifted around so he was looking straight at her. 'I know the magistrates don't usually interfere between husband and wife, but I promise you, Susan, I'll do everything in my power to make sure there won't be a next time.'

Susan gave them both a heart-wrenching smile as she wiped her eyes.

A nurse in the familiar lavender uniform came out from behind the desk and walked towards them.

'Theatre has just phoned to say Mrs Turner is in recovery and is doing well,' she said, brightly.

'Can I see her?' asked Susan.

The nurse shook her head. 'She's not awake yet. But if you can get a neighbour to bring you in during visiting times tomorrow you can see her then. If you wait a few moments I have her clothes and you can take them home so that someone can wash them.' The nurse looked at Alex. 'And Dr Oliver has just been called away but he is keen to talk to you, Inspector.'

'Thank you,' said Alex. 'I'll come back later when I've taken Miss Turner home.'

'Well,' said Millie gathering her nurse's bag from under the bench. 'Now I know your mum's on the mend I'd better be off myself.'

She stood up. As she did so, Millie's nurse's jacket swung open. Alex's gaze latched on to her growing stomach, and then he looked up to her face.

'Oh, Sister Smith, you're in the family way,' Susan said what Alex was obviously thinking. 'When's the baby due?'

Millie dragged her eyes from Alex and smiled at the youngster. 'Just over four months.'

'Congratulations, Millie,' Alex said, in a low voice.

'Thank you,' Millie replied, feeling oddly uncomfortable. She pulled the two Mars bars from her pocket and handed them to Susan. 'And these are for you and Sidney, and don't forget to tell your mum that I'll pop around to see her once she's home.'

Susan's small fingers closed around the chocolate bars, and she smiled. 'Thank you, Sister.'

Millie gripped the handles of her bag firmly and looked at Alex. 'Nice to see you, Alex.'

'You too, Millie.' He gave her that slightly crooked, utterly charming smile of his. 'And mind you take good care of yourself and the little one.'

After hooking her coat on the hall stand, Millie went into Miss Gardener's parlour. The old gas lamps were trimmed low, cutting shadows across the darkened room, and a faint hiss from the jets could just be heard. Miss Gardener lay on the chaise longue with her eyes closed and her chest moving slowly up and down.

Miss Moncrieff was sitting on the far side of the couch, hunched up in an oversized cardigan and gently holding her friend's hand. She was staring fixedly at the dying woman. Dr Masterson was standing nearby.

He looked up as Millie walked in.

'Ah, Sister Smith,' he said. 'Punctual as always.'

'Good evening, Doctor.'

If asked, Millie would have put Dr Masterson in his late fifties or early sixties, but with only a few wisps of grey hair creeping over his ears and a few fine wrinkles criss-crossing his face, it was difficult to tell. He wore his usual tweed jacket with the leather-patched elbows and baggy moleskin trousers, and he had a thin cigar clasped between his lips.

He stubbed out the half-smoked cigar in the huge crystal ashtray sitting on the dresser. 'Would you excuse me for a moment, Miss Moncrieff?'

She nodded, not taking her gaze from Miss Gardener's ashen face.

The doctor hobbled over to Millie, who was standing beside the table with his Gladstone bag on it. 'I've given her a decent dose of morphine,' he said in a low voice. 'So I'd like you to stay until it's done its job. I don't expect it will be more than an hour or so, but I'd like you here just in case.'

Millie looked puzzled. 'In case of what?'

His gaze flickered on to Miss Moncrieff's grief-stricken face. '*She* does something reckless, like make a funeral pyre in the back garden or smash in all the windows.'

Millie looked surprised. 'I really don't think Miss Moncrieff would do anything like that, Doctor.'

'Mr Kite, Miss Gardener's nephew, seems to think Miss Moncrieff is capable of anything, and I'm inclined to agree with him,' Dr Masterson replied. 'Artistic temperament, you see.' He snapped his case shut. 'I'd be obliged, Sister, if you would ring the surgery in the morning and tell me what time she departed this world so I can write out the death certificate.'

He went over and muttered something to Miss Moncrieff and then he left. Millie walked around to the other side of the couch and discreetly slipped her hand under the cover.

Thankfully Miss Gardener wasn't wet, so Millie wouldn't have to cause her further pain by moving her. She withdrew her hand and, with a practised eye, looked the dying woman over. Her face was almost as white as the pillowslip under her head and the fine purple veins on her temples and eyelids were clearly visible through her transparent skin. Dr Masterson was right; it wouldn't be too long.

Millie straightened the sheet and walked back around to Miss Moncrieff's side of the couch.

'Would you like me to make you a cup of tea?' Millie asked.

Miss Moncrieff stood up abruptly and left the room.

Millie perched on the edge of the chair, wondering if she should go after her. After a couple of moments the door opened and Millie's eyes opened wide with surprise as the artist swept back into the room.

She'd changed out of the kneed trousers and baggy knitwear into a dramatic red and black dress with a drop waist, handkerchief-pointed hem and twinkling jet beads sewn on it. Slung around her neck and pinned in a loop on one side with a diamond brooch were half-a-dozen pearl necklaces. But by far the most extraordinary item she wore was the tight band around her head just above her eyebrows, out of which curled two ostrich feathers. She held an armful of garments.

Miss Moncrieff strode to the chaise longue and draped the clothes and frippery she was carrying in her arms on the back of the chair she'd been sitting in. She grabbed the top of the sheet and stripped it and the blankets off Miss Gardener, and threw them behind her.

'What are you doing?' Millie exlaimed, lunging out and catching the covers just before they touched the ground.

Miss Moncrieff's piercing eyes looked at Millie in amazement. 'I'm not letting my beautiful Dodo die in rags.' She hooked her arm behind her friend's neck and lifted her up.

Miss Gardener flopped forward, but mercifully she didn't make a sound.

'Let me help you, please,' Millie said, as Miss Moncrieff grasped the back of the winceyette nightdress and tried to pull it off.

Millie scooped Miss Gardener into her arms and gently removed the nightdress. She grabbed a towel nearby and covered the dying woman's skeletal frame.

Miss Moncrieff handed across a gossamer silk under-slip from the top of the pile. Millie took the undergarment, and gently slipped it over Miss Gardener's head, feeling her soft white hair beneath her fingers. Millie rolled the under-slip down and then removed the towel from beneath Miss Gardener.

Miss Moncrieff smoothed out a crease in the silk, and then lifted up a diaphanous lilac gown and passed it over. Millie eased it over Miss Gardener's head and then worked her arms through carefully. 'I can do up a few of the buttons but I don't want to cause her unnecessary pain.'

Miss Moncrieff nodded.

Millie reached under Miss Gardener and fastened the back of the gown as far as she could. When she'd finished, Miss Moncrieff rolled a pair of old-fashioned silk stockings up Miss Gardener's wasted legs and then combed her hair into a semblance of her bobbed style. She covered it with a little cap with a fringe of crystal beads and dripped six strings of beads around her neck, arranging them carefully between Miss Gardener's breasts. She lifted from the chair an ornate shawl decorated with exquisitely embroidered Chinese lotus flowers and deep tassels around the edge. She stood for a moment gazing down at Miss Gardener and then laid it in gentle folds over her friend's lower half. Millie rescued a dried long-stemmed rose that had fallen from the chair and rested it on the pillow beside Miss Gardener.

'She looks beautiful,' she said softly.

A sad smile lifted the corners of Miss Moncrieff's lips. 'Lilac was always Dodo's colour.' She sat down and smoothed her paint-stained hand over Miss Gardener's.

Millie busied herself tidying the equipment left by Dr Masterson away and then sat on the footstool at the end of the chaise longue. Miss Gardener's slow, laborious breaths punctuated the silence and soon Millie's eyes started to feel heavy. She yawned.

'We met in Paris in 1920,' Miss Moncrieff said, so suddenly than Millie jumped. 'And it was as decadent and licentious as they said it was – and more. There was art and music in cafés that never closed and I grasped at that wicked city with both hands.' She gave a hard laugh. 'Between the drink and opium I was barely in my right mind, imagining wild images by night and then buying paint and oils instead of food to capture them during the day. I was on the edge of death and didn't know it until an angel fixed her lovely blue eyes on me, and saved me.'

'Miss Gardener.'

'My love.' Miss Moncrieff raised her friend's hand to her lips and kissed it slowly. 'She'd lost her fiancé in the war and had come to visit his grave. Her aunt, that brute Freddie's grandmother, had just been widowed and decided to tack on a trip to Paris with Dodo. From the moment we met we were inseparable.

I moved in as her permanent houseguest. Although people thought us an odd combination, her, a classic English rose and me as wild as a gypsy, no one would have questioned our friendship if I hadn't displayed my portrait of her in the 1923 Royal Academy Summer Exhibition.'

'Is that the one you painted of her …' Millie couldn't bring herself to finish the sentence

Miss Moncrieff raised an arched eyebrow and smiled. 'Of course. If I'd been wise, I'd have dressed her in a demure flowery print and sat her on a garden bench instead of paddling naked in a meadow stream like a water spirit. But I was sick of the pretence.' Amusement lit the older woman's eyes. 'Are you shocked, Sister Sullivan?'

'A little. And I can't say I blame her family for being angry,' said Millie, trying to imagine aunt Ruby's reaction to such a thing.

Miss Moncrieff laughed drily. 'Never fear, Sister, they had their revenge. They engaged a barrister with the aim of having dear Dodo incarcerated in an institution for mental instability. But in the end, to keep it out of the papers, they just cut off her money. We escaped to this little house her great-grandfather left her. I set up my studio to pay the bills and sometimes I couldn't, and so we starved or froze, or both.' She held Miss Gardener's lifeless hand against her cheek and gazed at her. 'But we had each other and neither of us ever had a moment of regret.'

A lump formed in Millie's throat.

Miss Gardener gasped and then gave the faintest of sighs as her breathing ceased. Millie took her hand and caught the last beat of her heart. She looked across at Miss Moncrieff.

'I'm sorry but she's gone,' Millie said after a moment, resting the dead woman's hand gently at her side.

For a moment Miss Moncrieff didn't move. Then she stood up and, bending over, she brushed her lips against her friend's.

'Goodbye, my heart, my reason and my life,' she said, with tears just visible on her lower lids. She blinked them away, stood up and marched towards the door.

'Don't you want to sit with her for a moment to say goodbye?' Millie asked, wondering if Dr Masterson was perhaps right.

Miss Moncrieff shook her head sharply. 'I have to paint.' She tore open the door and, with the points of her red gown swirling around her, she crashed up the stairs to her studio.

'How much longer, Jim?' asked Millie, as the late afternoon sunlight dappled the insides of her eyelids and the car turned left.

'Another few moments, I promise,' Jim replied. 'And then you can look.'

'I hope so,' Millie replied.

Although it had been no more than ten minutes since Jim had told her to close her eyes, as they drove past their turning a combination of disorientation and a baby pushing upwards meant she was beginning to feel a little sick. But she shouldn't complain.

When she'd got back from her afternoon rounds and found a message saying Jim would be meeting her from work, Millie was relieved. Now just shy of six months, she didn't feel particularly safe on the Gadabout, but she found the forty-minute journey on the tube followed by a ten-minute walk at the other end had started to take its toll in the past few weeks. But no matter: it was Holy Week in two weeks, which meant she had only a week and a day until she finished on Ash Wednesday.

'Just one more corner and you can look,' Jim said, as the car turned right.

It slowed and then stopped. Jim put the brake on and turned off the engine. His arm slid around the back of Millie's seat and he kissed her cheek.

'We're here.'

Millie opened her eyes.

They were parked with a row of tall four-storey houses on the right and the green grassy expanse of Wanstead Flats on the other.

'Is that Forest School?' she asked, seeing a solid brick building through the budding trees.

'The very same,' said Jim, grinning at her in the same way he had since they'd left Munroe House.

He got out and came around to Millie's side to open the door.

'If madam would care to step out,' he said, offering her his hand.

Millie took it and, gripping it firmly, pulled herself out of the car. 'I thought we were going to dinner, not a walk in Epping Forest.'

'We are,' replied Jim. 'But I want to show you something first.'

He tucked her hand in the crook of his arm and then escorted her to the house at the far end. It had a small paved area at the front and was by far the grandest dwelling in the row. Judging by the tall sash windows and weathered brickwork, it had probably stood on that spot since the time the horse-drawn stagecoach to Cambridge passed along the road. There were a couple of similar buildings along Cable Street still, but they had at least half-a-dozen families living in them, which clearly wasn't the case for this house.

Jim opened the wrought-iron gate. 'After you.'

Millie walked through and up to the black-lacquered front door with a brass knocker. Jim joined her and pulled out a set of keys from his pocket.

He unlocked the door and pushed it wide. 'Welcome to your new home, my sweetheart.'

Millie could only stare at her husband.

'I hope you like it,' Jim said, smiling down at her.

Taking her hand, he led her through the door and into the carpeted hallway.

'This,' he guided her through the open door to their left, 'is the lounge. I had it decorated in the style of the house,' he said, running his hand down the Regency-striped wallpaper. 'And the sideboard and sofas are from Tollshunt,' he said, indicating the two button-backed Chesterfields on either side of the marble fireplace. 'But if you don't like them you can buy others and I'll send these back.'

Jim led her back into the hall and into the next room, which had an oval dining-table in the middle with six chairs tucked in around it, and then through to the back of the house.

'And this is the kitchen,' he said, letting go of her hand and standing back.

As she stepped in, Millie's eyes opened wide with astonishment. 'Oh, my goodness!'

She rushed past him, and then stopped abruptly.

Unlike the upright dresser in her current kitchen, this one had cabinets sitting flush against two walls, with a sink set in more cupboards under the window. Millie ran her hand along the smooth laminated surface and then opened a cupboard door. 'It's just like the American kitchen they featured in *Ideal Home* last week.'

Jim strolled to the cooker. 'The salesman in the gas company showroom assured me this Parkinson oven is the latest model.'

Millie followed him across the room. 'It's got a drop-down door,' she said, pulling it open. 'And is that a refrigerator?'

Jim nodded. 'It means you won't have to collect your meat from the butcher's each day. I've had a new hot water and heating boiler—'

'Heating!' squeaked Millie.

'There's a radiator in every room.' Jim's grin was broad. 'Shall we look upstairs?'

Somehow Millie tore her eyes from the cupboards and appliances, and she followed Jim back into the hall and then up the stairs to the first floor. He showed her into three large bedrooms, all of which were unfurnished, and then into a bathroom with a new streamlined bath and basin, as well as a separate toilet. Then he took her into a smaller room at the back overlooking the garden.

'I thought this could be the baby's room and of course, you can decide on any decoration and furniture you like,' he said, standing back so she could walk into the room. 'What do you think?'

Millie stood open-mouthed and looked around the airy room for a moment and then walked to the window and stared out at the long lawn. 'It's perfect, Jim. In fact, the whole house is just perfect.'

He crossed the room and took her hand.

'I'm glad you like it, Millie,' he said, slipping his arm around her waist. 'It's no more than you deserve for all you've had to put up with from me in the past few months.'

The feeling of betrayal tugged at Millie's heart again and she looked away.

Jim tucked his finger gently under her chin and raised her head. 'And I hope this house goes some way in making it up to you, my darling.'

A tear threatened to roll down Millie's cheek.

'Ideal for raising our family,' Jim said as he looked deep into her eyes.

Millie smiled at him and nodded.

He gathered her closer. 'So, can we put the past behind us and have a new start?'

The pain and grief of the past few months tried to surge up, but Millie cut it short. Jim had made a mistake and hurt her, that was true, but he was her husband and she did care for him.

'Yes,' she replied, looking squarely at him. 'I'd like that very much.'

His blue eyes held her brown ones for a moment longer and then he lowered his lips on to hers. And for the first time since he came back from Oxford, Millie's mouth opened under his.

Chapter Fourteen

Doctor Gingold took Millie's hand and looked fondly at her over half-rimmed glasses. 'I can't say I won't miss you, Millie, but I wish you all the best.'

'Thank you, Doctor,' replied Millie. 'It's been a pleasure working with you, too.'

Doctor Gingold laughed and opened the top drawer of her desk. 'Just a little something,' she said, handing Millie a white paper bag.

Millie pulled out a tiny pair of white bootees and a bonnet, both with lemon ribbon fastenings. 'Thank you, Doctor. They are beautiful.'

'You can put them with all the other little somethings you've been given,' the doctor said.

Millie smiled. 'People have been very kind.'

'Around here they always are, and they're very fond of you, Millie,' said the doctor.

Millie couldn't argue with that. She'd been given so much in the past week as she went around saying her goodbyes that she'd returned home each day with bags full of knitted matinée coats, leggings and mittens. One of the chemists had given her a tub of zinc and castor oil, while Letterman, her regular pharmacist, had presented her with half-a-dozen terry-towelling nappies and the same number of rubber cover-overs. With just tomorrow to work doing home visits, Millie would spend her remaining four days at Munroe House in the office sorting out the handover of rotas and setting out the programme for the next batch of QN trainees who would be arriving after Easter.

Doctor Gingold squeezed her hand. 'And we've been through some times and seen some sights together, haven't we?'

Millie smiled. 'You can say that again. Remember the triplets born on the eastbound platform in Stepney station with bombs shaking the walls?'

Releasing Millie's hand, Doctor Gingold leant back and chuckled. 'And we only had two towels and had to wrap the boy in his mother's underslip. And then there was the old couple in Hanbury Street buried under the rubble.'

'I still don't know how we managed to squeeze through to them in the dark,' Millie said.

Doctor Gingold patted her paunch. 'Well, I couldn't do it now.'

'Neither could I,' Millie laughed, running her hands over her swollen stomach.

'You'll snap back and you won't be long in labour either,' Doctor Gingold said. 'So you be sure and get your husband to take you to hospital at the first twinge or he might have to do the job himself.'

Millie looked amazed.

The doctor gave her a shrewd look. 'After thirty years of delivering babies, I can tell.'

'Well, to use one of your favourite phrases, Doctor, from your lips to God's ears.' Millie stood up. 'I ought to be getting back to Munroe House. I've got a pile of paperwork to do before Friday.'

'Nice to see you, Millie,' said Doctor Gingold, picking up her pen. 'And may Jehovah bless you and your little one.'

Leaving the doctor to write up her notes, Millie left the surgery and headed along Cable Street towards Cannon Street Road. As she turned the corner, she noticed a great deal of activity outside Miss Gardener's old house.

As she got closer, Freddie Kite walked out of the front door and threw an armful of rubbish into the open-backed lorry parked in the road.

Millie walked over and looked up at the old Georgian building stripped bare of the genteel lace curtains and with its windows gaping wide, like an elderly lady caught at her ablutions.

'Wotcha, Sister,' shouted Freddie from the doorstep as another man pushed past him and heaved an old chair into the back of the lorry.

'Hello, Mr Kite,' Millie said, as he joined her on the pavement. 'I see you're having a clear-out.'

His artful face creased in a broad smile. 'Freddie, please,' he said, as another piece of Victorian furniture crashed on to the street. 'Now I've finally got that old cow Harry out, I am. And would you Adam and Eve it? That poxy woman had the blind cheek to make me go to court to evict her. And then when we got to court she told the beak that because she and aunt Dot had lived together for so long that she was the old girl's "real" family. The judge, a silly old fart if ever there was one, started to um and ah, but I told him straight, is this what we fought a war for? To have a respectable family member diddled out of their rights by a dirty pervert in men's clothing?' Freddie grimaced. 'That shut the old buffer up, I can tell you, and he granted the eviction order without another murmur. But if Harry had buggered off like she should have, I could have had a nice little income out of this place long before now.'

'Where did Miss Moncrieff go?' Millie asked.

'I don't know and I don't care,' he replied. 'After all the grief she gave me, I hope she's took a long walk off a short pier.'

'I found another load of these things, Freddie,' a scruffily dressed man with bad teeth called as he carried an armful of papers out of the house.

'Chuck them on with the rest of the rubbish,' Freddie replied.

The worker swung around and threw them on top of the old Indian rug and the piles of leather-bound books and broken china in the back of the lorry. As he did, a couple of sheets escaped and floated on to the ground close to Millie's feet.

She looked down at a line drawing of what looked like a Parisian street scene. Millie picked it up.

'But these are Miss Moncrieff's sketches,' she said, glancing at the others in her hand. 'Look, there's a picture of the Embankment and another of Tower Bridge.'

'So what?' Freddie asked. 'I said I'd get rid of the lot. She should've taken them with her.'

'Where are her paintings?' Millie asked, thinking of the dozens of canvases she'd seen stacked up in the old dining-room next to the kitchen.

'Gone,' he grinned. 'Which I'm right sad about, as I was looking forward to setting them ablaze in the back yard.' He brushed his hands together in a workmanlike way. 'Still, I can't stand here chatting all day.' Freddie rolled his sleeves up his thickly hairy forearms. 'Nice to see you again, Sister, and,' he eyed her middle, 'good luck with the sprog.'

Freddie retrieved the rolled-up cigarette from behind his ear and turned back towards the house.

Millie stared down at the drawing for a moment. 'Mr Kite?'

He looked around.

'Do you mind if I have these?' She held up the sketches.

'Take what you like, ducks.' He struck a match on the wall, lit his roll-up and ambled back into the house.

Standing on tiptoe, Millie reached into the tailgate of the lorry and salvaged a handful of drawings, pastel sketches and a couple of unframed oils from amongst Miss Gardener's discarded belongings, including a sketch Miss Moncrieff had made of Millie with Miss Gardener. Rolling them in on themselves, she tucked them under her arm and continued her journey back to the clinic.

Hopping off the five-thirty bus from the station, Millie tucked Miss Moncrieff's roll of pictures more securely under her arm and crossed Snaresbrook Road. A little flutter of happiness started in her chest as she spotted Jim's car sitting outside the house.

Enjoying the rustle of the trees overhead and the sweet smell of newly mowed grass on the other side of the road, she picked up her pace and was soon turning the key in the lock of the front door.

'I'm home,' she called as she stepped inside.

'In here, sweetheart,' Jim said from his study.

Leaving the pictures on the hall table, she hung up her hat and coat and went into the room on the left.

Jim was sitting at his desk writing. He looked up as she walked in. 'Just let me finish this.'

Millie strolled over and tilting her head, looked down at the page of writing. 'I suppose it's some boring old report.'

'It is,' he said, scratching his signature at the bottom. 'But now it's done.' He shoved it away and smiled warmly up at her. 'Well, this is a pleasant surprise. You're early.'

'Yes,' replied Millie. 'Not only did I get away on time, but I caught every connection without waiting more than a minute.'

'And how are you, darling?' he asked, drawing her to him.

'A bit tired,' Millie replied.

'And what about James?' he asked, resting his hand lightly on her stomach.

'Playing football all day again,' Millie replied. 'Still, only another couple of days.'

'And then you'll be a lady of leisure and will be able to put your feet up all day long,' Jim said.

'What, with a house this size to clean?' Millie replied.

Jim looked thoughtful. 'Oddly, I was considering that earlier and wondered if as well as the maternity nurse for when you come home from hospital, we ought to get a char, too.'

'Jim, I haven't said yes to a maternity nurse yet, and I'm certain I don't want someone all the time,' Millie said. 'And I wouldn't want our neighbours to think I'm the kind of woman who can't keep her own house clean and so I really don't know about the char.'

Jim threw back his head and laughed.

'What's so amusing?' asked Millie flatly.

'You are,' he said, pressing the tip of her nose. 'Your funny ideas about what's right and proper.'

'But, Jim, what sort of woman is at home all day and still has someone in to clean for her?' asked Millie.

'Well, my mother, for one,' Jim replied. 'In fact, she has a whole army of people looking after the house.'

'That's different,' said Millie, trying to imagine Lady Tollshunt pushing a vacuum cleaner around.

'I don't see how,' replied Jim. 'And besides, you're not Millie Sullivan living in a two-up two-down terraced house on the Chapman Estate any more. You're Mrs Amelia Smith, wife of a Member of Parliament.'

Millie pulled a face. 'Amelia?'

'It has to be formal on the stationery.' He drew her to him and slipped his arm round her as far as he could. 'And,' he kissed the top of her bump through her dress. 'Having a woman-that-does will give you more time with the baby.'

Millie bit her bottom lip. Perhaps it wasn't such a bad idea. Although she couldn't wait to have her baby, Millie was already wondering how she was going to adjust to not seeing the girls at the clinic every day. It was lovely that their house faced on to the green and was surrounded by trees, but it was quite isolated. She might not have felt quite so trepidatious if her neighbours seemed friendly, but other than a polite hello, not one of them had invited her in for a cup of tea, which is the least anyone in Wapping would have done for someone new moving into the street. Millie had got quite chummy with a couple of pregnant women at the ante-natal clinic but most of them weren't within walking distance. Even her mother was now a forty-minute train journey away, and so couldn't easily pop in after work either.

Millie sighed. 'I suppose so, and it would mean I'd have time to do other things like join the Mother's Union or the WI to meet other mothers.'

'And there's the Party's women's branch too,' Jim said in a casual tone. 'It would be good to have you sitting on the committee so you can keep an eye on them for me.'

'I'll give it a go,' Millie said. 'But what if I really can't get on with our woman-that-does?'

'Then you don't have to keep her on.' Jim took his wife's hand and kissed it.

'All right.'

'I just want you to be happy, my darling,' he said, giving her a heart-stopping smile.

Millie ran her fingers through his blond hair and smiled. 'I am, Jim.'

She bent down and kissed his brow.

His arms wound around her and he hugged her to him. Millie kissed his hair and closed her eyes and Oxford faded a little further from her mind. He'd been right; this beautiful house had given them a bright new start.

She kissed him again and pushed him way. 'I could murder a cup of tea. Do you want one?'

'Sounds perfect.' Jim released her and stood up. 'You put the kettle on while I put the minister's report in my briefcase so that I don't forget it in the morning and I'll join you in the kitchen.'

Leaving Jim to finish off, Millie made her way to the kitchen.

'What's all this?' Jim asked a minute or two later, entering the room holding Miss Moncrieff's pictures in his hand.

Millie explained briefly about meeting Freddie Kite.

'Take a look if you like,' Millie said fetching the milk from the refrigerator.

Jim untied the string and then, unwrapping the dozen or so pictures from the examination-couch paper Millie had used to protect them, spread them on the table.

Millie put his tea next to him and sat on the chair opposite with hers.

'What do you think?' she asked, as he scanned the images of night-time Paris, interiors of theatres and portraits of singers and ballet dancers.

'They look like something a child of four would have painted,' Jim said.

'Miss Moncrieff's an Expressionist,' explained Millie.

Jim looked distinctly unimpressed. 'Just because some jumped-up art critic gives it a name doesn't mean they are any good.'

'But I think they are,' Millie said, pulling out a picture of people sitting in cafés next to the Seine. 'I thought I could get them framed properly and put on the wall.'

He looked amused. 'We've got several family portraits by Reynolds and a series of Hogarth prints at Tollshunt, not to mention a Constable hanging in the dining room, and so I think I can claim to know a little bit about art. But if you like them, well ...' he shrugged. 'You can put a couple of the landscapes up in the spare bedrooms if you like and perhaps some of the sketches on the upstairs landing. I don't really want them where too many people can see them.'

'What about this drawing?' She extracted a foolscap-sized sheet of paper. 'Surely you want this one in your office?'

Jim smiled. 'I admit it's a very good likeness, but you're in your uniform sitting on some old woman's bed, Millie.' He took the picture from her and tucked it in amongst the others. 'I would like a painting of you in my office, Millie, and once you've had the baby I'll commission a proper artist. What do you think?'

'That would be something quite special,' Millie said, imagining the look on her mother's and Ruby's faces when she told them. Indeed Ruby was still trying to get over the excitement of Millie living in such a large house.

An adoring expression spread across Jim's handsome face. 'Just think of it as my way of thanking you, my darling, for making me the happiest man alive.'

Millie smiled and decided not to point out that the Constable he claimed to be hanging in the dining room at Tollshunt Manor was in fact a Turner.

Millie drew a line through the entry in the message book and turned to the next page.

'Doctors Matheson and Frankham would like a nurse to call, so could you, Nurse Robb, and your sleepy friend Nurse Dare next to you, call in sometime on your rounds and see what they want?' Millie looked down the table of nurses and at Peggy yawning for the third time since morning handover started.

'Sorry, Sister,' said Peggy, blinking.

'Did you all have a nice time at the Palace last night?' Millie asked, looking at the three student nurses struggling to keep their eyes open.

Peggy's round face lit up. 'Oh, yes, Sister, it was brilliant.'

'I'm glad you enjoyed yourselves,' said Millie. 'In late, were you?'

'Oh, no, Sister,' replied Veronica, looking at Millie with pin-pricks for pupils. 'We were in bed by lights out.'

Millie suppressed a smile and wondered who they'd persuaded to sneak them in.

Her gaze returned to the list. 'Mrs McKay's son rang to say his mother's taken her bandages off.'

'What, again?' whined Judy, pulling a face.

'She's an old woman and doesn't understand,' said Millie sharply.

'As Mrs McKay lives right by the O'Tooles' yard, I'm sure Sister Fletcher would be happy to go,' smirked Judy.

Millie glanced at Annie. Even after almost two months and Millie's numerous attempts to apologise, Annie still refused to speak to her about anything other than clinic business.

'She would if Mrs McKay was Sister Fletcher's patient,' replied Millie, feeling a tightening in her throat as she said her friend's name.

'I'll do her for you,' Veronica told Judy. 'You've already got four full-leg dressings, and I'm over that way.'

Millie looked back at the list.

'And finally, if Nurse Isles collects the pharmacy supplies and pops in to St Katherine's to collect the list of pupils starting after Easter from the headmistress, that will cover everything until dinnertime. Are there any questions?'

'No, Sister,' the room replied.

'And lastly, before you set out pedalling those bikes, as you know, tomorrow will be my last day,' Millie said.

There were murmurs of regret from the dozen or so nurses around the table.

Millie put on her 'severe matron' expression. 'And because I know you lot couldn't organise a screaming contest on a delivery ward' – all the nurses except Annie laughed – 'I've done the allocation of tasks for next month, and I'll post them on the board this afternoon. Until the local board appoints a deputy superintendent, Sister Scott will be responsible for making sure you Queenies complete your workbooks properly and get to your exams on time next month, Sister Rogers will keep an eye on the equipment store, and Nurse Barrett will order the weekly lotions and potions.' Millie looked around the table and the corners of her lips trembled. 'And I've asked Vi and Bert Fallow to keep the snug free, as I'm going to have a little drink at the Boatman tomorrow evening after work to say goodbye to everyone.'

The nurses in the room showed their approval of the arrangement by clapping and cheering.

Millie looked pointedly at Annie. 'I would dearly love to see all of you.'

Her old friend held her gaze for a moment and then looked away.

The door opened and Miss Dutton's sour-looking face appeared. 'I'm sure you can't hear for all the racket you're making in here, but the phone rang, and so perhaps you could drag yourself away from the merriment, Sister Smith, and send someone to see a Mrs O'Toole. The caller didn't give an address but I assume someone knows where she lives.'

Millie's mouth pulled into a hard line. 'I do most certainly know where Mrs O'Toole lives.'

*

Half an hour later with a grumpy look on her face and her nurse's bag gripped firmly in her right hand, Millie all but kicked open the small door in the O'Toole's double gates and set the dogs barking as she marched across the yard. She'd just reached halfway when Seamus and Dougan burst through the garden gate and ran towards her.

'Thank goodness,' the elder brother said, as they skidded to a halt in front of her. 'It's me Mammy.'

'Isn't it always?' said Millie, a little breathlessly.

Dougan took off his cap and clutched it in front of him. 'No, this time she's really sick.'

The baby shifted in protest at the early-morning route march down Commercial Road and Millie's temper shortened still further.

'What is it this time?' she snapped.

'I don't rightly know, but she's not the full crack this morning, that's for sure,' Seamus replied. 'Will you come and see, Sister?'

Millie gave them an infuriated look. 'You know, I could have done without a morning stroll.'

'And we're sorry, for sure,' Dougan said. 'And I wouldn't have called, but she fair tore the ears off of Pat the Lad for saying he thought she needed the doctor, so we didn't know what else to do.'

The two brothers towering over her looked mournfully at Millie.

'Will you just take a look at her, Sister?' pleaded Seamus.

Dougan twisted his cap in his shovel-like hands. 'Please.'

Millie let out a long breath. 'Very well.'

'Thank you, thank you,' said Seamus, taking her bag.

Dougan opened the garden gate. 'May the Virgin herself keep you in her loving care, Sister.'

Millie walked past them and into the front garden swearing to herself that it would be Mrs O'Toole who'd need saintly protection after this latest shenanigan. Stepping into the hall, Millie found Mickey and Brendan waiting for her, along with a host of the wives and children, many of whom were sitting up the stairs peering anxiously through the banisters.

A door on the floor above opened and Patrick appeared at the top of the stairs. 'Good morning, Sister Smith.'

Although his expression was unfriendly, there was relief in his tone.

'Good morning,' Millie replied, smiling politely up at him. 'I believe you called Munroe House because your mother's unwell yet again.'

'It wasn't me who called.' He shifted his angry eyes on to his brothers. 'I was for getting the ambulance!'

'Well, I'm here now,' said Millie briskly, 'and so I'll take a look at her.'

She started towards the kitchen at the back.

'Mammy's still in bed,' said Seamus.

Millie couldn't help but look surprised as Patrick shooed the children on the stairs and they shuffled aside.

Holding on to the handrail, Millie picked her way through a sea of small bodies wondering what illness the old woman had concocted this time. Perhaps her vision had faded and so she needed a guide dog, or her head was too heavy all of a sudden and she needed a specially made pillow.

'This way,' said Patrick, heading for the door at the far end. He knocked and then opened the door. 'The nurse is here to see you,' he said gently.

A cup flew out of the door and smashed on the wall opposite. The crowd behind Millie cowered back but Patrick didn't flinch.

'Send her away!' Mrs O'Toole screamed from inside the room.

'It's Sister Smith, Ma,' he said, motioning Millie forward. 'She's in the family way so don't you be throwing anything in her direction, now.'

Clutching her bag in her hand and getting ready to dodge any flying crockery, Millie marched into Mrs O'Toole's bedroom.

Like the rest of the house, the old woman's bedroom was jam-packed with furniture. In addition to the ancient wardrobe against the far wall, there were two tallboys with various bits of ornamental china and a collection of photographs. They ranged from faded sepia portraits of men and women in stiff poses though to a faded photo of a cheeky chap with a trilby at a jaunty angle and a mischievous grin that was sitting on the bedside-table.

Mrs O'Toole, wearing a turquoise bed-jacket and a belligerent expression on her face, sat in the middle of the double bed like an Eastern potentate. She was supported by at least half-a-dozen pillows and had a patchwork bedspread draped across her.

'Good morning, Mrs O'Toole,' said Millie, putting her bag on the dressing-table. 'I understand you're not feeling very well.'

'I'm as fit as a fiddle,' the old woman said, waving the notion away. 'So you can pick up your bag, Sister, and be on your way.'

Millie opened her case and pulled out a jar. 'Well, now I'm here, why don't you let me take a look,' she said, unscrewing the lid and taking her thermometer out.

'I keep telling you, there's nothing wrong.'

'Do as Sister Smith says, Ma,' Patrick coaxed, before giving his mother a fierce look.

Mother and son glared at each other, and then the old woman opened her mouth.

Millie shook the mercury down and popped the thermometer between two brown teeth and under the old woman's tongue. Mrs O'Toole clamped her lips around it and continued to scowl at her youngest son.

Millie pulled out her sphygmomanometer. Hooking the stethoscope around her neck, she took the old woman's wrist and looked down at her watch. Ninety. A little faster than the last time she'd taken it, but not unusual, given her patient's advancing age.

Millie quickly wound the cuff around Mrs O'Toole's upper arm and, placing the earpiece of the stethoscope in her ears, she pumped up the machine. Pressing the percussion cup in the crook of the old woman's elbow, Millie released the valve slowly. It, too, was higher than the last time she'd taken it, although still within a normal range.

She took the cuff off, folded it back in the case, then placed it and her stethoscope back in her bag. She removed the thermometer and twisted the reed of glass against the light.

'Everything's as right as rain, isn't it, Sister?' said Mrs O'Toole as Millie read the gauge.

'To be honest, I can't find anything out of the ordinary in your mother's observations, Patrick, except that her pulse is a little fast and her temperature is up half a degree at 98.9.'

'That's 'cos I've just had a cup of hot tea,' Mrs O'Toole said.

'An hour ago,' Patrick replied.

Millie looked at Patrick. 'Why did you want to call an ambulance?'

'Because I can't remember one day in the last twenty years when Ma wasn't already in the kitchen when I got up.'

'For goodness sake, boy,' shouted Mrs O'Toole. 'Ain't I entitled to a lay in?'

She clutched a fist to her chest and coughed.

'How long have you had that cough?' said Millie.

'For the last time, Sister, there's nothing wrong with me.'

'How long?'

'I've had a bit of phlegm on me chest for a couple of days, but me breakfast fag soon puts paid to it.' Mrs O'Toole smiled sweetly. 'Now, Sister, if you don't mind, sling your bloody hook and leave me in peace.'

Millie studied Mrs O'Toole's face. It was pale but again, not alarmingly so, and the brightness of her eyes could just be her temper. But Millie couldn't help feeling concerned.

Millie picked up her stethoscope again. 'I need to listen to your lungs, Mrs O'Toole.'

'There's nothing wrong with my blessed lungs!' Mrs O'Toole squeaked out, before starting to cough again.

'Will you sit your mother forward, please Patrick?' Millie said, clambering on to the bed.

He knelt on the other side of the bed and supported his mother's shoulders.

'Ger off me!' she bellowed, trying to shrug him off.

'Just do as you're told, Ma,' he said, heaving her away from the brass headboard. 'And I'm sure Sister Smith would be obliged if you'd stop being contrary for a moment or two, for I know I would.'

Mrs O'Toole gave her son another furious look and clamped her thin lips together.

Millie lifted the bed jacket up and, putting the earpieces in place, positioned the cup of the stethoscope at the bottom of Mrs O'Toole's back on the side nearest to her. As Millie bent forward, the baby kicked. Millie gasped and her hand went to her stomach.

'Move forward and give Sister some room to move, Ma,' Patrick barked.

Millie gave him a grateful look. 'Take a nice big breath, Mrs O'Toole, and then let it out slowly.'

The old woman did as she was told.

There was the whoosh of air and then, as she exhaled, there was faint but distinct crackling, like screwing greaseproof paper. Millie scrambled over and positioned the stethoscope in the same place on the right side.

'And again.'

The old woman took another breath and Millie heard the same sound.

'You can sit back now,' said Millie, straightening up.

Patrick eased his mother back, then came around to Millie and offered his hand. Millie grasped it and got off the bed.

'Thank you,' she said, as she returned her instrument to the bag. 'And you can call that ambulance now, please Mr O'Toole.'

Patrick shot to the door. 'Brendan, Sister Smith say's you're to call the ambulance. Mo, you get the case from under my bed and pack Ma's things.'

A cry went up outside the room and heavy footsteps clattered down the stairs as Patrick came back into the room.

Mrs O'Toole's face went red. 'For the love of God, I'm fine. And you said yourself there was nothing out of the ordinary.'

'There isn't,' said Millie. 'But as we get older our responses change and sometimes that masks the symptoms. I'm certain if you were half your age you'd have a raging temperature and be coughing up all kinds of muck. I'm no doctor, but I'd bet a pound to a penny that you've got double pneumonia, Mrs O'Toole.' She snapped her case shut. 'I'll go downstairs and write my notes while I wait for the ambulance. And then I'll ring ahead and talk to the sister in Casualty.'

She went to pick up her case but Patrick took it from her. 'Let me be carrying that for you, Sister Smith,' he said, opening the door for her.

Connie banged on the bar with the flat of her hand and then raised her glass of port and lemon. 'As you know, Millie and I have been friends since we were wet-behind-the-ears students in the London, and then we were staff nurses in the evacuation ward during the war. Understandably, with the terrible twins of number one set still terrorising the night matrons three years later—'

The nurses packed into the Boatman's snug laughed.

Millie and her fellow nurses had been in the pub since the clinic closed two hours earlier at five-thirty. Connie had arrived shortly after that, and between them they'd managed to demolish the half-dozen plate-loads of sandwiches, scotch eggs and pork pies that Vi, the publican's wife, had provided as a buffet.

As nothing that happened between Gardener's Corner and Bow Bridge was ever a secret, along with the nurses a number of Millie's patients had dropped by to wish her well and buy her a drink. But of course not everyone she hoped to see was there.

'So they split us by sending Millie to Herts for her midders,' continued Connie. 'And me to Queen Lottie's. But they couldn't keep a winning pair apart.'

'What, like Laurel and Hardy?' Doreen shouted.

'Or Abbott and Costello,' added Eva.

'Watch it,' said Connie. 'Anyway, me and Millie were reunited on the district in Munroe House and spent the duration dodging bombs and GIs' wandering hands.'

Another burst of laughter.

'But,' continued Connie, 'all good things come to an end and I'm sure the old Nursing Board breathed a sigh of relief when I parted company with the St George's and St Dunstan's Association and moved to Fry House a couple of years ago.'

There was a collective sigh of 'ah' from the audience.

'Millie has been the deputy superintendent there for almost three years now and has worked tirelessly since last July to get the new health service up and running in the area while still carrying a full list and keeping you lot in order. Which is a full-time job in itself.'

There were a couple of catcalls and hoots.

'But now it's time for Millie to wave farewell to Munroe House because, in case you haven't noticed, in a few months she's going to take on the hardest job in the world, and I know you all would want to wish her the very best.' Connie's expression lost its jollity, and she raised her glass. 'I give you our very own Millie Smith. Loved by patients but the scourge of lazy GPs—'

'Lackadaisical QN students,' chipped in Daphne.

'And interfering neighbours,' added Sally.

The nurses lifted their drinks high. 'Millie Smith!'

'Speech,' shouted Eva, and a couple of others took up the call.

Millie stood up. 'Thank you, Connie, for saying such nice things and not telling them the story of the three Swedish sailors we met in the blackout in Wapping Lane.'

'I'm saving that one for later,' chuckled Connie.

Everyone laughed again.

Millie smiled. 'But seriously, thank you for all the lovely presents you've given me. I think this baby's spoilt before he or she's even arrived. As much as I can't wait to be a mum, I will miss seeing you every day and *most* of my patients. I know there are a few faces missing tonight but I just want to say—'

The half-glazed snug door opened suddenly, and Annie walked in with Patrick O'Toole behind her. She stared at Millie for a moment and then her eyes softened.

'I just want to say thank you for all your support and help, and I'm so pleased to see you all, and thank you so much for coming,' Millie concluded, looking straight at her friend.

The audience applauded.

'And there's still a plate of sandwiches to finish off,' shouted Connie over the noise.

Millie made her way across the room. 'Oh Annie,' she said as she reached her. 'I'm so glad you've come, and Patrick, too,' she said, looking at up at him. 'How's your mother?'

'Complaining to the bejesus about having her rear speared with "the devil's own pitchfork", as she calls it, three times a day,' he replied. 'But thanks to you at least she can complain. The doctor said if she'd gone another day without treatment the pneumonia would have taken her.'

'And that's why we've come,' said Annie, 'to thank you.'

'Don't be silly,' said Millie. 'I think everyone in the family thanked me at least twice, if not three times, in the hospital. Including you, Patrick.'

'Well, maybe I did, but it bears saying again,' he said. He slipped his arm around Annie's waist. 'Doesn't it Annie?'

'Yes,' said Annie. 'Yes, it does. And anyway we want to wish you well with the baby too.'

'And I want to say sorry for speaking out of turn about Patrick,' Millie said seizing her friend's hand. 'I was wrong and I hope that you'll accept my apology.' Millie looked from Annie to Patrick.

'I do,' said Annie. 'I'm sorry too for not letting you say it before, but I was very upset.'

'You had every right to be,' said Millie. 'But I hope we can put it behind us and be friends again.'

Annie smiled. 'I'd like that, especially ...' She glanced up at Patrick.

'Well, you'd better say, me darling, before you burst,' he said, giving Annie a wry smile.

Annie beamed at Millie. 'We're getting married.'

'That's wonderful.' Millie hugged Annie and felt her relax in her embrace. She put Annie from her and looked at the young couple. 'I am so very happy for you both, and I wish you a long and happy life together.'

'You will come to the wedding, won't you?' said Annie.

'As long as you're not planning it in the next couple of months.' Millie ran her hand over her bump.

Annie shook her head. 'No, we're thinking next summer – probably July or August. Isn't that so, Patrick?'

'That it is,' he agreed. 'I'm buying a couple of acres of land in Purfleet to set up on me own, so we'll be looking for a house in one of the villages close by, like Rainham or Aveley. We're marrying in Annie's church in Bethnal Green, though.'

'Well then, I'll be there throwing rice for all I'm worth,' said Millie, hugging Annie again.

'Did I hear someone is getting married?' said Connie, pushing her way over to where they were.

'Yes, our Annie,' laughed Millie. 'Our Annie's getting married.'

'Annie!' squealed Eva and Sally together.

The nurses crowded around Annie, hugging her and bombarding her with questions about rings and dates.

Patrick smiled at the good wishes coming his way, and then quietly stepped back to let Annie enjoy her moment.

Millie went over to him. 'I'm so glad you and Annie stopped by, Patrick.'

'So is Annie,' he replied.

'I hope you can forgive me for all the terrible things I said about you,' she said, looking him in the eye.

'I've been called worse,' he replied. 'But after what you did for Ma, I can forgive you anything. But tell me, Sister, how did you really know she was so ill?'

Millie laughed. 'That's easy! Because she was so blooming adamant she wasn't.'

'All the best, Millie,' said Sally, giving her a kiss on the cheek.

'And you,' Millie replied, hugging her back. 'And thanks for coming.'

Sally gave her another quick squeeze, and then she and three of the other nurses turned and hurried off towards Munroe House.

Millie looked down the street and then at her watch. Five past eight. Jim was supposed to be here half an hour ago. She pressed her lips together and wondered what his excuse would be this time.

The Boatman's saloon door swung open and Connie stepped out. 'Well, that went well,' she said, joining Millie under the street lamp. 'And I'm glad you and Annie have made up at last.'

'So am I,' Millie said with feeling. 'And I'm so pleased for her and Patrick.'

'Me too,' Connie replied. 'And it will be another excuse to buy a new outfit.'

Millie laughed. 'Well, at least by then I should have my waist back.'

Her friend looked around. 'No Jim?'

'I expect he's been caught in traffic,' Millie replied.

Connie glanced surreptitiously at the clock hanging outside the pawnbrokers opposite.

'Don't worry,' said Millie. 'You get off to your mum's.'

'I popped in on mum yesterday,' Connie explained. 'It's just that I promised Dr McEwan that I'd nip back to the surgery.'

'What? At this time of night?'

'It's only just gone eight,' Connie replied, a tad defensively.

'He's hoping to set up a special clinic for the local prostitutes and there's a couple of health board officials coming by tomorrow. He's hoping they will give him the thumbs-up, and I promised I'd give a hand checking everything through. But I don't like to leave you alone in the middle of Wapping.'

'Don't be silly,' Millie replied. 'It's only just gone eight and there are plenty of people around.'

'Are you sure? I mean, of course I don't mind staying if you'd like me to.'

'You go,' interrupted Millie. 'I'm sure as soon as you walk around the corner Jim will drive up in the car.'

'All right.' Connie gave her a hug. 'I'll see you at twelve on Saturday.'

A bus with the interior lights switched on passed the end of the road and a car turned into the street. It wasn't Jim's. Millie looked at it then looked at her watch again.

The sound of footsteps and a woman's giggling laugh made her look up as a couple, arm in arm, turned the corner.

Millie's heart thumped in her chest as her eyes fixed on Alex Nolan.

Wearing a fawn-coloured summer suit over a pale blue shirt and with a pastel diagonal striped tie knotted at his throat he looked as if he'd walked straight out of the pages of *Picture Post*. Without a hat his dark curls sprang about in the evening breeze as he matched his pace to the petite red-head on his arm.

Alex said something to her and she laughed adoringly up at him, and then he saw Millie. He stopped dead.

'Hello, Millie,' he said gently, as his eyes flicked on to her stomach and then back to her face.

'Alex, hello,' she replied, feeling slightly sick.

'Good evening, Sister Smith,' said a cheery voice into the space between them.

Millie dragged her eyes from Alex's face and looked properly at the woman beside him.

She frowned. The woman looked familiar but Millie couldn't quite place her.

'Wendy Lamb,' the young woman explained. 'I work at Fry House with your friend Connie. We met when you visited a little while back.'

Millie forced a smile. 'Of course, yes. You're the Sister on the Boundary Estate, aren't you?'

The young nurse nodded.

'I'm sorry,' said Millie. 'I didn't recognise you at first.'

Wendy giggled again. 'We look different out of uniform, don't we?'

'We certainly do,' Millie replied, running her gaze over Wendy's curvy figure and shapely legs. 'So how did you and Alex meet?'

'I was in the Rose and Punch Bowl with a couple of the girls a few weeks back and there was a punch-up. The police were called and Alex came and sorted it out.'

'Well, me and the rest of B relief,' added Alex, giving the wry smile that Millie had never quite forgotten.

Wendy giggled for a third time. The cheerful sound was now definitely setting Millie's nerves jangling uncomfortably.

'Oh, Alex,' Wendy compounded her crime by sending Alex a flirtatious glance from under her mascaraed lashes. 'You're such a laugh.'

Alex acknowledged her flattery with a stiff smile.

'Are you off somewhere nice?' Millie asked, frostily.

'We're going up West to celebrate,' Wendy replied, hugging Alex's arm.

A cold shiver ran through Millie. She glanced at Wendy's left hand but it was curled in the crook of Alex's arm.

'Celebrate?' she asked in a tight voice.

'Yes, I've just passed my Superintendent board,' Alex explained.

'Will this mean that you'll be transferring off the borough?' Millie said.

'Not for a few months.'

'Jack Goodman's band is playing at the Lyceum,' Wendy said. 'Alex is such a good dancer.'

'I would guess that he is,' Millie replied, as their first dance together on VJ night flashed through her mind.

Wendy's eyes narrowed for a split second, and then she smiled artlessly at Millie. 'When is your baby due, Mrs Smith?'

'At the end of May,' said Millie quickly.

'Well, you look blooming,' continued Wendy merrily. 'Doesn't she, Alex?'

Alex's expression softened. 'Yes.'

'And is your husband's looking forward to being a dad?' asked Wendy.

'We both are,' Millie replied. 'In fact, I'm just waiting for him.'

There was a roar as Jim's Ford Pilot tore down the road and screeched to a halt on the other side of the street.

'And here he is,' Millie said, smiling brightly.

Jim honked the horn.

'Well, we ought to be off then,' said Alex, not moving an inch.

'Have a nice time,' said Millie.

'I'm sure we will,' said Wendy.

Jim blasted the horn again.

Millie gave them a wan smile and stepped off the pavement.

As she brushed past Alex he spoke softly. 'All the best with the baby, Millie.'

She looked up. 'Thank you.'

Wendy and Alex walked away as she hurried across the road.

Jim leant across the passenger's seat and opened the car door.

'Sorry I'm late, sweetheart, but there was an accident on the Strand,' he said, as she climbed in. 'Who was that you were talking to?'

Millie slammed the door. 'Just an old friend.'

'I thought as much.' Jim put the car into gear and it rolled away. 'Pretty little thing.'

Millie peered through the windscreen at Alex's tall figure striding down the street with Wendy Lamb trotting alongside. 'You said it.'

Chapter Fifteen

Jim strolled into the lounge and put his suitcase on the floor just as Millie looked up from her knitting.

'Is that going to be enough for five days?' she asked, looking at the small tan case at his feet.

He looked quite dapper in a countrified sort of way in his moleskin slacks, Tattersall shirt and with what Millie called his hairy Harris Tweed tie knotted at his throat.

'It's just my spare shirts and underwear,' he said, shrugging on his jacket. 'I've already put my three-piece and dinner suit in the car.' He clicked his fingers. 'Talking of which, did my dickey shirt arrive from the cleaner's?'

'It turned up while you were still upstairs.' Millie swung her legs off the pouffe and started to rise.

'No, you stay there, my darling, I'll get it,' he said, smiling lovingly at her. 'The doctor said you have to rest as much as you can.'

'It's on the hall table,' Millie replied, sinking back in the comfortable chair.

The combination of a warm night and a baby doing the fandango on the top of her bladder since first light meant that Millie had been not so much singing as yawning while she worked her way through the household chores.

Jim returned holding the paper bag on the flat of his hand. He opened the case and slipped it in on top of his other shirts.

'Now, have you got everything?' asked Millie. 'Cufflinks? Bow tie? Shaving kit?'

'I think so,' Jim said.

Millie sighed. 'You're bound to have forgotten something. I wish you'd let me pack for you.'

Jim smiled warmly at her. 'The doctor said you've got to rest.'

'I bet he says that to every pregnant women who walks through his door,' Millie replied.

Jim pressed his lips together. 'Well, he is the consultant obstetrician.'

'He might be, but he barely glances at me,' said Millie. 'He asks me the same questions each visit but he never remembers the answers.'

'Doctor Prendergast is the best there is,' Jim replied patiently. 'An Oxford man and he's published papers in the *Lancet* as well as being on the government's Advisory Committee for Women's Health.'

'But when did he last deliver a baby?' Millie asked. 'Some of his advice is very out of date. All the modern textbooks agree that, as long as the mother is well, it's better for her to stay active, and I don't think packing a few shirts for my husband constitutes heavy labour.'

'Perhaps not, but Hoovering the whole of the downstairs and washing the kitchen floor certainly would do,' Jim said. 'And all that despite the fact Mrs Everett is coming tomorrow.'

Millie looked horrified. 'I can't have her going through the house if it isn't spotless, and I'm not used to having time on my hands.'

Jim came over and hunkered down beside her. 'You are a funny little thing sometimes,' he said pressing the tip of her nose playfully. 'But, seriously, you should make the most of having a bit of time to put your feet up. From what I hear, you'll have precious little after the baby arrives.' He rested his hand on her stomach. 'Are you sure you'll be all right here while I'm away?'

'Of course,' she said, enjoying his tender attention. 'The baby won't be here for at least three weeks and probably more. And Blackpool isn't the other side of the world.'

Jim gave her a crooked smile. 'You wouldn't say that if you'd ever been there. All the landladies sound like Gracie Fields and look like Old Mother Riley.'

Millie laughed. 'Well then, it's as well you're staying in a hotel and not a boarding house.'

Jim looked at his watch. 'I said I'd pick Sid Humberson up at Stratford at half-past.' His anxious expression returned. 'Are you sure you're going to be all right?'

'I'll be fine. I've got my mum and aunt Ruby at the end of the phone.' She reached up and moved a stray lock of blond hair from her husband's brow. 'Now, you go off and enjoy your first Labour Party Conference as an MP.'

Jim kissed her lightly on the lips then stood up. He picked up his jacket and his suitcase.

'Oh, and where are you staying?' Millie said, picking up her knitting again.

'Didn't I tell you?'

'No,'

'Oh, the Royal.' Jim patted his pocket. 'I don't think I've got the number, but directory enquiries will have it listed.'

'It doesn't matter,' said Millie waving the notion away.

'I'll ring you when I get there and see you on Friday evening, darling.' Jim blew her a kiss. 'Love you.'

Millie smiled. 'Love you too.'

The baby started as the door banged behind Jim and Millie ran her hand over her stomach. Imagining the little hands and feet tucked tightly together inside her, she smiled. The clock on the mantelshelf struck two o'clock. She reached out, turned the wireless on and then wound the thin strand of three-ply wool around her little finger and slipped the stitch.

As the insistent pain encircling her middle brought Millie awake, she realised it wasn't Ruby trying to squeeze her into a new girdle in Bearman's, but her own stomach muscles instead. In the dark she rolled on her back and put her hand on her bump only to find it hard and unyielding. As she'd instructed countless women to do, Millie raised her chin and took shallow breaths to stay above the pain. Focusing on remaining calm, she counted to thirty before the contraction subsided.

She stretched out tentatively and switched on the bedside light. Shielding her eyes from the glare of the forty-watt bulb, Millie looked at the clock. It was almost two-thirty in the morning.

Wide awake now, she realised that the sudden urge to tidy the house yesterday wasn't the weather lifting her spirits but the pre-delivery surge of energy, and the niggling ache in her back since lunchtime had nothing to do with her long walk back from the library. And she called herself a midwife!

The muscles in her back quivered again and Millie focused on the fringes of the lampshade above as another contraction gripped her.

What on earth had possessed her to tell Jim she'd be all right at home while he was at the Party conference? She of all people should have known that babies were notoriously unpredictable in their arrival; and first ones were often the very worst.

Another pain started in the small of her back and radiated around her stomach. She glanced back at the clock. Just five minutes since the last one.

As Doctor Gingold's warning about not tarrying flashed through her mind, Millie waited for the pain to abate, then threw back the covers and swung her legs out. Quickly, she put on her day clothes and then, gripping her hospital case firmly in one hand and the banister in the other, carefully she made her way downstairs.

Putting the front door on the latch and leaving her case next to it, Millie sat down on the chair by the hall table, picked up the telephone and dialled 999.

'Which service do you require?' asked the operator.

'Ambulance.'

She was put straight through.

'Ambulance. What address?' asked the controller at the other end.

Millie gave it and then a swift run-down of her situation.

'All right, don't you worry none, ducks,' the controller assured her. 'I'll send one of our wagons straight away. It should be there in about ten minutes to take you to Whipps Cross. Will your husband coming with you?'

'No, he's away on business,' Millie explained.

'Well, you stay put and our lads will be there in a jiffy.'

'Thank you,' whispered Millie.

The line went dead and Millie put her finger on the handset cradle for a moment, and then dialled anew. The telephone rang a couple of times and then an operator picked up the phone.

'Directory enquires,' said a sleepy-sounding voice.

Another contraction swept through Millie. She put her free hand on the wall and closed her eyes.

'Would you give me the number of the Royal Hotel in Blackpool, please?' she asked, forcing out every word.

'Just a moment.'

The contraction reached its peak and then subsided as the operator returned.

'There's no Royal Hotel listed in Blackpool, madam.'

Millie frowned. 'But my husband's staying there.'

'I'm sorry.'

'But it is the hotel where the Labour Party delegates are staying,' said Millie, as the muscles in her back knotted again.

'You want the Westmoreland.'

'Yes, thank you,' said Millie. 'Could you put me through?'

The operator dialled the number and someone picked up the telephone at the other end.

'Westmoreland Hotel, night porter speaking,' said a man with a northern accent.

'I have a caller for you,' said the operator as she put Millie through.

'I'm trying to contact Mr James Smith, who I think might be staying at your hotel,' Millie said, breathing out between contractions.

'Let me see.' There was a pause, then the porter spoke again. 'I can't see—'

'He might be registered as Woodville Smith,' Millie said. 'His home address is fifty-five The Forest, Wanstead.'

'Ah yes, I have him,' said the porter. 'Room three-one-four. One of our best, overlooking the sea. Churchill stayed there in forty-three when he was—'

'Could you put me through?' Millie interrupted brusquely.

'We don't usually disturb our guests after midnight, madam, unless it's urgent,' the porter said stiffly.

'I wouldn't be ringing if it wasn't,' said Millie through gritted teeth as her whole body tightened ready for the next assault.

'Very well, hold the line.'

As the telephone in Jim's room rang, Millie braced herself for the next contraction, but instead of a vice-like grip seizing her this time, an overwhelming urge to push swept through her. She raised her head and with a monumental effort resisted the urge to bear down. Beads of perspiration sprang out on her forehead and as the contraction reached its zenith, Millie felt a pop and warm fluid flooded down her legs.

Straining her ears for the sound of the ambulance bell she gripped the receiver tightly as she willed Jim to answer the telephone.

The ache started in her back again and Millie drew a breath.

The phone was picked up and hysterical relief flooded over Millie.

'Oh, Jim—'

'Room 314,' a woman's drowsy voice said.

Millie froze. Another contraction swept over her but she barely registered the pain gripping her body as something akin to a rip-saw cut deep into her chest.

Millie heard some grumbling in the background, then she heard Jim's voice. 'What on earth? Give me the phone.'

There were some muffled sounds of the bed creaking at the other end of the line.

Some way down the road, the sound of an ambulance heading towards her filtered through the still night towards her.

'James Smith,' he said, groggily.

'It's me.'

'Millie!'

'I thought you'd like to know I'm just off to hospital to have your baby,' she said calmly. 'And please apologise to your friend for waking her.'

'Sweetheart! I can—'

Millie dropped the receiver back in the cradle and waddled to the front door to meet the ambulance.

Without opening her eyes, Patricia Woodville Smith gave a little hiccup. Millie's mother and Ruby, who were sitting on either side of Millie's hospital bed, rose up in their seats and peered at the newest member of the family just to check once again that she was all right.

Her mother and aunt had burst through the door ahead of all the other visitors for afternoon visiting five minutes ago and had done nothing but comment on Patricia's perfection ever since. And Millie couldn't help but agree with them.

'She's just such a poppet,' said Doris, looking adoringly at her grandchild.

A sentimental expression stole over Ruby's powdered face. 'I don't think I'm exaggerating when I say that our Patricia is the most beautiful baby in the world.'

Millie gazed down at her ten-hour-old daughter, asleep in her arms. 'Yes, she is, isn't she?' she replied, as love that hurt with its intensity surged up again.

She was in the third bed down on the left on the long Nightingale maternity ward in Whipps Cross Hospital. She was close to the nurse's station so she could be easily observed for signs of infection, and she would be shifted down the ward as the risk of puerperal fever decreased.

The ward was run by a jolly Irish sister who seemed to spend all day dashing up and down the ward with the lacy frills of her hat trailing behind her. The half-a-dozen maternity nurses concentrated on the newly delivered mothers, helping them to feed their babies and show them in the correct way to clean new-born eyes and attend to the cord. Thankfully, as Millie was skilled in both, she was let off the daily childcare lesson.

'And you look lovely, too, my dear,' added Doris, smiling at Millie. 'Motherhood really suits you. Doesn't it, Ruby?'

'Oh, yes,' replied Ruby, opening her handbag and taking out her cigarettes.

'I'm afraid Sister doesn't allow smoking on the ward, aunt Ruby,' said Millie.

Ruby looked amazed. 'What, not even for the mothers?'

Millie shook her head. 'They have to go in to the day room at the end of the ward. She says it affects the babies' lungs.'

'What a ridiculous idea,' replied Ruby, shoving the pack back in her bag and snapping the clip.

Doris put her little finger into her granddaughter's tiny hand and watched her fingers curl around. 'Your granddad would have loved you.'

'And spoiled her rotten,' said Millie, as a lump formed in her throat as she thought of her father.

Ruby laid her hand on Millie's arm. 'Was it very bad?'

'To be honest, I can hardly remember,' Millie replied. 'It was all very quick once the ambulance arrived. Her head was crowning as I got into the delivery suite and the doctor only just got his mask and gloves on in time.'

'My goodness,' said Doris. 'It's lucky that you didn't hang about.'

Ruby glanced over both shoulders and then leant forward. 'What about ...? You know. *Down there*?' she mouthed.

'Just a little tear, but it's nothing and I'll be fine in a day or two,' Millie replied in a hushed tone.

Her aunt pressed her hand to her chest. 'Thank goodness, you hear such stories.' She looked at Millie. 'Even so, don't let Jim, er, do anything before the doctor says it's safe.'

Millie's mouth pulled into a hard line. 'Don't worry, aunt Ruby, Jim won't be coming near me for a long time.'

Doris laughed. 'We all say that, but you'll soon forget.'

Millie gazed down at Patricia and didn't reply.

Her mother glanced anxiously at the large ward clock above the door. 'I thought he would have been here by now.'

'I expect he had a few loose ends to tie up before he left,' said Millie flatly.

Doris frowned. 'He should have come straight away.'

'I'm sure he wanted to, Doris,' said Ruby, 'but a man in his position can't just drop everything and run home. He must have rung the ward?'

'Three times,' Millie said, gazing down at Patricia's delicate features again as tears sprang into her eyes.

Her mother stood up and put a comforting arm around her daughter. 'Oh darling, he'll be here very soon, I'm sure.'

'Your mother's right,' said Ruby, rubbing Millie's arm. 'He's probably caught in traffic. It took me and Anthony almost ten hours to drive back from Blackpool last time we were there.'

Millie took the handkerchief from her bed-jacket sleeve. 'I don't want him to see me like this.'

Doris tucked a stray lock of hair back behind Millie's ear. 'I'm sure—'

'Here he is,' cut in Ruby excitedly. 'Jim! Over here!'

Millie turned.

Jim was standing by the nurses' desk at the end of the ward holding a large bunch of red roses in his hand. He'd clearly stopped at the barber's before coming to the hospital, as his cheeks were smooth from the razor. He'd also dropped in at the house, as he was wearing the chocolate pinstripe suit she'd collected from the cleaner's the day after he'd left. As their eyes met across the space, Millie saw apprehension flicker briefly in his blue eyes before an assured smile spread across his face.

He caught one of the nurses as she walked past and she took the flowers from him. Jim gave her a dazzling smile that made the young nurse blush, and fury lodged itself at the base of Millie's throat. He adjusted his tie and strolled over.

'Doris, Ruby,' he said embracing both women in turn. 'Nice to see you both and thanks for holding the fort until I got back.'

His gaze shifted to Millie. 'Hello, sweetheart,' he said kissing her awkwardly on the cheek.

Millie didn't answer and Jim's easy-going expression faltered a little. He cleared his throat and looked at the bundle in her arms.

'So this is my little girl, is it?' He hooked the shawl away from the baby's face with his finger. 'She is very beautiful.'

Doris smiled fondly at Patricia. 'Just like her mum.'

'And we haven't heard her cry once,' cooed Ruby.

Jim ran his finger over his daughter's cheek. 'Thank you, darling.' He raised his eyes and met Millie's implacable gaze. He looked away and straightened up.

'It's time we made ourselves scarce, Ruby,' said Doris, putting her handbag on her arm.

Ruby rose to her feet and, after assuring Millie they would be in the next day and congratulating Jim again, they left.

The nurse came back with a vase containing Jim's bouquet and set it on the locker next to Millie. Jim thanked her and she headed back to the nursery.

Millie waited until she was out of earshot and then glanced at the blooms. 'I thought being caught in a hotel room with another woman would be worth more than a bunch of flowers.'

'I can explain.'

'French perfume or perhaps even a mother-of-pearl compact case,' said Millie crisply.

'Millie, darling, if you'd—'

'Or,' continued Millie giving him a glacial smile, 'perhaps, as I was actually in labour when your fancy bit answered the phone, something gold and dripping with diamonds might be more appropriate. What do you think?'

Jim hung his head. 'I'm not proud of what I did, Millie. But you have to understand. She was just some girl I met in the bar and she means nothing to me, honestly.' He shrugged. 'In fact, I can't even remember her name. It's you I love. You and our little girl.'

He took Millie's hand, but she snatched it back and turned from him.

'I think you'd better go,' she said, feeling his presence beside her like an oppressive weight.

Jim didn't move for a moment or two and then the chair scraped on the polished wooden floor as he rose to his feet. Millie didn't look around.

'I know you're very tired, my love,' he said, raising his voice so those around them could hear. 'So I'll leave you to sleep, but I'll be in to see you both tomorrow.' He reached across to tickle Patricia's hand, then kissed Millie on the top of the head. 'I do love you,' he whispered and then walked out.

Millie felt tightness in the corners of her eyes and her nose tingled. She pressed her lips on to Patricia's forehead in a gentle kiss as tears fell into her daughter's downy hair.

'I tell you, Millie, she is the very image of you,' Connie said, who was sitting beside Millie's bed and admiring her soon-to-be goddaughter through the bars of the hospital's iron cot.

This afternoon the old Victorian ward was bathed in a warm glow of early summer sunlight which shone through the tall windows above the beds. Nearly everyone had a visitor sitting next to them, mostly anxious-looking young men trying to grapple with the correct way to hold their new offspring, but there was the occasional mother or friend keeping the new mum company for an hour before the enforced rest period between three and four o'clock.

'That's what my mum and aunt Ruby say, but I don't know how you can tell at this age,' replied Millie.

'Of course you can,' said Connie. 'She's all you, from the shape of her face to her turned-up nose and she didn't get that mop of brown hair from Jim, did she?'

Millie smiled down at her daughter, who was now looking around peacefully after a feed and nappy change. 'I suppose not.'

'And you're looking more like your old self too, too.' Connie ran her gaze over Millie. 'It won't be many weeks before you can fasten your skirt waistbands again.'

'I don't know about that,' said Millie. 'My stomach still feels like a half-set blancmange.'

'Pushing a pram to the shops each day will soon sort that out,' said Connie knowingly.

'Annie came in yesterday,' said Millie.

'How is she?'

'Full of wedding plans,' Millie replied. 'And she brought a lovely little pink bonnet and a good-luck charm from her future mother-in-law, with instructions to hang it over the baby's head to keep the pixies away.'

'Are pixies a problem in Wanstead?' giggled Connie.

'According to Mrs O'Toole pixies are a problem everywhere there is new-born babies' breath to steal,' replied Millie. 'But I suppose it was kind of her to send something.'

Connie's gaze returned to Patricia, who had now drifted off to sleep. 'I can't believe she's almost two weeks old already.'

Millie studied her daughter's tiny fingernails. 'No, neither can I.'

'Is she still feeding all right?'

Millie nodded. 'And going for almost four hours between. I've only had to go to the nursery once for the past five nights.'

'I thought the night nurses gave the babies a bottle in the night,' said Connie.

'I told them I wanted to be called,' replied Millie. She reached in and lightly smoothed her fingers over Patricia's soft hair. 'And she's certainly getting enough, as she's put on four ounces already.'

Connie looked impressed. 'I don't suppose Jim's quite got used to the idea of being a father yet.'

The hard lump of betrayal lodged in Millie's chest reasserted itself.

'Not quite,' she replied quietly.

'And I bet your daddy rushes up here every day just to see his little girl,' Connie said to the sleeping baby in her newly acquired auntie voice. She raised her head. 'He must be counting the minutes until he can take you home tomorrow. I tell you, Millie. If Malcolm is half as good as your Jim.'

The wave of desolation Millie had fought to keep at bay for almost two weeks suddenly burst and before she could stop them, tears welled up.

'What's wrong, Millie?' asked Connie anxiously.

'It's ... it's ... J–Jim,' Millie sobbed.

Risking the ward sister's wrath, Connie sat on the bed and put her arm around Millie. 'There, there. Don't upset yourself and this time tomorrow you'll be home.'

'You don't understand,' said Millie, reaching for her handkerchief. 'I don't want to go home. Everyone thinks Jim's such a wonderful husband. But I know different now.'

Starting with Beth's son and finishing with ringing Jim's room at the Westmoreland, Millie told Connie everything, her words tumbling out between gasping sobs.

'So you can see why I'm not relishing walking out of the hospital with Jim tomorrow,' Millie concluded, feeling utterly exhausted.

'But you've not been married two years,' said Connie when her friend had finished.

'I know,' replied Millie, feeling the searing pain of his betrayal cut through her again. 'He says it didn't mean anything and it's me he loves. He even swears he'll never do it again, but he said that last time. And as for coming in to see us, Connie, he visited the first three days after Patricia was born for half an hour, then, despite all his apologies and promises to make it up to me, he only made it in three times last week and one of those was just ten minutes before the bell rang at the end. He phoned on Monday to say he'd been kept late at the House, but he hasn't shown his face since.' She blew her nose. 'Not that I'm complaining. If I never set eyes on the Honourable James Percival Woodville Smith again, it'll be too soon.'

'What do your mum and aunt Ruby say?'

'I haven't told them. It would break their hearts.'

'Go around and punch him on the blooming nose more like,' said Connie.

Millie covered her eyes with her hand. 'I should never have married him. But at the time he seemed ...'

'Everything Alex wasn't,' Connie finished for her.

Millie looked up. 'What's Alex got to do with it?'

'It's no coincidence that you accepted Jim's proposal on the day you found out Alex was getting married, is it?' said Connie.

Millie held her friend's gaze for a moment and then looked down. 'Maybe you are right. Perhaps it's because I married Jim on the rebound that I was blind to what he was really like.'

Connie shrugged. 'Who knows, but what can you do?'

Millie's mouth pulled into a determined line. 'I haven't decided yet.'

Connie's eyes stretched wide. 'You're not thinking of leaving him, are you?'

'It's crossed my mind,' Millie replied, feeling a little shock that she felt bold enough even to say such a thing out loud.

Although the number of divorces had shot through the roof since the end of the war, the street-corner gossips still shook their heads in disgust at a woman walking out on her husband. Even the women who got the worst of their husband's fists after closing time were thought to lack moral fibre if they didn't stand by their wedding vows.

'But what about Patricia? Surely you don't want her to come from a broken home?' said Connie.

'Of course I don't.' Millie's gaze returned to the dozing child in the crib beside her, and tears sprang into her eyes again. 'But I don't want her to grow up with a drunken, womanising liar for a father, either.'

Chapter Sixteen

Jim swung the car right into The Forest and drew to a halt outside their house. The sinking feeling that had started the moment she'd set eyes on him an hour ago hit the pit of Millie's stomach.

She had already dressed Patricia in a lacy matinée dress and light cardigan and herself in her red and white polka-dot dress by the time Jim had arrived on the ward at ten. He was wearing his new tailored navy suit and a debonair smile, and he had used their combined monthly sweet ration to buy the nurses the traditional box of chocolates. Having thanked the staff and said their goodbyes to the other mothers, Millie and Jim, just like dozens of other new parents that morning, strolled out of hospital.

Pulling the handbrake on, Jim turned to her. 'There we are, sweetheart, home sweet home.'

Millie didn't reply.

He jumped out and came around to her side of the car. As he opened the door for Millie to get out, a middle-aged woman in an old-fashioned matron's uniform and elaborate white frilly cap stepped out of their house. Ignoring Jim's outstretched hand, Millie got out of the car.

'Who's that?' she asked, shifting Patricia's weight in her arms.

'Nurse Browne,' Jim replied, retrieving her suitcase from the boot. 'She's the maternity nurse and she is going to look after you and the baby.'

He beckoned the woman over.

'Good afternoon.' A supercilious smile spread across her face, lifting her downy cheeks. 'Perhaps Mummy would like me to take Baby for her,' she said stretching out her arms towards Patricia.

Millie held her daughter closer. 'No, thank you.'

The maternity nurse shot a glance at Jim and he shook his

head slightly. Nurse Browne stepped back. Jim guided Millie into the house.

'Perhaps you'll be so kind as to unpack my wife's suitcase and then make us a cup of tea,' he said, handing Millie's weekend case to the nurse as they passed.

Nurse Browne's thin lips drew together, but she took the suitcase nonetheless and followed them in at a discreet distance. As the nurse's brogues thudded up the stairs, Jim closed the front door.

'You look tired, my dear; you should have let Nurse Browne take her,' Jim said as they entered the lounge.

Millie sat down in the fireside chair. 'I told you I didn't want a maternity nurse, Jim,' she said curtly, resting Patricia on her lap. 'And especially one who addresses me as "Mummy".'

Jim dismissed his wife's words with a casual wave of his hand. 'Browne's a bit quaint I know, but she comes with solid references and you know that I hired her to take the burden from your shoulders.'

'I don't consider caring for my own child a burden,' replied Millie.

Jim gave her his most charming smile. 'I was only thinking of you, sweetheart.'

Patricia sneezed and Millie made a play of straightening her daughter's cardigan.

He picked up the newspaper from the coffee table and flicked it open. The clock on the mantelshelf ticked out the seconds until Nurse Browne returned with a tea tray. She put it on the low table on the fireside rug and set out the cups.

'Mr Kirby telephoned while you were out, Mr Smith, and he asked that you ring him as soon as you have a moment,' she said, handing Jim a cup. 'Your secretary also called, as did a Mrs Harris, saying she and Mrs Smith's mother would be visiting tomorrow afternoon.' She looked at Millie. 'Sugar?'

'No, thank you,' Millie replied.

Nurse Browne tutted. 'You must keep your strength up while you're feeding, Mummy.'

'I'm well aware of that,' replied Millie tightly. 'But I have recently given up sugar in my tea, Nurse Browne. Also, my name is Mrs Smith, and so please address me as such.'

Bristling with offence, Nurse Browne placed Millie's tea on the table next to her. Patricia stirred and started to niggle.

'She'll be wanting her afternoon feed soon,' said Millie squeezing her daughter's nappy. 'And a new nappy.'

Jim looked up from his paper. 'Nurse Browne can change her for you, my love.'

The nurse sprang forward, but Millie stood up. 'No, I'll see to her myself.'

Jim frowned. 'But your tea will get cold.'

'Then Nurse Browne can make me another,' replied Millie and, without waiting for either of them to reply, she swept out of the room with Patricia in her arms.

By the time she'd reached the nursery on the first floor, Patricia was fully awake and rooting for her feed. With a sure hand Millie changed her nappy and then settled herself into the chair by the window. Unbuttoning her blouse, Millie cradled her daughter in the crook of her arm and offered her breast.

As Patricia started sucking, Jim appeared at the door. 'Nurse is only trying to help, darling.'

'I'm sure she is,' Millie replied pleasantly. 'But Patricia's my daughter and I'm looking after her.'

'At least let Nurse Browne attend to her at night to save you traipsing in and out of the nursery at all hours,' Jim said in a voice loaded with concern.

'Patricia's not sleeping in the nursery; she's going to be in with us,' Millie said.

'But don't babies wake three or four times a night?' Jim said.

'Don't worry,' Millie replied. 'I'll sleep between feeds.'

Patricia unlatched and a small rivulet of milk escaped out of the side of her mouth.

Jim's eyes flickered down on to Millie's breast and then back to her face. 'Aren't you going to bottle-feed her?'

'No,' Millie replied, changing Patricia on to the other side.

For a long moment Jim studied his daughter fussing to get settled. 'Maybe it would be better if I slept in the spare room.'

'Perhaps it would,' Millie agreed, turning her attention back to the child in her arms.

The floorboard creaked as Jim shifted his weight. 'Millie, I am sorry about the business at the Westmoreland and I'll make it up to you. I promise.'

Millie raised her head and regarded him coolly. 'I thought Ted was waiting for you to call him back.'

Millie lay awake in the dark gazing down at Patricia in the cradle beside her. It wasn't the old wooden one Jim's mother had brought with her from Essex when she'd finally deigned to visit last week. That had been consigned to the box-room, along with the rickety wood-wormed highchair she'd also given them. This was the pink wicker crib festooned with lace and ribbons that Ruby and Tony had brought in Bodgers for their great-niece.

By the faint glimmer of light streaking under the curtains, Millie guessed it must be close to four o'clock in the morning. And if the warm early-morning breeze was anything to go by it was going to be another lovely day.

Patricia made little sucking noises in her sleep. Millie's breast tingled and she smiled. Silently, Millie got out of bed, collected a fresh nappy from the pile on the dresser, then reached in and picked the sleepy child up. Quickly, before Patricia could wake fully, she changed her and, settling her in the crook of her arm, rested back against the wooden headboard, pulling aside her nightgown and unfastening her nursing brassiere. The baby latched on immediately, her little chin moving up and down rhythmically as she worked for her nourishment.

The let-down reflex tightened almost immediately and a glow of happiness settled over Millie. Somewhere in the forest at the back of the house a woodlark started its trilling song. Cuddling Patricia closer and, enjoying the complete and wonderful feeling of motherhood, Millie closed her eyes. After a few moments Patricia started fidgeting and so Millie shifted her on to the other breast. She ran her fingertips lightly over her daughter's cheek and a little hand reached up and curled on her breast. A lump of pure joy caught in Millie's throat and she pressed her lips to Patricia's forehead.

After a few moments Patricia's head fell back and a dribble of excess milk escaped from the side of her mouth. With an expert hand Millie burped her, laid her back in the cot and lifted gently over her the pink knitted blanket with bunnies on it. Patricia pulled a couple of faces as she drifted back to sleep. Millie repositioned her own clothing and got back into bed. Lying on her side, she tucked her hand under the pillow and gazed down at Patricia, imagining all the wonderful things they would do together.

She was just on the edge of sleep when Jim's key turned in the front door. Millie's eyes snapped open and her heart pounded as she heard the door scrape over the coconut mat.

There was faint click as it closed. Something thumped and the glass in the hall stand rattled. There was a low grumble and some shuffling then the second stair from the top creaked as Jim put his weight on it. The door to the bedroom smashed open and Millie sat bolt upright.

'There you are, my little darling,' he slurred, stumbling into the room.

Millie threw back the covers and got out. Crossing the room, she caught him as he lurched towards the chest of drawers.

'For goodness sake, Jim, you'll wake Patricia,' she said, trying to steer him back to the door.

He belched, sending a combination of brandy and stale perfume wafting over her.

'You're drunk,' she said, trying to pull away.

He caught her and jerked her towards him. His hand grasped the back of her head as his mouth closed over hers. The bitter taste of spirits filled her mouth. Fighting the wave of nausea, Millie forced her hands between their bodies.

'Stop it,' she shouted shoving him away.

Jim staggered back a few steps, then regained his balance. Shaking his head as if to clear it, he lunged at her. She sidestepped but he caught her and they crashed on to the bed.

Pressing her on to the mattress with his body, he leered down at her. 'What about us having a bit of a cuddle?'

Millie's heart thumped uncomfortably in her chest. 'Stop it, Jim, the doctor said we couldn't. Not until—'

He caught her hands, twisted them behind her back and pressed a sloppy drunken kiss on her lips.

'You're hurting me,' said Millie.

Jim chuckled. 'Don't pretend you don't like it.'

He tried to kiss her again, but Millie turned her head to avoid his lips. He shifted his weight to hold her on the bed then as he did, his foot slipped and he kicked the crib. It crashed on the floor. Her daughter's terrified scream cut through Millie as Patricia tumbled out.

Millie prised a hand free and slapped Jim across the face. 'Get off me, you pig.'

Digging her heels into the bed, she heaved him sideways. He fell heavily, crashing against the bedside table before hitting the floor.

Millie scrambled to her feet and hurried over to her daughter. Gathering her from the floor, Millie turned to face Jim, who was sprawled on the floor.

'Get out,' she spat at him as she rocked Patricia.

'What?' he asked, padding his hands around on the wooden floorboards as he tried to figure out how to get up.

Scrambling on to all fours and using the chest of drawers for leverage, Jim rose unsteadily to his feet.

'Now yoooous slook here, Mil–Millie,' he slurred above the cries of his frightened daughter. 'I'm your huss … band—'

'You're a disgrace, that's what you are,' Millie cut in, glaring at him. 'A bloody drunken disgrace. Now get out and leave us alone.'

Hugging Patricia closer, Millie stepped sideways to use the bed as a barrier. Jim's eyes lost focus and he put his hand out to steady himself, sending the china dressing-table set her parents had given her for her twenty-first crashing to the floor. Patricia jumped in Millie's arms and started crying again.

As Millie tried to soothe her distressed daughter, Jim crunched over the broken china towards her for a couple of strides, and then put his hand over his mouth.

'Oh, God,' he groaned, and wheeled around and stumbled out of the room.

Millie crossed the room and slammed the door. Turning the key, she looked down at her daughter. Secure in her mother's arms, Patricia had stopped crying and she was beginning to drift back to sleep. Pressing her lips on to her daughter's forehead, Millie leant back against the door and listened to Jim retching in the bathroom across the hall. Staring at the dawn light creeping under the curtains Millie contemplated glumly the future of Patricia, Jim and herself.

*

Putting the basket of clean washing she'd just brought in from the garden on to the table, Millie went to the sink and filled the kettle.

As she lit the gas ring under it, the sound of heavy footsteps overhead told her that Jim was finally awake. She collected two eggs from the larder and half a loaf from the crock, placing it on the breadboard. Pain stabbed across the back of her eyes. Millie put her hand over her eyes and willed it to go.

It was hardly surprising she had a headache, given that once Jim had finally crashed into the spare room, she'd lain watching the second hand of the clock tick around until Patricia's eight-o'clock feed.

She heard the letter-box snap shut as Jim collected his newspaper before striding into the kitchen. Millie raised her head to look at her husband.

Although he had washed, shaved and Brylcreemed his hair, his putty-coloured complexion and bloodshot eyes showed he hadn't yet recovered from the effects of too much brandy.

He pulled out the chair and sat down. 'Where's the baby?' he asked, shaking open his paper.

'In her pram in the garden,' Millie replied. 'Do you want breakfast?'

Jim paled and shook his head. 'Coffee will do. Have we got any aspirin?' he asked, squinting slightly at the sunlight streaming through the kitchen window.

'Got a headache, have you?' Millie asked, opening the small cupboard over the sink and taking out a medicine bottle.

'Just a bit of one.'

Millie opened the bottle and shook out two white tablets. 'That's what you get when you give yourself alcoholic poisoning,' she said, filling a glass and offering it and the tablets to him.

He took the painkillers. 'I didn't have that much.'

'Well, not if you're comparing it to three nights ago when you passed out in the hall,' she replied, taking back the glass.

'Can't a man have a few drinks?'

'You could barely stand,' said Millie incredulously.

'Don't exaggerate.'

'You were blind drunk, Jim!' Millie said. 'So drunk, in fact, that you tried to force yourself on me.'

'For goodness sake, Millie, you make it sound as if I was some sort of pervert,' he said in an exasperated tone. 'All I was after was a bit of affection. I don't see how you can be angry at me for that.'

Millie looked at him stony-faced. 'I'm angry with you because you were so drunk you kicked Patricia's cot over with her in it.'

'It was an accident and it wouldn't have happened if she was in the nursery where she belongs,' Jim replied. 'And anyway, she's all right, isn't she?'

'Yes, but no thanks to her father, who then staggered off to the bathroom to vomit his guts up.'

Jim held her gaze for a moment and then sprang to his feet.

'If it's too much trouble for you to have a civil conversation over the breakfast table, I might as well go to work,' he said, snatching his jacket from the back of the chair as he marched out to the hall.

Millie followed. 'As you've only been home for supper three nights in the last ten, I don't suppose there's much chance of seeing you tonight, either.'

'Probably not,' he said, flicking a speck of dirt from his sleeve. 'And who can blame me? Since you had the baby—'

'Her name is Patricia,' said Millie in a rigid tone.

'Since you've had *Patricia,* then, there's been no pleasing you. I hire a nurse and you won't let her near the baby, so I had to pay her a whole month's wages for two weeks' work. Then, despite the fact I have to be on top form for the House, I'm forced to make do with the old bed in the spare room because you insist on having the baby in with you despite the fact I've spent a fortune on an up-to-date nursery. And there's washing everywhere,' he indicated the basket on the table. 'And instead of worrying about me and all the pressure I'm under, you spend most of your time fussing over the child. And the pram is making ruts in the lawn.'

'Patricia's only four weeks old and too young to be in the nursery. Babies have a lot of washing. And you volunteered to sleep in the spare room,' Millie replied. 'And I don't fuss over Patricia, I care for her. New babies take a lot of looking after and I haven't got into a routine yet.'

'I know, and who's suffering because of it?' Jim asked sullenly. 'Me, that's who. The breadwinner. And Patricia! My mother is furious that her only grandchild has a Catholic name.'

'Well, she'll have to put up with it, won't she,' Millie shouted, 'because that's what I'm calling my daughter. And what do you care? You're not the slightest bit interested in her, me or anyone else except yourself.'

Jim regarded her coolly. 'Don't think I don't know what this is really about. You're trying to get your own back because of Blackpool. Sorry is not good enough for you, is it? You want to keep turning the knife.'

'This has nothing to do with finding out about your sordid affair,' Millie replied. 'This is about you being the most selfish person I have ever met.'

'Don't lie.' Jim's mouth pulled into an ugly line. 'I told you it didn't mean anything, but you won't let it rest. I had a few drinks with someone and we found ourselves in bed together. It happens, and that's an end to it,' he said, slicing his hand through the air to emphasise his words.

'Betraying someone's trust might mean nothing to you, Jim. But after the promises you made after Oxford, I'm afraid I can't just carry on as be—'

The back of Jim's hand smashed across her face and Millie staggered backwards with the force. Her arm hit the table as she stumbled to keep her balance, but her knees buckled and she crashed to the floor.

Black spots started at the edge of her vision and threatened to crowd in. Millie shook her head to keep them at bay. Forcing her eyes to remain focused, she gazed up at Jim, who loomed over her.

'I've got a head that feels as if it's been cut in two by a blunt meat-cleaver, a burning stomach and a sore throat, added to which the minister is expecting me to brief him in less than an hour as to why the stevedores in the Royal Docks are on strike again, so just shut up if you know what's good for you,' he yelled, furiously jabbing his finger in the direction of her face. 'I've given you a home most women can only dream of, I allow you double what you need for housekeeping each week, you've got a wardrobe stuffed with clothes and shoes, and a jewellery box spilling over. And so you had better get all the business about the hotel out of your head and start treating me with a bit of bloody respect. Do you understand?'

Millie stared up into his furious face for moment, then nodded.

A hint of satisfaction lifted the corners of his mouth. 'Good.'

He jammed his hat on, picked up his briefcase and stormed out of the house, banging the door behind him.

As the front gate squeaked closed, Millie scrambled to her feet and, after checking that Patricia was still asleep, she made her way upstairs to her bedroom. Pulling out her dressing-table chair, she dragged it over to the wardrobe, climbed up and pulled down her large leather suitcase.

Chapter Seventeen

Putting her foot on the back wheel axel to control the pram, Millie backed it out of the taxi door.

'Hold on a moment, love, I'll give you an 'and,' the red-faced taxi driver called as he jumped out of the cab's door.

'I've got it,' Millie said, glancing at Patricia who was laying on her front, fast asleep.

The taxi driver unstrapped her large and small suitcases and vanity case from the baggage platform.

'Are you sure this is close enough?' he asked, glancing at the traffic thundering east and westwards along Commercial Road.

'Yes it's fine, thank you,' Millie replied. 'It's only a short walk through the alley.' She indicated the narrow passage between the Ship and Compass pub and Rosen's garment factory.

The driver set her luggage beside the pram. His gaze flickered under her scarf and on to her bruised cheek and badly swollen eye.

'How much do I owe you?' Millie asked.

He glanced at the metal meter fixed above the parcel rack. 'Three and nine.'

Opening her handbag Millie took two florins from her purse and handed them to the driver. 'Keep the change.'

'Ta, missus,' he said, throwing the coins up and catching them in a hairy-knuckled hand.

He flipped his tweed cap back on, got back in his taxi and then rumbled away towards the City.

Trying to ignore the odd looks she was getting from passers-by, Millie squeezed the smaller suitcase into the pram's shopping rack and then set her large case across the coach-built body and grasping the vanity case in her left hand, Millie pushed the pram through Star Court to her mother's street.

As she emerged from the shadows, Millie's heart sank. She'd

stupidly hoped to make it to her mother's front door without too many people seeing her loaded down with all her worldly goods. But the bright morning had tempted everyone out from their houses.

Mrs Willis, who was on the other side of the road cleaning her window with a sheet of newspaper, paused mid-wipe and studied her. Mrs Greenburg, two doors down from her mother's house, looked up from beating her rugs on the doorstep and gave her a sideward look, while two women outside the corner shop with scarves over their curlers stopped talking and glanced over.

Turning her head slightly in an attempt to hide her injury, Millie pushed her pram along the narrow pavement towards her mother's house.

Stopping outside, she stared at the polished lion's-head knocker for a moment, then hammered it on the stud beneath as she knew Doris was having the morning off to visit the dentist later. It echoed through the hallway for a bit before the latch turned.

Her mother's mouth formed a perfect O as the door opened. 'Millie, what a lovely surprise.'

'Hello, Mum. Can I come in?' Millie said, keeping her face turned from her mother's view.

'Of course you can, my darling,' Doris said. 'Is Jim parking the car?'

'No, I got a taxi here.'

'You should have rung to say you were coming,' said Doris, planting a kiss on Millie's cheek.

'I hadn't decided to until an hour or two ago,' Millie replied, lifting the large suitcase off the top of the pram and putting it and the vanity case by the stairs.

Doris looked at the luggage. 'The church jumble's not for another three weeks and so you didn't need to struggle here with all that stuff and the baby.'

Patricia sneezed and Millie stretched her arms towards her.

Doris leapt forward. 'I'll take her.'

Lifting her granddaughter out, Doris tucked her in the crook of her arm.

'Hello my little precious,' she said, rocking her back and forth.

Parking the pram by the coat rack, Millie followed her mother down the hall taking off her scarf as she walked.

'I've just put the kettle on and I'll ...' Doris caught sight of Millie's face. 'For the love of Mary, what's happened to your face?'

Millie flopped into the fireside chair and closed her eyes. A black cloud whirled around her head a couple of times and then descended like a physical weight, stopping her breath and draining her spirit. With a Herculean effort she shook off the oppressive emotion, and opened her eyes.

'It's Jim.'

An hour, three cups of tea and half-a-dozen handkerchiefs later, Millie finished telling her mother exactly what her life with Jim had been like since Christmas.

Her mother stared incredulously across at her for a few moments and then her face clouded thunderously. 'Did he hit you when you were carrying Patricia?'

Millie shook her head. 'Today was the first time, I promise.'

The harsh lines of her mother's mouth relaxed a little. 'Well I suppose we should be thankful for small mercies. But, for goodness sake, why didn't you tell me, Millie?'

Millie shrugged. 'I thought our differences were just those adjustments you have to make in married life, and then Jim was so full of remorse after the business in Oxford that I gave him a second chance. Since then he's been a perfect husband, and so kind and considerate, and of course the new house is lovely. I'd almost started to believe that it had all been just a stupid mistake, as he said, and that we could put it behind us. But when that woman answered the phone I knew the truth, although I couldn't quite admit it.' Tears welled up and a couple escaped and rolled down her cheeks. 'And now it's come to this.' Patricia gave a little cry and Millie took her daughter back from her mother. 'Mum, I know it's going to put you out a bit, but can I stay here with Patricia, until I work out what I'm going to do next?'

The eight o'clock pips went and the modular tones of the radio announcer began the morning news bulletin with a report of more industrial trouble on the newly nationalised railway.

Millie rested Patricia long-ways on her thighs as she rebuttoned her blouse. The baby hiccupped and then stretched and yawned.

'I don't know why you're still tired, Miss,' Millie said, hooking her fingers in Patricia's hands. 'You've been asleep most of the night, unlike your poor mother.'

She stood up and, holding Patricia over her shoulder, Millie strolled through to the kitchen.

Her mother was standing by the sink washing up their breakfast bowls before she did what every other woman in the area did Saturday morning: join the queue at the butcher's to buy the Sunday joint. She turned her head as Millie walked in.

'All finished?' Doris said, shaking the suds from her hands and wiping them on a tea towel.

'Indeed,' said Millie, smiling at her daughter. 'That should keep her happy for a few hours.'

She went over to the pram, squeezed between the dresser and the mangle and, giving Patricia a quick kiss, Millie laid her on the mattress. She crossed the kitchen, opened the larder and pulled out the OXO tin that served as her mother's first-aid box.

'Headache?' asked her mother.

Millie nodded as she rummaged through for the bottle of aspirin.

'I'm not surprised,' Doris replied, taking an upturned cup from the draining board and turning on the tap. 'I don't suppose you slept much last night.'

'Not much,' Millie replied, taking the drink her mother offered her.

There was a knock on the front door and Millie's heart lurched uncomfortably in her chest.

Doris smiled at Millie. 'It's probably the milkman after his money.'

She took her purse from her handbag and left the kitchen. The front-door latch clicked and the door opened.

There was a pause and then Millie heard Jim's voice.

'Good morning, Mrs Sullivan,' he said from the hallway. 'May I come in?'

Millie's mouth went slack for a moment. Then she gathered

herself, pulling her shoulders back firmly as she waited for her husband to appear.

He was neatly dressed in a charcoal three-piece suit and he held a large bunch of red roses in his hand.

'Hello, Millie,' he said, giving her the repentant yet roguish smile that she'd once thought so appealing.

'Hello Jim.'

He offered her the flowers. 'These are for you.'

Millie didn't move and so Jim looked around in a confused manner before putting them on the kitchen table.

Doris was unable to contain herself any longer and swept into the room, her face a picture of fury.

'You've got a nerve showing your face around here, Jim Smith, after what you've done,' Doris burst out. 'If my Arthur was alive he'd knock you into the middle of next week for the way you've treated my daughter.'

'I'd like to speak to my wife alone, Mrs Sullivan,' Jim said in the same imperious tone his ancestors may well have used to order their peasants around.

'It's all right, Mum,' said Millie.

Her mother's lips pulled tightly together and she picked up her purse and two shopping bags. Giving Jim another scalding look, she marched to the front door, banging it behind her.

Jim extended his hands wide. 'Darling, I'm sorry. I don't know what came over me.'

'I expected you yesterday,' said Millie dully.

'I thought it might be better to give you a day to cool off,' Jim said.

'Oh, really?' Millie raised an eyebrow. 'And there was me thinking it was because you didn't make it home on Tuesday night, and so you only realised that I'd left when you got home yesterday.'

Jim's assured demeanour wavered a little, but then his appeasing expression returned.

'Look, Millie, I know we said some terrible things to each other.'

'No! You said a lot of terrible things,' she said resolutely. 'Just before you hit me.'

'All right, *I* said some terrible things. And it goes without saying that I know I shouldn't have let my temper get the better of me. But I didn't mean any of it.' He sighed and looked truly contrite. 'I'm sorry, if I could take back all of what happened, I would. But you know that I've been under a lot of stress at the ministry and that I'm snowed under with constituency issues. Look, sweetheart, I know you're angry, but you must forgive me.'

'No, I'm not angry, Jim. Not any more,' Millie replied quietly. 'I'm just finished. Finished with your drinking, throwing away good dinners night after night, finished with your bullying, deceitful ways and selfishness. And, most of all, I'm finished listening to your lies.'

Jim shifted his weight on to his other foot. 'I know I made a mistake, but I swear I'll never so much as look at another woman from now on, or lay a finger on you in temper ever again.'

'I don't believe you,' Millie replied.

Jim raked his hair with his fingers. 'For goodness sake, Millie, I'm sorry. What else do you want me to say?'

Millie shrugged. 'Whatever you like, Jim. It doesn't matter in the slightest any longer to me what you think or do.' She went to the lounge door, and held it open. 'Now, if you don't mind.'

Jim took her hand. 'All right, sweetheart, I can see you're still upset. But I promise I'll stop drinking and come home every night without fail and we'll do things as a family and be happy once more.'

Millie shook her head sadly. 'Just go, Jim.'

Jim looked bleakly at her for a moment and then his shoulders sagged. He retraced his steps to the door but as his hand rested on the handle, he turned.

'I mean what I say, Millie,' he said, determinedly. 'And just to prove I've turned over a new leaf, I'll make arrangements with the Whitechapel branch of my bank for you to take as much as you need from my account for you and Patricia. I'll do it today and then you can just go down any time you like and take out as much as you like.' He put his hat on and set it at its usual jaunty angle. His eyes travelled sadly over Millie's stiff stance.

'I know you don't believe me, my darling, but I love you, Millie, and I swear that if you come back to the home I bought to make you happy, I promise I'll be the very best of husbands from now on.'

*

Millie rolled the pram back and forth and watched Patricia's pale eyelids flutter downwards. Although it was not yet ten it was already shaping up to be a hot day and so Millie had parked the pram facing away from the direct sunlight in order that her daughter could have her morning sleep in the fresh air.

The women in the street had already completed the daily ritual of scrubbing an arc of pristine whiteness on the pavement around their front door step. In addition, there were already a number of upper windows flung wide open that had bed linen and blankets hanging out for airing.

The door of Doris's next-door neighbour opened and Olive Morris stepped out. She was dressed as she always was in a nondescript-coloured dress covered by a faded wraparound overall. She was still in her slippers, and her brassy golden hair was wound round a selection of rollers and gathered under a nylon chiffon scarf.

As she spotted Millie the well-padded mother of five threaded the key tied to string back through the letter-box and then waddled over.

Olive smiled indulgently at Patricia. 'Such an angel.'

Millie suppressed a yawn. 'Not at three o'clock in the morning, she's not.'

Olive gazed at the sleeping baby for a few more moments and then she eyed Millie suspiciously. 'So you're still staying with your mother then?'

'Yes,' replied Millie.

'I only ask 'cos, Rene at number eight said she saw your old man turned up last Saturday.'

Millie forced a smile. 'He just popped in on his way to somewhere else.'

Olive studied her for a few more moments, and then crossed her arms and adjusted her sizable bosom. 'Well, I better get going or there'll be nothing on the shelves.'

She turned and hobbled off down the street.

Millie sighed. It had been too much to hope that Jim's sudden appearance and equally swift departure the week before had gone unnoticed. But at least it would give Olive something to talk about while she waited for her greens.

As Millie snapped the pram hood up a car roared around the corner, scattering the pigeons pecking in the gutter.

Millie's heart sank as she recognised Tony's sea-green Hillman Minx with Ruby sitting, po-faced in the passenger seat.

The car stopped alongside her and Tony jumped out. Ruby regarded Millie coolly through the side window as she waited for her husband to open the door.

Shaking the creases from her box-pleat skirt, Ruby swung her legs out and planted her two-inch heels on the pavement in front of Millie.

'Aunt Ruby,' said Millie. 'I thought you and Tony were in Devon.'

'We were.' Ruby tilted her head. 'Come back for me at twelve, Tony. I should have things sorted by then.'

'Right you are.' Tony gave her a quick kiss and sneaked Millie a sympathetic look before jumping back behind the wheel.

Ruby unclipped her handbag, took out her silver case and extracted one of her beloved Mayfair cigarettes.

'Which "things sorted" might you mean?' asked Millie.

Ruby flicked her lighter and, clasping the cigarette between her Coral Burst lips, lit it with a satisfied inhale. 'Is your mother in?'

'Yes, she's got a couple of days off work.'

'I'd prefer not to discuss family business on the street if you don't mind, Amelia,' Ruby said, walking passed Millie.

Ruby put her hand on the door latch, and then paused and looked over at Patricia lying with her little fists clenched either side of her head and a peaceful expression on her face.

A tortured expression flitted across Ruby's face. 'You poor child,' she said meaningfully and then strode inside.

Millie followed her into the front room.

'Ruby,' Doris said with surprise, looking at her sister. 'I thought you were in Devon.'

'We were until I phoned Edie to see how Martha's legs were doing, and clearly it's just as well I did,' Ruby replied, blowing a steam of smoke toward the central lampshade.

'Get what sorted out, aunt Ruby?' repeated Millie.

Ruby's pencilled eyebrows rose. 'You and your husband, of course. And in fact, I'm surprised you're still here. I thought you'd have come to your senses by now and gone home where you belong. Especially with the christening in two weeks.'

'Don't worry, Patricia is still being baptised,' Millie replied. 'But at St George's, and not now at Tollshunt. I spoke to the vicar yesterday.'

Ruby looked horrified. 'What on earth did Jim's mother say?'

'I don't know and I care even less,' Millie replied. 'Anyway, there's nothing for you to sort out because I'm not going back to Jim under any circumstances.'

Ruby laughed. 'Don't be ridiculous. You can't come running home to your mother after a little tiff, Amelia.'

'Tiff!' exclaimed Millie. 'I'd hardly call have my husband's mistress answer the phone when I call to tell him I'm in labour a tiff.'

Ruby looked slightly taken aback.

'And that wasn't the first time he'd been unfaithful either,' continued Millie. 'Do you remember when he went to Oxford that weekend?'

As Doris ferried in a tea tray and a plate of garibaldi biscuits Millie repeated a shorter version of the story she'd told her mother the week before, leaving out none of the salient facts.

'And so there you have it, aunt Ruby,' she concluded. 'I'm not prepared to put up with a husband who rolls home drunk every other night, is having a string of affairs and then, worst of all, lashes out when he loses his temper.'

Ruby nodded thoughtfully and stubbed out the cigarette butt. 'Of course I quite understand but . . .'

'But what?' asked Doris.

Her aunt extracted another cigarette and flicked a flame from her Ronson lighter. 'Well, twice is hardly a string; and he's only hit you the once, and it does sound like tempers were very heated at that moment.'

'Ruby!' Doris cried, looking incredulously at her sister.

'All right,' said Ruby, waving the words aside. 'It's clear that Jim hasn't behaved as he should have.'

'He hit me, aunt Ruby! He didn't push in front of a queue, or do something minor. He hit me, and it hurt.'

'I know, I know,' Ruby blew a long stream of smoke from

the side of her mouth. 'But some women put up with far worse. And the fact that he is a good provider should go a long way.'

Doris rolled her eyes. 'For goodness sake.'

'Well, he is,' retorted Ruby, looking put out at her sister's tone. 'Look at that house and the clothes and jewellery he's given Amelia.'

'And all to salve his conscience,' Millie pointed out.

'Maybe so, but many women have it much worse. And you can't just walk out on your marriage now you've got Patricia to love and provide for,' replied Ruby. 'What are you going to do for money? Because I'm pretty sure Jim won't give you any if you insist on this separation.'

'If I have to, I'll go back to work,' Millie replied.

'And who's going to look after Patricia then, may I ask?' Ruby asked, flicking the ash from her cigarette into the ashtray at her elbow.

'I'll find someone to mind her for me,' Millie replied, already feeling a harsh ache at the mere prospect of leaving her daughter.

Ruby looked horrified. 'You'd leave that precious angel with a stranger!'

'For goodness sake, aunt Ruby,' said Millie, with more than a touch of exasperation. 'I'm not farming her out to the workhouse.'

'And if your poor child's welfare isn't enough to get you to see reason, Amelia, have you even given one moment's thought as to what will people say?'

'They can say what they like,' replied Doris.

Ruby stubbed out her cigarette. 'It's all right for you, Doris, but what about me?'

'What about you?'

'Well these things get about, you know,' replied Ruby. 'It said in the *Daily Mail* only the other day how divorce was double what it was before the war. But I never dreamed the article was talking about *our* family.' Ruby drew a lace handkerchief from her sleeve. 'That my own niece would think about doing such a thing.' Ruby blew her nose noisily. 'When it gets out, I'll be the talk of the whole Conservative Club.'

'Well, when you put it like that, Ruby,' Doris said, sharply. 'I'm sure Millie will be only too glad to be beaten black and blue on a regular basis in order to preserve your reputation with the Ilford Tories.'

Feeling like a spectator at Wimbledon Millie turned from her aunt to her mother.

'I don't think that's what aunt Ruby meant, Mum.'

'What I'm trying to explain, Doris,' added Ruby, 'is that it might not matter around these parts. But amongst the people of quality and good breeding I'm acquainted with now, divorce is regarded as something no respectable Christian would ever be associated with.'

'Are you saying we're not respectable?' asked Doris in a low voice, rising to her feet on one side of Millie.

'Mum!' said Millie.

'Well, as you told me yourself there's a women in the street with six kids with three different fathers and that the woman at number six is living in sin with a Maltese sailor, I'd hardly call the Chapman Estate a stronghold of decent morals,' jeered Ruby from the other side of Millie.

'Now, now, aunt Ruby,' rang Millie's conciliatory tones. 'Perhaps we should all calm down before someone says something they later regret.'

'Don't give me all that rubbish, Ruby,' Doris spat across at her sister. 'You might be able to swank about with your fancy friends now in your fancy clothes, but I remember you when you had hand-me-down shoes on your feet and no knickers around your backside.'

Ruby's face went as red as her name. 'How dare you?!'

'And as for Christian respectability, was that what you and Cyril Mulligan used to get up to in the dark at the back of the graveyard?'

The two sisters glared at each other.

'I know when I'm not wanted,' Ruby said, tightly fiddling with the clasp of her handbag.

'Good. And make sure you shut the door on the way out,' Doris muttered.

She and Ruby exchanged a caustic look, and then Ruby turned to Millie.

'I'll see you at Patricia's christening, Amelia,' she said, planting a light kiss on Millie's cheek. 'And tell your mother if that's her attitude then she's not to come crying to me when she's in trouble again.'

'And tell your aunt,' Doris said from over Millie's shoulder, 'that I'd rather jump off Southend pier with a rock tied around my neck before I ask her for help.'

The two sisters exchanged a lengthy hostile glare. And then with her nose almost horizontal, Ruby stormed out.

'Come on, you've held her for quite long enough,' Annie cajoled, stretching out her arms to take Patricia from Sally.

Millie smiled as her sleeping daughter was passed from one nurse to another. She and Patricia were in the nurses' lounge in Munroe House for afternoon tea. They had been there for forty minutes already and, as Patricia still had a dozen young women waiting to cuddle her, it would be at least another half an hour before she could tuck her in her pram and walk home. But Millie didn't mind; it was good to see the girls again.

'And she's just six weeks,' said Annie, rocking Patricia back and forth in her arms while Phyllis chucked her under the chin.

'Seven on Thursday,' Millie replied.

Annie had rung Millie at Wanstead the day after she'd left and had spoken with a terse Jim, who had explained that Millie was staying with her mother while he was working away. But when Annie popped by the next day, Millie had confided the whole sorry tale.

Of course, everyone would know the truth sooner or later, but until she worked out all the details with Jim, Millie had decided to keep up a general pretence for those outside her inner circle.

'Are you all set for the christening on Sunday?' Eva's question brought Millie back to the here and now, and she watched Eva tucking her finger inside the curve of Patricia's small fingers.

'Yes, except my mum's still not talking to my aunt Ruby,' Millie replied.

'Why not?' asked Eva.

'Oh, some nonsense or another, you know what families are like,' Millie replied vaguely, watching her daughter gaze up at the sea of faces surrounding her. 'But it's going to be a bit of a strain having to relay messages between them.'

'I'm surprised she's still coming then,' said Annie, pulling a happy face at Patricia.

'The only way my aunt Ruby wouldn't be there is if she was behind bars,' said Millie. 'I doubt she's missed a family occasion since 1921.'

The lounge door opened and Miss Dutton entered. The nurses put down their cups and stood up.

'Good afternoon, Miss Dutton,' they chorused.

She acknowledged their greeting with the slightest of smiles. Her eyes flickered over Millie.

'Good afternoon, Miss Dutton,' Millie said, taking Patricia back from her friend. 'I hope you don't mind me popping in for afternoon tea.'

'Of course not.' An uncharacteristic welcoming smile spread across the superintendent's narrow face. 'You look a little tired, Mrs Smith.'

Millie shrugged. 'Well, you know babies.'

Miss Dutton looked concerned. 'I've heard how difficult it can be until the little one gets into a proper night routine.'

Millie smiled non-commitedly.

In truth Patricia had now started to go straight through from her last feed until six in the morning, and so it was thoughts of their uncertain future that were to blame for driving sleep from Millie's mind rather than her daughter's demands.

'And are you still at your mother's?' asked Miss Dutton, digging further into Millie's troubled thoughts.

'Yes, I am.'

Miss Dutton looked perplexed. 'You seem to have been there a very long time. You must be missing your lovely house in Wanstead by now?'

'Of course,' Millie replied as she made a play of straightening Patricia bonnet. 'But with Jim away so much on government business it's easier for me at my mother's.'

'I'm sure it is,' said Miss Dutton.

'I bet you're looking forward to getting him back this weekend for the christening, Millie,' chipped in Eva, as the other nurses admiring Patricia muttered their agreement.

'Yes, I am,' replied Millie woodenly.

Miss Dutton's ice-blue eyes ran over Millie for a second, and then she spoke again. 'You know it's funny, Mrs Smith, but I was only talking about you yesterday.'

'Really?' said Millie.

'Yes, at the health board's weekly meeting,' said Miss Dutton. 'Miss Webb, the superintendent at the Old Ford clinic happened to have a copy of this week's *Leyton and Walthamstow Bugler* and it had a feature on Hoe Street's recent parade.'

Millie shifted Patricia in her arms. 'I didn't know you took an interested in local events, Miss Dutton.'

'It took up the whole of the centre page of the paper,' continued Miss Dutton pleasantly. 'With photos of floats decked out in crepe paper and children dressed as flowers.'

'How nice.'

'Yes, absolutely.' Miss Dutton's wide smile was causing the area between Millie's shoulder-blades to prickle. 'But you can imagine my surprise when there, smack bang in the centre of the whole piece, was a picture of your husband opening the event.'

Somehow Millie managed to maintain a calm expression. 'Jim's often called on to open local events.'

'I'm sure he is,' said Miss Dutton smoothly. 'But is having his arms around the local beauty queen part of his job, too?'

Millie's cheeks had high spots of colour as the pain of Jim's various betrayals flared again.

A smug smile hovered on Miss Dutton's lips for a few seconds, before she cast a bossy gaze over the assembled nurses. Quickly, they threw back the last mouthfuls of the tea and gathered themselves together in readiness to resume their duties.

Miss Dutton gave Millie a final smirk. 'Lovely to see you again, Mrs Smith, and please do remember to give my regards to your husband when you eventually do see him.'

Closing Munroe House's front door behind her, Millie pulled up the pram's canopy and then turned in the direction of Watney Street. She'd picked up her green ration book for pregnant and nursing mothers, along with Doris's ordinary buff one, on her way out earlier, and was hoping to get a bit of liver and a couple of onions for their tea, along with anything else that might be available, such as broken biscuits, as these were sold off-ration because they were damaged.

As there was a queue for the cold-meat counter that stretched around to the outside of Sainsbury's, Millie headed for Mullins, the butcher opposite. She'd delivered Mr Mullins' third child the year before and now he always cut her a little bit extra when paring her meat.

A new display of frilly underslips in Shelston's window caught her eye, but as Millie stopped to admire them, someone called her name.

'Sister Smith!'

Millie turned and saw Dorothy Joliffe with her hand resting lightly on the handle of a dove-grey pram. She was dressed in a loose-fitting summer frock, but although her hair was neatly permed and she wore lipstick, her completion was pale and there were dark blots under her eyes.

'Nurse Scott told me that you'd had your baby,' Dorothy said, peeking into the pram. 'A little girl, isn't it?'

'Yes. I called her Patricia.' Millie reached in and moved the cot sheet a little away from her daughter's face.

'She got your colouring,' Dorothy said.

'And my temper,' laughed Millie, gazing tenderly at her sleeping baby. 'I can't believe how quickly she's growing. She's almost out of the first-size clothes already.'

'Well, they'll do for the next one,' Dorothy replied. 'How's your husband coping with a baby in the house?'

'Oh, you know.' Millie gave a casual shrug. 'How's Mr Joliffe?'

'As busy as ever,' Dorothy replied. 'There seems to be a new directive from the Ministry of Education every day about one thing or another.'

'Well, they must be great friends with the Ministry of Health, because by all accounts the same thing's happening day in and day out at Munroe House,' said Millie. 'In fact, I've just taken Patricia there for tea so that the girls could see her.'

'I bet they made a fuss of you, young lady,' Dorothy said, smiling down at Patricia.

Millie laughed. 'They certainly did. How's your William?'

Dorothy's face clouded. 'Better now the warmer weather has come, but he was in hospital again two weeks ago with another bout of bronchitis.'

'I'm sorry to hear that.'

Millie looked down at William, who was swaddled up in a powder-blue blanket with a floppy-eared bunny beside him. Although William fidgeted with interest at a new face, he didn't attempt to lift his head.

'But they are marvellous on the children's ward.' Dorothy gave a plucky little smile. 'And the new matron allows parents to visit Monday, Thursday and Sunday.'

Millie looked surprised. 'That's a bit of a change. When I was a student it was once a week, and no exceptions.'

'It's the third time William's been in since Easter,' continued Dorothy. 'But thank goodness for the new health service. They are so efficient. We carried William into Casualty at two-thirty and by two-forty-five he was on the ward in an oxygen tent with doctors around him.'

Millie wasn't surprised. One look at William's medical notes would have told even the most junior doctor that he'd be dead by three if they hadn't.

'It's his chest,' Dorothy said with a sigh. 'Mr Lamming, the consultant, a lovely man with six children of his own, said William has a weakness because he was born early.'

'It's a common problem with premature babies,' Millie replied.

'He told us that, and he advised me to keep William warm and well-fed and to bring him straight into Casualty at the first hint of wheeziness, but that he'd grow out of it by the time he went to school.' Dorothy gazed down adoringly at her son. 'And then you'll be kicking a ball around with your dad in the park on Saturday morning like the rest of them.'

A lump formed in Millie's throat. 'I really ought to get to Sainsbury's before everything's gone.'

Dorothy nodded. 'Me too. William's due his afternoon feed. It's such a bother and he hasn't got the hang of solids yet.' She smiled apologetically. 'Always seems to go down the wrong hole. It's been lovely to see you and Patricia, Sister Smith. I hope to see you again.'

'Nice to see you too,' Millie replied.

Dorothy gave her another smile and continued on her way. Millie stared after her.

It was a commonly held belief amongst doctors that an

incurable diagnosis could cause a patient to give up hope, and so it was usual to keep such news from them and their relatives, as it was deemed to be the kindest course of action. But, as Millie watched Dorothy Joliffe push her pram down the market, Millie concluded that withholding the truth about the grim extent of their son's condition from Derrick and Dorothy Joliffe was, in fact, nothing short of cruel.

Chapter Eighteen

The photographer, a chubby young man with thinning hair and shiny demob suit, rolled the film ready for the next picture.

'Right, now hold our little celebrity nice and still,' he called as he peered through his viewfinder. 'And on the count of three, all please say cheese.'

Millie straightened Patricia's lawn-cotton christening robe with one hand and then held her a little higher so her face was in full shot.

They were in the memorial gardens at the side of the bombed-out shell of the Hawksmoore church of St George's on a bright August morning. Behind the photographer the congregation were still leaving the wooden hut sitting snugly inside the grand exterior walls that was serving as the church until funds were raised for the restoration work.

To Millie's right was her mother dressed in a dog-toothed check suit with a smart velvet collar and new felt hat, while to her left stood aunt Ruby, resplendent in a wine-red dress and jacket, and a pork-pie hat trimmed with such a long pheasant tail feather that it had almost taken the vicar's eye out when she took her place at the font.

So far her mother and aunt had contented themselves with chilly glares at each other. Millie prayed it would stay that way, especially as just to the left of the photographer stood Jim's mother, who was equally frosty.

Lady Tollshunt had pushed the boat out too though as to what she was wearing and looked resplendent in a stylish apricot day dress, a hat that would have kept her shoulders dry if it had been raining, and a long loop of pearls. She blended into the East London congregation like a poppy in a cinder tray.

Trying though her mother-in-law's presence was to Millie, it was nowhere near as disconcerting as having Jim there, pretending to be the attentive husband and father. He'd arrived just as the service was about to start which saved Millie from having to speak to him at all initially, and now they were surrounded by four other christening parties and so there was too much going on for anyone to notice they'd not exchanged more than a handful of words.

Millie's eyes strayed beyond Lady Tollshunt and the photographer to where her husband stood relaxed and smiling behind the main family party.

Elegant as ever, he wore a linen suit in oatmeal hues that were perfectly complemented by a chocolate-brown Fedora and tan brogues. Predictably, he was oozing charm as he chatted to a couple of pretty young women who were kitted out like seaside rock in pastel striped dresses. Millie could only wonder, yet again, how it was that she had ever been so completely taken in by him.

'One two three,' shouted the photographer.

'Cheese!' Millie's nearest and dearest called back.

'Good,' yelled back the photographer. 'Now if we could just have mum and dad, with the little lady of the day.'

Millie's heart thumped uncomfortably. Someone must have told Jim that he was required, as he touched his hat at the giggling girls and hurried over to his wife.

'Sorry darling,' he said, smiling cordially at her.

Millie regarded him dispassionately. 'Don't mention it. I'm just sorry to have dragged you away.'

Jim shot her a sharp look, and then laughed a mite too loud. 'I suppose it's time for me do my bit for the old family album,' he joked to those within earshot.

He stepped in alongside Millie and she had to try hard not to inch away.

'That's nice,' said the photographer as he lined up the shot. 'Now if you could just move a little closer.'

Jim's arm slipped around her waist. Millie shifted Patricia on to her other side so she was between them, and Jim loosened his hold.

'Big grins, please,' said the photographer, hunching down behind the camera.

He snapped the shutter and turned the side handle. 'Perhaps dad could hold his little princess for this one?'

Millie offered Jim his daughter, with a whisper, 'I think she might need changing, so best mind your suit.'

Alarm flashed across Jim's face and quickly he turned to the photographer. 'Thank you. I think perhaps we have enough for now.'

While the photographer explained to Jim when the proofs would be ready to collect Millie carried Patricia across to where she'd parked the pram by the hedge. The verger had let Millie use the vestry to feed her daughter before the service but now, after being passed from one doting relative to another for what must have seemed to her like a very long time, Patricia was starting to get grizzly.

Millie tucked her in, then released the brake to rock her back and forth gently. Unfortunately, Patricia was now red-faced with indignation at having her morning routine disrupted and so she continued to scream.

'Is she always so colicky?' asked a voice that would have made a BBC announcer sound common.

Millie turned to face her mother-in-law. 'No, Lady Tollshunt. She's just unhappy at missing her morning nap.'

Lady Tollshunt's gaze flickered testily over her granddaughter, and then back to Millie.

'You know you'll have to come back sooner or later, don't you?' said Lady Tollshunt.

'Will I?'

'Of course,' Jim's mother snorted. 'And when you do come to your senses, I'd advise you in future to ignore any little distraction my son might have from time to time.'

'You think I should turn a blind eye to Jim's philandering?' said Millie.

'Of course,' replied her mother-in-law, looking surprised at the question. 'It's ever been the way with men like James.'

'You mean men like James, who can get their housemaids in trouble and then marry them off to their tenants,' Millie replied.

Lady Tollshunt flicked an imaginary speak of fluff off her sleeve. 'I assure you that Beth Scarrop, Tillie Reacher and that frightful gardener's daughter from Trinity, all have nothing to complain about in the way they or their babies were cared for.'

Millie regarded her mother-in-law coolly. 'Bought off, you mean, so Jim could avoid his responsibilities.'

Lady Tollshunt gave a harsh laugh. 'His responsibilities are to his family, and obviously not a handful of silly girls he's sown his wild oats with.'

'And what him about hitting me?' asked Millie angrily. 'Should I turn a blind eye to that too?'

Lady Tollshunt's cool, assured expression faltered just a little. 'That was unfortunate, I grant. But you have now his sworn word as a gentleman that it will never happen again.'

'That's what he said when he was caught with his pants down in Oxford; and three months later he was up to his old tricks in Blackpool,' Millie replied. 'Frankly, I can't believe anything he says any more.'

Lady Tollshunt's neck went from pink to purple and back to pink again in a flash, as a furious expression contorted her powdered face.

'You ungrateful little chit. He's given you far more than a girl like you could ever hope for,' she hissed.

'Here you are, mother,' Jim's voice halted their conversation.

Millie and Lady Tollshunt glanced around, each looking slightly guilty.

'Oh, Jim,' fluttered Lady Tollshunt, the ostrich plumes around her hat swaying like a feathery hula skirt around her brow. 'I was just explaining to your wife how she should—'

'I know you're keen to get back, mother dear,' Jim said, pleasantly, 'and so I had Peters bring the car to the front of the church.'

'Oh, yes, thank you,' his mother replied, as she busied herself adjusting the fox-fur pelt draped around her shoulders. 'That is very considerate of you, as always.'

James kissed his mother briefly on the cheek and then stepped aside to let her pass.

Lady Tollshunt sent Millie a final withering look before marching across the churchyard to her waiting car.

Jim turned to Millie. 'She's right, you know. You'll have to come back eventually.'

'You think so?'

'Of course.'

'Is that why you've still not sent instructions to your bank?'

Jim shrugged apologetically. 'It slipped my mind.'

'That's convenient.'

'Look Millie, this it's getting beyond a joke,' he said, cajolingly. 'I've had no end of flak from the chief whip, not to mention that mealy-mouthed bunch of blue-stockings on the women's sub-committee. You need to understand, Millie, that if word gets out in the House that you've walked out, in all likelihood it will ruin my chances of getting the junior post in the Ministry of Works at the next reshuffle.'

Millie regarded him impassively. 'It's a shame you neglected to think about that when you invited that woman back to your hotel room.'

'For God's sake, Millie,' Jim said, exasperatedly. 'Be sensible, damn it. Didn't you hear what my mother said about occasional lapses?'

'And very informative she was, too,' Millie replied. 'I thought Beth Scarrop's boy was your only illegitimate child. But now I now know you have at least two others.'

Jim blanched.

'So I'm afraid, Jim,' Millie continued, 'that you can talk at me until you're blue in the face, but hell will freeze over before I'm coming back.'

'Look here, Millie. I've been more than patient with you, but now enough is enough.' A spiteful expression twisted Jim's mouth. 'You've got just one more week to think through where you're best interests lie. But – and you mark me well – if you don't come home by next Saturday, you'll regret it.'

Millie kicked off the pram breaks. 'I don't think so. But I do expect you to put the financial arrangement in place that you promised faithfully you'd do six weeks ago,' she said, strolling past him. 'And don't worry. I'll make your excuses as to why you couldn't come back to Mum's for tea.'

Millie took the pink-topped safety pin from her mouth, stuck it through the thick nappy and then smoothed down the frills of Patricia's beautiful christening dress.

'There you are, darling,' said Millie smiling at her daughter. 'All done and dusted.'

Patricia, who was lying on a towel on the edge of her mother's bed, looked up with a dreamy look in her eyes. Millie wasn't surprised.

Patricia had been well past her feed when they arrived back, and so leaving her mother, Connie and Annie to sort out a cup of tea for everyone, Millie had dashed upstairs.

Downstairs her family and half of Munroe House, as well as Doris's immediate neighbours, were assembled in her mother's front room. Well, in truth not so much assembled as packed like sardines into the compact space.

Checking in the dressing-table mirror that she'd buttoned her blouse properly, Millie scooped Patricia up from the candlewick counterpane and carried her downstairs.

She and Doris had moved all the furniture back against the wall to make as much space as possible in the middle, and they had extended the dining-room table in front of the unlit fire to accommodate the buffet, which had a square pink-and-white iced christening cake at its centre.

The men of the family had already taken their pints out into the street, and from the window they could be seen laughing and joking. Doris was putting the last few paper serviettes between the assortments of tea plates at the far end of the table while Ruby, legs crossed and cigarette balanced in nail-polished fingers, perched on the chair beside her looking pointedly in the opposite direction.

'Mind your backs,' called Connie, holding a plate of sandwiches aloft, with Annie bringing up the rear carrying a platter of cold meat.

'Oh, there's that darling little angel,' called great aunt Martha, as she saw Millie holding Patricia. 'Can I have a cuddle?'

'Of course,' said Millie, handing Patricia to her great aunt. 'She's just been fed and so you'd be best to hold her a little upright.'

Martha tucked the dozing baby into the crook of her arm. 'Isn't she the prettiest baby?' she said to her sister Edie sitting next to her on the sofa.

'And so good,' said Edie. 'It must be nice for your mum to have you both here, especially as babies change so quickly at this age.'

'She loves it, and it's so helpful having her around,' said Millie.

Martha gave her a querying look. 'I'm surprised your husband doesn't mind you being away from home?'

Although the truth would be out very soon Millie had decided to keep up the pretence that she was just staying with her mother until after the christening, although she knew that sooner or later she'd have to write a long letter of explanation to the rest of her family.

Millie forced a pleasant expression on to her face. 'He's away so much for work it's the best for all of us. And that's why he's not come back with everyone as he had to catch a train.'

Her aunts looked astounded.

'Not come back to the house?'

'It couldn't be helped,' explained Millie, with a regretful shrug. 'It has just worked out that way.'

'Millie!'

Millie looked up and was relieved to see her mother beckoning her over. 'I'd better help Mum. Are you all right to hold her?'

'Of course,' Martha replied, still looking oddly at Millie.

'And can I get you anything while I'm there?' she asked her elderly aunts.

Edie shook her head. 'But we could do with a top-up.' She held up an empty sherry glass.

Millie joined her mother.

'I think that's everything,' said Doris, scanning anxiously the array of plates and dishes.

Millie cast her eyes over the triangular fish paste and egg-and-cress sandwiches, liver sausage and tinned salmon bridge rolls, and the cubes of cheddar cheese that were jostling for space beside scotch eggs, pickled herrings, and a large golden-crusted pork pie. There was even an enormous salmon complete with head and tail sitting in the centre of the table.

'It looks right grand, as Little Nan used to say.' Millie slipped her arm around her mother's shoulder. 'Thanks Mum.'

Ruby swung around. 'Do you want me to cut the salmon before you start, Millie, so everyone gets a bit?'

'That's a good idea,' Millie replied. 'And thank you for bringing it. Goodness knows where you got one that size.'

'Not for coupons that's for sure,' muttered Doris.

Ruby glared at her. 'Millie, could you tell your mother please that a friend of Tony's caught it in Scotland?'

'Tell your aunt to pull the other one as it's got bells on,' replied Doris, matching her sister's hostile look.

The two sisters glowered at each other.

'Perhaps I ought to say a few words before people start tucking in?' said Millie.

'I'll get the knife to cut the "legally acquired" salmon,' said Ruby.

'I don't know why you don't save on the washing up and use your tongue instead,' replied Doris.

Ruby gave Doris a crushing look before sweeping off towards the kitchen.

'Honestly, Mum! I really wish you and Ruby would just make up. I've already got a headache from having to deal with Jim and his mother, and you two sniping at each other is just making it worse.'

'Not until she apologises,' Doris replied. 'And if that fish didn't fall off the back of a lorry then I'm a Chinaman. And someone should tell her that that colour lipstick is too young for her.'

Millie rolled her eyes. She then clapped her hands. 'I just want to say a few words before I open the food.'

The muttering stopped and the men stepped into the house.

'Do you want me to fetch Jim from outside, Millie?' asked May, Millie's cousin on her father's side.

Millie forced a nonchalant smile. 'Thanks May, but he's had to go.'

'Go?'

'He's got a conference,' explained Doris.

May look puzzled. 'On a Sunday?'

'He's driving there ready for tomorrow,' Doris added.

'I thought he was catching a train?' said Martha from the sofa.

A flush started around Doris's throat. 'I meant he had to catch a train.'

'Honestly, Doris, you'd forget your head if it wasn't screwed on,' laughed Ruby. She cast her eyes around dramatically, and there were a couple of snickers.

Doris's nostrils flared and she looked as if she was about to reply when Connie butted in.

'He told us outside the church how upset he was that he had to rush off, didn't he Annie?' she said.

'Yes. Yes, he did. When we came out after,' agreed Annie, trying to look as if Jim had said any such thing.

Millie shot her friends a grateful look.

People in the room exchanged mystified glances and May frowned. 'But even so I would have thought he'd want to be here.'

'Millie's husband is a Member of Parliament, May, and not a clerk at the town hall,' interrupted Ruby, flicking ash from her cigarette with a nail-polished finger.

Millie's cousin, whose husband was a clerk at the town hall, glared at Ruby but then she pressed her lips together and said nothing more.

Millie took a deep breath.

'Firstly, I want to thank you all for coming today, and I say this also on Patricia's behalf,' said Millie. 'And I want to thank you too for the many wonderful presents she's received.'

There was a collective 'ah' as everyone gazed towards the baby fast asleep in her great-aunt's arms.

'And thank you to my aunts Martha and Edie for the veritable mountain of sandwiches. And to Gwen,' Millie smiled across at her cousin who was trying to keep her two boys from kicking each other's shins. 'for the giant sherry trifle she balanced somehow on her knee all the way from Billericay.'

A murmur of appreciation went around the room.

'And my cousin Bob, who can't be with us today, for sending around a crate of Double Diamond and Mackeson from the Britannia,' the men in the doorway cheered and raised their glasses, 'uncle Billy for the bottle of port, and aunt Ruby for the salmon.'

Ruby smiled benevolently as everyone admired the silver and pink fish sitting on a bed of cucumber.

'And lastly,' Millie turned to her other side, 'to my dear mother for helping me put the spread together. Now, please help yourselves.'

The party moved forward, and after she had replenished her aunts' sherries, Millie relieved them of Patricia.

Patricia was now fast asleep and Millie carried her through the kitchen into the back yard and laid her into her pram, pulling the blankets over her. Patricia pulled a face and started to stir. Millie took hold of the handles and rocked her back and forth.

Doris came out from the house holding a plate of food and joined Millie beside the pram.

'She's so adorable,' said Doris, smiling down at her granddaughter.

Someone else came out of the house and Millie turned and saw Ruby stepping out of the back door. She exchanged a polar look with her sister, and then came over and stood on the other side of the pram.

'I'm pleased you and Tony came, aunt Ruby,' Millie said softly, rocking Patricia back and forth.

Ruby smiled down at the sleeping infant. 'I wouldn't miss my grand-niece's christening for the world.' Her glacial expression returned as she looked up at Doris. 'Even if *some* people wish I wasn't here.'

Doris matched her sister's icy stare. 'I suppose your posh friends think you're taking tea at the Palace.'

A red splash appeared on Ruby's powdered cheeks. 'Just because some of us want to move up in the world doesn't mean—'

'That my Millie has to put up with a drunken husband who beats her,' Doris replied.

Ruby bristled. 'You're twisting my words, Doris.'

'Perhaps I'll see how Annie and Connie are getting on with the teas,' said Millie, her headache flaring again.

'You've been the same since you were a kid, Ruby,' snapped Doris. 'Self, self, self.'

Ruby's eyes opened wide. 'Me! What about the time you made our poor mum ...'

Millie heaved a sigh and leaving her mother and aunt to bicker over the sleeping Patricia, she turned and made her way inside to search for the aspirin.

Millie placed the still-warm and smoothed sheet on top of the other four sitting on the kitchen table and took the next one from the pile stacked in the wicker basket. She flicked it out then, folding it in half, laid it over the ironing board.

Wiping the sweat off her forehead, she dipped her fingers in the jug of water and flicked them along length of the sheet before grasping the iron from the cooker plate and pressing it on. There was a faint hiss and a jet of steam escaped from the side as Millie ran it over the white cotton.

Usually the washing wouldn't have been ready to iron on a Monday but with the temperature soaring into the 70s by mid-morning the smalls that she'd hung on the line first thing were now bone dry.

Millie glanced at the mid-morning post that had been sitting on the front-door mat when she returned from the market. There were the usual collection of bills and family letters, most telling her what a lovely time that had been had by all at Patricia's christening the week before. Of course none of them were from Jim. But then why was she surprised? Hadn't she learnt by now that all his promises were just empty words? He was a politician, after all.

The unpaid electricity bill sticking out from behind the clock on the mantelshelf caught her eye. As much as she was loath to, if she didn't hear something from him by next week Millie knew she would have to eat her words and contact him. It was inescapable that her mother's wages wouldn't stretch to supporting them all for very much longer.

Millie put the iron close to her face to test the heat but just as she was about to apply it to her underslip there was a loud knock at the door.

Returning the iron to the stove, Millie hurried down the hall and opened the door.

On the white doorstep stood a smartly dressed man wearing a tailored jacket, pin-striped trousers and a bowler. Behind him two burly-looking men wearing tan-coloured knee-length overalls stood beside a dark green van with an elaborate crest painted in gold on the side.

'Mrs Millie Smith?' he asked.

'Yes.'

'Mr Willis,' he said, raising his hat. 'I represent D'Pole, Chivvers, Chivvers and Marchant solicitors. I'm here on the instructions of your husband, Mr James Smith, to return certain items to you.'

He signalled over his shoulder. The two men went to the back of the van and opened the doors. Jumping into action, they started heaving tea chests out of the van.

Doors all along the street started opening.

Jim's brief appearance at the christening and her continued presence at her mother's house had alerted the neighbourhood to the fact that it was worth keeping an eye out for any further goings-on at the Sullivans', and a liveried van rolling up would certainly fall into that category.

'Where shall we put them?' asked the first delivery man as he stopped in front of doorstep.

'Er, in the lounge to the right,' Millie said, opening the door wider.

He squeezed past her.

'Don't wake the baby,' Millie begged, as his colleague followed him in.

The delivery men repeated the process twice more under the gaze of various neighbours now gathered around, before they closed the van doors and climbed back into the front cab.

'Your husband also asked that I deliver you this.'

Mr Willis handed Millie a stuffed manila envelope before, raising his hat again, he climbed into the van and it rolled away, leaving the smell of diesel in its wake.

Sensing the morning's drama had concluded, the crowd opposite started to go about their business.

Millie closed the door and went into her mother's lounge, where six bulky tea chests were now sitting. She tore open the paper covering on the nearest chest and looked in to find some of her clothes and shoes. She ripped the cover to the second chest, and spotted the teapot her cousin May had bought them as a wedding present and the set of glass dessert dishes aunt Martha had given them amongst the sawdust, along with a couple of Miss Moncrieff's unframed sketches Millie had stored on top of the wardrobe.

Millie stared at these possessions for a moment and then turned over the envelope, slipping her finger underneath the flap to open it.

There were four pages of thick, expensively watermarked paper with an embossed address on the top. She scanned down the first page quickly. It went over the events leading up to and since she'd left, but when she turned it over and read the second page, Millie's heart lurched. As she scanned down the bold black words for the second time, the floor rose up to meet her and her knees began to fold. Collapsing on to the sofa, with dizziness swirling around her head, she closed her eyes and lay back until the queasiness passed, and she was able to stand up.

Kicking off her slippers, Millie slipped her feet inside her shoes and shoved the solicitor's letter into her handbag on the sideboard and hooked the bag over her arm, kicked the brakes off the pram and manoeuvred it out from behind the sofa and into the hall and out through the front door.

Chapter Nineteen

After a forty-minute train journey and with her temper still at boiling point, Millie turned the corner of Church Street into Leytonstone High Street. With the afternoon sun full on her back Millie stormed along the street towards the Labour Party offices at the far end of the road. Without pausing she shoved open the door and stormed in.

Miss Frances, the soberly dressed receptionist looked over her glasses in alarm as she saw Millie. 'Mrs Smith, how—'

'Is he in?' Millie asked as she headed for Jim's office at the back of the reception area.

Miss Francis sprang to her feet. 'Yes, but he's very busy.'

'Good,' said Millie, without breaking her stride.

The receptionist attempted to fling herself across the door like a tweed-clad starfish but Millie got there first.

As she burst through into Jim's office, he was reading the paper with his feet up on the desk, and he looked up with a startled expression.

He swung he legs down. 'Millie, I wasn't expecting you.'

'You despicable bastard,' she yelled, rattling the glass as she slammed the door behind her. 'How dare you say that you're not sure you're Patricia's father?'

She threw the solicitor's letter on the table.

Jim stood up and resting his hands flat, he faced her across the table. 'I warned you, Millie, I wouldn't just stand idly by and let you ruin my political career.'

Millie grabbed the letter up and shook it in his face. 'But how can you do this to your own child!'

'I've only got your word on that,' Jim replied, grimly. 'And by the way you've been behaving since she was born I'm beginning to wonder. And I'm sure any fair-minded judge would agree, especially if details of your past liaisons were brought to the court's attention.'

'My past!' screamed Millie. 'That's rich coming from someone with the morals of a tom-cat.'

'And of course the fact you didn't mention you were intimate with that policeman chap until after we were married can only attest to your personal morals.'

'That's a lie, and you know it, Jim Smith,' cried Millie, forcing away the furious tears that were gathering. 'I told you all about Alex when you proposed.'

He smirked. 'I'm sorry but I can't recall any such conversation.'

The door burst open as Ted hurried in. 'What's all this screaming and shouting? Oh it's you, Millie.'

'Did you know about this?' Millie asked, shaking the solicitor's letter at him.

Ted's eyes shifted from her face. 'Now, now, ducks, calm down as we don't want everyone to hear, do we?'

'Hear what?' yelled Millie. 'Hear that the honourable James Percival Woodville Smith, Member of Parliament for Leytonstone and Wanstead, is a wicked liar?'

'Look, I know you're upset, Millie,' said Ted, taking his handkerchief from his top pocket and mopping his forehead. 'But it's over now, and she's gone.'

Millie gave Jim's right-hand man a puzzled look.

Jim came out from behind the desk. 'It's all right, Ted. I can handle this.'

'Who?' asked Millie.

'Daphne. Daphne Montgomery,' replied Ted hastily. 'The blonde intern who helped with Jim's campaign.'

Jim glared at him. 'I *said* I can handle this.'

'The girl in the red beret?' asked Millie innocently.

'Yes,' Ted said. 'I blame myself for not realising what she was about,' he continued, oblivious of Jim furious expression, 'but I should have known she'd be trouble, what with those legs. You can't really blame a man when it's offered on a plate, can one? Anyway, Jim's dead sorry, aren't you?'

Jim didn't reply.

Millie stared at her husband. Suddenly the penny dropped. What a fool she'd been!

She should have realised all along that Jim's real reason for marrying her wasn't because he loved her, but because he needed her working-class background to show himself to be a man of the people.

He'd used her just as surely as he had used Edwina, Beth and Tilly – and probably countless other women before and since – purely for his own selfish ends.

All Jim was ever interested in was Jim.

'Thank you, Ted, for telling me about Daphne and, believe me, the only thing that dear old Jim is ever sorry about, is being found out.' Millie tucked the letter back in its envelope and returned it to her handbag. 'But I'm sorry, too, Jim. Sorry that I ever set eyes on you.'

She grasped the pram handle and headed for the door. Ted sprang forward and opened it for her. Millie paused and looked at her husband. 'And don't worry. You won't hear from me again because Patricia is better off not having a father at all than having one like you. And if I never set eyes on you again, believe me when I say that it will still be too soon.'

As Doris's eyes made their way down the page a crimson flush appeared at her throat. She turned to the next sheet and the flush spread upwards until it reached her cheeks.

'I can't believe it,' Doris said, looking incredulously across at Millie.

'I know, I had to read it twice myself,' Millie replied.

Her mother's hands flopped on her lap. 'But didn't he promise you could have as much money as you needed for Patricia?'

'He also promised never to be unfaithful again, and to be a good husband,' replied Millie. 'So I shouldn't be surprised now that he intends to cut off all funds.'

Doris frowned. 'But what I can't understand is why he says he's not sure if he's Patricia's father.'

'To cover himself if I take him to court,' Millie said.

'I don't understand.'

'You might have noticed that he mentions three times in that letter that I had had an intimate relationship with another man prior to our marriage.'

Doris looked pensive. 'I suppose he means Alex?'

'Yes,' Millie said wearily. 'I slept with Alex. I know we should have waited, but we were engaged to be married after all, and we were so in love. But if I ever got Jim to court, of course his barrister would have me admit on oath how far my relationship with Alex went.'

'But how does Jim know about him?'

'I thought the best way to start married life was to be completely honest with Jim about Alex. And it's not as if Jim hadn't had plenty of pre-marital experience himself.'

Her mother signed resignedly. 'I'm afraid that even in this day and age, it's a different story for men. It always has been.'

'I can see that now, and of course if I'd known then what I know now about Jim, then I would never have mentioned it. Although, if I'd cottoned on to what a complete and utter bastard Jim could be, I wouldn't be sitting here now with his ring on my finger, would I?'

Doris patted her hand. 'Don't worry, dear, if we have to drag him through every court in the land, he won't be allowed to get away with treating you like this.'

Millie sighed. 'I'm afraid it would cost thousands and even if we did have that sort of money, which we don't, I wouldn't put it past him to pay some low-life to say on the stand that he'd slept with me.'

Her mother looked outraged. 'But the judge would only have to look at you to know that was untrue.'

'I wouldn't bank on it,' Millie replied, 'as you'll probably only find he was in the same college as Jim at Oxford. I'm already the talk of every street corner as it is, and I'd never be able to hold my head up again if my relationship with Alex Nolan was plastered all over the front pages.'

'But I still can't see what Alex has to do with anything,' said Doris. 'I mean you haven't seen him for over three years.'

Millie gave her mother an apologetic look, and then she told Doris about running into Alex again.

'For goodness sake, Millie! Why on earth didn't you tell me? I'm your mother and there's nothing that you need keep from me.' Doris said when she'd finished.

'I didn't say anything, because there wasn't anything to tell.'

'Does Jim know that you've seen him?'

Millie shook her head firmly. 'I was going to tell him, but it was the day that I found out about the Oxford business and so in the end I didn't. As I say, there was nothing to tell anyway. My relationship with Alex was over before I even met Jim. When I saw Alex again, I was married and I'd just found out I was carrying Patricia. I found out then that he'd been back in the country since before Christmas. And now I can see that even if we did manage to get Jim to court, the chances are that he would find out that Alex was in London at about the time Patricia was conceived, and then I wouldn't put it past him to have Alex summoned to court, too. Even though Alex couldn't say anything that could incriminate him or me, it would blight his career nevertheless, and I just couldn't do that to him. His life has moved on since we were in love, and in any case he's probably left Arbour Square by now.'

Patricia gave a little squeak. Wearily Millie stood up and went over to the pram. Patricia kicked her legs and smiled. Millie picked up her daughter and kissed her on her forehead.

'As much as I'd like to expose Jim for the lecherous, lying scoundrel that he most definitely is, the reality is that I'm afraid, Mum, I think he would stop at nothing to hurt me. And so I can't take the chance of him raking up my past,' Millie said, rocking her daughter gently to and fro and making happy faces at her to make her smile. 'The more I think about it, the more it seems that the most sensible way for me to use my time and energy right now would be for me to try and get my old job back at Munroe House.'

As she turned into Sutton Street, Millie paused briefly as the familiar sight of Munroe House came into view, before jutting her chin determinedly and marching forward. Pushing open the large oak front door, she stepped into the quiet hallway.

As it was mid-afternoon, most of the nurses were out on their late rounds and although the four chairs outside the treatment room were empty, the low hum of voices told Millie that the afternoon clinic was still running. Wiping her feet on the coconut mat, Millie walked towards the door.

The astringent smell of undiluted Dettol and iodine made her nose tingle as she stood in the doorway. Eva was at the far end scrubbing something in the butler sink, while Annie was by the white enamel lotions cupboard instructing a mother, who was holding on tightly to a small boy, on the correct way to use a nit comb.

The screens were pulled around the examination couch at the far end, but in the gap beneath Millie could see a pair of hobnail boots with rough canvas trousers gathered around them. From behind the flimsy fabric, Sally's soft tones instructed the patient to bend over.

Eva looked up and immediately a bright smile spread across her face. 'Millie, how lovely to see you!'

Millie smiled. 'I'm not disturbing you, am I?'

'Of course not,' said Annie, setting a kidney bowl upside down on the draining board to dry. 'And I hope you've brought that little sweetheart with you so that we can have a cuddle.'

'Not today, I'm afraid,' Millie said. 'I left her with a neighbour. Is Miss Dutton in?'

'As far as I know,' Annie replied.

'Good. I'll catch up with you later,' said Millie, and left them to their tasks.

Stopping in front of the superintendent's door, Millie straightened her skirt and after tucking a stray lock of hair behind her ear, knocked. There was a shrill 'come' from the other side and Millie turned the handle.

Miss Dutton looked up as Millie entered. 'Mrs Smith.'

Millie closed the door behind her. 'I'm sorry to disturb you, but may I have a quick word, Miss Dutton?'

The superintendent glanced at the watch on her modest bosom. 'As long as it is quick.'

Tucking her skirt under her Millie sat on the chair in front of the desk.

Miss Dutton put down her pen and folded one hand over the other on the desk. 'To what do I owe this pleasure?'

'Well,' said Millie, 'I noticed that you're advertising for two experienced district nurses in last week's *Nursing Mirror*, and so I'd like to apply.'

A chilly smile lifted the corner of Miss Dutton's lips. 'Would you indeed?'

'Yes. My situation has changed recently and so I need to return to work,' said Millie.

'Has your husband suddenly taken ill, or lost his job?' Miss Dutton asked with a look of uncharacteristic concern.

'No, it's nothing like that. It's personal.'

Miss Dutton regarded her for a long moment, and then her expression changed to what Millie could only think of as a smirk. 'So the rumours are true then.'

Millie felt something akin to ice water flood over her. 'Rumours? I don't know what you mean.'

'I heard a whisper that you were back with your mother because your husband threw you out,' said Miss Dutton, not bothering to hide her relish.

'It not like that at all,' said Millie over the sound of the blood pumping in her ears.

Miss Dutton flicked the lace on her cuff 'I can't say I'm surprised. Marriages across the classes are doomed to failure of course.'

'But I left him.'

Miss Sutton's pale eyebrows rose. 'Did you?'

'Yes,' Millie replied. 'I'd rather not go into the details, other than to say that from now on I will need to support myself and my daughter. I've already spoken to a young mother around the corner who is happy to look after Patricia while I work.'

'So you have it all worked out then, do you?'

'Yes,' replied Millie firmly. 'I know you're still three staff nurses short and that Sister Yates is leaving at the end of the month. I could start at the beginning of September.'

'That's very accommodating of you.'

Millie gave a tentative smile.

Miss Dutton studied her for a long moment, and then lowered her eyes to her paperwork. 'I'm afraid it's out of the question.'

Panic surged up in Millie's chest. 'You know that I've got the qualifications and the experience. In fact there can't be many more suitable candidates.'

Miss Dutton looked up. 'You're probably right, but it isn't your suitability that is the issue.'

'Well, what is the problem?' asked Millie, hoping the superintendent couldn't hear the panic in her voice.

Miss Dutton sniffed. 'Firstly, you've got a child, which means you'll be unreliable.'

'No, I won't,' retorted Millie. 'And Sister Wilson and Sister Norris both have children, and you couldn't meet two more conscientious nurses.'

'Well, if I'd had my way I'd never have employed them, but you overrode me at the interview board, and now I'm saddled with them,' replied Miss Dutton. 'If it isn't one of them absent to look after a snotty infant, then it's the other,' she continued irritably. 'So if you think I'm taking on anyone else with a child, then you've got another thing coming.'

Millie looked aghast. 'But I've just explained that I have already organised my daughter's care.'

'Even if that is so, Mrs Smith, my conscience wouldn't let me employ a nurse who is estranged from her husband.' Miss Dutton's lips drew tighter. 'Munroe House has a reputation to uphold and I have to consider what our patients might say. They could very well object to having a nurse in their homes who has turned her back on her marriage vows.'

Millie's jaw dropped. 'But there are hundreds of women who are separated from their husbands and who are raising children alone.'

'There are. But I don't have to employ them. However,' Miss Dutton glanced at the rota sheet to her left, 'as I am experiencing a temporary shortage of staff at the moment I would be willing to take you on as one of our casual bank members of staff.'

Millie stared at the superintendent in disbelief.

'As you know, we ask our bank staff to call in each Friday evening at four o'clock to see if we have any need of them the following week,' continued Miss Dutton. She smiled condescendingly. 'Of course, I couldn't guarantee we would want you every week, as I do like to offer work to our long-standing bank staff first. And nor could I tell you which area you would be allocated to until you arrived on the day. But I am sure you would get used to that.'

Millie stared at Miss Dutton's smug face.

Bank work!

Millie wondered how could she manage, never knowing quite what her income was going to be from one week to the next? The rent didn't vary and neither did the housekeeping costs. Millie knew she could probably do the occasional night shift at the East London Lying-in Hospital to supplement what she could bring in; but that would be on the bank too and, worse, it would pay even less than doing bank work for the District. Millie needed a proper full-time job and not an odd day here and there; but with Patricia to care for, she couldn't even return to the hospital and so her best option had to be the District, where Miss Dutton should have been delighted to welcome back someone with Millie's experience. And after all, she *was* a very experienced Queen's Nurse.

'Of course, Mrs Smith,' Miss Dutton's sharp tones sliced Millie's bitter thoughts, 'if you'd rather not then I do understand.' The superintendent's supercilious smile widened.

Millie swallowed and forced herself to look gratefully at the superintendent. 'Thank you, Miss Dutton. I'd be happy to be put on your bank list.'

'Good. Come back on Friday and I'll see if I have anything for you.' The superintendent took the top off her pen and her eyes returned to the work on her desk. 'Good day.'

Millie watched the lace on Miss Dutton's frilly cap jiggle as she wrote for a couple of seconds before she stood up and, running though the weekly household expenses in her head, swiftly left the office.

Chapter Twenty

Millie had just turned the key in the door when Janey Frazer, her mother's neighbour on the other side, stepped out of her own front door.

'Hello, duck,' she said, pushing her door to make sure it was locked. 'How are you finding it then being back to work, and how is the little one taking it?' she asked, indicating the pram beside Millie.

'Not as badly as I thought,' lied Millie, trying not to relive the dark moment the previous Monday when she'd handed Patricia over to the child-minder for the first time.

There had been a disapproving look or two when she'd arrived for morning report, due no doubt to Miss Dutton telling the whole of Munroe House about her changed circumstances and the end of her marriage. According to Annie, who'd popped around for a cuppa after work the previous Friday, Miss Dutton had hardly been able to keep the smile from her face when she informed everyone that they should forget that Millie had ever been the deputy superintendent, and that they should treat her as casual staff.

Janey, who was a friendly soul with five children of her own, gave Millie a sympathetic look. 'I'm sure Patricia didn't even notice you weren't there.'

Millie gave a wan smile.

She knew that with Cora Tweedy, a good-natured mother of two small girls, who had a spotless home and spacious garden, Patricia would want for nothing while she was at work. But it didn't make it any easier for Millie to wave her goodbye each morning.

'Anyway, I'll let you get on,' said Janey, as she threw a nylon scarf over her curlers and tied it loosely under her chin.

Millie turned the key and pushed the door wide and then manoeuvred the pram through.

'Is that you, Millie?' called her mother from up the stairs.

'Yes,' Millie replied, taking off her mac.

She lifted Patricia out and taking off her daughter's knitted jacket and hat, she made her way upstairs. As she walked into her mother's room Doris was lifting down a cardboard box from the top of the wardrobe.

'You're home in very good time,' said Millie, sitting on the dressing-table stool with Patricia.

'Well, it's Friday and so we finished early,' her mother replied. 'I thought I'd have a bit of a clear-out so that I can move that old dresser of Gran's out of your room into here in order to give you a bit more space. With a bit of luck you'll be able to get a small wardrobe in the corner for Patricia.'

'That would be very helpful,' said Millie.

With the cot wedged between Millie's bed and the wall, the room she shared with Patricia was a squash for the two of them, and that was even before the tea chests had been sent over from Wanstead.

Setting Patricia on the bed to kick about, Millie lifted the box lid and peered in.

Although it had been perched on top of her mother's wardrobe, it was in fact full of old nursing textbooks and odd copies of the *Nursing Mirror*, along with fairground knick-knacks and long-forgotten trinkets. Stacking the half-a-dozen books on the dressing-table, Millie dropped the journals on the growing pile of rubbish.

'So,' said Doris, making a happy face at her granddaughter, 'how was your day?'

'Not bad, but I'm thankful I'm not back until Monday.' Millie rubbed her thighs. 'I tell you, Mum, I've rediscovered muscles I'd forgotten I had.'

Doris laughed as Patricia wriggled her hands at her. 'And how's my little angel been today?'

'As good as gold, so I'm told,' Millie replied. 'And she's started swinging her legs, so I think she'll be rolling over soon.'

'It's when she starts crawling that we'll have to worry.' Leaving Patricia to play Doris stepped up on the chair again. 'And have you got any work for next week?'

'Monday, Tuesday and Thursday. But I rang the lying-in

hospital and they want me for a night on Tuesday and a late next Saturday, and so I'll be OK next week.'

Doris looked concerned. 'Will you be all right? I mean, you won't finish on Tuesday until six in the evening and then have to go on night shift again at seven-thirty, ninety minutes later.'

'Of course,' said Millie, brightly. 'And I'll save myself two bob by not sending Patricia to Cora on Wednesday.'

Doris didn't look convinced. 'But you'll be exhausted.'

'Don't worry,' Millie replied. 'It's only one night and I can put my feet up when Patricia has her morning nap.'

Her mother gave Millie a dubious look, and then grasped the handle of an old tan suitcase. As she eased it forward a photo album, that had been sitting on top of the case slid off and fell with a crash to the floor. Millie bent down to scoop up a couple of photos that had fallen out. She froze as her eyes fixed on the strikingly handsome face of Alex Nolan.

'Where did this come from, Mum?' she asked, her hand shaking as she held the image.

'Oh, my goodness,' said Doris, taking it from her. 'I'd forgotten quite what a handsome chap he is.'

As the memory of how fine he'd looked on Wendy's arm was never far from her mind, Millie frowned. 'But I threw it in the bin the day I married Jim, and so what's it doing in gran's old album?'

Doris looked a bit sheepish. 'I know you might think it's silly, but I didn't want to destroy Alex's picture when he was being shot at by the Zionists, and when I saw it in the rubbish I pulled it out. To tell you the truth, I'd forgotten I had it.' She handed the photo of Alex back to Millie.

Patricia started to niggle.

Doris turned and scooped her granddaughter up. 'I think someone's getting ready for their bedtime.'

Millie slipped the photo into her pocket. 'I'll go down and get her bath sorted, and I'll make us a cuppa while I'm about it.'

Doris kissed Patricia. 'Leave her with me. I'm putting this lot in the rubbish, and then I can fetch her down with me.'

Millie went downstairs to the kitchen. Although it was only the second week in September once the sun had gone down the air quickly chilled. Doris had lit the fire in the lounge when she'd arrived home and some of that heat had filtered through to the back of the house, but now Millie lit the rings of the cooker to make sure the kitchen was warm enough for Patricia's nightly bath.

After cleaning the sink with bleach, Millie turned on the Ascot and the cold tap, and filled it. She went back into the lounge, collected the towel and Patricia's nightclothes she had just draped over the fireguard to warm and went to the foot of the stairs.

'I'm ready when you are,' she called up.

'We're just coming,' her mother said.

Millie returned to the kitchen and tested the water.

'There she is, sweetie.' Doris carried Patricia into the kitchen on her arm.

Millie took her and, sitting on a kitchen chair, started undressing her. 'I thought I'd pop around to the chippie and treat us to a fish supper to celebrate my being back at work.'

'That sounds nice,' Doris replied. 'But I'm off out to the pictures tonight and we're having supper beforehand.'

'What are you and Peggy seeing this week?' asked Millie, as she lowered Patricia gently into the sink.

'That new one about the Scottish island and the ship full of whisky.' A slight flush appeared in Doris's cheeks. 'Actually, Millie, it's not Peggy I'm going with. It's Charlie.'

Millie swirled the soapy water around Patricia. 'Charlie?'

'Charlie Hawkins, the chap I work for,' her mother replied, her colour deepening. 'It was funny, really. We were just chatting over a cup of tea the other day – you know how it is – and I spotted an advert for the film and said I fancied it, and then he said he did too. And it wasn't long before he said why don't we go together, and I agreed.' Doris twisted a cardigan button back and forth. 'You don't mind, do you?'

Millie broke from her mother's gaze and lifted Patricia out of the sink. 'No, of course not.'

Doris wrapped the towel around the baby and then handed her back.

'I mean, it's just for a bit of company,' she said, looking uncertain.

Millie smiled her widest grin, and gave her mother a peck on the cheek. 'Of course. You go out and enjoy yourself, Mum.'

Doris smiled happily and jiggled Patricia in her arms as she carried her into the lounge to get her ready for bed. After cleaning the kitchen sink, Millie relit the burner under the kettle and then, leaving it to come to the boil, spooned in two measures of tea into the pot and got two cups out of the dresser.

As the steam started to curl from the spout Millie pulled Alex's picture out of her skirt pocket. She studied it for a long moment and then the kettle whistled. Deep in thought, Millie slipped the photo back in her pocket and switched off the gas.

As the rain lashed the bare window Millie made a start at cleaning the gash running the length of Maureen Turner's lower arm.

Unfortunately the downpour that had started just after lunch had continued relentlessly, and after cycling around all afternoon on one of the bicycles belonging to Munroe House the damp had finally seeped through the shoulders of Millie's mac. She couldn't help cast a wistful thought towards the much faster Gadabout presumably still sitting in the shed at Jim's house.

Maureen winced.

'I'm sorry,' Millie said, patting the Dettol-soaked gauze as gently as she could, 'but I have to make sure I get all the grit out.'

'I know,' Maureen said, giving her a little smile and revealing the gap where her right eye-tooth had been until the day before.

Millie had pedalled the twenty minutes' journey from Canning Town to the Turners' house and had met Susan and Sidney as they arrived home from school. Susan had gone straight to her mother in the scullery.

Millie had followed and found that in addition to the bump on her head from yesterday that Dr Robinson had asked her to call about, Maureen, after exchanging words with her husband that morning, now had a huge patch of the skin from her right arm missing too.

Millie had made them all a cuppa and prepared a slice of bread and jam for each of the children. This disappeared in the blink of an eye while Millie changed their mother's head dressing. But while Sidney scooted out to play, Susan stood beside her mother holding her hand while Millie dealt with the latest injury.

At last Millie dropped the dirty dressing on to the newspaper at her feet, took out a tub of Germoline and, using a clean square of gauze, dabbed it on the raw flesh.

'I'm afraid it's going to be sore, Mrs Turner, but as long as you keep it clean in between dressings, it should heal in a couple of days,' Millie said, putting on the final dressing and applying a bandage.

'Thank you, Sister. It feels better already,' said Maureen.

'I'd like to scrape his face along the outside wall and see how he likes it,' Susan burst out.

'Susie!' Maureen gasped. 'Don't talk about your father like that.'

'Why not?' Susan retorted. 'All he does is shout and lash out at us.'

'Has your father hit you or Sidney, Susie?' Millie asked as she started to tidy away her equipment.

Susan shook her head. 'No, because Mum always puts herself between us and him.' Tears formed in her eyes and she looked away.

Maureen put her arm around her daughter. 'Don't worry, love. Once Dad gets some work, things will get better, I promise.'

Susan broke free from her embrace. 'That's what you say every time. And he never does get any work.'

Maureen caught her daughter's hand. 'You don't understand, Susan, love.'

'I hate him!' Susan yelled, jumping off her chair. 'And I wish the coppers had locked him up and thrown away the key 'cos we'd all be better off without him!'

The door burst open and Susan and Maureen froze as Mickey Turner staggered in, colliding with a couple of chairs on the way.

Mickey stood around middling height but his squat frame and massive fists made him appear shorter. He had a full head of russet hair and regular, almost handsome features – well, they had been before drink had raised the fine veins on his cheeks and in his eyes – and he was dressed in the rough clothing typical of an East End workman, but without the dirt on his boots that a day's work would have put there. It was clear from his unsteady gait that he'd been downing pints in the Flag and Sword for some hours.

His gaze fixed belligerently on his daughter. 'Who're you

shouting your mouth off about?' he bellowed, spit flying from his mouth.

Maureen rose to her feet and stepped in front of Susan.

'Hello, dear, I didn't hear you come up the stairs. Fancy a cuppa?' she asked, giving him an appeasing smile.

Mickey shoved her aside and grabbed Susan's arm.

'Answer me!'

Susan twisted out of his grip. 'We'd be better off without you.'

Clumsily, Mickey took a swipe at her, but Susan sidestepped and he careered forward, narrowly missing the end of the sofa.

'You're nothing but a drunk and bully,' Susan screamed. 'And we'd all be better off if you were six-foot under.'

Mickey lunged at Susan, catching her hair in his oversized hand.

Maureen grabbed his arm. 'She's only a kid, Mickey, and she doesn't know what she's saying.'

'Well, I'm going to teach her so that she knows better,' he replied, balling his fist.

'Let go of your daughter, Mr Turner,' Millie commanded authoritatively in her best matron's voice.

Mickey turned slowly and glowered at Millie, then lumbered across the room towards her.

Millie stood her ground.

'Who the bloody hell are you?' he barked, breathing a mix of stale beer and tobacco into her face.

'I'm Sister Smith from Munroe House,' Millie replied. 'And you're hurting Susan.'

'She'll do more than hurt when I'm done with her,' he said, shaking the girl.

Susan screamed and clawed at her father's fingers.

'Let go of her,' Millie snapped.

Mickey's mouth pulled into an ugly line, but he released Susan, who fell sobbing on to the mat. Maureen gathered her daughter up and bustled her out of the room.

Mickey burped. 'What you want?'

'Doctor Robinson asked me to visit.'

'I might have fucking guessed this was your doing,' Mickey shouted, rounding on his wife. 'I suppose you've gone running to the bloody cop-shop, too.'

'You know I wouldn't do that.'

Mickey drew back his hand and Maureen shrank away.

Millie stepped between them. 'Don't you dare!'

Mickey's whole body trembled as he glared down at Millie, who stared furiously back. 'Get out of my way or I'll—'

'Or you'll what?' Millie said with an icy calm although she was quaking inside.

Mickey shook his fist in her face just inches from her nose. 'I'm warning you!'

'And I'm warning you, Mickey Turner. Lay one finger on me and find out how long you'll be locked away for when the magistrate hears how you struck a district nurse going about her duty.'

Mickey drew his arm back further. Memories of Jim's hand smashing across her face flashed through Millie's mind. A knot of fear tightened in her stomach but she forced herself to hold the drunkard's gaze.

He glowered at her for a long moment, and then smashed his fist on to the square of sterile paper that was Millie's dressing area, sending her pots and tubs flying around the room. He stumbled forward, falling against the end of the sofa as he struggled to keep his balance.

Maureen slipped her arm in her husband's. 'You're worn out, Mickey. Why don't you put your feet up while I get supper ready?' she said, guiding him down on to the settee.

Mickey belched again and let his head fall back as his wife lifted up his legs up on to the cushion. Before Maureen had taken off her husband's second boot, Mickey was snoring.

She looked at Millie. 'I'm sorry about your stuff,' she said, picking up a set of tweezers from the floor.

'I'm not worried about my equipment,' Millie replied, quickly collecting up the rest of her scattered pots and dressings from the floor. 'It's you and the children that I am concerned about.'

'We'll be just fine,' said Maureen. 'His temper's always better once he's had a kip.'

Millie's gaze returned to Mickey Turner sprawled across the sofa. 'You know, Mrs Turner, you really should go to the police.'

A sad smile lifted the corner of Maureen's lips. 'They won't do anything. 'Es my husband and that's just the way things are.'

*

With the rain water dripping from her hat and down the back of her neck Millie swung her bicycle through the back gates of Munroe House and straight through a puddle in the middle of the old courtyard, inadvertently spraying dirty water up her legs.

Millie cursed under her breath and came to a halt at the shelter by the back door to the clinic. Hopping off, she lifted her nurse's bag from beneath the plastic cover of the basket and hurried into the house. She glanced at the grandfather clock at the bottom of the stairs.

Panic started in her chest.

Twenty past five! She had to pick Patricia up at six but she still had to clean her instruments and get them ready for tomorrow.

Shrugging off her coat Millie hooked it on the hall stand and hurried down the hallway.

In the treatment room Sally was dealing with the last of the afternoon patients, a boy about ten years old. He was sitting on the tall stool with his head tilted to one side and an anxious-looking mother hovering behind. Sally loomed over the child with a set of extended forceps in her hand.

'Right,' she said. 'Hold still.'

The boy started to squirm but his mother grabbed his shoulder and shook him. 'Didn't you 'ear the nurse, George? Sit still!'

George stopped moving.

Grasping the boy's head with her free hand Sally eased the end of the forceps into his ear a little way and then extracted a blue and yellow flecked marble.

'That's out,' said Sally, handing the boy his marble. 'But don't do it again. Not even if it is to win a bag of bulls' eyes.'

George grinned and hopped off the chair.

'Thanks Miss,' he called cheerfully as his mother led him away.

Millie took her bag to the butler sink and emptied out her used instruments into the bowl.

'You look wet through,' said Sally.

'I am,' said Millie with a shiver, turning on the tap and throwing in a handful of carbolic soap flakes. 'Right down to my blooming underwear. And I've cycled from Dock Street to Devons Road and back again twice this afternoon, and that's in addition to my trips to Valance Road and Back Church Lane this morning.'

Sally pulled a sympathetic face. 'Yes, it's not fair. Miss Dutton has sent you to all points of the compass today.'

'And not just today,' said Millie, picking up a pair of scissors from the soapy water. 'I had the same the day before yesterday as well as all of last week.'

'She's doing it on purpose,' said Sally in a conspiratorial voice, pushing the stainless steel trolley over to the sink.

'I know,' Millie replied, scrubbing furiously at the dirty instruments. 'And she's given me all the heavy patients. I nearly broke my back moving Mrs Alwin out of bed yesterday.'

Sally looked shocked. 'But you're not supposed to shift Bertha by yourself.'

'Miss Dutton said there wasn't anyone to help.'

Sally uncorked a bottle of surgical spirit and tearing off a length of paper wipe from the roll on the workbench started cleaning the trolley. 'You should say something.'

'I would, but I know if I did she wouldn't offer me any work at all next week,' said Millie putting the clean scissors on the draining board. 'And I need the money too much.' She plunged her hands into the soapy water and pulled out her brass ear syringe. 'Still, never mind, as it could be worse.'

Sally gave her a querying look.

Millie smiled brightly. 'I could still be with Jim.'

Sally laughed and Millie joined in.

The door opened and Gladys strolled in with Judy at her shoulder.

'Oh, this is where you're hiding, Smith,' Gladys said pointedly as she looked at Millie.

'I'm not hiding anywhere,' Millie replied. 'I've only just got back.'

'Well, at least you're here now,' continued Gladys officiously. 'Miss Dutton wants to run through a few things with me and Judy, and so you're to take our last couple of patients. There's Mr Eggerton at Limehouse Cross—'

'But he's got bi-lateral leg ulcers!' groaned Millie.

Gladys shrugged. 'And there's Judy's afternoon insulins, Miss Braithwaite and Mrs Kenward.'

'But I have to pick my daughter up in half an hour,' Millie said, imagining Patricia in her coat and hat waiting to be collected.

'Well, you'd better be get a move on then, hadn't you?' snapped Gladys. 'Unless, of course, you'd rather I tell Miss Dutton that you can't make these visits because you've got to pick your child up.'

Millie's shoulders slumped. 'All right, I'll go.'

'I thought you might.' Gladys smirked.

Giving Millie a condescending glance she and Judy flounced out of the room.

'I'll finish your equipment,' said Sally, when the door had closed. 'And I'm going that way so I can do Miss Braithwaite, if that helps.'

'You're a pal,' said Millie, shaking the water from her hands. 'And have you got a couple of coppers as I'll have to ring my child-minder from the telephone box on the corner? Her husband works for the council road department and so they have a party line.'

'Sure. In my purse,' Sally replied, indicating her nurse's bag on the desk.

'Thanks.'

Millie quickly restocked her bag from the cupboard and headed back into the hall. Her damp coat clung to her as she eased it on and the Petersham hat felt chilly as she pulled it down on her brow.

She glanced at the clock.

Half-past-five. If she got her skates on she could finish in an hour.

Millie hurried down the hall to the back door but as she opened it lightning cracked across the sky. A deep booming shook the glass in Munroe House's Victorian window frames as rain swept across the backyard in an icy sheet.

Squaring her shoulders and with her mouth set in a determined line Millie turned her collar up and stepped out into the deluge.

The streetlights were glowing when Millie finally turned into her mother's street.

Thankfully Mrs Eggerton had already set out the equipment

for Millie so Mr Eggerton's dressing had taken half the time it usually did, but it still meant that Millie arrived flustered and almost an hour late to collect Patricia. Luckily Cora had given her a bottle and a soaked rusk and so that was one thing Millie didn't have to worry about this evening; but she'd have to pay Cora extra at the end of the week to cover this, which Millie knew she could ill afford.

The rain had finally eased off by the time she'd parked her bike at Munroe House but it was still a wet walk home with lorries throwing up spray as they passed and deep puddles underfoot. Of course Patricia didn't care as she was wrapped up like a knitted parcel under the blankets and slept the whole way home.

As she reached the door Millie was surprised that the front window was still dark but thinking her mother was probably in the kitchen preparing dinner, she put the key in the lock and let herself in.

'We're home!' she called, pushing the pram over the threshold.

There was no answer and the house was decidedly chilly.

Millie picked up the half dozen letters on the mat and snapping the canopy down, she manoeuvred the pram through in to the front room, parking it in its spot behind the sofa.

After quickly shuffling the letters into two piles she put them on the mantelshelf and then set about lighting the fire. Satisfied that the kindling was beginning to glow Millie threw on a couple of small lumps of coal, stripped off her sodden coat and lay it over the metal guard standing around the hearth. She was just about to go into the kitchen to put the kettle on when there was a knock at the door.

Millie opened it to find a stout middle-aged woman in a gabardine mac over a tweed suit standing on her mother's white doorstep and holding an umbrella. With her blue eyes, wispy fair hair and soft round face, she reminded Millie of an old-fashioned china doll.

'I hope I'm not disturbing you, dear, but is your mother in?' she asked, giving Millie a friendly smile.

'No, she's not home from work yet,' Millie replied.

The woman frowned and glanced at her watch. 'She said to call at seven. It's about the cake stall at the Christmas bazaar.

Your mother's volunteered to run it, but the Vicar's wife wants a list of the donated cakes by Sunday.'

'Of course. I recognise you now,' said Millie. 'You're Mrs English from the St George's Mother's Union. We met at the summer fate.'

'Yes, we did,' Mrs English replied. 'When you were considerably larger.'

She looked pointedly at Millie's middle.

'I was,' laughed Millie. She opened the door. 'Why don't you come in and wait? She shouldn't be too long.'

'Well, if I'm not putting you out at all,' said Mrs English, stepping over the threshold.

'Not at all,' said Millie. 'Let me take your coat.'

After helping Mrs English off with her mac and hanging it up Millie showed her into the front room.

'I'm just going to make a cuppa; would you like one?'

'That would be lovely, dear,' replied Mrs English amiably. 'But only if it's not too much trouble.'

Millie shook her head. 'I'll be back in two shakes.'

Leaving Mrs English making herself comfortable in the fireside chair Millie quickly put on the kettle and laid the tea tray with her mother's barely used best china; she even remembered to put milk in a jug rather than splash it in the cups beforehand.

'There we go,' Millie said, as she returned to the front room. 'I found us a couple of digestives to soak it up.'

Mrs English wrinkled her nose. 'How lovely. You had a little girl, didn't you?'

'Yes, Patricia. She arrived a couple of weeks early,' Millie replied, pouring the tea.

Mrs English looked alarmed. 'She didn't have to be put in an incubator or anything?'

Millie shook her head. 'No, she was fine.' She handed her a cup of tea. 'I'm sorry if it's a little chilly in here but I've only just got home myself. I was called out to a patient at Limehouse Cross. I'm a nurse at Munroe House.'

Mrs English's friendly expression wavered a little. 'So your mother said. But who looks after your baby while you're working?'

'I have a woman who minds her for me,' Millie replied.

Patricia gave a little cry. Millie went to the pram and lifted her out.

A maternal expression stole over Mrs English's face. 'All my babies have grown up and flown the nest. Do you think she would mind if I had a little cuddle?'

'I shouldn't think so,' Millie replied, handing Patricia to her. 'How many children do you have?'

'Seven. Four boys and three girls, and eighteen grandchildren,' Mrs English said. She settled Patricia in the crook of her arm and tickled her under the chin. 'And each one a little miracle, like you,' she told the baby.

Patricia studied her solemnly for a moment and then smiled.

'Ah, bless your little heart,' continued Mrs English, hooking her finger in Patricia's chubby little hand and wiggling it. 'You're as good as gold, aren't you, even though your mummy leaves you all day?'

Millie's face lost some of its smile. 'Let me take her so that you can drink your tea.'

Mrs English relinquished Patricia with a sigh and picked up her cup and saucer.

Propping Patricia up on a pillow beside her, Millie took up her drink too.

'Have you come far?' she asked.

'Stepney Green. I live in the houses next to the Jewish Hospital. It's convenient for my husband. He works in the City.'

'Straight in on the number 25, then.'

'Yes.'

Millie glanced at the clock on the mantelshelf. 'I can't imagine what's keeping mum. She's usually home by now.'

Patricia started fretting and so Millie picked her up and, as the room was now warm, peeled off her outer clothing and sat her on her knee. Slipping her hand under the rubber pants and judging the nappy would last until bath time in an hour, Millie finished off the last of her tea.

Mrs English made a play of putting her cup and saucer back on the tray and then looked at Millie.

'My dear,' she said. 'I hope you won't take this the wrong way but you do know that it is common knowledge that you've left your husband.'

Millie forced a polite smile. 'People like to gossip.'

A tortured expression spread across Mrs English face. 'But my dear, are you sure you haven't acted too hastily. I've been married for over forty years and I can tell you marriage is not like they show you in the cinema. It takes hard work.'

'I'm sorry, Mrs English,' said Millie, struggling to keep the irritation from her voice. 'I don't see it is any concern of yours.'

'Marriage is a sacrament entered into in the sight of God.' Her gaze moved to Patricia playing with the buttons of her mother's blouse. 'Don't you think the innocent child in your arms deserves to be raised in a loving home?'

'I do,' replied Millie. 'And that why I left.'

Mrs English stretched over and rested her hand on Millie's. 'I urge you, Mrs Smith. For the sake of your daughter's happiness and your reputation, return to your husband.'

Millie opened her mouth to reply but there was a click as a key turned in the front door.

'Cooeee! I'm home,' called Doris.

Millie snatched her hand from the old lady's and stood up.

'In here!' she shouted. 'You have a visitor.'

Removing her rain bonnet as she entered, Doris walked in to the sitting room.

'Oh Mrs English,' she said. 'I'm so sorry. Three buses went past before I could get on one. I hope you haven't been waiting long?'

Mrs English smiled. 'Don't worry I've had a nice cup of tea and I've been admiring your precious little granddaughter.'

Doris gazed down fondly at Patricia and then started unbuttoning her mac. 'Just let me get out of these wet things and I'll be with you.'

Millie picked up her daughter. 'I'll leave you to it while I get Patricia ready for bed. There's probably a cup left in the pot if you want it, Mum.'

'Thank you dear. I'll get myself a cup.'

Leaving her outer coat over the back of the upright chair to dry Doris went into the kitchen.

Adjusting Patricia in her arms Millie went to follow.

'It was nice to talk to you,' said Mrs English. 'And I hope you'll think over what I said.'

Millie gave her a cool look. 'I hope you don't get too wet on your way home.'

Passing her mother coming the other way Millie fled to the kitchen. She closed the door behind her. Resting against it and hugging Patricia tightly to her, Millie closed her eyes and took several deep breaths as she fought the urge to scream.

As her pulse and temper steadied Millie straightened up and flicked the switch on the wireless. Putting Patricia in the middle of the kitchen table she rested her hands on either side of her daughter and smiled. Patricia smiled back and Mrs English's words and any lingering doubts fled.

There had been many moments in the past month or two, such as when she waved her daughter goodbye or when Miss Dutton allocated her the hardest of tasks or when she'd had to miss a night's sleep to do a shift at the maternity hospital, that almost made Millie cave in under the weight of her responsibilities.

But at times like this, with her daughter's large brown eyes gazing trustingly up at her, Millie knew as surely as she knew the sun would rise in the East tomorrow, that come what may she and Patricia were better off without Jim Smith.

Thankfully Mrs English had left by the time Millie returned from bathing Patricia, and her mother was stacking the cups back on the tray.

Doris looked up as Millie walked in. 'All done?'

'Yes,' said Millie, putting her daughter on the chair by the fire to keep her warm. 'You?'

Doris nodded. 'But I still can't believe it's Christmas in just six weeks.'

Millie slipped her arm through her mother's and smiled fondly at her. 'I know she won't really understand, but I can't wait to see Patricia's face when she sees the tree.'

'I remember what you were like about Christmas.' Doris laughed. 'As soon as Guy Fawkes Night was done you used to nag Dad for weeks on end to put the decorations up.'

'Do you remember how he used to stagger home with the largest tree he could get for half a crown and then teeter at the top of that old house ladder to pin paperchains across the room?' said Millie.

'Remember!' Doris put her hand on her chest. 'I used to have palpitations every blooming year.'

They laughed.

Millie squeezed her mother's arm. 'Have you had another think about the family get-together on Boxing Day, Mum? I know it's at aunt Ruby's, but aunt Martha and Edie haven't seen Patricia since the christening. And cousin Gwen and her crowd will be coming from Wickford, too.'

Her mother's mouth became a stubborn line. 'I'm sorry, Millie, I know it's the season of goodwill and all that, but until *she* apologies for what she said I'm not setting foot in *her* house.'

'You don't think perhaps that it's time to forgive and forget?'

Doris folded her arms resolutely. 'I'm not going, Millie.'

'All right, Mum,' Millie hugged her mother. 'And I'm sure it will be just as much fun with just me, you and Patricia.'

A flush spread up her mother's throat. 'I've been meaning to mention this for a couple of days actually. But Charlie Hawkins has only a sister in Leeds and they're not close, and so he'll be all by himself over the holidays. I hope you don't mind too much, Millie, but I've invited him to join us for Christmas.'

Chapter Twenty-One

'Hold the flannel tight over your face, Annie, while I dab on the last bit,' Millie said, squeezing what remained of the Toni Quickie Perm lotion on to the tightly pinned rollers.

They were in the larger of the three upstairs bathrooms in Munroe House and had forgone their monthly trip to the cinema for a night in so that they could give Annie's dead straight hair a little festive lift. As the first part of the operation was almost complete, Connie had popped down to the kitchen to make them all a cocoa to drink while the perming lotion was doing its work.

'It's making my eyes water,' mumbled Annie through the thickness of the towelling square.

'Almost done.' Millie discarded the cotton wool into the bin and wrapped the towel from Annie's shoulders around her head.

Annie sat up. 'That's better.'

She was sitting in front of the old Victorian sink in her underwear just in case some of the permanent lotion or fixer splashed. Millie was in one of her old petticoats, too.

Millie picked up the instruction leaflet. 'It says leave for a quarter of an hour and then check.'

'Check for what?'

'To make sure your hair hasn't turned green,' answered Connie, coming through the door carrying a tray with three mugs and a plate of biscuits.

Annie's eyes flew open. 'It couldn't, could it?'

'Don't be silly,' laughed Millie, winding the egg timer to fifteen minutes.

Connie set the tray on the floor between them and then, taking her cocoa, perched on the side of the bath.

Millie handed Annie hers and then, cradling her own hot drink, sat on the small cabinet where the housekeeper stored the spare toilet rolls.

Connie wrinkled her nose. 'That old paraffin heater's getting worse,' she said, giving the old pot-bellied stove a sidewards glance.

'I know, although without it our teeth would be chattering,' Annie replied. 'But as soon as the perm sets, we can take the rollers out back in my room as it's much warmer there.'

Millie picked up a custard cream. 'It won't be long now, you two, before you can both start telling people that you're getting married *this* year.'

'I know, it's now only a month to Christmas.' Annie laughed. 'This year just seems to have flown by.'

'Yes,' said Millie, overwhelmed at how she'd gone from being a happy wife to a single mother since the last time she had sung 'Auld Lang Syne'.

'But, Annie will be the first down the aisle, in August,' said Connie, quelling Millie's dispiriting thoughts.

'But it's you soon after,' Annie chipped in.

'I wouldn't call October soon,' Connie replied. 'And we've got Veronica and Judy's big days in between.'

'You don't sound very keen,' said Annie, picking up on a downbeat tone in Connie's voice.

'Oh, I am. But Malcolm's mother is being decidedly awkward about the arrangements, and we've still got half a year to go.' Connie spent a moment retying her dressing-gown sash. 'Sometimes I think it might be easier all around if I just postponed the whole thing until the following year, as his mother wants. Of course, then I'd have to fight with Mum and my sisters, as they've already started organising the table settings and are discussing caterers.'

'That's what mums do,' said Millie.

'Your mum didn't.'

'Don't tell me you've forgotten what my aunt Ruby was like!' said Millie, looking pointedly at her friend.

'Oh, yes.'

Both of them took a large mouthful of cocoa.

Ruby's precision, second-by-second planning of Millie's big day had made the D-Day landings look like a day trip to the beach.

Connie sighed. 'Isn't it supposed to be the happiest day of your life?'

Millie stretched over and squeezed her friend's hand. 'It'll be all right, Connie, you'll see.'

Connie gave another sigh and turned to Annie. 'Has Patrick taken you to see the house yet?'

Annie shook her head. 'He says it's a man's job to present his wife with a home and not a pile of bricks, but he promised me it'll be finished by Easter and so I'll have a few months to set it to rights. And he's just got the licence from the council for his scrap yard in Purfleet, too.'

Millie put on a cheery smile.

She was very happy for Annie and Connie, and the other girls, of course. But she knew that seeing her friends arm in arm with their fiancés or new husbands would just highlight her own woefully unattached situation, especially when couples were invited to join the happy pair for the first dance.

Millie took another sip of cocoa. 'Are you at your mum's for Christmas dinner, Connie?'

'Yes,' laughed Connie. 'It's compulsory. But we're at Malcolm's mum's for tea. I suppose you're going to Ruby's?'

'No, because they are still not talking,' replied Millie. 'So we're staying at home.'

Annie's pretty face took on a sentimental expression. 'Aw, that's nice. Just you and your mum enjoying Patricia's first Christmas together.'

The timer sprang into action. Millie switched it off.

'As it happens, Mum's invited a friend to join us,' she said, turning to unfasten one of Annie's metal curlers to see if the perm had taken. 'Mr Hawkins. Her boss. He's all by himself and so she asked him to spend the day with us, which I think is jolly kind of her.'

'Won't it be a bit awkward, seeing how she hardly knows him?' asked Connie.

Millie studied the kinked golden strands for a moment and then rewound the curler. She carefully reset the timer before looking up again.

'Actually,' she said, putting on her brightest smile. 'Mum and Mr Hawkins have been having supper out and going to the pictures every Friday since the beginning of September.'

'That's nice,' said Annie.

'Yes it is, isn't it?' replied Millie, her smile growing even wider. 'She's had a rough time of it since Dad died and I think it's terrific she's got a male friend she can enjoy an evening out with.'

'You're right,' said Annie. 'Your mum's been through a hell of a lot and I'm sure it's only a bit of fun.'

'I think so, too,' agreed Millie, trying not to imagine the sort of fun her mum might be having.

'And at least you know your mum won't do anything daft like run off to Gretna Green,' added Connie.

She and Annie laughed as Millie tried to join in.

The hall telephone rang a couple of times before Sally's head popped around the edge of the nurse's sitting room. She surveyed the room and then spotted Millie. She beckoned to her.

'I swapped with Felicity and so she's covering the late,' Millie said, taking a sip of tea.

'It's not a call-out; it's Doctor Gingold.' Sally replied. 'She wants to speak to you.'

Millie's heart leapt into her throat. She'd told Cora that if Patricia ever started a fever and she couldn't get hold of her, to take her daughter to Dr Gingold, who was Doris's GP.

Putting her tea down Millie hurried out into the hall and picked up the telephone receiver. 'Sister Smith.'

'Ah, Millie, I'm glad I've caught you before you go home,' Doctor Gingold's distinctive voice said down the phone. 'I know you were closely involved with Mr and Mrs Joliffe and so I thought you would want to know. I'm afraid that very sadly their son William passed away this afternoon.'

Dorothy put the teapot down. 'Please, help yourself to sugar, Sister,' she said, handing Millie a fine bone-china cup and matching saucer.

'Thank you,' said Millie, taking it from her.

She'd dashed through her afternoon visits to ensure she had a full hour for the after-funeral bereavement visit to the Joliffes and she was now sitting in their front room.

With Christmas just over a week away, there were paperchains hanging from the ceiling and a fully dressed tree complete with baubles, tinsel and presents beneath in the far corner. Having laid William to rest on the previous Thursday, no amount of mistletoe and holly was going to raise Dorothy and Derrick's spirits this year, Millie knew.

Dorothy moved the tea strainer to the next cup to pour her husband's drink.

He sat next to his wife on the sofa with the same grey, haunted expression etched on his face. Both of them seemed to have aged ten years overnight.

'Thank you, my love,' he said softly, taking the cup from his wife.

Their hands touched.

Derrick gave his wife the tenderest of looks and somehow Dorothy mustered a ghost of a smile in return.

The lump that had formed itself in Millie's throat as she walked up the front steps grew further.

Putting his cup on the side table to cool, Derrick took his wife's hand and looked at Millie. 'Knowing how busy you all are at the clinic, we were touched that you attended William's funeral, weren't we, Dorothy?'

'Yes.' The expression in Dorothy's red-rimmed eyes softened. 'We were greatly comforted to see you and the other three nurses at the back of the church.'

'William was a very special baby,' Millie said.

Although nurses were supposed to keep their emotions in check, she and Annie had wept unashamedly as Derrick, carrying the little white coffin down the aisle in St Dunstan's, had laid it on the altar with the utmost gentleness. He'd stood stoically through the brief service with his arm around his wife, who wept uncontrollably.

'That's very kind of you to say, Sister,' Derrick said. 'And we will always be grateful for what you did the night he was born.' He squeezed his wife's hand. 'Our little chap wouldn't have even got started if it hadn't been for you.'

'Yes,' said Dorothy. 'And the doctors and nurses at the hospital have been marvellous, too. Nothing was too much for them and the matron even allowed us to come and go as we pleased, regardless of the visiting times.'

'That was very kind of her,' said Millie.

Dorothy gave a mirthless laugh. 'It was, but in fact, since the cold autumn weather set in, the Joliffe family was more or less a permanent fixture on the ward.'

Dorothy's gaze drifted to one of half-a-dozen photographs of William in the room, which was sitting on the bookcase beside her. She picked it up and, resting it on her lap, ran her fingers gently over his image.

'I still can't believe he's gone,' she said, her lower lip trembling as she spoke.

'I know,' said Derrick, his nose looking suddenly pinched and his eyes bright. 'But we must be grateful we had him, even if only for a short while, as it's more than we ever hoped for. And he's at peace now, and he isn't having to fight for every breath.'

Tears shimmered in Dorothy's eyes. 'I know, I know. But every time I close my eyes all I see is his little chest rising and falling and hear the rasping sound he made at the end.' She covered her face and sobbed.

Millie picked the picture up and looked at it.

'Come on, old thing,' said Derrick in rallying tones. 'There's nothing to be done except to square up and carry on.'

Dorothy pulled a handkerchief out of her sleeve and dabbed her eyes. 'You're right.' She looked at Millie. 'I'm so sorry.' She blew her nose and tucked the cotton square away again. 'And how rude of me not to ask you how your little one is.'

Millie gave the Joliffes a brief rundown of how Patricia was almost sitting up and was already trying to feed herself. They held each other's hands and smiled politely.

Finishing her tea, Millie glanced at her fob watch. 'And talking of Patricia, I ought to go or I'll be late collecting her.'

She stood up and so did Derrick and Dorothy. The photo of William slipped off her lap and landed at Millie's feet.

She bent down and picked it up.

It was a studio picture and must have been taken sometime in the summer when William was about the same age as Patricia was now. He was wearing a romper suit with ducks embroidered across the smocking. He was propped up on a large pillow with a teddy bear almost as big as him sitting alongside, and he was smiling. As Millie gazed down at the baby she'd delivered less than a year ago the injustice of the Joliffes' situation almost overwhelmed her.

Day after day she dealt with women who, without a second thought, tripped along to backstreet abortionists to rid themselves of unwanted babies; and if the child escaped the knitting needle and made it into the world, they were at best ignored by their parents and at worst abused.

Had he lived, William would never have been left to cry in a soaked nappy or expected to sleep in a filthy cot. He wouldn't have had to dodge his father's fists or been taken out of school to mind younger siblings while his mother went down the pub.

No, William would have been encouraged, nurtured and loved every moment.

Instead of which he was now mouldering in his grave, while his parents had nothing but a few brief memories and studio photographs, and a lifetime of shattered dreams. To Millie's way of thinking it was just bloody unfair.

Putting her foot on the pram's back axle, Millie pushed down on the handlebar so the front wheels could clear the kerb.

'Right now, young lady,' she told Patricia, who was wrapped up like a pink Eskimo against the brisk weather, 'it's the butcher first to collect the chicken, and then we'll go to Al's for the spuds and sprouts.'

In her nest of pillows and blankets, Patricia waved her mitten-covered hands in response.

Being Christmas Eve morning and a Saturday, the market opposite the London Hospital known as The Waste, from when it was the rough ground between Aldgate and the old Essex Road, had really pulled out all the stops this year, and it looked very festive. Even the stalls selling blocks of soap and loo brushes had twinkling lights on their awnings that were powered by heavy black cables strung overhead. Street vendors had fired up their trolleys early and the oniony smell of hot dogs, a much-loved GI legacy, mingled with the more traditional aroma of roasting chestnuts.

Although it was only just after nine, the street was packed already with women pushing prams loaded with toddlers and dragging children in their wake as they brought their last-minute bits and pieces for the big day tomorrow. And everyone, from the road sweeper pushing his broom along the gutter to the conductor hanging off the back of the passing number 25 bus, seemed to be brimming over with Christmas spirit.

It was as if the approach of a new decade, the 1950s, had finally helped people throw off their wartime make-do-and-mend and waste-not-want-not attitudes. Although the bombs had stopped more than four years ago in 1945, it seemed for the people Millie lived and worked amongst that now, at long last, the gruelling war was finally over.

Passing the hat shop and then Lipton's in the parade of shops alongside Whitechapel station, Millie took her place at the back of the queue outside the butcher's as the half-a-dozen customers shuffled forward. A woman, wearing a headscarf over her rollers, stopped behind her.

'She's a little darling,' she said, cooing at Patricia. 'How old?'

'Six months,' Millie replied.

'They're lovely at that age, aren't they?' she said, a sentimental expression spreading across her face. 'Is Father Christmas going to bring you something nice?'

Patricia answered by blowing a series of bubbles.

The woman looked curiously at Millie. 'Ain't you one of the nurses from Munroe House?'

'Yes, I am,' replied Millie, stamping her feet to warm them up.

'I thought you looked familiar. You delivered Winnie Rogers in King John Street. I'm her sister Joan,' said the woman.

To be honest Millie had delivered so many babies since the end of the war, and at least a dozen in the old streets just off Stepney High Street, that she was unable to remember either of the women, but she smiled anyway.

'How's she doing?'

'Fine,' Joan replied. 'He's at school now and a right little tearaway.' She gazed back at Patricia. 'And now you've got one of your own.'

The queue shuffled forward and an old woman lumbered up behind Joan, causing Millie's heart to sink. That's just what she needed.

'Hello, Mrs Lennon,' she said, with a friendly smile.

Pat Lennon, mother of six and grandmother to countless others, was a thin, sallow faced woman with sharp knees and elbows, and an even sharper tongue.

The old woman's close-set eyes gave Millie the once-over. 'Did I hear right that you're back living with your mother,' she said, raising her voice to include the other women in the queue.

Somehow Millie maintained her pleasant expression. 'Yes, I am.'

Mrs Lennon's mouth became a disapproving line. 'I don't know what the world's coming to. In my day you married for life. Better or worse, that's what we said and that's what we did.'

There was a murmur of agreement. Millie's cheeks burned.

Ignoring Mrs Lennon, she looked at Joan. 'Give your sister my best when you see her.'

Millie turned around to face towards the front of the queue.

'I blame the war for all this so called marriage break-up,' Mrs Lennon's harsh tones continued. 'Time was when a woman would count herself lucky if their old man put their housekeeping on the table each Friday, never mind anything else. But now!' As Mrs Lennon expounded her views on marriage Millie stared doggedly ahead.

The woman in front of Millie moved into the shop and Millie followed, leaving Patricia and Mrs Lennon outside. After collecting the large chicken she'd chosen earlier in the week for their Christmas dinner, she moved to the cold meat counter and bought a quarter of tongue and some best ham for tea. She handed over one and six with the appropriate number of coupons. And then, ignoring the four pairs of disapproving eyes staring at her as she passed, Millie left the shop.

As she tucked her purchases in the shopping rack beneath the pram she spotted Susan and Sidney with their eyes cast down, carrying a heavy shopping bag between them.

Kicking off the pram's brakes Millie hurried over.

'Hello, Susan,' she said cheerily. 'What are you and Sidney up to?'

'Getting mum's veg,' Susan replied.

Millie looked over her head and scanned the crowd. 'Is your mum behind you?'

'No, she's at home because she's not well,' Susan replied.

'Not with this chesty cough that's going around, I hope,' probed Millie.

Susan's care-worn eyes looked at Millie. 'No. Just the same

old thing. *He* got his Christmas money yesterday lunchtime, and then spent the rest of the day propping up the bar in the Old Rose. He staggered home after chucking-out looking for a fight. Mum shut the door on him, and so he kicked in the front window. Winnie next door called the police. They tried to calm him down, but he thumped the sergeant and so they carted him away. I thought they'd let him out like they usually do when he'd sobered up, but the policeman in charge turned up and said they were charging him with assaulting an officer and as the courts weren't open until Boxing Day, he'd have to stay in the cell until then.'

'The copper gave me this,' piped up Sidney. He thrust out his hand and showed Millie a threepenny piece. 'He gave Susie one too, and we're going to get a toffee apple, aren't we?' He looked expectantly up at his sister.

Susan smiled weakly. 'Yes, we are, but only when we've got all Mum's shopping.'

Satisfied with the assurance, Sidney slipped the coin back in his pocket, and then looked over the edge of the pram and pulled a funny face at Patricia.

Millie put her hand on Susan's thin shoulder. 'I'm so sorry.'

'I know,' Susan replied softly. 'Everyone is.'

Patricia started to grizzle.

'She's getting cold. I'll have to go,' she said. 'Will you give your mum my regards and wish her a Happy Christmas from me? And I hope you and Sidney have a jolly time too.'

Susan gave Millie a heart-breakingly plucky smile. 'We will now 'e's banged up in the nick.' She tugged her brother's hand. 'Say goodbye to Sister Smith.'

'Goodbye, Sisser Smif.'

Millie smiled. 'Enjoy your toffee apples.' The children walked off.

'And Susan,' Millie called. The young girl looked around. 'Remember that you can always get hold of me at the clinic if you need to.'

Chapter Twenty-Two

Charlie Hawkins untucked the napkin from the front of his cardigan and wiped his mouth. 'Well, I can honestly say, Doris, I haven't had a Christmas spread like that since I lost my dear Ida. And that Christmas pud was nothing short of marvellous.'

Doris's cheeks flushed. 'Why, thank you, Charlie, it was my mother's special recipe,' she replied, basking in his admiration. 'It's so nice to cook for a man again. But have you had enough?'

'I couldn't eat another mouthful,' Charlie replied, patting his stomach over his straining waistband.

They smiled warmly at each other across the table.

Charlie had arrived just after midday, dressed in his best bib and tucker, a brown chalk-striped suit with a contrasting orange tie, and carrying a bunch of flowers, a box of Terry's Empire chocolates and a bottle of cherry brandy.

Had he lived, Millie's dad would have been in his late fifties. She guessed Charlie was probably around that age too, but that's where the similarity ended. Whereas her father had managed to hold on to his hairline, Charlie's had slid back way past his crown; and even after twenty-eight years of Doris's tasty cooking, her father had only a hint of a spare tyre, which certainly couldn't be said about Charlie.

'Yes, Mum, it was delicious, and Patricia agrees with me,' Millie said, wiping the custard from her daughter's mouth.

Patricia was sitting next to Millie in the new highchair that aunt Ruby had bought her for Christmas. She had scatter cushions wedged on either side to keep her upright and a tea towel around her neck to save her new dress. Patricia squirmed in protest at Millie's efforts to clean her face.

'Such a little darling,' said Millie's mother, reaching across and taking her granddaughter's hand.

Doris and Charlie exchanged a fond look.

'Yes,' agreed Millie. 'It's a pity Dad didn't live to see her.'

Her mother withdrew her hand and Charlie smoothed back what remained of his hair, although none was out of place.

Charlie leant back and the chair creaked under his weight. 'Your mum was telling me how upset she's been about all the shenanigans with your old man.'

Millie looked pointedly at her mother. 'Did she?'

Charlie nodded. 'Rotten sod. Treating you like that, and him an MP too. Mind you, don't matter what colour their politics, they're all in it for themselves, I say.'

Doris stood up. 'The King's Christmas speech will be on soon, and so I'll clear away and make us a cup of tea to have while we listen.'

Millie picked up her and Patricia's crockery. 'I'll help.'

'No, it's all right, dear,' Doris replied. 'We don't want to neglect our guest, do we?'

'I'm sure Charlie doesn't mind, do you?' Millie asked, as she snatched his plate away.

'No, of course not. It'll give me a chance to get to know this little lady.' He stretched his hands toward Patricia.

She smiled and happily reached up for him to hold her. Charlie lifted her out of her highchair and, with a joyful 'wheeee', hoisted her above his head.

Millie followed her mother into the kitchen and found Doris was already up to her elbows in the sink.

'It's all right, dear, I can manage,' she said, lathering up the block of Sunlight with the washing-up rag.

'How could you discuss my private business with every old Tom, Dick or Harry, Mum?' asked Millie, as she joined her mother at the sink.

'I'm sorry. But he found me crying over the filing cabinet one day and, well, it just spilled out.' Doris lifted a plate from the suds. 'I couldn't help it, Millie. You've got Connie and Annie to talk to, but I don't have anyone since me and Ruby fell out. And he's not any old Tom, Dick or Harry – he's Charlie.'

'Someone call me?' said Charlie as he strolled into the kitchen.

Doris turned and smiled at him. 'I was just telling Millie how much I've enjoyed our weekly trips to the pictures these past couple of months.'

Charlie's heavy features lifted into a cheery smile. 'Me too,' he said softly. 'And I thought perhaps when the weather picks up we can motor out one Sunday afternoon to Southend, or even Clacton.'

Doris's eyes lit up. 'That would be lovely. I haven't been to the seaside since Arthur died. We can take a picnic.'

'And I'll buy you a stick of rock.'

They smiled happily at each other. Millie looked away and picked up a plate to dry.

Patricia started fretting. 'I think she's had enough of uncle Charlie, and wants her mum.' He offered her to Millie.

'She's ready for her afternoon nap,' Millie said, taking her back. 'Leave them, Mum, and I'll do them when I've got her to sleep.' She indicated the pile of dinner plates on the draining board.

Charlie took a dry tea towel hanging on the oven door. 'Don't worry. I'll help your mum. It's the least I can do after such a dinner.'

He took up position alongside Doris at the sink. 'Got room for a little one?' he asked, playfully nudging her mother.

'Oh, Charlie, you are a one,' Doris giggled.

They smiled at each other again.

Millie positioned Patricia on her hip. 'I'll turn the wireless on then, shall I?'

'Yes, dear,' said Doris, without taking her eyes from the man beside her. 'We'll be in shortly.'

Millie went back into the lounge and after settling Patricia in her pram in the corner she flipped the switch on the wireless and plonked herself on the sofa.

A peal of her mother's laughter followed by a deep chuckle from Charlie escaped from the kitchen, and Millie slumped further into the upholstery lost in thought at how much life had changed for them all in the last couple of years.

Millie squeezed the clean bandages she'd just re-rolled into the tin alongside the other dozen and snapped on the lid.

Usually the tedious job of winding the bleached crepe bandages after they came back from the laundry ready for steaming in the steriliser was allocated to the junior members of staff.

However, with Miss Dutton prowling around outside Millie was quite happy to be out of the firing line in the treatment room. Added to which the January weather had changed from being merely dull to bitingly cold two days ago and so a couple of hours inside before the end of the day was most welcome.

The icy weather had done nothing to hinder her mother and Charlie's growing friendship, however, as since Christmas they had added a midweek drink and a drive out to the country most Sunday afternoons to their Friday-night pictures routine.

To be fair, there wasn't actually anything wrong with Charlie; he was always a perfect gentleman towards her mother and, goodness knows, after what she'd been through in the last few years, Millie completely agreed that her mother deserved a bit of happiness.

But although the last thing on Millie's mind at the moment was looking for another man for herself, she couldn't help but feel when she saw the way Doris glowed under Charlie's attention that her own lonely situation was highlighted.

Other than a terse letter from Jim's lawyer turning down once more her carefully worded request for financial support for Patricia, Millie hadn't seen or heard from Jim for months and she didn't expect to. Apart from anything else, he was probably campaigning night and day to retain his seat at the General Election in three weeks' time.

As Millie picked up another bandage to roll the door opened and Peggy rushed in. 'I'm sorry, Millie, but I've just had Susan Turner on the telephone. She was hysterical and I couldn't catch what she was saying, but she kept asking for you. Shall I whizz round and see what's happened?'

The image of Mickey Turner staggering around Maureen's front room and lashing out at Susan flashed through Millie's mind.

She stood up abruptly and took her hat and coat from the stand behind. 'No, I'll go. But if I'm not back by five o'clock, call the police.'

The sun had just given up the last of its pale midwinter light as Millie shot through Munroe House's back gates into Commercial

Road. The fog swirled around her as the mute yellow headlights of the lorries and cars loomed out of the thick miasma.

Keeping to the kerb, Millie sped her bike forward towards the City until she came to Watney Street. With her nurse's case bouncing in the large front basket as she rattled over the cobbles, she wove between the stalls and pushed on until she saw the railway arches emerge from the gloom. She swung right and skidded to a halt outside the newspaper shop.

Quickly chaining her cycle to the nearest lamp-post, she snatched her bag and ran to the Turners' front door, but as she raised her hand to knock, Millie noticed the door was unlatched. She pushed and it creaked open.

'Susan? Sidney? Mrs Turner?' she called, her voice echoed up the stairs to the living quarters above.

She switched on the hall light and then, with her heart pounding in her chest, hurried up the stairs. Stopping on the half-landing where the stairs turned, she called again. 'It's me, Sister Smith. From Munroe House.'

A muffled cry came from the back room where the family slept.

Millie grabbed the handle and slowly opened the door. 'Don't be afraid, Susan. I'm here now,' she said, groping along the wall for the electric switch and flicking it on.

The single bulb fizzed into light, revealing a double and two half-size children's beds, one with a teddy propped up on it. All three were neatly made with fresh, clean sheets. Above the adult bed was a picture of the Virgin Mary with a rosary looped over it and a school picture of Susan and Sidney wedged into the frame.

There was some shuffling under the child's bed in the far corner. Millie knelt down on the worn rug and lifted the bedspread, peering underneath. Susan and Sidney were huddled together against the wall.

Sidney had his head tucked tightly under his sister's chin, while Susan stared wide-eyed over his head. When she saw it was Millie, the young girl's frightened face relaxed.

'Goodness, what on earth are you doing?' Millie asked, stretching under the bed to reach them.

'We're hiding,' said Susan's shaky voice.

'It's all right. You can come out. I'm here now. ' Millie said.

Susan tried to move towards her, but Sidney's grip on his sister tightened.

'It's all right, Sid,' Susan said, stroking his wayward hair. 'It's Sister Smith. She'll make mum better.'

Sidney scrambled out from under the bed alongside his sister. He snatched the teddy and, sticking his thumb in his mouth, buried his face in the soft toy. Susan put her arm around her brother.

'Where is your mum?' Millie asked.

'In the other room. I think she's hurt. I wanted to go in, but Sidney was too scared, so I ran to the phone box on the corner and called you as you told me to.' She looked anxiously at Millie. 'Did I do right?'

'Yes, you did.' Millie took the eiderdown from the double bed and wrapped it around the children. 'Now you two stay here while I go and look after your mum.'

Susan nodded and tucked them both a little further into the quilted counterpane.

Picking up her bag, Millie retraced her steps back on to the landing. Adjusting her grip on her bag, she climbed the remaining half-dozen steps to the main living area.

As she pushed open the lounge door her heart lurched.

Maureen Turner lay sprawled on the floor with the furniture overturned around her. Her left arm was bent at an odd angle and her lifeless eyes stared out of an ashen face at the central light. There were a multitude of fresh bruises on her cheeks and forehead, while blood oozed across the carpet from the back of Maureen's head where the spikes of the fender had impaled it.

A wave of nausea swept over Millie. She dropped her bag and, taking a deep breath, turned and stumbled out of the room.

'I'm sorry it's taking so long,' said PC Mills, a lean individual with deep-set eyes. 'But we can't touch anything until the CID arrives, and they're out on another job.'

Millie gave a wan smile.

It had been at least twenty minutes since she'd burst into the newsagent's below and demanded they call 999. The two patrol cars had arrived very soon in a flourish of clanging bells and squealing brakes, followed by the divisional surgeon who, without taking his hands out of his pockets, pronounced Maureen dead and then strolled out again.

'I've telephoned the clinic as you asked, Sister,' Officer Mills explained.

Millie looked at her watch.

Officer Mills shifted his size-ten hobnail boots uncomfortably. 'They shouldn't be too much longer.'

'I'm thinking of the children.' Millie indicated Susan and Sidney, who were sitting in a stupefied daze on either side of her.

PC Mills shrugged apologetically. 'I'm sorry, but the crime scene has to be left as it was found and the parties who found the body can't leave.'

Sidney tucked his head into Millie further and sucked furiously on his thumb. Millie gave both children an encouraging hug. Neither responded.

'DS Pugh likes to question witnesses at the scene while things are fresh in their minds. Would you like another cup of tea while you wait?' said PC Mills

Millie shook her head. 'I'm fine.'

The officer thumbed over his lapels. 'Honestly, it's no trouble.'

The front door banged and manly footsteps marched up the stairs.

'What the bloody hell are you doing, Hanson?' boomed an authoritative male voice from outside the bedroom.

Goosebumps ran down Millie's spine as she recognised it.

The officer in the room stood smartly to attention. 'Gawd 'elp us, it's the guvnor,' he muttered under his breath.

'Guarding the crime scene, sir ' warbled an officer stationed outside the lounge door.

'I can see that, man,' roared the superintendent. 'Where's Pugh and his lot?'

'On another case,' Hanson replied.

'Well, get them out of the Ship and Compass, and tell them to attend. And I understand there are children involved.'

'Yes sir.'

'So where's A4 Branch?'

'I don't rightly know.'

'Ring Inspector Ogden and tell her I want one of her woman constables here in five minutes. Step to it.'

'Sir!'

'Well, get on it!' the superintendent barked, his deep tones sending Millie's heart racing.

Wide-eyed, Millie stared at the door. And then Alex marched into the room.

'Right, Miss—' He stopped dead and stared at her in disbelief.

As her gaze swept over his tall and muscular frame Millie felt dizzy as she wordlessly looked back at him.

PC Mills saluted.

'Sir. This is Sister Smith, sir,' he said, cutting into Millie's jumbled thoughts. 'She discovered the body. And these are the victim's children.'

With a monumental effort Millie pulled herself together. 'Good afternoon, Inspector.'

Alex, too, got a grip of himself. 'Good afternoon, Sister.' His gaze lingered on Millie for a few seconds more and then moved to the two children beside her. He stepped forward and hunkered down in front of them.

'Hello, Susan,' he said, in a soft tone. 'Do you know what's happened?'

Susan nodded. 'Sister Smith told me.'

Alex looked up at her and Millie noticed that in addition to the long-standing scar on his chin, there was another cut deep into his left cheek.

Alex's attention retuned to the children. 'I'm very sorry about your mother, but now it's my job to find out who did it, and to punish them.'

'I want my mummy,' said Sidney, without taking his thumb from his mouth.

Alex tousled the boy's hair. 'I know you do, lad. But right now we have to search around and find some things out. Then I'll need to ask you and your sister a few questions at the station, but I'll make sure there's some lemonade and cake for you both. What do you say?'

Sidney looked up at Millie. 'Will you come with us?'

'Yes, of course I will,' Millie replied, squeezing Sidney once more.

Alex smiled, and then raised his eyes to Millie. 'Are there any relatives who can care for them, rather than the welfare taking them in?'

'Mrs Turner's sister lives in Canning Town,' Millie replied. 'Although she doesn't know about . . .'

Their eyes meet again for two heartbeats as footsteps clattered up the stairs again.

Alex stood up as a policewoman with bright blonde curls appeared in the door. Her blue eyes flew open excitedly when she saw him and then she saluted briskly.

He returned her greeting. 'Collins, isn't it?'

'Yes, sir,' the woman constable replied, a little breathlessly.

'Tell my driver to take you and the children to their aunt and break the news about her sister; Mills here will fill you in on the details,' Alex instructed. 'Stay for as long as you think necessary, then report back to me at the Shop. I will need to speak to the children at the station, but it might not be today.'

The woman police officer saluted again. Millie told her the address and WPC Collins gathered the children together and gently coaxed them towards the door, but as they walked past Alex, Susan stopped.

'I wish you'd put *him* away last time,' she said.

Alex rested his hand lightly on the young girl's slender shoulders. 'So do I, Susan,' he said sadly. 'Now off you go.'

The children left and Alex turned to Millie.

'You've had quite a shock, too, and so I'll arrange for a patrol car to take you home.' A polite smile lifted the corners of his mouth. 'Will your husband be in to look after you?'

With some difficulty Millie held his gaze. 'No, he's working away at present, and so I'm staying at my mother's.'

They stared at each other again, and then the door downstairs banged open and this time several pairs of feet thumped up the stairs.

Alex raised an eyebrow. 'That will be the Creeping Insect Department.'

A red-faced man in a grey suit, with his trilby hat riding on the back of his head, came in, followed by two other individuals with their hands in their pockets.

'Nice of you to join us, Sergeant Pugh,' Alex said, conversationally.

The sergeant's stubby neck flushed when he saw Alex, and immediately he stood to attention. 'Sorry, guv, but me and the boys were making enquires.' He took a packet of twenty from his pocket and lit a cigarette. 'So, what's occurring?'

'See for yourself,' Alex replied. 'But you'll need your fingerprint equipment and camera.'

Sergeant Pugh and his plainclothes officers trooped out again.

'I'd better leave you to it, and don't worry about me, I've got my bicycle outside.' Millie reached for her bag.

Alex beat her to it. 'Nonsense. I'll get one of the constables to return the cycle to the clinic and to tell them what's happened.'

He stood back to allow her to pass.

Millie walked out of the room and made her way back down the stairs, acutely aware of Alex walking behind her.

A crowd of onlookers had gathered outside. Alex spoke to a young constable about Millie's bicycle, and then he guided Millie towards one of the police Rovers parked under the railway bridge.

'Just give the driver the address,' he said, opening the back door for her. 'Someone will call tomorrow and arrange for you to come to the station to make a statement.'

He handed her the bag and as Millie took it their fingers touched with a jolt of electricity.

'Thank you,' Millie said, climbing into the car.

She went to pull the door to, but Alex put his hand on it.

'And I'm glad to see you are well, Mrs Smith,' he said.

Their eyes locked for a final second, and then Alex closed the car door as the driver started the engine.

As the BBC Singers warbled the last few bars of 'Some Enchanted Evening', Millie scooped up what remained of the scrambled egg on to the spoon and offered it to Patricia. 'There you go, last one for mummy.'

Her daughter obediently opened her mouth and Millie popped

the egg inside, praying that the two aspirin she'd taken half an hour ago would soon stop the thumping in her head.

Although when she finished in the Turners' home it was almost time to pick up Patricia, she'd got the police driver to drop her at the clinic instead of her mother's house, as she didn't want the driver reporting back where she might be found. Which, she realised now, was stupid, as why on earth would Alex be interested anyhow, and in any case, being a policeman, he could easily find her regardless.

Thankfully, her mother and Charlie were going up West straight from work, and so Millie only had to feed and bathe Patricia before falling into bed exhausted herself at nine. Unfortunately, her eyes pinged open sometime between two and three in the morning, and remained stubbornly open until the alarm went off at six-thirty.

At breakfast, after Millie had recounted the events of the previous day without reference to Alex, Doris had insisted that she stay at home, which she gladly did.

Now, putting aside thoughts of Alex, the main reason for her sleepless night, Millie gave Patricia her tea-time milk before wiping her face and lifting her out of the highchair.

Sitting Patricia on the rug in front of the fireguard with her toys, Millie picked up her half-finished cup of tea. 'I've got half an hour before I have to start dinner,' she told her daughter.

Patricia babbled a reply and then rolled on to her knees and crawled to the collection of toys on the rug. Millie closed the curtains, switched on the light, and sank into a fireside chair and put her feet up on the leather pouffe. With Patricia quietly amusing herself, Millie rested her head back as the strains of the BBC Concert Orchestra drifted over her. The four o'clock pips had just finished when she heard her mother's key in the lock.

'Only me,' her mother called from the hallway.

'In here,' Millie called back.

The lounge door opened and Doris came in. 'How're you feeling?'

'Not too bad now,' Millie replied.

Patricia laughed and bounced up and down to attract her grandmother's attention. Doris smiled at her and pulled a surprised face, which started Patricia giggling.

'She's really finding her feet now, isn't she?' Doris said, turning her attention back to Millie. 'I reckon she'll be walking soon.'

'I think you're right.' Millie swung her legs off the footstool. 'There's tea in the pot. Do you want a cuppa?'

Her mother raised her hand 'You stay put, love, and I'll sort myself out.'

She went through to the kitchen and Millie put her feet up again. A minute or two later her mother reappeared with a drink in her hand.

'You're home early,' said Millie as her mother sat in the chair opposite.

'I would have been home at two if that new driver had returned to the yard on time,' Doris replied, putting her drink to cool on the side table at her elbow. 'Did the police call?'

'Yes, a constable knocked on the door just after dinner,' Millie replied. 'I'm going in tomorrow to make a statement,' she continued.

'Do you want me to come with you?'

'Thanks, but I'll be fine, honestly.' She forced a smile. 'And you took a day off two weeks ago when Patricia was poorly, and so you mustn't take off any more time or Charlie will start docking your wages.'

'He wouldn't do that,' said Doris. 'And he said I shouldn't come in until I was sure you were over yesterday's shock.'

'That's kind.'

A girlish expression spread across Doris's face. 'That's Charlie, you know; he's always thinking of others. He reminds me of your dad in that way, looking to do a good turn if he can. And he's very fond of you and Patricia.'

Millie smiled at her mother.

Doris glanced down and picked a speck of fluff off her skirt. 'In fact, he'll be coming down as soon as he's locked up the yard, which is another reason why I left work early. I wanted to have a little mother and daughter chat before he arrives.'

Patricia scrabbled over and Millie lifted her on to her lap. 'Yes?'

'I had hoped to catch you last night when I got in but you'd already gone to bed; and after you told me about that poor woman this morning, it didn't seem right to mention it. Anyway, I want you to know before I tell anyone else that,' Doris plucked nervously at her skirt again and then looked intently at Millie, 'that me and Charlie are getting married.'

Millie stared at her mother.

'He proposed last night, and I said yes,' continued Doris, barely pausing for breath. 'He's a lovely chap, generous to a fault and always a gentleman.' A coy smile raised a rarely seen dimple in her right cheek. 'And, well ... you know how these things go. Let's just say we've grown very fond of each other and as we're not getting any younger, we've decided we might as well enjoy the time we've got left together. We're not planning a big do, just family plus a few friends, probably sometime after Easter.'

'But that's only a couple of months away,' said Millie.

The colour heightened in Doris's cheeks. 'As I say, you have to make the most of this life while you can.'

There was a long silence as Millie continued to stare at her mother.

Doris shifted in her chair. 'Well, say something!'

'I wasn't expecting ...' Millie started, struggling to imagine her mother as Charlie Hawkins' wife rather than Arthur Sullivan's widow. 'Not that there's anything wrong with him or it ... or you ... And it's not as if you're old, or ... I ... I ...' Millie ground to a halt.

Doris's happy face crumpled, and she looked into the fire.

Immediately guilt surged through Millie. She reached across and grasped her mother's hand. 'I'm sorry, Mum, that was shabby of me and I'm sorry. I was just a bit surprised, that's all. Charlie's a lovely man and of course I wish you both all the happiness in the world.'

Doris rose to her feet and opened her arms. 'Oh, Millie.'

Millie stood up and warmly embraced her mother, and the two women clung together.

'Knock, knock,' called Charlie's voice from behind them.

Millie turned to see his ruddy face poking around the edge of the kitchen door. 'I thought I'd use the family entrance,' he said, thumbing over his shoulder at the back door. He winked. 'She's told you, then?'

'Yes,' replied Millie, smiling her cheeriest smile. 'And I'm delighted for you both.'

Millie let go of her mother and Doris hurried to Charlie's side. He put his arm around her and gave her a noisy kiss on the cheek. Doris blushed furiously.

Charlie's round face took on a serious expression. 'I want you to know, Millie, that I respect your father's memory and that I will do everything I can to make your mum happy.'

'I'm sure that you will,' said Millie.

'And I know it'll be a bit of a trek for you to see your mum, but I promise I'll bring her down at least once a week to see you both.'

'Don't be daft, Charlie,' laughed Millie. 'Forest Gate's only twenty minutes on the District Line. I can pop up any time.'

Charlie and Doris glanced at each other.

'Millie, Charlie's bought three more coaches and he is moving his yard to Harold Wood in Essex,' her mother explained. 'It's just right for Charlie's business, as it is on the Colchester and Southend roads and so he'll be able to corner the holiday-camp trade along the east coast. There's a bungalow at the back of the plot, and we're going to live there. There's a station, but it's on a branch line and so you'll have to change at Romford. We'll be right in the country. You'll love it, I promise, and so will Patricia.'

'It sounds lovely,' said Millie in a subdued tone.

Charlie and Doris hugged again as a feeling of deep loneliness swept over Millie.

Happy as she was for her mother, Millie couldn't help but feel that Doris's rosy future with Charlie served to highlight once again her own solitary situation. And now Millie could see that it wasn't just the emotional side of things that she had to fret about now.

Once her mother moved out, her own day-to-day expenses would almost double, Millie saw in a flash. Apart from the worry as to whether she'd be allowed to take over the tenancy of her mother's house, she'd now have to find all the rent from her own meagre wages, and this would be at the same time as she'd be paying Cora. Even in the unlikely event that Miss Dutton gave her a full week's work each and every week, it still wouldn't leave her more than a bob or two spare at the end of the week. It was a gloomy scenario, whatever way Millie looked at it.

Spotting her grandmother making a fuss of someone other than her, Patricia discarded her wooden stacking cups and crawled over to Charlie. Grasping at his trouser leg she pulled herself into a standing position. He disentangled himself from Doris.

'Hello, young lady,' he said, scooping her off the floor and holding her above him. 'Guess what?' Charlie asked as she waved her arms and giggled. 'I'm going to be your granddad.'

Chapter Twenty-Three

Sergeant Pugh scanned down the statement sheet and then looked up at Millie. 'And you didn't see anything else?'

'No,' Millie replied.

She was in one of the first-floor interview rooms in Arbour Square police station. As it was on the west side of the building, the setting sun, low on the horizon, streamed through the window grilles, illuminating the pre-war grey and white emulsion in all its dismal glory. She'd been there an hour and had now been through Tuesday's events twice in detail.

The sergeant's florid face lifted into an appealing smile. 'Not even just a little glimpse of Mickey Turner running away?'

Millie shook her head. 'I'm sorry.'

'Pity.' Sergeant Pugh sucked on his teeth. 'You see, if we had a witness who actually saw Mickey running from the scene, we'd have him bang to rights. As it is, we only have what we in the job call circumstantial evidence. And you can bet your grandmother's false teeth, once his brief knows that, he'll get the sod to plead "not guilty".'

'I'm sorry, Sergeant.' Millie shrugged apologetically. 'I'm afraid that I just didn't see him.'

The sergeant sighed. 'Oh, well. We've got him tucked away below, and so perhaps me and the boys can persuade him around to our point of view, and he'll come clean over what he did.' The sergeant splayed a fat hand on the paper and twisted it around so that Millie could read her statement. 'If I could just 'ave your moniker, on the bottom, Mrs Smith.'

Millie took the pen from the inkwell and scratched her signature along the dotted line he'd indicated.

Sergeant Pugh took it from her, slipped it in to the manila file next to him and smiled. 'Thank you for your time.'

Millie stood up. 'Not at all.'

The sergeant led her from the room, but as she emerged into the corridor the door to the office opposite opened.

A female police inspector, dressed in a tailored jacket very like her male colleagues' but with an A-line skirt instead of trousers, stepped out of the room opposite. Her mousy-coloured hair was cut or, more correctly, cropped to just under her ears and even in the poorly lit corridor the down on her top lip was clearly visible. Her close-set eyes looked Millie over.

'Mrs Smith?' she asked in a clipped, nasal tone that was unpleasantly similar to Lady Tollshunt's.

'Yes.'

'Inspector Grierson.' The corners of her mouth lifted a fraction. 'I wonder if you'd be so good as to spare me a few moments before you head off as I'd like to discuss the Turner children.'

'Of course,' said Millie.

'I'm just chaperoning one of the Cable Street toms while she's being cautioned, so perhaps you could wait in the canteen until I've sent her on her way,' the inspector said.

Millie looked at her watch: it was a quarter-past four. 'I have to be back at the clinic by five and elsewhere at half-past.'

'I shouldn't be more than a few moments,' Inspector Grierson replied. Her eyes darted on to Sergeant Pugh.

'If you'd follow me, Mrs Smith,' he said, indicating the stairs to the police refectory.

Wondering if she should call the shop on the corner of Cora's street so the shopkeeper could pass on the message that she might be late picking up Patricia, Millie plodded up the stairs.

Pugh opened the door and Millie walked into a haze of cigarette smoke and a wall of male voices. Being late afternoon, the evening shift, who'd come on duty at two, all seemed to be packed into the oak-panelled room for their afternoon cuppa at the same time. Nearly every one of the two-dozen tables had a group of officers, most of whom had a mug in one hand while they wrote up their pocket-books with the other.

The sergeant showed Millie to one of the last remaining free tables at the back of the room and then, ignoring the noisy protests, pushed to the front of the queue and fetched her a welcome cup of tea.

'Inspector Grierson won't be too long,' he said, setting it in front of Millie.

He left. Millie stirred her tea and waited. She'd only taken the first sip when the canteen door opened and Alex appeared. There was a scrape of chairs as the officers stood to attention.

In the two days since he'd strolled through Maureen Turner's bedroom door and back into Millie's life, she'd tried to convince herself that she'd exaggerated the breadth of his shoulders, the admirable length of his legs and the manly set of his jaw, but now, looking at all six-foot of him in his uniform, Millie realised that in fact she'd underplayed Alex's physical aspects.

Alex glanced casually around the room until his eyes alighted on Millie.

'As you were,' he said to the officers.

They sat down and Alex walked towards her.

'Good afternoon, Mrs Smith,' he said politely. 'Pugh said you were up here, and I thought I'd pop up and see if you'd recovered from the other afternoon.'

'Well, I didn't sleep at all well that night,' Millie replied.

He nodded. 'It's the shock, I expect.'

'I'm sure,' replied Millie. 'Sergeant Pugh told me you've arrested Mickey Turner.'

Alex pulled out the chair opposite and sat down. 'Found him drunk as a skunk in the Anchor, but it still took six officers to take him into custody. Have you seen the children?'

Millie nodded. 'I popped down yesterday. Maureen's sister seems a kind soul and Sidney is happy enough with his cousins, but Susan's still not saying much. I'm waiting for Inspector Grierson to talk to me about them.'

'Poor kids,' Alex said. 'I found the report you filed a couple of months back about Mickey Turner, when you witnessed him threatening the family.'

Millie put her hand on her forehead. 'Maybe back then I should have realised how dangerous Mickey Turner was and insisted that the station sergeant took more notice.'

'You couldn't have known that it would end like this, Mi–, er, Mrs Smith,' Alex replied, softly. 'It's not right, not by a long chalk, but it's not as if Mickey Turner isn't the only man to take his temper out on his wife.'

Millie's rubbed the underside of her wedding ring with her thumb.

Alex's eyes flickered on to her hand and then back to her face. 'I hope we won't make you late getting home.'

Millie's heart pounded, but she kept her amiable expression. 'No, I just need to be somewhere at five-thirty. I thought you'd transferred to C division on your promotion.'

Alex gave her a wry smile. 'Some Freemason from E division got in first.' He stretched out a long leg and leaned back in the chair. 'So, what did you have?'

'A little girl,' Millie replied. 'Patricia.'

He smiled. 'That was my nan's name.'

'Mine, too,' replied, Millie.

'Who does she look like?'

'Everyone says me,' Millie replied.

'I bet she's pretty then,' Alex replied, casually.

'Flatterer!' Millie scoffed. 'Unfortunately she has my temper, too.'

Alex laughed and then a tender expression stole into his eyes. 'I'm really happy for you, Millie. And your husband too, of course.'

Millie's throat tightened, but she forced a smile. 'Thank you.'

Their gazes locked for a couple of heartbeats – in fact Millie did wonder if her heart was going to stop – and then the canteen door swung open.

Millie tore her eyes from Alex to see WPC Collins walk in.

The policewoman looked around the refectory until she spotted Millie, then she noticed Alex and a glimmer of excitement flashed across her face. She marched over.

'I'm sorry, Inspector Nolan,' she said demurely while contriving to give him an impish look. 'Inspector Grierson is ready to see Mrs Smith.'

Alex stood up. 'That's all right. Mrs Smith and I have finished chatting now.'

He smiled down at the WPC with something approaching his old rascally smile, and a sharp pang twisted in Millie's chest. Alex's gaze returned to Millie. 'Congratulations again on the birth of Patricia, Mrs Smith. And I'll see you in court in a month or so.'

He gave Millie a final nod and marched across the canteen. Millie's eyes greedily watched his every step.

The woman sitting next to Millie stood up and made her way towards the dull green door at the far end of the corridor. She and the rest of the people sitting on the row of chairs stood up and moved along one. Millie was on the second floor in Stepney's Victorian town hall. Built somewhere in the middle of the previous century, the vaulted ceilings and fiddly cornices helped the building retain some of its former grandeur despite the curly ended notices instructing people not to spit in public places and to wrap their rubbish to discourage rats. As her eyes ran up the green half-tiled wall opposite, Millie yawned.

She'd been awake since just after six, which wouldn't have been so bad had she not also woken up briefly on the hour every hour since two.

It was now the end of February and four weeks since Millie had been called to the Turners' house and, to be truthful, she'd hardly had a full night's sleep since. And needless to say, it wasn't just because she'd discovered Maureen's body.

She might have had some respite from her nocturnal restlessness had it not been for the fact that, having willingly agreed to accompany the children to the police station to be interviewed, she'd met Alex on all four occasions. And if that wasn't enough, he'd dropped in to the clinic twice to clarify a couple of points in her statement. Thankfully, as it was official police business, Miss Dutton couldn't object.

It was also exactly a week after Maureen Turner's murder that, much to Millie's irritation, Jim had narrowly scraped back in at the general election as the MP for Leytonstone and Wanstead. And now it was just over four weeks until her mother became Mrs Hawkins, which is why Millie had been waiting for forty minutes in the draughty corridor of the housing department.

The office door opened and the previous applicant came out looking decidedly less than cheerful.

Millie stood up, walked the twenty feet to the room and knocked. There was a gruff reply so she walked in.

Behind the desk sat a stick-thin middle-aged woman, head bent, scribbling furiously in the file on her desk. She wore a gabardine suit that shone with wear and an unadorned buttoned-up blouse beneath. She'd once been a brunette but only a few brown streaks remained in her steel-grey bobbed hair.

Without looking up, she waved Millie to the chair on the other side of the desk. Tucking her skirt under her, Millie slipped into the seat and put her handbag on her lap. After a few moments the woman she was there to see slapped the file shut and, placing it on the pile to her left, took another from the pile on her right.

'Name?' she said, finally looking at Millie over her half-rimmed glasses.

'Mrs Amelia Smith,' Millie replied.

'Present address, if any?'

'And good afternoon to you, Mrs ...?'

The woman rested her forearms on the desk. 'Farleigh. Now if you don't mind, you're the fifteenth person I've seen since dinnertime and there's a dozen more behind you, and so if I could have where you're residing at the moment, it would do us both a favour.'

Millie told her Doris's address.

'Is that your place?' the housing officer asked as she wrote the previous answer.

Millie shook her head. 'I live with my mother.'

Mrs Farleigh ticked a box halfway down the page. 'Children?'

'One,' Millie replied. 'She's just coming up to a year.'

A sour expression tightened Mrs Farleigh's narrow face. 'I'll put it down, but you won't get many points for one baby.'

'Points?'

'Everyone applying for a council house gets points for different things, such as how many kids they have, how many rooms they have, how many other families share their lav and is it inside or outside, if they have hot water or just cold, and that sort of stuff,' Mrs Farleigh explained wearily. 'So, do you share the khazi with anyone else?'

'No, we have our own toilet.'

'Hot and cold?'

'Yes.'

Mrs Farleigh's top lip curled slightly. 'Lucky you. Me, me husband and four kids have to share with the Branhams upstairs. How many adults are there?'

'Two.'

The housing officer looked suspicious. 'I thought you said you were living with your mother?'

'I am,' Millie replied. 'It's just me, my mother, and my daughter.'

Mrs Farleigh's eyes narrowed. 'You are legally married, aren't you? Because the council can't allocate houses to women who—'

'Of course I am!'

The housing officer didn't look convinced. 'You'll have to produce the certificate if we offer you something.'

'That's fine.'

'Widowed, then?' said Mrs Farleigh, ticking another box.

An uncomfortable prickling started between Millie's shoulder-blades. 'Separated.'

Mrs Farleigh put down her pen and looked up. 'Your husband walked out on you?'

'No, it was me who left,' replied Millie, forcing herself to look the woman in the eye.

'Well, that puts a different complexion on things,' said Mrs Farleigh, scratching out her last entry.

'Why? I still need a council house.'

'You, and thousands of others. For a start you need to have to have a reference from an employer to get a council house, and your husband isn't there for us to get the reference.'

'I'm working as a district nurse at Munroe House and nights at the East London Lying in Hospital as a midwife, and therefore I can get a reference on my own behalf,' said Millie.

'Can you now?' Mrs Farleigh replied. 'My husband's been out of work for two years because of married women undercutting his job at the refinery.'

'Well, if he's a qualified nurse or midwife, please send him to me because we've got plenty of vacancies,' snapped Millie.

She glared across the table at the other woman and after a couple of seconds Mrs Farleigh shifted her gaze.

'Yes, well,' she said, crossing off another couple of boxes, 'even if you have an employer's note, it won't help you, because as far as I can see, you and your mother are ten times better off than most of the poor souls who come in here.'

'But the house must be two hundred years old if it's a day, and it has damp in every room,' said Millie.

'So has the rest of the Chapman Estate. We allocate our housing to the most deserving families first, and once the chief officer sees you've voluntarily left your marital home, that you've already got a roof over your head, you're not sharing facilities and you've got only one kiddie, you'll be right at the bottom of the list.'

'But my mother is getting remarried in four weeks,' Millie explained, 'and the landlord's said he's going to up the rent by twelve shillings a week. I'll never be able to afford to keep the place, let alone heat it and put food on the table for me and my daughter. I was hoping you might be able to offer me something by the summer.'

'Well, perhaps you should have thought of that before you decided to flit off.' Mrs Farleigh closed the folder and crossed her arms over her imperceptible bosom. 'As I say, we only give homes to those most deserving and, from what you told me about your circumstances, you probably won't even be looked at for a couple of years. And even then they'll be giving priority to proper families – you know, families with a mother, father and a couple of kiddies, and so there's no guarantee you'll get anything even then.' She gave Millie a condescending smile. 'I'm so sorry I couldn't be more help, Mrs Smith.'

Millie stared at Mrs Farleigh's wilfully unhelpful face for a moment. Then, with all the composure she could muster, she stood up and left the room.

As she opened the door, the next applicant stood up to take her place with the housing officer. Millie stepped aside to let him through and heard Mrs Farleigh bark 'Name!' before the door closed behind her.

With her feet feeling like lead and her mind spinning with worry Millie trudged the half a mile back from the Town Hall to Watney Street market.

Taking a string shopping bag from her pocket she headed past Shelston's and the Britannia Pub and on towards Johnny Philipp's rabbit stall in the middle of the market. After selecting a plump white one from the top rack Millie went to the stall next door for five pounds of filling potatoes, half a cabbage and a pound each of carrots and onions while the proprietor of the rabbit stall skinned and cleaned it for her.

After collecting her supper and buying some rosehip syrup for Patricia and some Dr Whites for herself, Millie started home along Chapman Street. But as she reached the corner Pete Moss, who ran the hardware shop on the corner dashed out and beckoned her over.

'That's a bit of luck,' he said, as Millie crossed the road. 'Your uncle Terry, I think he said, called for you on this number.' He handed her a torn-off corner of brown paper.

'Thanks – it must be my uncle Tony who rang. I'll ring from one of the boxes at the end of the road,' Millie said, slipping the scrap of paper into her pocket.

'He said it was urgent and so you can ring from here if you like,' Pete replied. Millie followed him in and with the smell of paraffin mixed with carbolic tingling her nose, wended her way past the lino and zinc buckets right to the back of the shop. Passing through the raised section of counter she entered the small hallway leading to the living quarters behind and walked to the telephone sitting on a small hall table.

She picked up the receiver and dialled the number. It rang a couple of times and then it was picked up.

'King George V Hospital. How may I help you?' said the woman at the other end.

Millie's heart lurched. 'I've had a message to call extension 446.'

'Putting you through.'

The phone clicked again and another voice answered.

'Valentine Ward, nurse Gee speaking.'

'My uncle Mr Harris told me to ring on this number.'

'Oh, he's in the waiting room. I'll just call him.'

There was a clunk as the phone was put down but within a few moments it rattled as someone picked it up.

'Hello,' said Tony's gruff voice.

'It's Millie, Tony,' Millie replied.

There was an audible sigh of relief.

'What's happened?'

'It's Ruby. She was rushed in with bronchitis about an hour ago and the doctors have put her on the critical list. They told me to get the family.' Millie heard a shuddering sob. 'It's not looking good.'

Millie gripped the mouthpiece. 'Don't worry, Tony, me and mum will come straight away.'

While the quiet hum of the afternoon routine on Valentine ward continued on the other side of the portable screens, Doris straightened the mushroom-coloured hospital counterpane for the fourth time in a quarter of an hour.

Stripped of make-up and with her hair plastered to her forehead, poor Ruby looked every day of her fifty-nine years and uncannily like Millie's grandmother.

'Your father had a blue one,' Doris said, without taking her eyes from the poorly woman lying in the bed.

'Yes,' Millie replied.

Millie knew exactly what her mother was thinking of because the thought had crossed her mind several times too. She had sat with her mother in very much the same position on VE day, almost four years ago, in St Andrew's hospital, staring at a blue counterpane. Her father breathed his last just as Churchill addressed a joyful nation. But so far, mercifully, Ruby was hanging on.

It was three days since Millie had rung the hospital from the hardware shop, and apart from popping out to ring Cora to check on Patricia, Millie, her mother and Tony had been at Ruby's bedside ever since. As only two people were allowed at the bedside during visiting time, she and Doris had taken it in turns. Tony was manfully carrying on, with the occasional joke about how Ruby would give him a 'right telling' if she found that he'd been slacking, but he had been persuaded to nip out for a much-needed break.

With pneumonia clearly rattling in both lungs and her chest barely moving the sheets, the doctor had already told them to prepare for the worse if Ruby's fever didn't break very soon.

Doris took her sister's limp hand and lovingly stroked it. 'I shouldn't have been so sharp with her at Patricia's christening,' she said, in a little cracked voice.

'Oh, Mum,' said Millie. 'You weren't to know she was going to be so ill.'

A tear escaped from Doris's right eye and rolled down her cheek. 'But she's my sister. We argued like mad from when we were kids, but we always loved each other too.'

The casters squeaked as the curtain parted. A young woman in her late twenties who was wearing a white coat at least three sizes too big and who had a stethoscope around her neck, stepped in. She lifted Ruby's chart from the end of the bed and glanced at it.

'How is she, doctor?' asked Doris.

'There's very little change,' the doctor replied. 'Under the circumstances I have authorised Sister to allow family members to stay beyond the usual hours.' She hooked the observation chart back on the footboard and smiled professionally. 'We just have to hope for the best.'

She disappeared back through the screens, closing them behind her as she went.

Doris and Millie resumed their vigil.

'That was kind of her,' said Doris, taking Ruby's hand again. 'Letting us stay like that.'

Not wanting to say it was usual practice to let the relatives of a dying patient remain at the bedside, Millie didn't reply. They sat silently for a few moments, and then Doris spoke again. 'Shouldn't that Pen-cilly stuff be working by now, Millie?'

'I'm sure it is.'

Doris's chin wobbled. 'When we were kids she was always looking out for us younger ones,' she continued, her eyes not leaving her sister's sallow face. 'As the oldest girl our mum used to rely on Ruby to help her with the young ones. I remember her, when she was no more than a child herself, getting us some bread and scrap for tea. Mum used to work as an office cleaner until seven,' Doris continued, smiling as the childhood memories flooded back. 'And dad always had a beer or two to clear the coal dust from his throat before walking home from Limehouse Basin, and so it was Ruby who washed behind our ears and tucked us in. And when our mum was gripped by the melancholy after little Bette died, it was Ruby who got us up in the mornings as well.'

'She told me how she used to gather the discarded fruit at the end of the Saturday market so you could all have a treat,' Millie said.

'And we had to pare the rotten bits out before we could eat them.' Doris smiled. 'I remember when Martha bit through two maggots in a Cox's apple once. You should have heard her scream! And one Christmas, when dad hadn't had work for days, Ruby crawled under a stall on the market to pinch a jar of jam from the display so we could all have a treat.' Her eyes drifted back to the woman in the bed. 'She always looked after us, did Ruby.' Doris's expression softened further as she watched her sister. 'She took me to the Lying-in Hospital when I was having you.'

'Because you couldn't fetch dad from work,' replied Millie, having been told the story on every birthday.

'She helped me make my wedding dress and she was my chief bridesmaid when I married your dad. And after all that I …' Doris's face crumpled, 'I wasn't even going to invite her to my wedding to Charlie.'

She pressed her forehead on to Ruby's motionless hand and sobbed.

'Oh, Mum,' said Millie, rising to her feet and moving around the bed.

She put her arm around her mother's shoulder.

Doris looked up. 'What will I do without her?'

'Now, now, Mum, it's not over yet. The doctor said she was stable, remember,' Millie said. 'And I'm sure the penicillin will kick in soon. It got Mrs O'Toole back on her feet, and she has to be well over seventy.'

'Did it?'

'Yes,' Millie said firmly. 'I promise you that she's as right as ninepence now.'

Doris's gaze returned to Ruby and a sentimental expression stole over her face. 'I know she can be bossy and overbearing sometimes, but underneath she's got a heart of pure gold.'

Ruby's arm raised a couple of inches from the cover before it flopped back.

Millie ran a professional eye over her aunt. Although she was still the colour of old putty, there was now a frown across her brow, and the black rubber mask covering her nose and mouth was moving.

Doris stood up and they both moved closer to the bed.

'Ruby?' Doris whispered, leaning close to her sister.

Ruby's fingers twitched, and the mask moved again.

Tentatively Millie lifted it.

Ruby coughed. 'For God sake, Doris, stop snivelling,' she rasped. 'I'm not gone yet.'

Chapter Twenty-Four

Patricia, dressed in a pink organza and satin dress, shifted on Millie's lap and pointed at her grandmother sitting next to Charlie at the table that had a spray of flowers at each end.

'Yes, it's Nanny and uncle Charlie, poppet,' Millie whispered in her daughter's ear. 'They're getting married.'

Millie, along with the rest of her family, was sitting on the bride's side of the oak-panelled registry office in Poplar Town Hall. The spring sunlight streamed through the tall Art Deco windows, and it seemed to cover the couple about to become husband and wife in a mellow glow.

Looking very snazzy in a new double-breasted grey suit with a red rose buttonhole, Charlie had obviously visited the barber's earlier, as his hair was trimmed and his cheeks were still flushed from the razor.

But all eyes were on the bride. And Doris looked truly lovely in a dove-grey two-piece with a matching hat. She held a posy of white bud-roses and lily of the valley, and she looked very happy.

The first Sunday after Ruby was released from hospital her mother and Charlie had taken the hour-long journey to Ilford so Doris could introduce Charlie to Ruby and Tony. Millie had gone too and she was relieved to see that although her aunt's brush with death had left her a great deal thinner, it hadn't stopped her making it to the hairdresser for a perm nor getting made up with a new shade of lipstick to complement the vibrant orange of her blouse.

Millie had been a little worried before they arrived that her aunt would disapprove of Charlie's tattoos and his liking for sharp suits, but instead they got on like a house on fire. Sometime during the afternoon Tony and Charlie discovered they had several business acquaintances in common, and when it was revealed that Charlie was a dab hand on the piano, all four of them gathered around Ruby's old upright for a boisterous sing-song.

Aunt Ruby had sent out a three-line whip as regards the wedding, and so all Millie's immediate family were in the wedding party. Millie, wearing an apple-green cropped jacket over a candy-striped pink, green and white dress with a half-circle skirt and stiffened petticoat, sat in the front row with Tony and Ruby, who was togged up in a chocolate-brown dress and jacket with an enormous hat. Behind them were Uncle Bill, Doris and Ruby's younger brother, looking like something from a bygone era in his pre-war wide-lapelled suit. He was flanked by his younger sisters, Martha and Edie. They were on the wrong side of fifty, but clearly had made an effort. Martha sported a red hat with foliage around the brim while her sister had gone to town with the rouge and lipstick.

Cousin Gwen and her husband Len were there, along with their two boys, who were smartly dressed in their school uniforms. Cousin Bob, well off, thirty-seven and still unmarried, sat behind them. Much to Ruby's annoyance, May, who was Millie's other cousin, and her husband Wilfred, were on an Easter camp with their Scout troop and so weren't able to attend.

The registrar sitting behind the desk offered Doris his fountain pen. She signed the two elongated registers in turn and then passed the pen to Charlie, who did the same. The official rolled the blotter over the paperwork a couple of times and then handed the certificate to Doris.

'It is now my great pleasure to pronounce you man and wife.' The registrar grinned. 'You may now seal the matter in the traditional manner.'

Charlie put his arm round Doris and kissed her as the whole room clapped unreservedly.

Patricia wriggled and Millie stood her on the floor. Patricia promptly dropped down on all fours and scrambled off.

'No, you don't, young lady,' Millie said, catching her daughter before she disappeared between a dozen pairs of legs.

Squealing and arching her back, Patricia protested. Millie turned her around so she could see Doris and Charlie.

'Look at Nanny,' she said brightly, hoping to avert the threatened tantrum.

Patricia's lower lip trembled and she tucked her face into Millie's shoulder. Millie stepped forward and embraced her mother with her free arm.

'Congratulations, Mum,' she said, kissing her on the cheek and feeling the edge of the veil tickle her nose. 'I'm so happy for you.'

'Thank you,' her mother replied, fizzing with excitement. 'Hello, Patricia dear,' she said to her granddaughter.

Patricia pressed her face further into the shoulder padding of Millie's bolero.

'She's sulking because I won't let her crawl off.' Millie explained. She reached across and caught Charlie's arm. 'Congratulations, Charlie. I know you and Mum will be very happy together.'

He turned and grinned. 'Ta, love, and don't you worry none,' he put his arm around Doris and squeezed her, 'as I'll take proper care of your mum.'

Millie smiled. 'I know you will.'

Someone else came forward to congratulate the newly-weds, and Millie stepped back. After she'd exchanged a few words with her mother's old friends and introduced herself to a couple of people on Charlie's side, the party started moving into the main lobby and Millie followed everyone out.

Poplar Town Hall sat like the prow of a Portland stone cruise ship on the corner of Bow and Fairfield Roads. It had only been finished fifteen years or so before and was a masterpiece of 1930s modernity, with a decorative frieze of squarely fashioned industrial workers hammering, sawing and welding the brave new world into shape. In addition there was a mosaic representation of the river and the surrounding area around the main entrance, which was where the party assembled to take photos.

Millie took her place when asked and stood patiently while the photographer added immediate family, then cousins and friends, until the whole party were arranged up the four steps in front of the main door.

As the photographer reloaded his camera, Ruby threaded her way through the well-wishers to join Millie.

'Your mum looks happy,' her aunt said, taking her cigarette case out of her handbag.

'Yes, doesn't she?' Millie replied as her mother and Charlie struck up another pose. 'How are you, Ruby?'

Ruby lit the cigarette and regarded Millie thoughtfully. 'I'm feeling well, thank you. But are you all right with your mum moving out, Amelia?'

'I will be once I've sorted everything,' Millie replied. 'I've got a month before I officially take over the tenancy, and so that should help.'

'I still don't understand why your mother couldn't have kept the house in her name so you didn't have to pay the extra rent,' said Ruby.

'Because if the council knocks the street down, unless my name's on the rent book, I'll be out,' Millie replied.

Her aunt blew a mouthful of smoke upwards. 'Bloody socialists.'

The photographer started to pack away and Charlie guided his new wife around to the other side of the building where the cars were parked. Millie followed the rest of the party around but just got to Tony's Hillman when she realised she was missing something.

'Blast! I've left my handbag.' She held Patricia out. 'Can you take her, aunt Ruby, while I pop back?'

Putting her cigarette between her lips Ruby took her great-niece. 'You wait with me and uncle Tony until mummy gets back.'

While everyone decided which car they were going in and the best way to the Spotted Dog, Millie dashed back to the front door. Without pausing, she sped across the foyer and up the central stairs to the main assembly room above. Thankfully, there was no one in the room, so she slipped through the gap between the tall oak doors.

She spotted her handbag immediately and had just retrieved it from under the chair when footsteps sounded behind.

Thinking it was probably the registrar returning to get ready for the next wedding, Millie turned around.

'I'm sorry, I forgot ...'

Every thought vanished from her mind as she saw Alex standing in the doorway.

The tailored suit he wore showed off his athletic physique to perfection, while the bold Windsor knot at his throat emphasised his firm chin. If that weren't enough to stop every breath in her body, the pristine white collar underscored the thick blackness of his hair and made a striking contrast to his green eyes.

'I left my handbag.' Millie held it aloft.

'Did you?'

'Yes.' She laughed. 'Luckily, I realised before we set off in the car.'

Alex frowned. 'Is your husband here?'

'No. Tony and aunt Ruby are driving me.'

'Oh.'

There was a long pause.

'So, apart from rescuing your handbag, what are you doing here?' he asked eventually.

'Mum's just got remarried.'

'Has she?'

'Yes,' Millie replied. 'To Charlie.'

'Who?'

'Charlie Hawkins, the chap she works for,' Millie explained. 'You wouldn't know him.'

Alex smiled. 'That's nice.'

'It is,' replied Millie, returning his smile. 'What about you?'

'Me?'

'Yes, why are you here?' She forced a laugh. 'Not getting married, are you?'

Alex chuckled. 'No, it's Georgie Tugman who's tying the knot. I'm just the best man.'

Millie's gaze ran over him. 'How funny that we should both be attending weddings on the same day in the same place.'

'Yes,' he said seriously. 'What are the odds?'

They stared wordlessly at each other as the second hand on the wall clock made another full circle.

'Well, I'd better be off,' said Millie, tearing her gaze from Alex. 'Or they'll be sending out a search party.'

Alex raised his eyebrows. 'And I'd better make sure everything is in order before the bride's mother arrives.'

They laughed again.

Millie hooked her bag over her arm and walked towards the door, but as she drew level with him, Alex spoke.

'Please give your mother my best wishes,' he said softly, his eyes locking with hers. 'And green always was your colour.'

Watching the happy couple with their family and friends crowded around, through the open door of the Old Spotted Dog, Millie rolled the pushchair back and forth in the rear garden.

Once the formalities of the sit-down and speeches were finished, Charlie had put a wedge of pound notes behind the bar and now everyone had either a pint or a short in their hand. The pub pianist had taken up their place at the old upright in the corner and was now bashing his way through the chorus of 'My Old Man Said Follow the Van'.

Patricia grizzled as she fought sleep and then, as the motion of her pram took effect, her eyelids finally closed. Millie continued rocking for a moment or two longer, and then she parked the pram under the crab apple tree. Settling on the bench alongside the pub wall she picked up her G&T and took a sip. Leaning back, Millie closed her eyes.

As she knew it would, the image of Alex as she had seen him three hours before floated into her mind. For once she didn't try to dislodge it but allowed herself the pleasure, if only in her head, of enjoying his masculine figure and strikingly handsome face. Her thoughts moved inevitably away from their most recent encounter and on to other more exciting, breath-taking rendezvous. Tears gathered in the corners of her eyes.

Hopelessness hovered over Millie for a second, and then Connie's voice interrupted her thoughts. 'I wondered where you'd got to.'

Millie opened her eyes as her friend slipped on to the bench beside her.

'Patricia was getting over-tired, so I thought I'd try to get her asleep out here,' she replied.

'Well, it looks like you're succeeded.' Connie smiled fondly at her godchild for a couple of seconds. 'She's such an angel.'

Millie nodded in agreement.

Connie studied the slumbering child for a little longer and then looked closely at her friend. 'Are you all right, Millie?'

'Of course,' replied Millie quickly. 'Why do you ask?'

'It's just that you were a little tearful during the speeches and you looked so unhappy when I was just coming to sit down.'

Millie put on her brightest smile. 'Don't be silly. I always cry at weddings.'

Connie closed her hand over Millie's. 'It's not Jim again, is it? I mean he's not sent you another horrible letter or anything like that, has he?'

'I haven't heard from Jim since that visit I paid to his office,' Millie replied.

'Is it your mum then?' Connie persisted. 'I know how close you were to your dad and so it must be difficult for you to see her getting married again.'

'No, no, Connie,' Millie insisted. 'I'm really pleased she's got the chance to be happy again with Charlie.'

'Well, are you worried about coping with everything now she's not around the corner? Because you know I'll always pop down and give—'

'It's Alex.'

'Alex!'

'He was at the Town Hall,' Millie explained. 'He was best man at the wedding after mum's.'

'Did he say anything?'

Millie smiled wistfully. 'That I always looked good in green.' From nowhere tears welled up.

Connie squeezed her hand. 'Oh, Millie.'

'It's ridiculous, I know,' she said, with a little sob. 'How can running into him make me so unsettled and weepy?'

'Because you still have feelings for him,' replied Connie gently.

Millie opened her mouth to argue, but then the weight she'd been carrying around for weeks pressed down on her shoulders.

'Before all this business with Mickey Turner I only saw him in passing half a dozen times at most and then usually with some blonde or redhead on his arm. And so I'm telling myself "you can't possibly be in love with him", and yet now all I do is remember how his eyes twinkle, the shape of his lips as he smiles, and the way his hair curls around his temple. As I was talking to him in the register office all I kept thinking about was how I'd like to run my fingers over his jaw to feel his bristles.'

'Good grief. You've got it bad,' said Connie, with a wry laugh.

'It's not fair, Connie!' sobbed Millie.

Connie gave her a sympathetic smile. 'No, it's not.'

'And if it wasn't bad enough bumping into him all the time, now I've got to spend goodness knows how long hanging around at the Old Bailey with him in only a few weeks.' Millie rubbed the wetness from her cheeks. 'It's all right for Alex bloody Nolan. He's all footloose and fancy free, waiting to be promoted again, while I'm running around like a blue-tailed fly as a bank nurse, while unavoidably shackled to a drunken letch.'

Connie opened her handbag and pulled out a clean handkerchief. 'Here you are.'

Millie took it and mopped her face. 'Sorry.'

'Don't be silly.'

'Talking of sad,' said Millie, studying Connie a little closer. 'You don't look on top of the world yourself.'

Connie gave her a forlorn look. 'I've broken off the engagement.'

Millie's jaw dropped. 'Why?'

'I don't feel about Malcolm the way you feel about Alex,' Connie said simply, catching Millie's eye to signal someone was approaching.

Millie turned and smiled at her mother. 'Hello Mum, how's it going?'

'Swimmingly,' Doris replied, beaming at them both. 'Me and Charlie are thrilled that so many people have made the effort to come. Although I think poor Gwen's had enough of Basil and Rex fighting.'

'Yes I saw her split them up again as I came out,' said Millie. 'And it's a shame Charlie's great aunt and nephew had to go straight after the service.'

'Yes, wasn't it,' Doris agreed. 'But at eighty-seven, Hoddesdon is a bit of a trek.'

'The spread was delicious,' said Connie. 'And the cake was beautiful. Who made it?'

'Someone Ruby's knows,' Doris said. 'And it's nice to have proper icing instead of a white cardboard cover with plaster edging. It's a pity your Malcolm couldn't come, Connie. I suppose it's his mother again.'

'Something like that,' said Connie. 'I'm sorry to be a wet blanket, but would you be terribly offended if I made a move?'

'Of course, not, Connie,' said Doris cheerfully. 'I'm just glad you came.'

'Thanks, Mrs Sull ... I mean Mrs Hawkins.' Connie kissed Doris on the cheek. 'You have a lovely day.'

The pianist struck up the chord for 'Slow Boat to China' as Connie hurried back inside the public house.

The warm afternoon breeze lifted Doris's blush-tinted curls and Millie slipped her arm through her mother's.

'Have you had a lovely day, Mum?' she asked quietly.

Doris laughed. 'I have.' She gazed across at Charlie who was talking to Tony just inside the door and her expression softened. 'You know the terrible time I had of it when I lost your dad, Millie, and I never thought I could be happy again. And then I met Charlie.' She squeezed Millie's arm and winked. 'And even at my age there's nothing better than having a man to keep you warm on a cold night.'

The image of Alex in his uniform that was never far from her conscious thoughts drifted back into Millie's mind. She hugged her mother.

'Oh, Mum,' she said smiling through the tears that were once again gathering in her eyes. 'You're so right.'

A loud hammering on the back door awoke Millie. Forcing the sleep from her eyes, she switched on the bedside lamp and peered at the alarm clock. Two o'clock!

The backdoor thundered again and this time Patricia screamed.

Millie jumped out of bed and hastily scrambling into her dressing-gown. Tying the sash firmly around her waist, she hurried into her daughter's room at the rear of the house and picked Patricia out of her cot. Holding her daughter in one arm Millie threw up the bottom half of the window with the other and poked out her head.

Below her in the yard, illuminated by the street lamp on the other side of the wall, stood Ted Kirby with Jim slumped against the coal-hole beside him.

'What the hell do you think you're doing?' Millie demanded, as loud as she dare.

Ted looked up. 'Jim's been in a bit of bother,' he said, struggling to keep Jim from sliding on to the floor.

'He's drunk, you mean,' Millie snapped.

Next door's dog suddenly launched itself at the side fence snarling and snapping.

Jim jolted into life as if a puppeteer had just pulled all his strings. 'Tally ho!' he yelled, swinging his arm wildly and almost unbalancing himself in the process.

The bedroom light in the house opposite went on as did two others, and wood scraped against wood as windows were shoved upwards.

'Keep the noise down, will yer?' a man shouted from the other end of the street. 'Some of us have to get up for work in the morning.'

'Come on, Millie, love, let us in just for a few moments,' Ted pleaded.

Millie glared at them. 'All right, but keep Jim quiet until I come down.'

After rocking Patricia for a few moments Millie laid her back in her cot and then she made her way downstairs. Throwing back the bolt, she opened the door. Ted lurched in with Jim draped around his shoulders.

Jim was, as ever, dressed in an expensive charcoal-grey three-piece suit, although the sartorial effect was marred somewhat by the right collar being all but detached, and him having several buttons missing from his waistcoat. Jim's Royal Air Force tie was twisted around, and there was a deep rent in the knee of one leg of his trousers. But what really drew Millie's attention was the encrusted blood around his mouth and the bruising around his eyes and cheeks.

Jim frowned as his sodden brain tried to make sense of what his eyes saw then he belched.

Millie gave him a disgusted look. 'Take him into the front room.'

Ted staggered into the lounge and off-loaded Jim into the fire-side chair, where he laid sprawled in an untidy heap.

'He got into a fight with some shop steward from the Steve-dores & Dockers Union,' said Ted, puffing from his exertion.

Millie wrinkled her nose. 'Where? In a brewery?'

Ted shook his head. 'Poplar Baths. Jim was addressing a meet-ing, and I admit he'd had a couple too many before it started. But then this big Irishman started questioning him. Jim got annoyed, someone threw a punch, and in a minute things got out of hand and the Old Bill were called. They steamed in and arrested half a dozen, including Jim. Well, not all of them because the Irishman was carted off to hospital. Nothing too serious,' Ted added, seeing the look of horror on Millie's face, 'just a mild case of concussion and a busted nose. But would you Adam and Eve it? The bloody inspector wanted to charge Jim with GBH. Cheeky bugger. But as luck would have it, the Borough Commander and me are in the same lodge, and so a swift chat on the phone, and that was that.' Ted chuckled. 'You should have seen that copper's face when he got the call telling him to drop all the charges he was trying to pin on Jim.'

'Which police station?' asked Millie, wondering how she'd ever look Alex in the face again if it were his.

'Limehouse.'

Her shoulders relaxed. 'But why come here?'

'Someone tipped off this blasted reporter from the *News of the World* who's been nosing around for a month or two,' Ted explained. 'He saw us coming out of the nick and followed us. We gave him the slip in Salmon Lane but I'd bet a pound to a penny he'll be waiting for us at home. Jim's in enough trouble with the party executive, and so if there are pictures of him looking like a prize fighter all over the front pages, he'll be finished.'

Millie folded her arms. 'You've got a blooming nerve, Ted.'

'Come on, Millie, 'ave a heart,' he said cajolingly. 'How am I going to get him anywhere in that state?'

'I don't care,' Millie replied. 'But you'd better, or I'll call the *New of the World* myself.' Ted started to speak but she cut him short. 'I mean it. You are forgetting that he refuses to support his own daughter.'

'All right, love, I'll find a taxi,' Ted capitulated quickly as he headed for the front door.

'If you can't, you'd better fetch a handcart,' Millie called after him. 'Or I'll be putting the MP for Leytonstone and Wanstead straight in the gutter outside, and then phoning the press.'

Ted closed the door and the house fell silent again.

Glaring at the oblivious Jim lying spread-eagled in the chair, Millie pulled her dressing-gown a little tighter and sat in the chair opposite. There was a rumbling grunt with each indrawn breath and then a faint whistle as he exhaled. As she studied her drink-sodden husband, scenes from their brief life together played over in her mind, and Millie wondered for the umpteenth time how she could ever have been so stupid.

Jim snorted and woke up. He looked around blearily until his barely focusing eyes reached her. 'Issss that you, Millie?'

'Yes. More's the pity. Ted's gone to fetch a taxi.'

An inane grin spread across his face. 'Good old Ted.' He looked sideways at Millie. 'I sss ... uppose he told you all about ... about my bit of bother?'

Millie raised an eyebrow.

Self-pity flashed across Jim's face. 'It wasn't my fault,' he whined. 'I didn't know she was—'

'Shut up, Jim.' Millie snapped. 'Just shut up. I'm not interested.'

He gave her an indignant looked and slumped further in the chair.

Millie turned away and watched the second hand of the mantelshelf clock mark off the minutes. After three circumferences of the dial Jim started snoring again. Millie closed her eyes. She must have drifted off to sleep as a faint knock on the front door brought her back to the present. Rubbing the sleep from her eyes she stood up.

Ted was standing on the doorstep with a taxi idling behind him.

'Sorry I took so long, Millie,' Ted said.

Millie gave him a sour look as he went into the lounge.

'Wake up, old chum,' he said, shaking Jim to rouse him. 'Time to go home.'

Jim opened his eyes and tried to get to his feet. Ted hooked his shoulder under Jim's armpit and heaved him up. Jim swayed for a moment and then found his balance.

'There you go,' said Ted, jovially. 'We'll soon have you home.'

Beads of sweat sprang out on Jim's forehead and his hand went to his mouth.

'Don't you dare, Jim Smith,' Millie yelled, grabbing the empty coal-scuttle from the hearth. But it was too little, too late.

Jim gagged, retched, then pitched forward and vomited

violently into the middle of Millie's rug. The combination of stomach acid and half-digested whiskey filled the room.

For the first time Millie could ever remember, Ted look shamefaced. 'I'm so sorry, Millie, I'll pay for a new one.'

'Just get out,' Millie said resignedly.

Ted half-carried, half-dragged Jim out to the waiting taxi, and with relief Millie turned the lock behind them and then walked back through the house to fetch the mop and bucket from the kitchen, trying not to think that she would have to be getting up in less than three hours.

Packing the last tin into the Little Sister steriliser sitting on the sluice bench, Millie turned the handle down firmly and set the dial for a full steam cycle.

'Why don't you get yourself ready for dinner, Eva?' Millie said, to her friend who was wiping the last of their four stainless-steel trollies down with surgical spirit.

'No, it's all right,' said Eva. 'I'll help you finish off as you're not feeling all the ticket.'

'It's just a bit of a headache, that's all,' said Millie as cheerily as she could. 'Go on. I'll be all right.'

'If you're sure?'

Millie nodded.

Eva gave Millie a grateful smile and collected her bag from under the desk as she headed off to refresh herself before the dinner gong sounded.

As the treatment-room door closed Millie's shoulders sagged. Her bit of a headache was in fact a blinding, head-splitter that two doses of aspirin hadn't dented. But after the night she'd had, Millie was hardly surprised.

After Jim and Ted's departure at gone three o'clock she'd scrubbed the rug for many minutes before concluding it was beyond saving and throwing it in the backyard. The pink pre-dawn light was already streaking across the horizon when she'd finally fallen into bed and had slept fitfully until the alarm clock started up at six.

Millie stretched across the sink and threw open the sash window to let the smell of feet, leg ulcers and surgical spirit out. Tilting her face towards the sun Millie took in a deep breath of warm, summer air in an attempt to shift the jagged pain behind her eyes.

Drying her hands, Millie headed for the door into Munroe House's courtyard. As she stepped outside she found Peggy, a newly appointed Queenie, standing by the bike rack crying.

Millie went over. 'Whatever's the matter, Peggy?'

Peggy looked up with red-rimmed eyes. 'It's her. Miss Dutton. The old battleaxe. She's cancelled my weekend off.'

'Well, we are nurses and that means having to put our patients first,' said Millie, carefully.

'I know, but it's the third time she's done it to me since Easter. It's not fair.' Peggy blew her nose, and then looked appealingly up at Millie. 'I don't suppose that you could you have a word with her?' She grabbed Millie's hand. 'Oh please! It's my mum's birthday and I promised to take her out to tea, and she'll be so disappointed.'

Miss Dutton had only given Millie three shifts that week and two the week before, and although it would mean paying Cora, Millie thought that if Miss Dutton allowed her to cover Peggy's day, it would give a much-needed boost to her income.

'Well, I could offer to do your shift.'

'Thank you, Millie.' Peggy bobbed up and down on the spot.

'Don't get your hopes up, Peggy,' cautioned Millie. 'She's just as likely to say no to me.'

Leaving Peggy in the yard, Millie made her way back into Munroe House. As it was Wednesday, the smell of steak and kidney stew drifted out from the kitchen and, judging by the chatter from the refectory at the far end of the hall, most of the nurses were already back.

Millie looked at Miss Dutton's office door at the far end of the corridor and the band of pain tightened around her temples. Tempted through she was to just collect her lunch from the locker room and slip into the dining room without seeking out Miss Dutton, she couldn't ignore the fact that if she could cover Peggy's shift it would make this week's housekeeping a little less worrisome.

Ignoring the tired fog in her head, Millie walked briskly up to the door and knocked.

'Come.'

Squaring her shoulders, Millie walked in.

With her pen poised over her paperwork, Miss Dutton raised her head and a tart look pinched her face. 'Yes?'

Millie smiled. 'I understand you're short of nurses this weekend and—'

'Who said that?'

'Oh, I just overheard someone say that you'd had to cancel some weekend leave,' said Millie.

'Well then, we're not short of nurses, are we?' Miss Dutton flicked her hand at Millie dismissively and concentrated once more on her correspondence.

Millie stared at her white cap for a moment and then spoke again. 'It's just that perhaps I could cover Sister Dare's shifts as she's arranged to take her mother out for a birthday tea.'

The superintendent looked up again. 'You can't. She's nurse-in-charge.'

'But I've done it hundreds of times.'

A thin smile lifted the corners of Miss Dutton's lips. 'When you were a sister here you did. But you are forgetting that now you're *just* a bank nurse. And obviously bank nurses can't run the clinic.'

'Well, then put Sister Scott in charge, and I'll take her list,' said Millie.

Miss Dutton's eyes narrowed. 'Are you telling me how to run this clinic?'

'No,' replied, Millie, 'I'm just saying that I could cover for Sister Dare so she can visit her mother.'

'Well, you can't, and that's an end to it. It's about time Sister Dare learnt that patients come first at Munroe House,' snapped Miss Dutton. 'And if I hear of anyone else moaning about their shifts, then I'll cancel their weekends for the next two months.'

Millie's mouth narrowed. 'I'm sure that will make for a very happy workplace.'

Miss Dutton sniffed. 'That's not my concern. My job is to run the clinic efficiently.'

'And even though you've already had four nurses leave since Christmas, and despite the fact that half of those that remain are looking for other jobs, you think the best way of doing that is repeatedly cancelling their rest days?'

A crimson flush stained the superintendent's throat. 'I suppose if you were in charge you'd let nurses do what they like willy-nilly, would you?'

'No, but I wouldn't spend my time trying to find new ways of making everyone as miserable as I was,' Millie answered, the band of pain around her head tightening a little more.

Miss Dutton's eyes bulged, and then a syrupy smile spread across her face.

'Well then, perhaps I should look at the rota again just to see if I can be a little more even-handed.' Miss Dutton opened the desk diary and glanced at the list of names. 'Nurses Willis and Hogan, for example. They're bank nurses like you, but it would seem that they don't have any shifts next week whereas you have at least three during the week.' Miss Dutton picked up her pen and scratched through the three days Millie had already been allocated for the following week.

Millie stared at her in horror. 'But ... but I need those days.'

'I'm just being fair,' Miss Dutton said, closing the book. 'If you still want me to consider you for some shifts the following week you can pop by next Friday and I'll see if I've got anything.' Her sickly smile widened. 'Now, if you don't mind, I have a clinic to run and so please shut the door behind you when you leave.'

Chapter Twenty-Five

Millie placed Patricia on the floor in the middle of a new fireside rug that Doris had given her, and then set bricks and rag toys around her. Patricia seized her favourite doll and started babbling at it.

Millie had collected Patricia from Cora's an hour before, and after a detour to Watney Street to get a basketful of end-of-day spring vegetables, she'd arrived home just as the BBC pips announced the six o'clock news. After giving Patricia her supper of scrambled egg and toast, Millie had bathed her and got her into her nightclothes, ready for her bottle and bed.

Leaving her daughter to her imaginary game, Millie opened the front window to let in the early-evening May air and then, taking the brown envelope containing her weekly wages from her pocket, settled herself at the fold-down dining-table next to her cup of tea, a battered Friar's Custard tin and the household notebook.

Tearing open the flap, Millie took out a green pound and brown ten-shilling note and counted out three copper pennies and set them aside for when the rent man called on Saturday morning. Then she took the other ten-shilling note and popped a florin next to it for Cora and a further ten shillings for the man from the Pru. Putting aside seven shillings for the electricity meter and another one for the gas, the familiar pay-day anxiety fluttered in Millie's chest. £1 1s 9d was all that was left from this week's income of £3 14s 6d.

Thankfully the new crop of summer vegetables were cheap if she shopped at the end of the day, and so by careful management she was able to keep the weekly food bill to under fifteen bob, and she didn't switch on the light until almost nine and therefore the meter money was eked a bit further, but goodness knows what she'd do when the clocks went back. A half-hundredweight of coal would cost her half her spare money a week, added to which Patricia would certainly need a winter coat, not to mention a new pair of shoes and if from now on Miss Dutton only gave her the odd shift or two, the consequences didn't bear thinking about.

There was a knock at the door.

Patricia looked up and pointed.

Millie popped her money back in the tin. 'It's open!'

Footsteps sounded along the hallway. Thinking it must be a neighbour Millie looked up but the smile froze on her lips as saw Jim standing in the lounge doorway.

He was wearing a hopsack shooting jacket, cream slacks, a Tattersall shirt and tie, topped off with a tweed trilby.

He removed his hat. 'Hello Millie. I need to talk to you.'

'You've got a nerve showing your face around her after the way you behaved the other night,' she said.

'I know, and I'm sorry,' he said, sincerely. 'Did you get the postal order for the carpet from Ted?'

'Yes,' Millie replied.

It had arrived three days after that grim night, and as Miss Dutton hadn't given her any work this week she had put the £1 2s 6d aside to top up this week's housekeeping.

Jim turned his attention to his daughter. 'And how is little Patricia?' he asked, bending down and offering her his hand.

Leaving her toys, Patricia crawled to her mother. Millie picked her up and Patricia buried her face into her shoulder.

'Don't be shy,' said Jim, dodging to one side to see her averted face.

'Why would she be anything else?' Millie replied resignedly. 'She doesn't know you.'

Jim's genial expression slipped a little but then he rallied. 'And how have you been, Millie?'

'What is it that you want, Jim?'

'I've been thinking things over these last few months, and I realise now that I treated you abominably.'

'Do you?'

'Yes, and I can't blame you for leaving as you did,' he continued, apparently sincerely.

'Is that why you're here?' asked Millie.

'Yes, and to say I'm sorry.'

'Well, you've said it now, and so you can go.'

Jim shifted his weight from one foot to the other and stayed put.

A wry smile lifted the corners of Millie's mouth. 'So, what else do you want?'

He swallowed. 'Perhaps I could sit down?'

'If you like,' Millie replied.

'It's a bit embarrassing really,' said Jim perched on the edge of the sofa. 'I'm in a bit of bother.'

'I thought Ted's masonic chum got all the charges dropped,' Millie said.

'He did, but it's not that I'm talking about.' He twisted his signet ring back and forth. 'It's just that I need a divorce.'

Slowly, Millie raised an eyebrow. 'And, tell me, why do you *need* one, Jim?'

'Look, Millie,' he said, giving her his most disarming smile, 'I won't beat about the bush. I know I've acted like a cad towards you and Patricia.'

'Bastard is probably the word that I'd use,' said Millie, kissing her daughter's dark curls lightly.

Jim gaze wavered. 'The truth is, Millie, I'm in a bit of a tight corner. There's this young woman and ...'

'You've got her pregnant.'

'Well, yes.'

Millie looked puzzled. 'So, why don't you marry her off to one of your tenant farmers like you usually do?'

'It's not as easy as that,' said Jim, struggling to control his irritation. 'Hermione's the daughter of the Viscount of Rutland.'

Millie stared at him for a couple of seconds, and then she burst out laughing.

Jim's expression lost any final traces of amiability. 'It's not funny.'

'No, it's not funny,' replied Millie. 'It's bloody hilarious. That's stupid, even for you.'

'I didn't know she was Sir William's daughter,' Jim protested angrily. 'I thought she was just the under-minister's little secretary. But anyway that's not the point. Sir William is one of the Labour peers Churchill created at the start of the war to balance up the House of Lords. He's a big noise in the party, and if I'm to have a hope in hell of making minister, I simply have to marry Hermione as soon as possible.'

'So you want me to divorce you to save this poor woman's good name?' said Millie.

'No, that's not quite it.' An odd expression was on Jim's face. 'Actually, Millie, Sir William insists that I divorce you. And the quickest and quietest way is for me to divorce you for adultery.'

Millie froze.

'These things can be arranged. For a fee there are people who are willing to be cited in divorce proceedings as the co-respondent,' Jim said, as casually as if he were explaining how to have the house redecorated.

'And what about my reputation?' snapped Millie. 'My name is already mud on every street corner around her.'

'Don't worry,' said Jim calmly. 'It will be discreetly arranged somewhere well out of town.'

Millie jumped to her feet. 'Get out.'

Patricia screamed and clung to her mother.

Jim stood up and looked confidently at her. 'I'll get my lawyers to draw up a proper settlement for you and Patricia.' He glanced pointedly at the damp patch above the window, and then at the flaking plaster in the corner. 'You can move then to a nicer house, a home with a proper garden for Patricia to play in. And you'll be able to give up work to look after her instead of palming her off to a stranger every morning.'

Millie stared at him for a couple of seconds and then, ignoring her daughter's voluble protests, she sat Patricia carefully on the chair.

Stepping forward, Millie slapped Jim as hard as she could across the face. 'I said get out.'

Jim picked up his hat, and touched his jaw. 'You'll get a letter from my solicitor in a few days. I'm sure once you've had a chance to think it through, you'll see what's best for all of us.'

Millie glanced at her watch and then back at the doors to number one court, which had remained firmly closed for almost an hour.

Even though much of the interior hall of the Old Bailey was covered by scaffold because of the restoration of the classically styled frescos that had been damaged in the Blitz, the classic, lofty arches and ornate plasterwork left no one in doubt of its once grand design. This was a building that had been built to impress, and no amount of draped tarpaulin could disguise that.

The rumble of male voices filled the space that was packed with black-gowned young men talking in small groups, the tails of their cream-coloured horsehair wigs quivering as they moved their heads. Dotted between them were police officers checking their evidence in their notebooks. Nervous-looking members of the public, like Millie, were waiting to be called into the witness box.

Millie recrossed her legs and sighed as she contemplated a second long day of doing nothing, going nowhere and loosing another bank shift at the maternity hospital. The group of lawyers just to her right moved aside, and Alex emerged from behind them.

Like most of the other officers, he'd clearly put on his best uniform to appear in England's foremost law court. The newly pressed jacket fitted him like a glove, while the epaulettes with their single pips drew her eyes to his shoulders. The belt fastened around his slim waist seemed to extenuate the breadth of his chest, as did the silver whistle chain hanging from his breast pocket.

He spotted her and smiled.

Before she could stop it, Millie's heart gave a little leap.

'There you are,' he said, sitting beside her on the long bench.

'Yes, I'm still here,' she said, her eyes flickering on to Alex's thigh that was so very close to hers. 'Any news?'

He shook his head. 'The judge is still hearing arguments in his chambers. It's almost twelve now, and so you must be getting hungry?'

'No, I'm fine,' Millie replied.

'Well, I'm starving,' he said. 'Let me buy you lunch.'

'But shouldn't we stay in case we're needed?' asked Millie.

'I doubt the court will be called back in this side of three o'clock,' he replied. 'There's a pub around the corner that does cracking pies. My treat.'

Millie was about to protest when her stomach rumbled.

Alex laughed and stood up. 'I'll take that as a yes,' he said, smiling down at her.

Millie hesitated for a couple of seconds then rose to her feet. 'Very well. I never could say no to a plate of steak and kidney.'

As he promised, the King Lud on Ludgate Circus was just a short walk away. He guided her to a round table at the back of the long bar, and then went off to order their meals.

The pub reminded Millie of a wedge of wood hammered between the two stone-fronted buildings on either side. Somehow it had survived the firestorm that had engulfed the area around St Paul's in December 1940 and, if the low ceilings and blackened timber were anything to go by, it had escaped the Great Fire of London, too. Like the foyer she'd been sitting in for the past three hours, the tavern was packed with lawyers and policemen talking loudly and smoking whilst holding glasses and pints respectively.

Within a couple of moments Alex returned.

'One fruit juice,' he said, putting her drink on the table.

'What are you drinking?' she asked, as he took a sip from the half-pint glass in his hand.

'Lemonade.'

Millie laughed. 'Lemonade!'

'I only have the odd pint or two at the weekend since I worked abroad,' he said, squeezing into the chair beside her. 'There wasn't much else to do in the officer quarters and as I didn't want to end up with a pickled liver, I decided to cut right back.'

'Was it very bad in Palestine?' asked Millie.

Alex's jolly mood was quelled in an instant. 'It was hell. We were at war but the top brass didn't have the guts to call it that. We weren't raw recruits, but some of the things we saw were stomach-turning.' He shook his head dolefully. 'It certainly wasn't like being in the desert with Monty and the Eighth when we were fighting Rommel. You had snipers shoot at you while you talked to children, and wedding parties were blown up in hotels.'

He popped another piece of pie in his mouth.

'Did you carry on with your studies?' Millie asked, gathering up the last of her carrots. 'It was history, wasn't it?'

'Art history,' he said. 'And, yes, I did. I ended up with a first actually.'

Millie's eyes stretched wide. 'A first!'

He gave an ironic smile. 'Not bad for a jack-the-lad from Shadwell School.'

'I'm not at all surprised,' said Millie, oddly proud. 'I remember how I was amazed at all the stuff you knew about Rubens and Holbein when you took me to the National Gallery that time.'

'I was just showing off,' Alex said, with his old cheeky grin.

'Well, I was impressed,' said Millie. 'Do you remember how the waitress in the tea shop kept taking our cups and plates away as soon as we'd finished?'

Alex's eyes twinkled. 'And how you confessed you thought I was an East End gangster?'

They laughed.

Alex's eyes locked on hers and Millie's heart paused mid-beat. He held her gaze for a few moments longer and then Millie looked down.

'Perhaps we should get back,' she said, rested her fork on the side of the plate.

Alex glanced at his watch. 'We're fine for another half an hour, and anyway you haven't told me what you've been up to these past four years.'

'Nothing as exciting as you, I'm afraid,' said Millie, as Alex mopped up the last of his gravy. 'As I said, Mum got better and was almost back to her old self by the Christmas of 1946. We froze like everyone else after that winter and ...'

As Alex finished off his meal, Millie ran through the problems the NHS had caused them at Munroe House. About Miss Dutton and Mr Shottington. She moved on to Connie's train-spotter fiancé, and finished off with a full description of Doris and Charlie's new house in Harold Wood.

'So, you see, there have been lots of changes since you've been away,' Millie concluded.

'There have,' he agreed, putting his cutlery together and wiping his mouth. 'But what about you becoming Mrs Smith? How did that happen?'

Something akin to ice water seemed to run through Millie's veins. 'Oh, the usual way, you know.'

'And is he a travelling salesman or something?' asked Alex.

Millie looked confused. 'Why would you think that?'

'Because when we were in the Turner house you said you were staying with your mother because your husband was away on business,' he said, in a light tone. 'I just assumed he was a salesman of some sort.'

'Actually, I'm married to the Honourable James Percival Woodville Smith, member of parliament,' Millie said. 'His father is Lord Tollshunt and they own land in north Essex.'

Alex looked puzzled. 'Do you mean Jim Smith, the Member of Parliament for Leytonstone and Wanstead?'

'Yes, that's him,' replied Millie, feeling distinctly uneasy discussing her estranged husband to her erstwhile fiancé.

'Someone mentioned something about him a little while back,' said Alex, conversationally. 'In connection with one of the big unions, I think it was.'

'Probably the Stevedores and Dockers Union,' said Millie, hoping that Alex hadn't read Jim's name on a charge sheet. 'He's often away on union or party business, and so that's why I often stay with my mum.'

'Of course,' said Alex.

'And we have a house in Snaresbrook,' she continued. 'And a little car. A Ford Pilot.'

'I'd hardly call that a *little* car,' Alex laughed. 'It makes my Morris Oxford look like a Dinky toy.'

Somehow Millie managed to laugh, too. 'Put like that, I suppose so.'

'I'm glad things have turned out so well for you, Millie, and that you're happy,' Alex said softly.

A tremor of emotion ran through Millie as the pain she'd kept locked away for so long threatened to well up.

'Yes I am,' said Millie. 'Very happy. Very happy indeed.'

They stared at each other for a moment or two, and then Alex looked at his watch again. 'We ought to go.'

Millie stood up. 'Okay, but have I got time to powder my nose?'

'Of course,' he replied, rising to his feet.

Someone pushed past Millie and her shoulder brushed against Alex's chest.

Millie looked up.

Alex, the man who she'd never stopped loving, smiled. 'I'm pleased we've had a chance to put the past behind us, Millie.'

'Me too.'

His smile widened. 'And I hope perhaps that we can now be friends.'

Willing away the tears menacing the corners of her eyes, Millie returned the smile. 'Friends. Yes, I'd like that, Alex. Will you excuse me?'

He nodded.

Screwing her serviette into a tight ball in the palm of her hand, Millie fled to the ladies.

Chapter Twenty-Six

The band-leader tapped the microphone and the happy hubbub in St Martha and St Mungo's church hall subsided.

'Now, ladies and gentlemen, please put your hands together and welcome Mr and Mrs O'Toole on to the floor for their first dance as a married couple.'

Millie shifted Patricia on her knee and clapped heartily as Patrick led his new bride out. As all brides should, Annie looked radiant in her long, full-skirted dress with cap sleeves and a sweetheart neckline. Patrick took her in his arms and the couple stepped on to the beat of an old-fashioned waltz. After a circuit of the dancefloor, others joined them.

The hall at the back of the Catholic church was not only festooned with balloons and bunting, but it was packed to the rafters with O'Tooles from all four corners of the British Isles, not to mention seemingly every state in Ireland. Now the formalities of the sit-down were over, as always seemed to happen, the men with pints of Guinness in their brawny hands were congregated around the bar, while their womenfolk had migrated to the tables at the other end of the room with their various offspring.

'Doesn't she look lovely?' said Connie as she re-joined Millie.

'Yes, and happy too.'

Connie put Millie's replenished drink on the table they'd secured for the Munroe House contingent at the edge of the dancefloor.

Millie picked up her glass and Patricia grasped at it. 'No, it's mummy's drink,' she said, holding it out of her daughter's reach.

'Here, this is for you,' said Connie, giving Patricia a feeder cup of orange.

'How are you holding up?' asked Millie, helping Patricia with her beaker.

Connie forced a smile. 'So-so.'

Millie looked concerned. 'Has your mum been on at you again?'

Connie nodded. 'And our Liz and Doreen. They all keep going on about Malcolm's steady job and clean ways, and how he's my last chance before I'm left on the shelf. None of them will accept the fact that there isn't some big secret that I don't want to tell anyone. I can't get it through to them that I just don't want to marry Malcolm.'

Millie gave her a sympathetic smile.

The band stopped, and Millie and Connie clapped as the couples on the floor waited for the next dance. The bandmaster counted in the half-a-dozen musicians behind him and the opening bars of 'In the Mood' blasted out.

Millie jogged Patricia on her knee in time to the beat and she giggled. Millie looked at the newly-weds. As she watched them laughing and smiling, an image of another hall not so long ago, and another couple happy and gazing into each other's eyes flashed through Millie's mind.

Although she woke up every morning thinking how much better off she was without him, the raw wound of Jim's betrayal still hurt, and especially so on days like these.

'Are you all right, Millie?' asked Connie, perceptively.

'I'm fine,' Millie replied, although she was feeling anything but.

Connie studied her closely for a moment. 'Have you decided what you're going to do about Jim?' she asked, as if she knew Millie had been thinking of him.

Millie nodded. 'It's all set for the week after next. The sooner the better, as far as I'm concerned.'

'You're a better woman than I am,' said Connie. 'After the way he's treated you, if it were me, I'd do everything I could to blooming well make him suffer.'

Millie smiled sadly. 'My first reaction was to tell him to take a long walk off a short pier. But, really, what's the point? To be honest, for all his charm and money, the Honourable James Percival Woodville Smith is nothing more than a violent drunk like Mickey Turner, and I'm sick of being tied to him. I've decided to make a clean break of it once and for all.'

'A good settlement is the blooming least he can do after the way he's treated you,' Connie said. 'You're just lucky that aunt Ruby's got the money to foot the solicitor's bill.'

'Yes, aren't I?' said Millie, not quite meeting her closest friend's eye.

Although her immediate family knew the truth, as she was determined that the actual divorce wouldn't cause herself and her loved ones any more shame and embarrassment than strictly necessary, Millie had decided she would tell everyone else that she was divorcing Jim.

'And I hope your brief turns the screw and makes him really pay up.' said Connie.

'Jim has already agreed to pay an allowance for Patricia, but I don't want any of his money for me,' Millie replied.

'Why ever not?' Connie looked confused. 'You're entitled, if anybody is.'

'Not a penny, Connie,' Millie reiterated. 'He lied to me from the very start, and he was unfaithful to me on two occasions that I know of, and I daresay there were others. He was a drunk and violent, and frankly if I never saw him again it would be too soon. He can pay me for Patricia, but from the day we're no longer man and wife, I refuse to be beholden to Jim Smith for anything to do with myself.' Millie pressed her lips into Patricia's dark curls and closed her eyes for a moment, and then turned her daughter to face her. 'And we'll be fine, won't we, poppet?'

Patricia giggled and clapped her hands.

Millie smiled jollily. 'See, she agrees with me.'

A knowing expression crept across Connie's face. 'And of course, if you were the ex-Mrs Smith, there would be nothing to stop you becoming friendly with a certain someone in a police uniform again, is there?'

A dart of powerful emotion jabbed at Millie's chest, but she laughed. 'Will you give over, Connie?'

'I'm just saying,' her friend persisted. 'And he is unattached, and didn't he take you for a meal?'

'He is unmarried, but I doubt he will be for long if Woman Police Constable Collins at the nick has anything to do with it,' Millie replied. 'And just remember that he bought me pie and chips in a pub, not a candlelit supper at the Ritz.'

The music stopped again and Patrick, with Annie on his arm, came over.

'I hope you're both having a grand time,' he said, smiling at Millie and Connie.

'We're having a lovely time,' Connie replied.

Millie looked fondly at them. 'And Annie, you look so beautiful in that dress.'

Patrick slipped his arm around his bride and squeezed. 'Doesn't she just? I nearly fainted away at the sight of her standing beside me at the altar.'

Annie slapped his arm playfully and laughed. They exchanged an intimate look, and tears welled in Millie's eyes.

She made a play of straightening the bows on Patricia's dress and then, ignoring the despondent feeling lodged in her chest, smiled at the newly married couple.

The band started again.

'Will you do me a kindness and have a word with me ma, Millie?' Patrick asked, looping Annie's arm in his again.

'I know she'd love to meet Patricia,' said Annie encouragingly.

Millie glanced over to where Mrs O'Toole senior sat in the midst of her extended family. She was dressed in a long black dress with a huge floral fringed shawl draped over it. There was a contented smile on her wrinkled face, as well there might be, at being surrounded by her many grandchildren.

Millie stood up. 'It'll be my pleasure.'

She set Patricia on the floor and then, holding her hand firmly, she guided the toddler between the dozen or so children jigging about on the edge of the dancefloor.

'Good afternoon, Mrs O'Toole,' she said, as she reached the O'Toole end of the hall.

'And to you, Sister,' the old woman replied.

Millie acknowledged the relatives she knew who were clustered around, and then she was introduced to a number of Bredas, Colleens, Marys, Patricks, Brians and Michaels who were part of the extended family.

'And is this your little darling?' the old matriarch asked, smiling at Patricia.

'Yes, it is,' Millie replied, running her hand gently over her daughter's head.

Mrs O'Toole struggled forward and held her arms out. 'Come to see your old granny, then, my sweet child, and I shall tell you your fortune.'

'She's a bit shy with strangers, Mrs O'Toole.'

At that Patricia let go of Millie's hand and trotted straight into Mrs O'Toole's arms.

Her lined face wrinkled in a contented smile. 'Sure, I'm no stranger, am I now, me darling?'

Patricia produced the smile that she normally reserved for Doris and Ruby as she was scooped up and settled on Mrs O'Toole's expansive lap. Patricia took hold of the rosary cross around her neck and put it in her mouth.

'She's a darling child, so she is,' said Mrs O'Toole, gazing fondly at the tot on her knee. She looked curiously at Millie. 'But I'll not tell you her fortune, I'll tell you yours, Millie Smith. You think she's to be your only one, but you're wrong. You'll have two others.'

Patricia dropped the cross and wriggled off the old woman's lap. Laughing, she started trotting across the dancefloor towards Connie, who was dancing with some chap.

'I'd better catch her before she trips someone up,' Millie laughed as she started after her daughter. 'And I don't know about another two. I have enough trouble keeping up with one.'

'I'm sure you'll have two more,' Mrs O'Toole called after her. 'And one will have the green eyes of his father.'

A shiver ran down Millie's spine, and an image of Alex started to form in her head but Millie cut it short. A divorced woman with a full-time job and a child to support couldn't waste her energies on fanciful notions.

Millie lay fully clothed on the bed, staring up at the single light-bulb overhead. She'd been in much the same position for the past seven hours; her only concession to being a hotel guest was that she'd taken off her shoes. As the early morning light was already filtering underneath the threadbare curtains and illuminating the peeling wallpaper and spots of mould in the far corner, she guessed she wouldn't have to remain as she was for too much longer.

Outside the sound of seagulls harrying the fishing boats

coming home after a night's fishing cut through the early morning stillness. It was faint, as the Shangri-La Hotel was at least four roads back from Folkestone's pretty waterfront, which Millie knew, if she lived to be a hundred, she would never visit again. She turned her head to look at the alarm clock on the bedside table. Six-thirty at long last.

Her eyes drifted on towards the other side of the room where Mr Priestly lay on the beaten up old armchair, softly snoring. At least that's what he'd introduced himself as when they'd met in the Daisy Chain tea-room around the corner the evening before. He was a stocky man in his mid-thirties who said he worked in a bank, but his brash mustard zoot suit made Millie think he was more likely to have robbed one than worked in one. Still, in an hour whatever Mr Priestly did or didn't do wouldn't be her concern any longer.

Millie studied his slumbering form for a couple of seconds, and then resumed her contemplation of the bare lightbulb. She tried to imagine Patricia asleep in the pink-painted bedroom in Doris and Charlie's house.

Her mother had been cheerful enough when she'd taken Patricia yesterday, but Millie knew that although Doris understood why Millie had agreed to the charade, she was still heartbroken at the humiliation of it all.

With the ticking of the clock, Millie closed her eyes and must have drifted off, because she was jolted awake by the alarm. She swung her legs off the bed and sat up.

Mr Priestly scratched his head, messing his carefully Brylcreemed hair. He yawned and eased himself out of the chair.

'We'd better get ready,' he said, shrugging off his jacket.

He hung it in the wardrobe and took out the suitcase he'd carried in the day before. Setting it on the chair he'd just vacated, he flipped the catches and pulled out a blue and red striped pyjama top. He laid it over the back of the chair and then, sticking his thumbs in his braces, slipped them down.

He looked at Millie.

'Come on, love,' he said as he removed his shirt and put it back in the suitcase. 'The maid will be in soon.'

Millie picked the untouched nightdress off the bed and turned away. With trembling fingers she unbuttoned her blouse and quickly slipped it off. Keeping her face averted, Millie pulled the nightie over her head and tied the ribbons either side of the neckline tightly. It was an old winter one with long sleeves, but despite still having her underwear and skirt beneath, Millie felt bare.

There was a knock at the door.

'Just a moment!' Mr Priestly called. He looked at Millie. 'Quick, get into bed.'

He threw the suitcase into the bottom of the wardrobe and shut the door. Millie rolled up her blouse, tucked it under the pillow and then threw back the untouched bedclothes. She slipped under the covers.

Mr Priestly, now wearing his pyjamas over his vest, threw back the covers on the other side and hopped in, making the bed creak as he did.

His leg brushed against Millie's and her stomach heaved. She moved further over towards the edge of the bed.

He grinned at her. 'Ready?'

Millie nodded.

'Enter,' he shouted.

The door opened and the maid walked in carrying a tray.

'Morning, Mr and Mrs Priestly,' she said, putting the tea on the bedside table the other side of the bed from Millie. 'Did you sleep well?'

'Morning,' Mr Priestly replied cheerfully. 'And we slept very well.'

The maid returned to the door and, bending down, picked up a pair of men's shoes. 'And I believe these are yours,' she said in a monotone.

She held them up.

'Oh yes,' replied Mr Priestly in the same stilted tone. 'I left them outside last night for cleaning. Thank you very much.'

The maid put them down and left the room.

Mr Priestly flung back the covers and got out of the bed.

'Right, that's over,' he said, stripping off the pyjama top as he made his way to the wardrobe.

He dragged out the case and retrieved his shirt and then unhooked his jacket. Within a few moments he was dressed again.

'I hope you don't mind if I shoot off, but I've got a bit of business back in the Smoke and if I stretch me legs I can catch the seven-thirty.'

'No, not at all,' Millie replied.

'Ta, love.' He winked. 'All you have to do is sign out downstairs and then it's done.'

He snapped the case shut, flipped on his broad-brimmed fedora and left the room. Millie lay quite still until she couldn't hear Mr Priestly's footsteps any longer, then she threw back the bedclothes, staggered to the washbasin in the corner and vomited.

The gates of Munroe House were already open by the time Millie arrived and she headed through.

She was just about to open the back door when she heard something like a faint whine. She stopped and looked around.

Everything in the yard seemed to be as it should, with the bikes parked and chained in the rack by the old stable. The health board had deemed Miss Dutton's old living quarters unfit for habitation and had decided to convert them to offices as part of Munroe House's refurbishment. The builders had left their wheelbarrows upturned on the pile of sharp sand with a pile of bricks covered by a tarpaulin next to it, and both seemed undisturbed.

She listened for a couple of seconds, then shrugged and put her hand on the door again. The sound of whining rent the still air again, but this time it sounded more like meowing.

Millie smiled and opened the back door. She dropped her bag inside and then turned back into the yard. If she was going to have to hunt around to rescue one of the local cats, she'd need both hands.

She waited and, sure enough, in less than a minute she heard the small cry again. It seemed to be somewhere close to the boiler house at the far end of the yard and so, guessing some young cat had trapped itself in the rubbish behind the outbuilding, Millie headed over. As she did Cathy Worth, one of the trainee Queenies, walked through the gate.

'What are you doing?' she asked, curiously.

'I think I hear a kitten trapped under something,' Millie said, moving an old crate out of the way.

Cathy came over. 'Where did the noise come from?'

'From over here, I think,' Millie replied, stepping over the puddles that had accumulated on the cobbles overnight.

She and Cathy scrabbled over the delivery crates awaiting collection and around to the back of the outhouse. There was nothing but discarded equipment and broken cycle wheels.

'Perhaps it's found its own way out,' Cathy said after a long pause.

Millie nodded, after another pause. 'You're probably right. Let's go.'

There was a feeble whimper.

'In the boiler house,' said Millie.

The three-quarter-size door was part-way open, and Millie yanked it fully back. Ducking to avoid the low door-frame, Millie entered the warmth and low rumbling of the furnace room.

'Can you see it?' Cathy asked, following Millie.

'It's too dark.'

There was a feeble cry somewhere in front of her. Millie peered into the gloom and then groped towards it. In the dark she felt the corded paper handles of a carrier bag. She slipped her hand in and felt a little body.

'It's a baby! Call an ambulance,' she screamed, lifting the child out.

Cathy ran out.

By the size and lack of muscle tone, Millie judged the baby to be new-born or thereabouts. Cradling the small head against her, Millie ran her fingertips over its little face. It twitched under her touch but it was ice cold. She unbuttoned her coat and ripped open her uniform and then pressed the child against her skin. Whatever the baby was wrapped in was soaked through with urine, but as she covered the child with her clothing the infant started shivering.

Relief flooded over Millie and she leant against the water tank. Within a few moments Cathy was back.

'It's on its way and Sister Boscombe is sterilising one of the sample sets the Maws rep gave us and is making up six ounces of Cow & Gate full cream.'

'Good,' said Millie, holding the child securely as she stepped out of the low-roofed building.

Millie hurried into the clinic, where she headed straight to the treatment room, where Bette was spooning formula milk into a feeding bottle. Millie sat down on one of the chairs. The baby wriggled and its mouth brushed against the top of her breast as it rooted around. Millie felt unbearably sad.

That was another thing she'd never forgive Jim for: making her wean Patricia on to a bottle at three months.

'How is the little mite doing?' asked Bette, screwing the teat on and shaking the milk to mix it.

'Hungry,' Millie replied.

Bette smiled. 'Well, it can't have it for a couple of minutes.' She popped the bottle in a jug of cold water to cool.

Millie peeled the top of her coat back a little and looked down at the little head nestled against her chest.

'Do you think it's been there long?' asked Bette, pulling up a chair next to Millie.

'All night, judging by the soaking nappy,' Millie replied. 'It was lucky that whoever did this put the baby in the warm, or we'd have found a dead new-born rather than a frozen one.'

Bette stroked a finger lightly over the fuzz of fair hair. 'Poor little dear.' She stood up. 'I'll get a nappy and see if there's some dry clothes in the charity box.'

She put the cooling bottle on the table next to Millie and left the room.

Millie sat there cradling the child for a few minutes, then picked up the milk and sprinkled a drop on the inside of her wrist. Satisfied that it was the right temperature, Millie adjusted her clothing just enough to feed the baby without losing any warmth. She slipped the bottle in under her clothes and the baby latched on immediately.

Bette came back into the room holding an assortment of clothes and a clean nappy. 'There we go,' she said, setting them out on the table.

The child finished the feed in a few minutes and Millie put the bottle down. 'That's better, I'm sure, and a little warmer. I think I'll chance a quick wash and change of clothes.'

'I'll help,' said Bette.

Millie stood up and extracted the child from beneath her dress, but as she lifted it out Bette gasped.

Millie didn't blame her.

The baby abandoned in the boiler house was a boy and could have been no more than a few days old. He was wrapped in an old grubby towel with just the rudiments of a nappy and, judging by the ragged nature of the umbilical cord, his mum had delivered him without assistance.

Bette handed Millie a warm towel and hurriedly she washed and dried him, then quickly pinned a fresh nappy in place. Bette slipped a vest over his head, followed by a knitted top and matinée jacket. For her part, Millie manoeuvred him into a pair of knitted leggings then, finally, wrapped him, cocoon-like, in one of the cot blankets from the linen cupboard. The boy yawned and nodded off to sleep.

'Poor little lad,' said Bette, as Millie popped him on the table.

'He is,' said Millie. 'Look at him closely.'

Bette studied the child for a second. 'Oh dear. Are you sure?'

'Well, the paediatrician on the children's ward will have to confirm it, but I'm pretty certain,' Millie replied. 'You can't always see the characteristics in a new-born, but the oriental-looking eyes and the larger head made me suspicious, Plus this,' Millie gently opened the child's hand to show a single crease across his palm, 'so if the doctor does confirm this wee chap has mongolism, then he's a poor little lad indeed, because he'll probably spend the rest of his life in an institution.'

Chapter Twenty-Seven

Feeling as if her kneecaps were about to snap Millie eased herself up from the floor of the equipment room in Munroe House's basement. Dropping the scrubbing brush in the bucket of bleach she surveyed the six wheelchairs. They were Munroe House's rickety pre-war models with wooden armrests and bald tyres that the clinic lent out to appropriate patients. Miss Dutton had set her the task of cleaning them all before dinnertime, and she'd finished with fifteen minutes to spare. No doubt the superintendent would find her some other encrusted items of equipment to keep her fully occupied this afternoon. Still Millie knew that she shouldn't complain as at least she was once again getting regular work.

Just as she put her hands into the small of her back to relieve the tension the door opened and Ruth's round face appeared around the edge.

'Thank goodness I found you,' she whispered, shutting the door quietly behind her. 'There's an Inspector Nolan outside. He says he must see you immediately. It's urgent.'

Before Millie could stop it, her stomach gave a little flutter. 'Does Miss Dutton know he's here?'

'No, not yet. But if she comes out of her office she'll have something to say.'

Millie ripped off her apron and dashed up the stairs to the hall.

Alex was standing looking out of the side window with his hands behind his back. He was dressed in his full uniform and had his flat hat tucked under his arm. He looked around as she reached the top step.

'Good morning, Mrs Smith,' he said.

'Hello,' she replied, noting how the sun sparkled on the jade of his eyes. 'Ruth said it was urgent,' Millie said. 'If it's about

Mickey Turner's trial it might be more convenient if I came to the station?'

'It's not the trial.' He pulled a sheet of newspaper from his pocket. 'It's this.'

Millie took it.

It was an inside page from the *Chelmsford Herald* dated six weeks before. Millie opened it, and gasped as she read the headline.

The Honourable James Percival Woodville Smith, MP for Leytonstone and Wanstead, granted divorce

All Millie could see were the screaming bold black letters across the top of the page. She scanned the story detailing their divorce hearing, and then looked up.

'Where did you get this?'

The handle of Miss Dutton's door at the far end of the hallway clicked.

'Quick.' Millie grabbed Alex's arm and opening the door to the linen cupboard, dragged him in, quickly closing the door behind them. Alex put his hat on a pile of clean towels next to him.

'Where did you get it?' Millie asked again, in a subdued voice.

'Wrapped around six-pennyworth of chips and a portion of fish,' he answered in the same hushed tone.

Millie shook her head. 'I mean ...'

'The boys and me were playing a friendly against the Essex Constabulary the day before yesterday in Witham, and we stopped off at the chippie after the match.'

Millie refolded the newspaper and handed it back. 'Well, that explains the grease stains then.'

Alex glared at her. 'Is that all you've got to say?'

'What do you expect?' Millie replied.

'I don't know.' Alex raked his fingers through his hair. 'Some explanation. Some reason, some excuse even, but something.'

Millie matched his angry stare. 'You've got a nerve, turning up here.'

'And who is Vernon Priestly, when he's at home?' He hit the newspaper with his other hand.

'My co-respondent,' Millie replied with her eyes shut.

Alex looked incredulous. 'You had an affair!'

'That's what it says, doesn't it?'

He studied her face for a few moments, then shook his head. 'I don't believe it. Not you. But I would have thought your husband would at least do the gentlemanly thing and take the blame.'

Millie didn't answer.

'So what was all that rubbish about the posh house and swanky car, and the "I'm very happy, very happy indeed" then?' he asked.

Millie's eyes narrowed. 'You're the detective, Alex. Work it out for yourself.'

He ripped his fingers through his hair again. 'For goodness sake, Millie. Why didn't you tell me?'

'Because it's none of your bloody business,' she replied between tight lips.

Alex's jaw dropped.

'It's been none of your business since you walked out of my life some four years ago to find, as you wrote in your final letter, "the opportunities out there". You decided then that your career was more important to you than I was, and so how dare you march back now into my life and my workplace, and question what my life has been since you sailed off.' Her eyes flicked over him. 'Well, you've got what you wanted, haven't you? Pips on your shoulder, and a different girl on your arm every night.'

Alex could only stare silently at her.

The space between them seemed to close and suddenly Millie felt hot.

There was a rap on the door.

'Who's in there?' called Miss Dutton's imperious voice.

Millie put her index finger over her lips and glared at Alex. He glared back but stood still.

'Nurse Smith,' Millie answered.

'What on earth?' The door creaked open and Millie jammed her foot in it.

'I'm sorry, Miss Dutton,' Millie said, her heart thumping in her chest. 'I was just getting the linen ready for the afternoon clinic and a pile of sheets fell on the floor. They are right behind the door.'

'Well, I hope they don't have to be re-laundered because of your clumsiness, Smith,' Miss Dutton said through the two-inch crack. 'Or I'll deduct the cost from your pay.'

Millie's shoulders slumped.

'Yes, Superintendent,' she replied, mortified that Alex was witness to her further humiliation.

'Very well.' Miss Dutton relinquished the door. 'But when you've finished putting the linen back in proper order, report to my office.'

The door closed again and she and Alex stared at each other as the sound of the superintendent's tin-tipped heels faded.

Alex spread his hands. 'Millie, I, er, I—'

'Just go, Alex.'

He hesitated.

'Now!'

Alex held her unwavering gaze for a further long moment, then snatched up his cap and marched out.

As the door closed behind him Millie leant back on to the back of the door and closed her eyes as wave after wave of ignominy swept over her. She remained in the warm stillness of the linen cupboard until she was certain no tears would catch her unawares, and then with her head low she slowly made her way to Miss Dutton's office.

Letting the door swing shut behind her, Millie entered the main corridor of the Princess Elizabeth Hospital for Sick Children.

Although the temperature inside was cooler than outside, it was still quite warm, and so she unbuttoned her jacket. The weather had held out dry and fine until the day after her mother's wedding, but then it had become so cold that she'd even taken to bathing Patricia in front of the lounge fire. Thankfully, although the summer had been very late to arrive, it now seemed reluctant to leave, as even though it was already the beginning of September, it was still warm enough to go out without a jacket or cardigan.

Making her way between the visitors, nurses and porters milling around in the reception area, Millie approached the desk.

'Good afternoon, Sister,' the receptionist said, looking at Millie over the top of her wing-ended glasses.

'Morning,' Millie replied. 'I'm looking for Burdett Ward.'

'Top floor on the right,' she said, pointing a shocking-pink manicured finger in the direction of the main stairs.

The solid Victorian building occupied the corner plot on Glamis Street, just a short walk from Munroe House. It had been created in the grand manner, with a three-arched mock-gothic entrance flanked by two wings styled in the nineteenth-century interpretation of medieval architecture. Founded some seventy years before, it was the descendant of the Children Hospital's started in a sailmaker's warehouse, which Dickens had written about. Sadly, its glory days were long gone and now the peeling paintwork and dull windows showed clearly the many years of poor maintenance and neglect. Although it had been renamed in 1932, it was universally known as the East London Children's Hospital and was still greatly loved by the locals.

Although like all the other hospitals in the area – St George's, the Jewish, Bethnal Green, the Mildmay, and St Andrew's, where Millie's dad had died – the ELCH was now part of the NHS, it still felt like a charity infirmary as collection boxes could clearly be seen, as could charts showing the progress of donations towards a third iron-lung to treat children with polio.

Resting her hand on the stone banister, Millie made her way up the stairs and past the first floor where the general medical and surgical wards were, and up and into the specialist floor where the fever and incurable wards were sited.

Passing a grey-haired consultant with a monocle jammed in one eye and a paisley bow-tie at his throat, who was surrounded by his flock of fresh-faced young men, Millie continued to the end of a long corridor. She stopped at the door marked Burdett Ward, which had an added sign beneath, 'Mentally Deficient Children'.

She leant on the brass plate and pushed the door open.

Even though she'd taken the precaution of breathing through her mouth, the stench of bodily waste and boiled cabbage hit Millie in the back of her throat. The unintelligible uproar was the next thing to assault her senses as guttural grumbles, low groans and high-pitched screams that pierced the eardrums joined together in a wall of noise. The old Nightingale-style ward, with beds lined up facing each other on either side, was probably made to accommodate three-dozen cots, but there were at least half that number again squeezed into the space. The cots themselves were the heavy wrought-iron type favoured in the previous century, with flaking paint on the bars. Each contained a child, some with enlarged hydrocephalus heads and rolling eyes, others with contorted limbs and lolling tongues. All were dressed in washed-out garments with more than a touch of the workhouse about them.

As fresh air was good for growing children, the top skylights had been wound open, but as the ward was north-facing, this chilled rather than replenished the air.

The young nurse sitting at the report desk by the antiquated stove looked up from her task.

'Can I help you?' she asked.

'I'm looking for Robert Munroe,' said Millie, running her eyes down the blackboard with the patients' names on fixed to the wall. 'I believe he was transferred from the London yesterday.'

The nurse twisted around and studied the list behind her.

'There he is,' she said, pointing to a slot with the words 'six-week male mongol' scratched in chalk. 'He's in cot ten at the far end.'

Millie left the nurse to her paperwork and made her way towards the back of the ward.

Robert was lying on his back with his head turned towards the bare wall as he watched the shadows the cot bars made.

Resting her hands on the metal bar at the end, Millie peered into the cot. Now he'd lost his new-born wrinkles, it was clear to see he had the classic features of his medical condition.

'Hello, Robert,' she whispered.

The baby fidgeted in response. Millie ran her finger lightly down his cheek and he turned his head and opened his mouth.

There was a click of steel heel-tips on the polished floor. Millie looked up and saw the ward Sister striding down the ward in her direction, the wings of her starched hat flapping behind her.

She was a rounded woman in her late thirties with short brown hair, and she looked in imminent danger of bursting out of her navy uniform.

'Good afternoon, Sister Burdett,' Millie said.

'And to you,' replied the ward Sister. 'Was it one of your nurses who found him?'

'It was me, actually,' replied Millie. 'How's he doing?'

'Well enough, now he's over his chest infection,' the Sister replied. 'But I'm beginning to think those nurses on Buxton Ward have been spoiling him, as he's starting to niggle for his feed before it's due.'

'He's probably just hungry,' said Millie, looking down at Robert again.

The sister raised her thick eyebrows. 'I don't see how. He's already on three ounces of half-cream with two teaspoons of sugar as it is.' Her lips pulled together firmly. 'No, believe me, imbecile children are always looking for attention. But we'll soon cure him of that. It'll do him no good looking for special consideration when he gets to the asylum.'

'I don't know if any one's mentioned it to you, Sister, but the nurses on Buxton Ward got the chaplain at London to christen him. We at Munroe House named him Robert after our founder, Miss Robina Munroe.'

Sister Burdett gave a tight smile. 'I was told, thank you, Sister, but we don't call the children by their names here to stop the less experienced nurses getting too involved with them. Has his mother been found?'

'Not as far as I know,' Millie replied.

'She was probably one of those filthy women who hang about at the bottom end of Cable Street,' the Sister said.

'Or some poor girl who found herself in trouble and didn't know where to turn,' Millie replied evenly.

'Well, whoever she was, at least she left him somewhere where he could be found, I suppose, instead of just throwing him in the river,' said Sister Burdett, without a trace of emotion in her voice, 'Although in his case, that might have been a blessing. I mean, what sort of future has he got?'

'He's up for adoption,' said Millie, 'so, hopefully, a happy one with a new family.'

The ward Sister gave her a pitying look. 'Honestly, Sister. Who's going to take a dim-wit when they can take their pick of the dozens of curly-haired bright-eyed babies on the hospital welfare department's waiting list?'

Millie looked down at Robert flexing his hands as he listened to them speak. 'Surely there must be a charity who would care for him.'

The ward Sister regarded Robert dispassionately. 'He's better than some I've seen. His features aren't too pronounced, he hasn't got a cleft palate and he doesn't seem to have a defective heart. But Barnardo's is bursting at the seams and the Catholic Church, who I've heard have an excellent resettlement programme in Australia for orphans, will only take normal children, and so I'm afraid it's off to an institution in the country for this little chap. Now, if you'd excuse me, I've a ward round in half an hour and I have to get the notes ready.'

'Of course,' said Millie. 'Thank you for your time.'

Sister Burdett marched off and Millie turned back to Robert. She slipped her finger into his hand and he gripped it firmly.

Millie could only feel sad. Of course, the sister was right, there were already hundreds of babies waiting for adoption, and with Robert's condition it would indeed take a very special couple to take him on.

Millie pulled the curtains across her daughter's bedroom window and set the big blue bear with a satin bow around his neck in the corner of the cot.

'Come on, slowcoach,' Millie said to her daughter, dressed in a fresh nightdress and nappy after her evening bath. 'Big Ted's already in bed.'

Patricia laughed and ran along the landing towards her. Catching her, Millie swung her daughter into the air, then hugged her close. Patricia pressed her forehead against her mother's cheek.

'That was a lovely kiss,' said Millie.

Millie settled Patricia on her hip and then walked her over to the chair beside the cot. Picking up her daughter's beaker of warm milk as she passed the chest of drawers, Millie sat down and gave Patricia her night-time drink.

The September sun was on its last half-hour before disappearing behind the horizon, so Millie lay back to rest for a moment, enjoying the sensation of her daughter snuggled up close.

Patricia's head was already nodding by the time she'd finished her milk, so Millie kissed her forehead and then gently laid her amongst her knitted rabbits, ducks and golliwogs, and left the room.

By the time Millie had washed up the supper things, rinsed her stockings through and set them on the plate rack over the cooker to dry and made herself a cup of tea, *Take It From Here* had just started on the wireless. Although she usually enjoyed the comedy programme, she somehow wasn't in the mood for The Glums, and so she switched it off before settling down in the armchair. As she sipped her tea, Millie's eyes moved across the room and alighted on the bottom drawer of the sideboard. She stared at it for a couple of seconds, then put her drink down and went over.

Pulling open the drawer, she rummaged around amongst the fuse wire, balls of string, thumb tacks and brown paper, her fingers finally touching the smoothness she been searching for.

She pulled out the photo of her and Alex and ran her thumb along the line of his jaw and then across his smiling mouth. The stinging pain of loss flared again. Millie threw the photo back in amongst the rubbish and slammed the drawer shut. Thinking that as she had nothing else to do she might as well put her smalls in to soak, Millie went back into the kitchen.

No sooner had she lit the Ascot, than there was a knock on the front door. Turning off the tap, Millie wiped her hands on the tea towel and headed down the hall.

She opened the door and her head spun as her gaze fell, not on a neighbour asking to borrow a cup of sugar, but Alex.

For once he wasn't in uniform, but was wearing a charcoal double-breasted suit of some quality with a club tie knotted at his throat.

She noticed that, as always by this time of day, the bristles on his face were casting a shadow and that unless he visited the barber in the next few days his hair would start to curl around his temples.

He regarded her levelly from under his grey fedora. 'Hello, Millie.'

The urge to burst into tears welled up in Millie but she held it back. 'Good evening, Inspector Nolan.'

'May I come in?'

A chink of light flickered from the window opposite where someone had pulled a curtain back.

'I'm not—'

'If it's not too much trouble,' he persisted.

Millie heard a door along the street open.

'I suppose you'd better.' She opened the door wider.

Alex stepped in, bringing the faint smell of saddle soap and Sportsman aftershave with him. He took off his hat.

'Go through,' Millie said, indicating the front-room door.

Alex walked in and Millie followed.

She found him standing in the middle of her world.

'Is this an official visit?' asked Millie.

He smiled. 'No. I just wanted to say—'

'What? There's nothing to say is there, Inspector Nolan?' she said, bitterly. 'Not now you know about my failed marriage and my seedy trip to the seaside with Mr Priestly, my ruined reputation and my general humiliation.' Tears pressed the corners of Millie's eyes as she looked away. 'I'm sorry. Could you go please?'

'I will, but not until I've said what I came to say.'

Millie looked at Alex.

'You're right. What you've done in the past four years is none of my business.' Alex ran his hat through his hands again. 'And after treating you the way I did, I have no right to say anything. You needed me, but instead of standing by you as I should have, I left you and I've hated myself ever since,' he said bitterly.

'I was the one who finished it,' Millie said.

'But I, stupid and selfish bastard that I am, let you,' he replied vehemently. 'I should have refused to take back the ring and resigned my commission there and then, instead of leaving you to nurse your sick mother by yourself.'

Millie smiled sadly at him. 'Breaking our engagement was the hardest thing I've ever done, but you had so much burning ambition I knew you'd never be contented unless you made something of yourself. If I made you stay, you'd only have come to resent me.'

Alex gave a hard laugh. 'That's what I thought, too. And I forced myself to believe it all the way through the initial training in Cyprus and during the debacle in Palestine. I even tried to convince myself that I could fall in love with somebody else and have the family I desperately wanted, right up to a month before the wedding. Then I came to my senses and realised I couldn't have any of those things or that I could ever be happy without you.' His green eyes darkened and his gaze locked with hers. 'I love you, Millie. I always have and always will.'

Millie gasped. With his words and her emotions whirling around in her mind, she could only stare dumbly at him.

'I'm sorry, Millie. I know it's too late. But I had to tell you. I'll see myself out, then.'

He put his hat on and turned to leave.

'Alex!'

He looked around.

She smiled. 'Don't go.'

An expression of disbelief crossed his face for a second, before one of joy replaced it. Alex crossed the space between them and took Millie in his arms.

She slid her hands up and along his shoulders, enjoying feeling the hard muscles under her palms and then she wove her fingers together at the back of his neck. 'I love you, too.'

'Do you?' he asked, incredulously.

She nodded. 'I think, even when I was with Jim, I think I loved you even th—'

His mouth closed over hers and stopped her words. Millie moulded herself into his body and his arm tightened around her as she kissed Alex as passionately as he was kissing her.

Millie opened her eyes and looked up at Alex's firm jawline in the muted light of the bedside lamp, then snuggled in a little closer, relishing the feel of his skin against hers. Her head was tucked in the dip between his shoulder and neck, and his arm was curled around her. Her hand rested amongst his thick chest hair and as she moved her leg slightly the sensation of his hard muscular thighs on hers sent excitement pulsing through her.

On the floor her dress, underwear and stockings lay twisted around Alex's shirt and trousers, much as she had been for the past three hours with their owner. She stretched up and kissed Alex's stubbly chin. The corner of his mouth lifted slightly, but his eyes remained closed. Millie sighed and drew in a long breath, enjoying the mix of their bodies. She shifted slightly and Alex's arm tightened.

'Where do you think you're going?' he asked.

'Nowhere,' Millie replied.

'Too right you're not,' he replied, his fingers running lightly up her arm. 'In fact, I'm so comfortable I don't think I'll ever leave this bed again.'

'It's all right for you,' she said, playfully digging him in the ribs. 'I'm squeezed on the edge.'

Alex shifted on to his side and drew her close. 'Better?'

Millie ran her hand over his shoulder wove her fingers in his hair. 'Much.'

Alex smiled, then lowered his head and kissed her deeply. 'Don't worry, we'll have a double when we're married.'

'Married!'

He looked surprised. 'Of course. You don't think I'm letting you get away again.'

Millie grabbed his hair and shook his head. 'I think that should be the other way around, don't you?'

The satisfied expression on Alex's face vanished. 'Yes it should.' His eyes ran slowly over her face. 'But I promise, as long as I live, I'll never let you down again,' he said, moving a stray lock of her hair off her brow.

Millie smiled. 'I know.'

Alex studied her face for a little longer, then he pressed his mouth on to hers again. After a delicious moment he raised his head, and his lips started their journey to her ear. Millie ran her hand over his chest then, tracing the line of hair down the centre of his stomach with her fingers, moved lower. Alex's leg slid between hers and his erection nudged her hip as he tucked her under him.

'Maaaaa!' screamed a terrified little voice from across the landing.

Alex chucked and rolled on his back. 'I think someone wants you other than me.'

Millie threw back the covers and dashed across to snatch her dressing-gown from the back of the door. 'I won't be long.'

With the candlewick robe wrapped around her, Millie hurried to Patricia's room. In the dim light from the little Noddy and Big

Ears lamp, Millie reached into the cot and lifted Patricia out.

'Shhhh, darling,' she whispered, rocking her back and forth.

Alex strolled into the room wearing his pants, which fitted snugly around his hips.

Patricia stopped crying and looked at him with mild interest for a moment, and then stuck her thumb into her mouth

'Is she all right?' he asked in a quiet voice as he stood beside Millie.

Millie nodded. 'A bad dream I expect,' she replied in the same tone.

Alex smiled at the child in her arms and then pain flitted across his face. 'When I realised what a blooming idiot I'd been, I intended to come back as soon as my tour was up. I thought about asking Georgie Tugman to make some enquires before I shipped out of Haifa in May 1948, but then I lost my nerve, and so I just buried myself in my studies. When I re-joined the Met and they offered me my old stomping ground of H Division I said yes, not dreaming for a moment that I'd run into you again as I thought you'd be long gone.'

Millie shifted Patricia's weight to put her back in her cot.

'Let me,' Alex took Patricia in his arms.

'I can't regret the last four years. If you hadn't gone and I hadn't married Jim, I wouldn't have had Patricia,' Millie said, gazing at the man she loved holding her daughter. 'But she should have been yours.'

Alex smiled at Millie. 'As far as I'm concerned she is.'

Brushing his lips across Patricia's forehead, he laid her gently back in her cot and then took Millie's hand as a thrill of excitement and almost unbearable happiness rose up in her.

Alex drew her closer and pressed her fingers to his lips. 'How quickly can a wedding be arranged?'

Chapter Twenty-Eight

Doris's eyes opened wide with astonishment. 'So Sally's getting married, too?'

It was Saturday afternoon and, as usual, after several hours of shopping, Millie, her mother and Ruby were treating themselves to a nice cup of tea and piece of cake in Lunn's restaurant in Ilford.

Since Doris had moved out to the leafy lanes of Harold Wood, the three women had shifted their traditional Saturday shop and natter eastwards to Ilford, which was roughly halfway between Millie's house and her mother's.

'Isn't it wonderful?' Millie replied, breaking off a bit of her jam puff and giving it to Patricia.

'So that's another one down at Munroe House,' said Doris, catching her granddaughter's hand just before she plastered jam in her hair.

She refilled Patricia's beaker halfway with tea and then topped it up with milk before handing it back to her.

'You forgot the sugar,' said Ruby.

'I was telling Mum about an article in *Nursing Mirror* last week on a study that said children shouldn't have too many sweet things, and so I think she's had more than enough for today with the cake,' Millie replied.

Ruby rolled her eyes. 'I don't know. They'll be telling us these,' she held her half-smoked cigarette up, 'are bad for us next.' She flicked the end into the ashtray. 'Munroe House is more like a marriage bureau than a health clinic. How many weddings have there been this year?'

'Three, and ...' Millie hesitated for a second and took a deep breath. 'And Connie's eloped.'

Her mother and aunt stared at her dumbfounded.

'Two days ago,' Millie added. 'She phoned Munroe House and told me.'

Doris put her cup down. 'Never with Malcolm?'

Millie shook her head.

'Well, who then?'

'She swore me to secrecy,' said Millie. 'She wants to tell everyone herself when they get back.'

'My goodness.' Doris dabbed a clean hanky on her tongue and wiped the stickiness from Patricia's fingers. 'And her poor mother! Fancy not being there to see your daughter getting married.'

'At least you don't have to worry about that, Doris,' said Ruby as she stubbed out her cigarette and signalled to the young girl waiting tables to bring them a fresh pot of tea.

Millie smiled. 'No, you don't, Mum. Because when I marry Alex Nolan on the second of December at the Town Hall I want you all to be there,' she said, enjoying the sound of his name on her lips.

Her mother's jaw dropped while Ruby, a cigarette in one hand and her lighter aflame in the other, just stared while Millie told them about his appearance at Maureen Turner's and their meetings before and after the trial.

'Why on earth didn't you say that he'd come back, Doris?' demanded Ruby.

'Because I didn't know half of this, Ruby,' Doris replied.

Her mother and aunt looked reproachfully at Millie.

Millie shrugged. 'We weren't seeing each other. In fact, we went out for the first time the night I found out about Connie.'

Doris looked puzzled. 'But I don't understand.'

'We only really began speaking again because of that awful business with Maureen Turner. But nothing happened because I kept up the pretence that I was still happily married to Jim. It was only when Alex found out about the divorce that, well,' a mischievous smile tugged at the corners of Millie's mouth, 'things between us changed. He wanted to come with me to tell you our news, but I put him off, as I knew what you'd say.'

Ruby gave her a sour look. 'I suppose he told you he'd made a mistake and begged you to forgive him.'

'He did. And I have. And he's forgiven me for marrying

another man,' Millie replied. 'He did make a mistake, a big one; and later he wanted to put it right, but then he found out it was impossible as I was by then married to Jim.'

Doris looked pensive. 'But are you sure, Millie, really sure?' she asked, putting her hand over her daughter's. 'I don't want to see you get hurt again.'

'I am sure, Mum. Totally,' Millie replied, putting her hand over her mother's. 'I love Alex and I know he loves me. In fact, the truth is that I've never stopped loving him.'

'And what about Patricia?' asked Doris. 'I couldn't bear it if she wasn't happy.'

'No matter how much I love Alex, I would never marry him if I had any worries at all about the way he would care for Patricia,' Millie replied firmly.

'Can you?' asked Ruby. 'Marry? I mean, you've only just got divorced.'

'My decree absolute comes through on the twenty-fourth of November and so, yes, I can,' Millie replied happily. 'We booked the wedding in Stepney Town Hall this morning. I've been dying to tell you since last week, but we decided to wait until Alex got permission to marry from his borough commander, and that came through in the despatch yesterday.' Millie beamed at her mother and aunt. 'Well, aren't you going to congratulate me?'

There was a pause and then Doris smiled. 'Of course! If you are willing to give Alex a second chance, then so am I. When are you bringing him down to see us?'

'Next weekend,' Millie replied. 'I thought we could drive out to see you and Charlie for Sunday tea, if that's all right with you.'

Doris squeezed her hand. 'Why don't you come for dinner and make a day of it?'

'Thanks, Mum,' Millie said with a sigh of relief.

She and her mother exchanged a fond look.

Ruby snapped her lighter and finally lit her cigarette.

'Well, I'm not so easily convinced.' Her gaze shifted from Millie on to Patricia, who was playing with the beads strung across her pushchair, and her expression softened. 'I suppose one good thing will be that at least Patricia will have a father.'

Millie reached down and lifted her daughter on to her lap. 'Not only will Patricia have a father but he will be the best one she ever could have.' She kissed her daughter's dark curls and then looked over her head at her mother and aunt. 'And hopefully, she will have some brothers and sisters too.'

Turning into Arbour Square, Millie hurried along to the red door at the far end of the street. She mounted the three steps and knocked. Within moments she heard the lock being turned and the door opening.

'Sister Smith,' said Derrick Joliffe, with a gentle smile. 'What a pleasure to see you.'

He had clearly just returned from school, as he still had chalk dust on the cuffs of his suit. Although his smile was as warm as ever, Derrick seemed greyer and older since she'd last seen him a few months ago.

'And you,' Millie replied.

He opened the door wider. 'Come in, come in. Dorothy!' he called as Millie stepped into the tidy little house.

'Put the kettle on, love, we've got a visitor,' Derrick said to his wife as she came out of the kitchen.

She must have just come home too, as beneath her apron she was still wearing a smart heather-coloured linen suit. She, too, still had an air of residual sadness about her.

'Make yourself comfortable in the front room and I'll be with you in a few moments,' she said, giving Millie a brief smile before popping back into the kitchen.

Derrick showed Millie into the lounge. Again, this was unchanged since her last visit except that the only remaining picture of William was the professional photograph on the mantel shelf. He was sitting propped up on a shawl with a teddy beside him and smiling.

Millie took the chair while Derrick settled himself on the sofa. They chatted about this and that until Dorothy appeared with the tea.

'Well, this is an unexpected pleasure,' she said, setting the tray on the coffee table between them. 'How are you?'

'Well enough thank you,' Millie replied.

Dorothy's kindly face formed itself into a sympathetic expression. 'We were sorry to hear about you and your husband parting company, weren't we, Derrick?'

'We were,' her husband agreed. 'But I say it's his loss and that he doesn't deserve you.'

'Thank you,' said Millie seriously.

There was no point asking how they knew, because there were no secrets in East London, and with her so-called quiet divorce spread across the Essex newspapers, no doubt her swift marriage to the man she was to marry before long would be the next topic discussed on street corners.

Dorothy offered her the biscuit tin and Millie took one of Dorothy's shortbreads.

'And how have you been?' asked Millie, before taking a bite.

'Oh, you know,' said Derrick. 'Mustn't grumble. What with the new influx of teachers and the directives from the ministry every other day, the school keeps me out of trouble, and Dorothy has found herself something to keep her busy.'

Millie looked at her. 'So I'd heard. You're a volunteer at the special school, aren't you?'

'Yes, I've been there for what feels like a long time now,' Dorothy replied. 'I find teaching a deaf little one to use simple sign language or a spastic child to master a spoon so rewarding.'

'I heard you even started a choir with some of the older children,' Millie said.

Dorothy looked surprised. 'How on earth do you know about that?'

'The daughter of one of our patients has a child at the school and she was talking about it last week when I visited her,' Millie replied.

Derrick put his hand over his wife's. 'Dorothy's got a very special gift when it comes to children,' he said, smiling lovingly at his wife, 'especially handicapped ones.'

'I'm sure the headmistress at Jamaica Street School is very pleased to have you,' said Millie.

A melancholy smiled lifted the corners of Dorothy's mouth. 'Children, all children, are so precious and I wish I could do more. It helps me, too.' She glanced at the picture of her son. 'People keep telling me I'll get over it but I don't know.'

'They're wrong,' said Millie quietly. 'You'll never get over it; you just learn to live with it. But it's because of William that I've come to see you.'

The Joliffes looked at her curiously.

'When I arrived at work one morning a few months ago …' and Millie went on to tell them about baby Robert, finishing with, 'and so he was sent to the children's ward at ELCH.'

'How dreadful!' said Derrick.

'Not to mention wicked. To think of someone abandoning a new-born baby in an outhouse,' Dorothy added with feeling. 'I dread to think what would have happened if you'd not found him in time.'

'Yes it was awful. But in addition to everything else, Robert has mongolism.'

'The poor little lamb,' said Dorothy. 'We have a little chap, Trevor, at the school with the same condition.' She smiled fondly. 'He's such a loving little boy. He's only seven but has learnt all his colours, and so we've given him the job of sorting out the pencils at the end of the day. Do they know why some children are born that way?'

Millie shook her head. 'Some doctors think it's a defective egg, but others think it's caused by an infection the mother caught while she was carrying.'

'Like German measles?' asked Dorothy.

'Perhaps,' said Millie, 'But I'm not convinced, because if it were, children like Robert would be born to women of all ages instead of mainly to older mothers.' She shrugged. 'The truth is, no one really knows.'

'Well, I'm sure with all the new medicines and treatments the newspapers are for ever reporting, like the drops on sugar to prevent polio, some boffin will find a cure for it like they did with TB.'

'Probably so in time,' continued Millie, 'but the problem now for Robert is that when he gets to nine months old, the hospital will have to send him to a special institute.'

'Such a shame,' Derrick said, shaking his head. 'But what's that got to do with our William?'

Millie took another deep breath. 'With dozens of ordinary healthy babies in orphanages, Robert hasn't got a hope in hell's chance of being adopted unless some very special parents with love and patience decide to take him on.'

The Joliffes stared at her in astonishment.

'You mean us!' said Derrick.

'You and Dorothy are just the sort of parents who would give any child a happy life, but especially a dear little boy like Robert, who has had such a difficult start in life,' Millie said. 'I know it's a lot to ask of anyone, and I'm not expecting you to say or do anything right now. I'd just like you to think about what I've said.'

Derrick looked at his wife, but she shook her head firmly.

'I could never replace William.'

'Of course you couldn't, Dorothy. And you wouldn't be,' said Millie earnestly. 'What you would be doing is giving a poor child who will be locked away and forgotten in some old Victorian hospital in the back of nowhere the loving family that dear William couldn't live to enjoy.'

Dorothy gave a wan smile. 'I'm very sad for little Robert, but no.' Shaking her head, she pulled out her handkerchief and blew her nose.

Millie put her empty cup on the tray and stood up. 'I'm very, very sorry if I've upset you, Mrs Joliffe, and I do hope that you'll forgive me for asking.'

'Of course,' said Derrick.

Dorothy forced a smile. 'You've got a good heart, Sister Smith, and that's why Derrick and I are so very fond of you. But after the pain of losing William I don't feel I have the heart or the energy to love another child. I'm sorry.'

Chapter Twenty-Nine

Millie grasped the thin metal railing and looked at Alex, who was carrying Patricia plus Big Ted up the flight of steps to the third floor of Rowan House.

'Say "Come on, Mummy",' he said, as he reached the top and jiggled Patricia playfully in his arms.

Patricia clapped her hands as Millie smiled.

'Here I come,' she replied in a sing-song voice.

The police flats were built in blocks of eight, over four floors and with a central stairway. Like the storeys above and below them, the third-floor landing, where they were standing, was rectangular with two identical blue doors facing each other. The outer walls of the atrium were set together to form a lattice that raised the light in the communal space from dark to dim. There were four blocks of flats set around a central square, and they made up H Division's main housing accommodation.

Ducking to avoid the line of wet washing hanging on the line strung across the landing, Alex put the key in number fourteen and pushed the door. It opened halfway and then jammed.

'Probably the damp's made it swell,' he said, shoving it with his shoulder and then standing aside. 'Would *modom* like to inspect her new abode?'

Millie stepped over the threshold and on to a pile of tradesmen's leaflets. Alex followed her in and scraped the door closed.

The hallway was papered in a faded indeterminate design and it had lighter squares at regular intervals where pictures had once hung. The doors leading to the rooms were yellow with age and had dirty fingermarks around the handles.

He opened the door on his right. 'This is the kitchen.'

The kitchen was about the same size as her present one and, like the hall, hadn't seen a paintbrush for years. The floor was covered with brown lino that stuck to your feet as you walked across it.

'The estates office has promised to replace that,' he said with false joviality, nodding at a grease-covered cooker that wouldn't have looked out of place in a museum. 'And I think everything else will fit in.'

Millie cast her eyes around. 'The dresser might if I squeeze it along that wall, but I don't think the spin dryer will fit under there.' She pointed at the bleached-wood draining board. 'But it's all right because I can use the communal laundry on the ground floor. It will help me get to know the neighbours.' She opened the larder door and glanced at the dusty shelves and hanging cobwebs. Millie closed the door. 'Let's have a look at the bedrooms.'

Alex led her back into the hall. 'This will be Patricia's bedroom,' he said, opening the door.

As she stepped into the eight by ten room, Millie's stomach churned. 'What's that smell?'

'The paraffin heater,' Alex replied, pointing at the squat stove in the corner. 'I've borrowed two from the section-house sergeant to dry the bedrooms out a bit. I thought I'd decorate this room first.'

She forced a smile. 'I've seen some wallpaper with bunnies and bluebirds in Globe Paints.'

'I'll pop down tomorrow and get it. In fact, if you've got a moment, why don't you choose the paper for the lounge and we can get both at the same time? My shift is on a long weekend before starting nights next week, and so Georgie said he'd help me spruce the place up a bit. I'm aiming to get at least a couple of rooms done before we move in.'

He adjusted Patricia in his arms, and led Millie back into the hall.

'And this,' Alex continued, walking her into the next room, 'is ours.'

Again the smell of burning paraffin drifted over her.

Alex pointed at the space between the door and the wall. 'I thought the wardrobes could go here,' he continued, as Millie concentrated on keeping the contents of her stomach where they were. 'And the dressing-table will fit under the window. I'm doing an early on Thursday, so I thought we could go to

Wickham's after you've collected Patricia and order our bed.' He gave her a concerned look. 'Millie, are you all right?'

Millie nodded. 'It's just the fumes. Where's the facilities?'

Alex showed her the bathroom and toilet and Millie poked her head in. The antiquated china would need a good going over with neat bleach, but Millie judged it was sound enough. And they were inside, at least.

He led her into the room opposite and put Patricia down. She toddled off around the room, showing Big Ted the various points of interest.

'And this is the lounge,' Alex said, standing in the middle of the front room, which was only a little larger than her present one.

Millie strolled across to the window and opened it. The chilly air rushed in. She took a couple of deep breaths and her head cleared.

'It's a pity we're not facing the front,' he said as she gazed out at the concrete central quadrangle and the refuse bins overflowing with rubbish.

Millie turned and smiled. 'Well, it will be quieter away from the road.'

'It will look ten times better once I've decorated and got the lino down,' Alex went on, sweeping his arm across to illustrate the point. 'There's a carpet shop along Roman Road that does discount for police and so they will let me have it at cost, and this means that I can get the top stuff.'

'And the room is big enough to get the sofa, chairs and the sideboard in, and once the curtains are up it'll look snug and homely.' Millie put on her brightest smile. 'Aunt Ruby has offered to buy us a rug as a wedding present, and once that's down we can make this place look like something out of *Ideal Home*.'

Alex stood looking at her for a moment, and then his shoulders slumped. 'I'm so sorry, Millie.'

'For what?'

'For not having somewhere better for you and Patricia to live,' Alex replied.

'Oh, Alex.' Millie crossed the space between them and slipped her arms around him. 'It's fine, really it is.'

His mouth pulled into a line. 'No, it's not, Millie. Not by a long chalk, but I have to live in police accommodation and this is all the estate office could offer at such short notice.'

Millie took his face between her hands. 'It doesn't matter, Alex.' She stood on tiptoe and kissed him.

His stance remained rigid for a couple of seconds more, then he lifted her off her feet and hugged her. 'Are you sure?'

'Positive,' Millie replied, enjoying the strength of him surrounding her.

'Good.' He kissed her hard. 'Because I'm determined to marry you, Millie Patricia Smith, in four weeks and three days.'

Millie wound her arms around his neck. 'That's all right then, Alexander Patrick Nolan, because I'm determined to marry you too.'

He laughed and then closed his mouth on hers for another heart-stopping kiss.

'I promise this place won't be for long,' he said, releasing her lips. 'A few months at most. I have the allocation clerk's word that we'll get the next officer's house that falls vacant.'

Millie hugged him closer. 'We're together, and that's all that matters.'

She felt a small pair of arms hug her legs and Alex set Millie on her feet.

'I think someone's feeling left out,' he said, hunkering down to Patricia's level.

'More likely they're getting ready for their mid-morning sleep,' Millie said.

Alex took one of his soon-to-be-stepdaughter's hands and Millie caught hold of the other.

As they left the flat, he let go of Patricia to lock the door. She pulled away from Millie and ran giggling for the stairs

'No, you don't, miss,' said Millie, dashing after her and scooping her up.

She swung Patricia high, but as she did her head spun and she caught the handrail to steady herself.

Alex crossed the space between them in two strides. 'Are you sure you're all right, sweetheart?' he said, putting his arm around her.

'Yes, I'm fine,' she said, forcing a smile. 'I just lost my balance, that's all.'

Alex studied her face anxiously. 'You look a bit pale.'

'It's just the fumes, that's all.' Millie smiled. 'Honestly, Alex, I'm fine.'

He took Patricia from her and Millie slipped her arm in his.

As they made their way down the three flights of stairs to the street, Millie hoped to goodness that Alex was right about only being in Rowan House for a couple of months, because she didn't fancy lugging a pram plus a toddler up and down six flights of stairs each day.

Sneaking back along the hallway of the hotel, Millie slipped noiselessly back into the room. Alex was lying where she'd left him, sprawled across the bed.

As she closed the door, Millie crept across the bare floorboards to the small gas fire in the bricked-up hearth. Taking the box of matches from the mantelshelf above, she lit it. Standing up, she noticed the lacy nightgown bought especially for her wedding night lying unused in her overnight case. For a moment she considered slipping into it but then, throwing her dressing-gown over the footboard of the bed, she slipped back between the sheets naked, feeling wickedly wanton.

Alex turned towards her and his arm wrapped around her waist while his bare leg slid across hers, as if to anchor her beside him. Snuggled back beneath the warm bedclothes, Millie studied her husband's angular features in the pale winter light filtering under the heavy curtains. His hair was tousled, with several locks curled around his temples and ears. His eyes were closed and there was a contented smile on his lips.

The two nights' honeymoon at the Black Bull Hotel in Southwold on the Suffolk coast was her mum and Charlie's wedding present and after a frantic eight weeks of preparing for a wedding and putting together a home, both she and Alex needed the break. The landlord had given them the best suite at the top of the old coaching inn, but as the only other guests at this time of year were a couple of travelling salesmen, they had the entire third floor to themselves, which was just as well, considering the squeaky bed.

They'd arrived just after ten the night before and had fallen into each other's arms without bothering to unpack.

Alex shifted and his hold on her tightened. 'Morning, Mrs Nolan,' he said in a sleepy voice.

Millie reached up and pressed her lips on to Alex's cheek, enjoying the feel of his morning bristles on her mouth. 'Morning, sleepyhead.'

Alex pulled a face. 'It's all right for you, woman,' he said, running his fingers lightly over her hip and sending shivers through her. 'I was the one doing all the work last night.'

Millie shoved him playfully. 'All work, was it?'

Alex grinned. 'Carrying the cases up was.' He pressed his erection against her leg. 'The rest was all pure pleasure.'

Millie gave a throaty laugh and Alex raised himself up on to his elbow. He studied her face for a moment, and then covered her mouth with his. His hand smoothed upwards from her waist and cupped her breast. Millie ran her hands over the taut muscles of his arms and then wove her fingers through the springy thickness of his hair and kissed him back.

'God, I love you,' he said, releasing her lips.

'I know.'

'Are you happy?'

'I've never been more so,' Millie replied, running her fingers lightly over his dark chest hair.

They lost themselves in each other's eyes for a long moment, then his mouth met hers again as he shifted his weight over her.

There was a knock at the door.

'Breakfast!' a woman's voice called from behind the door.

Alex raised his head and smiled at her. 'Shall I send her away?'

Millie looked shocked. 'What and have the hotel staff talk about us? Not likely.' Her eyes twinkled. 'And besides, you've got to keep your strength up.'

Alex laughed, rolled out of bed and headed for the door.

'Put something on,' Millie told him in a loud whisper.

Alex grinned, snatched up his dressing-gown from the back of the door and shrugged it on. Tying it around him, he opened the door.

Tucking the sheet and blankets up to retain the warmth and her modesty, Millie sat up. She raised her left hand and twiddled her fingers, enjoying the sight of the thin band of gold on her third finger.

Alex thanked the maid and stepped back into the room carrying a breakfast tray with stubby legs at each corner. Setting it on the bed between them, he whipped off a covering cloth.

'I've got to see a man about a dog,' he said, winking at her. 'You make a start and I'll catch you up.'

Securing his dressing-gown again, he left the room.

Millie looked down at the loaded tray.

The kitchen had certainly pulled out all the stops. In addition to a rack of toast, butter, jam and a pot of tea, there were two plates each with two rashers of bacon, a fried egg, a sausage and a slice of fried bread cut into triangles. Millie's stomach protested at the sight.

She'd lost her breakfast yesterday for the first time, but thankfully her mother was seeing to Patricia and Ruby was on the telephone, so it had gone unnoticed.

Alex came back into the room. Discarding his dressing-gown on the chair, he got back into bed. Pouring them both a cup of tea, he picked up his cutlery. 'Go on, tuck in.'

Gingerly, Millie picked up a slice of toast, scraped a small knob of butter over it and popped it in her mouth. It stayed down, so she added a knob of plum jam and took another bite.

'Don't you want your bacon?' Alex asked, using the square of fried bread on the end of his fork to mop up a dollop of egg.

Millie shook her head. 'I've gone off it recently. You have it.'

'Are you sure?'

'Honestly, I couldn't eat it.'

Alex speared it and transferred it on to his own plate. 'I thought we could phone your mum before lunch to make sure Patricia's all right.'

'I bet she's having a whale of a time and is being spoilt rotten into the bargain,' Millie said.

'She's certainly got Charlie wrapped around her little finger,' he chuckled.

Millie laughed. 'And you.'

Alex grinned and cut through the centre of his egg. A dribble of yellow yolk oozed out and Millie put down her toast.

'Alex.'

'Mmmn?' he said, slicing through his sausage.

'I'm having a baby.'

He froze mid-cut and stared at her. 'You are?'

She nodded.

'But how? I mean, it's only been a couple of months.'

'It's almost twelve weeks since you stalked into Munroe House, and as I haven't had a monthly since then, by my reckoning I'm about ten weeks pregnant.'

'Are you sure?'

'Well, I haven't been to the doctor's yet, but I'm pretty certain.' A smile lifted the corners of Millie's mouth. 'Considering we've been making up for lost time, as you call it, on a daily basis, I'd be more surprised if I wasn't.'

Alex shoved his plate back on the tray and, lifting it off the bed, put it on the bedside table.

He gathered Millie into his arms and, cradling her gently, laid her down. He brushed his lips on hers in a tender kiss. 'Do you have any idea how happy you've made me?'

Millie reached up and curled a lock of his hair around her finger. 'As happy as I am, I expect?'

Alex caught her hand and pressed his lips on to her palm. His hand returned to her breast and he tucked her under him. As Alex's lips and hands sent excitement coursing through her body, Millie wondered if she would at last have a son with the green eyes of his father.

Chapter Thirty

Feeling the weight of the shopping bag dragging on her arm, Millie made the final two steps on to the second-floor landing and stopped as a little foot kicked her diaphragm.

There had been a few pursed lips, most notably aunt Ruby's, when they had returned from honeymoon and Millie had announced that she was nearly three months pregnant, but she didn't care. In fact, as happy as she'd been carrying Patricia, nothing could have prepared her for the added joy of having Alex just as excited as she was about the prospect of greeting their child. But as it had been just over four weeks since she'd stood in the Boatman and given another leaving speech to the girls at Munroe House, they didn't have much longer to wait.

Millie was holding tightly on to Patricia with her free hand, and now the little girl pulled forward.

'Just a moment, poppet,' Millie said, running her other hand over her thirty-three-week bump and catching her breath.

They had been allocated a pram shed in the adjoining yard where Millie locked Patricia's pushchair, but it wasn't large enough to house a coach-built pram, so when the new baby arrived, Millie would have to bounce her Silver Cross up and down the six sets of stairs each day.

The three women dressed in wraparound overalls standing by the first door stopped mid-conversation.

Millie smiled.

The brassy-looking blonde who lived on the ground floor flicked the ash from her cigarette, while the other two continued to regard her through narrow eyes.

The hierarchy of the Metropolitan Police Force was reflected in the social life of Rowan House. Constables' and sergeants' wives tended to clump together in their own groups, even having a loose subsection for the wives of CID officers. The three inspectors' wives in the flats kept themselves very much to themselves and so, despite her best efforts, as the only superintendent's wife in the whole block, Millie found herself excluded from all the day-to-day camaraderie between the other wives.

She took a deep breath and continued up the final flight of stairs, feeling the women's eyes boring into the space between her shoulder-blades as she did.

Letting go of her mother's hand as Millie opened the flat door, Patricia ran into the lounge to resume her game. Millie went into the kitchen and switched on the radio. Singing along to the tune, she unloaded the shopping and, as Alex would be home any time now, she put the kettle on in readiness.

As Patricia was playing contentedly in the lounge, Millie started preparing the vegetables for the evening meal. She'd just finished peeling the potatoes when there was a knock on the door. Hoping it wasn't a constable telling her that Alex had been called away to some incident or another, Millie wiped her hands on the tea towel and waddled to the front door. But instead of opening the door to a probationary constable with a shaving rash, Millie found Jim standing on her coconut welcome mat.

He was wearing a lightweight fawn-coloured summer suit and his usual Royal Air Force tie at his throat.

His mouth dropped open as his gaze fixed on her stomach.

'Surely you've seen a pregnant woman before?' Millie said, as excitable voices echoed up the stairwell from the landing below.

Jim pulled himself together. 'I'm sorry.' He raised his hat. 'Good afternoon, Millie. I need to talk to you. Can I come in?'

Out of the corner of her eye Millie caught sight of one of the women she'd passed on the stairs bobbing up and down as she peered through the wrought-iron banisters.

'I suppose you'd better,' Millie replied, holding the door back for him to enter.

Jim stepped in and Millie closed the door behind him, before leading him down the hall to the sitting room. Patricia stopped playing with her toys on the hearthrug and toddled over. Hugging her mother's legs, she stared suspiciously at the strange man.

Jim gave her a friendly smile. Patricia responded by pressing herself into Millie's leg a little tighter.

Jim raised his eyes. 'You're looking well, Millie. Positively blooming in fact.' His most charming expression spread across his face. 'When's the baby due?'

Millie regarded him coolly. 'What do you want, Jim?'

He ran his hat through his hands. 'It's a bit complicated, so do you mind if I sit down?'

Millie considered for a moment, then gave a sharp nod. Pulling his trousers up to prevent them kneeing, Jim sat in the fireside chair while Millie sat opposite him on the sofa. Patricia climbed on to what remained of her mother's lap.

He put his hat on the coffee table between them. 'I don't suppose you read about Lionel being killed in a car crash two months ago.'

'No, I hadn't. I'm sorry to hear that.'

'He was going too tight into a mountain bend just outside Monte Carlo in his new Jaguar,' Jim continued, 'which is typical of my brother. He always was one for the theatricals.'

Millie raised an eyebrow. 'So now you'll inherit it all.'

Satisfaction flit across Jim's face, swiftly followed by a frown. 'I'm afraid so, and that might be sooner rather than later. The doctor had already told Pater to lay off the drink or he won't last more than a year or two, but he's still getting through three bottles of Scotch a week.' Jim gave a resigned sigh. 'And so although it goes against every political grain in my body, it's my duty to take up the responsibilities of the estate when the time comes. Of course, I'll have to resign my seat.'

'What a shame,' said Millie evenly. 'You must be heartbroken.'

He regarded her suspiciously for a second, then his affable mask returned. 'I am, but I can still work for the cause in the Lords.' A hint of a smirk crept into his expression. 'And Hermione will be Lady Tollshunt: it's given me the upper hand with her father.'

'What's this got to do with me?' asked Millie.

'Well, it's like this, Millie,' said Jim, twisting his signet ring back and forth. 'Now Lionel's gone, everything rests on me, and after all the problems Hermione had after the pregnancy last time, she's expecting again. If it's a boy we want to make sure there's no hitch with him inheriting.'

'Problems?'

'She lost the first baby at five months. Something to do with the afterbirth, I think? I wasn't there at the time, as I'd just started a four-week fact-finding mission to Kenya, and couldn't get a flight back,' he explained in a matter-of-fact tone. 'Anyhow, at least it meant we could have the engagement announced in *The Times* and have a proper wedding instead of the hole-in-the-wall affair we'd planned to keep her condition hush-hush.' The smug smile returned. 'Now, there's every possibility of my son and heir making an appearance in a couple of months, so my solicitor feels I ought to tie up a few—'

The front door banged.

Patricia jumped off Millie's lap.

'Dadda!' she shouted as she dashed across the room.

Alex scooped her up as he stepped into the room. 'And how's my best girl today?' he asked, balancing her effortlessly in his arms.

Patricia responded by hugging his neck. He gave her a peck on the cheek and set her back on the floor. Patricia toddled off back to her game.

Millie stood up and went over to him. Alex slipped his arm around her waist and kissed her on the forehead, then his gaze rested on Jim.

'Alex, this is Jim,' she said, enjoying the feel of his hand resting lightly on her hip. 'His brother has died, so now he's going to be the next Baron of Tollshunt. He popped around to tie up a few loose ends.'

A hard-to-read smile spread across Jim's face as he stood up. 'Nice to meet you, old man,' he said, extending his hand.

Alex ignored it. 'We've already met,' he said flatly.

Jim studied him. 'I don't think so.'

'You probably won't remember,' Alex explained. 'Mainly because when we met I was covering for a colleague at Limehouse police station, and you were laying smashed out of your skull in a cell.'

Jim jabbed his finger at Alex. 'I bloody do remember – you're the inspector who wanted to charge me with assault.'

'It was GBH actually, chum. And you're the drunk who thinks that he's above the law because he's got friends with funny handshakes. I remember feeling sorry for your poor wife then. Of course, I never dreamed it was Millie; Smith, being such a common name. It's only when she told me she was married to an MP that the penny dropped.' Alex's mouth tightened. 'What sort of loose ends are you talking about?'

Jim withdrew his hand. 'As I was just explaining to Millie—'

'Mrs Nolan,' Alex cut in, his embrace tightening a little.

Jim's cordial smile flickered. 'Just so. I was explaining to your wife that I have some legal necessities to do with regard to Patricia in order to avoid any complications in the future.' His face formed into his earnest man-of-the-people expression. 'Naturally, I'll be happy to compensate you for your trouble.'

'Compensate me?' asked Alex.

'Indeed. And I'm prepared to be quite generous in order to speed the matter through.' He glanced around. 'It might help you provide something a bit better for your family.'

Alex's stance became rigid and his jaw muscles tensed.

Millie shot Jim a hateful look.

'Get out!' she shouted. 'We don't want your money and, as for signing anything, you can go to hell.'

'Now, hold on a moment, Millie,' Alex cut in. 'Let's not be hasty. Perhaps we should hear him out?'

Jim's smug expression returned. 'I knew we'd be able to come to some arrangement.'

'How generous are you actually prepared to be?' asked Alex.

'I thought perhaps to the tune of two thousand pounds,' Jim said.

Alex smiled. 'I was thinking more like five thousand. A nice round figure, don't you think, old boy?'

'All right,' said Jim without hesitation. 'Five it is.'

'And what is it you want my wife to do?'

'My solicitor needs Mrs Nolan to sign a few things on Patricia's behalf,' Jim replied blithely. 'I won't bore you with all the legal jargon, but it's just to tidy up Patricia's future. As soon as that's done, I'll write you a cheque. Or you can have cash if you prefer.'

Alex looked at Millie and smiled. 'Can you imagine that, Millie? Five thousand pounds in cash.'

Millie gazed up into her husband's dark-green eyes and a faint smile played around the corners of her mouth. 'No, I can't.'

'Are we agreed then, Mr Nolan?' Jim asked, thrusting out his hand again.

A hard, contemptuous expression flashed across Alex's face. 'I'd rather put my hand in a fire than take money from the likes of you.'

Jim flushed. 'Now look here.'

'No, you look here,' barked Alex. 'You must think we're stupid. "I won't bore you with the legal jargon",' he said, mimicking Jim's cultured accent to perfection. 'I bet you won't, because then you'd have to explain how you're trying to cut Patricia out of any claim on your family.'

'It not like that,' Jim protested.

'Isn't it?' said Alex. 'Well, we'll see, won't we? Because I'll tell you what we want before signing anything.'

Alarm flashed in Jim's face. 'Now hold on there. I'll not be blackmailed.'

'I'll get my solicitor to draw up the papers. I want to adopt Patricia,' Alex explained. 'And if you sign them and stump up for the court costs, then, and only then, will we help you tie up your "loose ends".' A hard glint flashed in Alex's eyes. 'Now, get out before I throw you out.'

Jim stared at them for a moment, then snatched his hat off the table and strode out of the lounge. Alex followed him and shut the front door firmly behind him.

'Cheeky bloody sod,' he said, glaring at the frosted glass.

Millie followed him into the hall. 'Do you think he'll do it?'

Alex nodded. 'I'll pop by to see my solicitors first thing and get them to draft the necessary. My bet is, we'll have his written agreement back within the week.'

Millie put her arms around her husband's neck, and then stretched up and kissed him.

His furious expression vanished instantly. 'What was that for?'

Millie smiled up at him. 'Because I love you.'

Alex pressed his lips on to hers. 'I'm glad to hear it.' His free hand rested lightly on her bump. 'And how's our little chap been?'

The baby answered by squirming around. Millie put her hand over Alex's and they exchanged a private smile. He kissed her again, and then let her go.

'I'd better get changed,' he said, unbuttoning his uniform jacket as he headed for the bedroom.

'I'll make us a cuppa while you do,' Millie replied.

Leaving Patricia to play, she went into the kitchen to reheat the kettle.

'What's this?' Alex asked, strolling into the kitchen holding an oil painting aloft in his right hand.

'Mum and Charlie brought them by earlier,' Millie replied, spooning tealeaves into the pot. 'I had them packed away in Mum's house and somehow then ended up on the van to Harold Wood. It's only because they are building an extension out the back, and Mum had to do some clearing out, that they came to light again.'

Alex looked astonished. 'Where on earth did you get them?'

She told him about Miss Moncrieff and Miss Gardener. 'I have four other paintings like that one and a dozen or so sketches in the box under the bed,' Millie said, handing Alex his tea

Alex laughed. 'So you saved them from the back of a lorry.'

'Yes,' said Millie.

He put his tea down. 'And there's more under the bed?'

'Yes, next to your old suitcase.'

Alex shot back into the bedroom and returned a few seconds later carrying the buff-coloured cardboard box in his arms. He put it on the kitchen table, pulled the lid off and took out a couple of chalk-and-ink sketches.

'This one *has* to go up on the wall,' he said, holding up the pencil drawing of Millie sitting beside Miss Gardener in her final hours.

'Do you like it?' Millie asked.

Alex nodded. 'I do. Very much.' He propped it up on the cruet set and stood back, regarding it as if he were in an art gallery. 'It captures your likeness but also your care and compassion.'

'Jim didn't agree,' Millie said. 'In fact, he called all Harry's work "childish rubbish".'

Alex looked up. 'Harry?'

'Miss Moncrieff's name was Harriet but all her pictures are signed Harry M,' Millie replied. 'I heard she'd died just a few months after her friend, in Paris. It was in the *East London Advertiser*.'

Alex peered at the signature in the bottom right-hand corner and an odd expression passed across his face. He picked up another oil painting and examined it closely.

'Would you mind if we put a couple of them up in the flat?' asked Millie.

Alex didn't reply but picked up the pen and ink studies of a very young Miss Gardener.

'Just in the lounge,' Millie continued. 'They'll brighten the room up no end.'

Alex looked up. 'Sorry,' he said, dragging his mind back from its wandering. 'Yes ... I mean no, of course I wouldn't mind.' His eyes drifted back to the pile of artwork. 'But I think they need a bit of attention first. Would you mind if I took a couple of them to a chap I know to get them reframed? Perhaps a black lacquer for the oils and polished beech for the sketches.'

Millie smiled as she took the picture from him. 'If you want to, but don't go mad and blow all our savings. They'll be hanging on a wall in number twelve Rowan House, not the National Gallery.'

Pushing open the door to Burdett Ward, Millie was hit afresh as the heat and foul smell of the ward enveloped her. The pleasant May sunlight streaming through the long windows had turned the usually cool ward into a greenhouse. The heat added to the pervading smell of human waste and unwashed bodies, and made the atmosphere in the long room more cloying than usual. Letting the door close behind her, Millie headed over to the nurse's station.

Nurse Connor, a well-rounded young woman with red-gold hair and a sprinkling of freckles over her nose, looked up.

'A grand afternoon to you, Mrs Nolan,' she said.

'And to you.' Millie looked around. 'No Sister this afternoon?'

'Herself's gone down in the almoner's office for something,' the staff nurse replied.

'Am I too late?'

Nurse Connor shook her head. 'I was sure you'd be in to give Robert his afternoon feed so, as he wasn't fretting for it, I left him for you. I've boiled the kettle and there's a sterilised bottle and teat in the tub.'

'Thank you,' said Millie.

She went into the milk room and quickly made up six ounces of Cow & Gate full cream then, collecting a clean muslin from the linen closet as she passed, Millie made her way to Robert's cot at the far end. He spotted her as she approached and waggled his hands by way of a greeting.

'Good afternoon, Master Robert,' Millie said, putting the bottle down and reaching in to pick him up. 'Time for tea.'

Robert's squat features lifted into a heart-melting smile as he gazed up at her. Millie smiled back, trying not to speculate if there would be anyone to cuddle him in the faceless institution he was bound for.

Giving him a swift kiss on the forehead, Millie settled him in the crook of her arm and offered him his afternoon feed.

He took a couple of mouthfuls and then let the teat slip from his lips, as he usually did. He was an unenthusiastic feeder at the best of times and the heat in the ward was adding to his lethargy. It would probably take him at least half an hour to polish off the six ounces.

The child in the cot opposite, a little chap with spasticity in all four limbs, started a high-pitched wail. Nurse Connor set aside her paperwork and came down the ward to investigate.

'Oh, Billy, me darling,' she said, reaching into the cot. 'You've gotten yourself in a right pickle and no mistake.'

Despite the Sister's insistence that the children shouldn't be called by their given names, many of the nurses, particularly the handful of Irish nurses on the ward, did. Millie noticed that since she'd brought in some clothes for Robert, some of the other children in the ward no longer spent the day dressed in the standard cotton nightdress.

Nurse Connor untangled Billy's stiff limbs from the metal bars and settled him back in the middle of the cot, before ambling over to Millie.

'Did the consultant do a round this morning?' Millie asked as she picked up Robert's feed again.

'That he did,' replied Nurse Connor. 'Came blustering in here at ten and was gone by twenty past. And ten minutes of that was writing notes in the office.'

Millie adjusted Robert in her arms and the baby inside her

protested at the squash. 'I supposed that paperwork included Robert's discharge letter for next week.'

Nurse Connor shook her head. 'I heard him muttering something about a month's deferment to Sister.'

'Did he?' A flutter of hope flared in Millie chest.

This must have reflected in her face because the nurse gave Millie a sympathetic look. 'I wouldn't be getting your hopes up, Mrs Nolan. It happens all the time. Probably something to do with not having a spare cot or having D and V in the orphanage. It's usually something like that.'

A child a few cots along from Robert started crying.

'I'll leave you to it,' said Nurse Connor and she headed back down the row of cots.

Picking up the bottle, Millie offered it to Robert again. He took a couple of mouthfuls and then pulled his legs up and grimaced.

Setting the bottle back on the locker, Millie sat him upright. Robert's head wobbled a little more than a normal nine-month-old baby's would, but he did what was expected of him and burped loudly.

'Good boy,' said Millie, pressing her lips to his downy head and closing her eyes.

A lump formed itself in her throat. She wondered if, for her own peace of mind, it would have been better if she hadn't taken such a personal interest in Robert's welfare. After all, it was drummed into nurses all through their training that only a bad nurse let her emotions intrude on her day-to-day work.

Millie dismissed the notion. Newly married and with a baby due, she wasn't able to give Robert a home, but she could make him feel loved, if only for his first few months.

She picked up the bottle again but as she did the ward doors swung open and the Sister burst through them.

'This way,' she instructed in a strident voice.

Millie's jaw dropped as she saw who was following the Sister.

Derrick and Dorothy Joliffe, dressed in their Sunday best and with expectant expressions on their faces, walked on to the ward.

'This way,' said Sister Burdett, ushering the couple between two cots. 'Now remember what Mr Edwards said. You're under no obligation to take the child and no one would think any the worst of you if that is your choice.'

As they reached the end of Robert's cot, Dorothy spotted Millie.

'Hello, Millie,' she said, smiling warmly. 'How are you?'

'Hello, Dorothy,' Millie replied, smiling back. 'I'm very well.'

'How long have you got to go now?'

'Just a couple of months, although Patricia was early, and so it could be sooner,' Millie replied.

Dorothy glanced around 'Is she with you?'

Millie shook her head. 'She's too full of beans to bring her to the ward, and so I popped her in to Cora, who used to look after her while I was at work.'

Dorothy smiled and then her motherly gaze shifted to the child in Millie's arms. 'And is this Robert?'

'Yes,' said Millie, sitting him up to face Dorothy.

Derrick reached out and tickled the infant's hand. 'Hello, young man.'

As if knowing he had to be on his best behaviour, Robert wriggled his hands and toes and gave a chuckle.

'He's certainly a happy little chap,' said Derrick.

'I have to confess,' the ward Sister said, 'I've rarely heard him cry, but of course you do realise that, like all mongol children, his mental age will never match his actual age.'

'But he has a very loving nature and with the right encouragement and patience who knows what he might be capable of?' added Millie.

Sister Burdett's lips formed a little bud. 'That may be so,' she conceded. 'But adopting a backward child is not something to be taken on lightly.'

'Believe me, Sister, we understand that, which is why we've asked to be considered as foster parents in the first instance,' said Dorothy.

The ward Sister clasped her hands in front of her and nodded approvingly. 'That's very sensible.'

'Would you like to feed him?' Millie asked Dorothy.

'If I may,' she replied.

Millie stood up and Dorothy took her place on the cot-side chair. Millie handed Robert to Dorothy, who tucked him into the crook of her arm. Robert wriggled a little until he was comfortable, then smiled up at the woman holding him.

Millie handed her the bottle. 'I'm afraid Robert can't take a huge amount in one go, so it takes a bit of time for him to polish off a bottle.'

'That's all right,' Dorothy replied. 'Our William was just the same.'

Derrick placed his arm around his wife's shoulders as she held Robert and they exchanged a bittersweet look. Dorothy offered Robert the bottle and obligingly he opened his mouth.

'What made you change your mind?' Millie asked softly, watching his little chin go up and down.

The Joliffes exchanged another look and then Dorothy spoke. 'A couple of days after your visit I was dusting William's photo, and kissed it as I always did without thinking, but when I felt the cold glass on my lips, the hard and dead feeling inside had gone somehow. I panicked, thinking I'd stopped loving William, but,' Dorothy gave a bashful smile, 'I know it might sound silly, but as I stared at the picture of him smiling, I knew the best way of remembering William wasn't to stare at a frozen image in a frame, but to give some other child, like little Robert here, the life we'd hoped to give William.'

'Since then we've talked to several families with mongol children,' Derrick continued, 'and the more we did, the more it seemed right to consider fostering Robert, with a view to adopting him eventually. We wanted to be absolutely sure we could give him a loving family life and that's why it's taken us so long to actually come to visit him. Isn't it, love?'

'Yes it is,' Dorothy replied, giving her husband a radiant smile.

The familiar lump reasserted itself in Millie's throat but this time for quite a different reason.

She straightened her dress over her stomach bump. 'Well, I ought to be off. I've got to pick up Patricia and get something for supper in the market before the head of the house gets home.'

'It's lovely to see you, Millie,' said Derrick, smiling warmly at her. 'And good luck with the little one when he or she arrives.'

'Thank you,' said Millie. 'And perhaps I'll see you, Dorothy, at the Thursday afternoon baby clinic at St Aiden's in a couple of weeks.'

Dorothy looked up. 'I'm sure you will.' A smile lifted the corners of her lips. 'And thank you again, Millie, for everything you've done.'

Millie rolled over and woke up as a band of pain tightened around her middle. Not again! she thought as her hands went on to her stomach, which was rock hard. As the tightness subsided, she turned her head on the pillow.

'Alex,' she said.

He grumbled something and changed position.

Her muscles tensed as the next contraction started and she grabbed his arm. 'Alex!'

He shifted again but this time opened his eyes. 'What?'

'The baby's coming.'

He sat bolt upright and looked at her. 'Are you sure?'

Millie gave him an exasperated look before pressing her lips together firmly to ride another powerful contraction.

'Call the maternity hospital,' she gasped as the wave peaked. 'And tell them the contractions are less than a minute apart and that they must hurry.'

Alex jumped out of bed and stripped off his pyjamas.

'Why didn't you wake me sooner?' he asked, dragging on his pants and trousers.

Millie let out a long breath. 'Because I've only just woken up myself.'

Alex looked relieved and his shoulders relaxed. 'Well, we've got a bit of time, then.'

'I wouldn't count on it. I only just got to the hospital with Patricia and second babies are often much quicker.' She clutched her stomach as another strong labour cramp took hold.

'All right,' said Alex, buttoning his shirt skew-whiff.

Millie nodded and a bead of sweat dripped off her brow.

'Will you be okay till I get back?' he asked, hopping on one leg to get his shoes on.

'Yes, but leave the door on the latch,' Millie replied, taking a deep breath in readiness for the next surge.

'I won't be long.' He gave her a swift kiss on the top of her head. 'I love you.'

As he dashed out of the room, Millie rolled awkwardly on to

all fours to ease the pressure on her back and then, spreading her knees to take the weight off a little more, she gripped hold of the headboard. By concentrating on her breathing she managed to stay on top of two more contractions and was just bracing herself for the next when the sensation faded for a long moment before the urge to push swept over her.

She raised her head and focused on the small blue and green flowers of the wallpaper as she fought the impulse to bear down. Gripping the headboard until her hands hurt she rode the wave until it finally subsided and her shoulders sagged. There was a damp sensation on the inside of her thighs but, thank goodness, not enough to indicate her waters had gone. At least with them intact there was a chance of holding on until the midwife arrived.

As the tight feeling gathered in her throat and chest again, Millie locked her jaw. Again the almost overwhelming urge to push caused her shoulders to curl, but she lifted her chin to reduce the downward pressure. Just as the surge reached its peak, she heard the front door open and Alex hurried into the room.

'She said she'll be about twenty minutes. What's happening?'

Millie gave him a wry smile. 'Then I reckon she's going to be ten minutes too late.'

'Oh my God!' Alex raked his hair. 'Shall I boil some water?'

'We haven't got time,' Millie replied. 'Just get some towels and my nurse's bag.'

Alex dashed out of the room but was back within seconds, clutching a handful of warm towels from the airing cupboard, and her case.

He put them beside her on the bed. 'What now?'

'Spread the largest towel under me, then help me to turn over,' Millie said, feeling a thickness pressing down through her pelvis.

He did as she asked and propped the pillows behind her. She flopped back for a second and closed her eyes.

'What shall I do?' Alex asked, kneeling beside her.

The full sensation spreading down between Millie's legs increased and she opened her eyes. 'The baby's head is low and I won't be able to hold back when the next contraction starts, so I want you to get between my legs and be ready to help the baby out.'

'I can do that.' he said, looking wide-eyed. 'It's going to be fine. Isn't it?' He shuffled around and took up position. 'I mean, women have been having babies for thousands of years before there were hospitals and doctors and—'

'Are you ready?' she asked firmly.

Alex rubbed his hand together and clapped. 'Ready.'

Millie lifted her nightdress and spread her knees apart as she felt the urge to push gathering pace. Gritting her teeth and grabbing her knees, she curled forward as her body squeezed around the baby to force it out. As she felt herself stretch wider, she focused on making every second of the contraction count.

'I can see the head,' Alex said.

The blood pounded through Millie's ears, muffling his voice.

As the cramp faded, Millie reached down and felt the baby's head. She ran an experienced finger around, feeling the position.

'Good. It's facing the right way,' she said with a sign of relief.

Alex grinned. 'And he or she has got lots of black hair.'

Millie gave a feeble smile.

'I'm sure everything's fine,' she said in as calm a voice as she could manage with the next wave already gathering. 'But to be sure, I want to deliver this baby in the next couple of contractions, so when I start pushing, you need to be ready.'

Alex shifted, cupped his hands together and gave her a determined nod.

The tell-tale sensation of her stomach muscles drawing down started again. As the instinctive force of the contraction engulfed her, Millie gripped her knees and closed her eyes. Tucking in her chin, she did what she'd instructed countless women to do over the years, and pushed into her bottom.

Alex's hands brushed the inside of her thighs. Millie felt herself stretch until she felt she would burst, then suddenly the tension went.

'The head's out,' yelled Alex manoeuvring between her legs.

The contraction subsided and Millie shook the sweat from her eyes. 'Just support the head until the—'

'It's turning! The head's turning!'

'That's good, Alex, now let it rest in your hands so I can check the cord.' Millie reached down, but then another wave gripped her.

She cried out and bunched forward.

'Come on, baby,' laughed Alex, his eyes shining with happiness.

Millie felt a popping sensation inside, then water gushed down her legs. The baby slithered down and out on the wave of the amniotic fluid.

'It's a boy,' Alex cried, holding his son firmly. 'Look, Millie, it's a boy!'

Millie looked at her son being held aloft by his father and her heart swelled with love for them both. The baby wriggled, coughed and let out a long wail. His colour went from bluey-grey to pink in an instant.

Alex laughed. 'He got a good set of lungs.'

'And probably his father's green eyes.'

Alex gave Millie a smile she would remember for a thousand years, and then he turned the baby on his back, cradling him lovingly in his outstretched hands.

'Lay him down on a clean towel,' Millie said, scrabbling for her nurse's bag on the bed beside her.

Alex kissed his son's damp head and then gently placed him on a fluffy white towel. Millie pulled out a packet with clean clamps and a sterile pack containing a cord ligature. With an expert hand she clamped off the cord and tied the length of silk around the cord three inches away from the root.

'Now wrap him up and put him on me,' Millie said, stretching out her hands to hold him for the first time.

Alex rested their son gently on her stomach and Millie cradled him to her warmth. Popping her little finger in his mouth, she checked for retained mucus, but it was clear. The baby stopped crying as his rooting reflex took over. Cradling him in the crook of her arm, she kissed his blood-smeared head then sank back exhausted on the pillows behind her.

Alex spread his hands. 'What should I do now? You know, with the afterbirth and everything?'

Millie gave a happy, tired smile. 'Just hold me.'

He shuffled up the bed beside her and, putting his arm around her shoulders, pressed his lips on to her forehead.

'Thank you,' he said, looking at her with tears in his eyes.

There was a knock on the front door. 'Yoo-hoo!' shouted a woman's voice. 'Did someone call the midwife?'

'In here,' shouted Alex.

Millie cuddled her son a little closer, rested her head on her husband's chest and closed her eyes.

Doris and Ruby stood either side of the Silver Cross, smiling down at Daniel Alexander Arthur Nolan, who was sleeping off his midday feed. His sister was standing on tiptoes with her head between the pram handles just to keep an eye on the proceedings.

'He's just such a darling,' said Doris, gazing adoringly at her grandson.

A dewy-eyed expression lit Ruby's impeccably made-up face. 'I don't think I'm exaggerating when I say that our Daniel is the most handsome boy in the world.'

They were right, of course.

After his son's hurried entrance into the world at three-thirty in the morning, he'd been introduced to his sister when she walked into the bedroom, rubbing her eyes, at seven o'clock. Patricia had taken her role as older sister very seriously and had been helping Millie by fetching nappies and holding the talcum powder ready. Alex had waited until a respectable hour before telephoning Doris to tell her about the newest addition to the family. She and Charlie had arrived four hours later to simper and coo over their grandson.

After Charlie had slapped Alex on the back at least a dozen times and shoved a bottle of Johnnie Walker in his hand, he'd departed, leaving Doris to help with the new arrival. She'd installed herself in Patricia's room on the camp bed and had taken over all the domestic chores, leaving Millie to concentrate on her new son.

Alex had managed to wangle a day off after the birth, but had to return to work the day after. Thankfully he was on an early week, so they had been able to spend the evening together as a family while Doris tactfully visited old friends in the neighbourhood.

'And he's so advanced, Amelia,' said Ruby, twisting her head to get a better look at the sleeping baby. 'I swear he understood his name when your mother called him.'

'Oh, aunt Ruby,' Millie laughed, 'he's only four days old.'

'Nevertheless,' continued Ruby, 'I can tell he's very intelligent.'

'And just so, so adorable I could eat him,' added Doris, wrinkling up her nose in girlish joy.

Millie laughed. 'Well, if he takes after his father in looks and brains, he won't go far wrong.'

Leaving her pram-side vigil, Ruby returned to the sofa and, tucking her skirt under her, sat down. Collecting her beloved golliwog from the chair where she'd left it, Patricia climbed on to Millie's lap.

'I must say,' Ruby picked up her teacup from the occasional table and took a sip, 'that although, as you know, I had reservations about Alex, he has turned out to be an excellent husband,'

'And father,' Doris chipped in, sitting next to her sister. 'I don't think Patricia could have a better dad, and yesterday he even changed Daniel's nappy.'

'Never!' gasped Ruby, as if she'd been told Churchill was really a Communist.

'Oh, yes, Ruby,' said Doris proudly. 'My Arthur would have jumped in the canal before he'd do such a thing, and yet there was Alex, a safety-pin in his mouth, folding a nappy. And it was a stinker.'

Ruby's red lips folded tightly together. 'Well, I suppose what with being a policeman he's got a stronger stomach than most. But I don't hold with these modern ways. When we were young you were scared stiff of your father. And a good thing, too.' She shook her head. 'Children are coddled nowadays and all it does is make them spoilt.'

Millie kissed Patricia's chestnut curls. 'Well, I'd rather my children have a father who'll change their nappies than take his belt off to them. And if that's spoiling them, then I'm all for it.'

'So am I,' said Doris emphatically.

Ruby rolled her eyes and took a new pack of twenty Kensitas Milds from her handbag. 'Any news on a house?'

Millie pushed the ashtray on the coffee table towards her aunt and shook her head. 'Alex has been on to the estates office for months now, but there isn't a police house in East London for neither love nor money and, according to the sergeant who allocates them, there's not likely to be for some time.'

'If you'd been a bit more sensible you could have your own place by now,' said Ruby.

Millie sighed. 'Aunt Ruby, we've been through this before. Alex was adamant he wouldn't take Jim's money out of principle, and I agree with him.'

Ruby flicked her gold lighter into flame. 'Having principles is all well and good but principles don't—'

The front door opened and a two-note whistle echoed through the house.

'Anyone at home?' Alex called from the hallway.

Patricia jumped off Millie's lap and rushed to greet her father.

'Don't mention anything about the house, aunt Ruby,' Millie said, giving her aunt a pointed look.

Ruby smiled and tapped her cigarette on the edge of the glass ashtray.

Alex walked in with Patricia in his arms. He'd taken his jacket off, loosened his tie and undone the detachable collar and the top button of his shirt. A little thrill of excitement ran through Millie as she imagined running her fingers under his police shirt.

'Hello, everyone,' he said, and then spotted Millie's aunt. 'And Ruby, too, nice to see you, love,' he said, laying on his Cockney accent.

Doris turned to hide a smile. 'I'll put the kettle on,' she said, heading for the kitchen.

Ruby's smile stiffened a little. 'Hello, Alex.'

His attention returned to Millie.

'Good day?' she asked.

He crossed the room and kissed her. 'All the better for coming home.'

They exchanged a private look and then he straightened up and strolled over to the pram in the corner. 'And how's the chip off the old block doing?'

'Eating and sleeping,' Millie replied.

Alex nodded. 'And how are you, Patricia? Have you been helping Mummy?'

She babbled a lengthy explanation of the day's events and pointed to the pram.

'I'm glad to hear it,' said Alex, kissing her again and putting her down.

She went over to her box of bricks in the corner and Alex flopped on to the chair beside Millie.

Ruby stubbed out her cigarette. 'Amelia says you haven't managed to get a police house yet,' she said, reaching for the packet on the coffee table and taking another.

'Aunt Ruby!' said Millie glaring at her aunt.

Alex's jaw tightened for an instant, and then he smiled. 'There's a housing shortage.'

Ruby looked puzzled. 'But I thought you were saving to put a deposit on one.'

'Fifty pounds is a lot of money,' he replied. 'Especially now Millie's not working.'

'What about all the extra hours you put in?' asked Ruby.

Although Alex's smile widened, his eyes took on a hard glint. 'Superintendents don't get overtime.'

Millie forced a jolly smile. 'Rowan House isn't half as bad as it looks, aunt Ruby, and once Daniel's a bit bigger, I'll sign on the midwifery bank at the London in order that I can do the odd shift or two when Alex is home.' She placed her hand over Alex's and smiled at him. 'We're happy as we are for the time being.'

Ruby ran her thumb over the flint of her lighter. 'That's all well and good, but—'

'I was reading in *Modern Science* the other day that cigarettes can make youngsters prone to asthma,' mentioned Alex conversationally. 'And so would you mind, Ruby, not smoking around my children?'

Ruby's Cherry Crush mouth dropped open and her neck flushed to match it.

Alex held her gaze then, after a long, heavy silence, she lowered her eyes and tucked the cigarette back in the carton.

Doris returned with a tray of tea and put it in the middle of the low table, then poured everyone a cuppa while Ruby regarded the wall closely.

'There's a letter from the solicitor for you behind the clock, darling,' Millie said.

'Good,' said Alex, taking the cup Doris was offering him. 'I reckon another month and we'll have the adoption signed and sealed.'

'That will be a weight off your minds,' said Doris.

'It certainly will be,' agreed Millie.

Alex picked up his cup again and was just about to take a sip when there was a knock at the door.

'Blast,' he said, dragging himself out of the chair.

'I hope you've not been called back,' said Millie.

'So do I,' he called over his shoulder.

Buttoning his shirt, collar and tie as he stomped out of the room, Alex grabbed his jacket from the peg to comply with police regulations for an officer opening his own front door.

Daniel gave a little cry. Millie stood up and went over to the pram. He was awake and looking around, and Millie picked him up. She heard Alex talking to someone at the door and then he came in holding a large manila envelope.

'It's a registered delivery,' he said, turning it over. 'From an address in King Street, Piccadilly.'

Millie looked puzzled. 'Do you know anyone in Piccadilly?'

Alex shook his head and tore open the letter. He pulled out a three-page letter and as he scanned through the pages, his eyes stretched wide.

'What's it about?' asked Millie.

Alex returned to the first page but didn't answer.

Millie and her mother exchanged baffled looks. And then Alex let out a loud 'Woo-hoo!' and raked his fingers through his hair.

'Alex?'

He grabbed Millie around the waist and planted a noisy kiss on her lips. Patricia jumped up and ran over. Alex lifted her in his arms and kissed her too, then, hugging them all, he threw back his head and laughed.

Millie laughed. 'What on earth has got into you?'

Alex stopped her words with his mouth for another long kiss and then released her. 'The letter is from Christie's, the big auction house up West.' He laughed again. 'When I said I was taking Harry Moncrieff's pictures to be reframed, I forgot to mention I also took them to my old professor at Birkbeck College to take a look at them.'

Millie looked puzzled. 'I don't understand.'

'When you showed me the painting you'd got from an old lady, I thought they were good – very good – but when you called her Harry, it rang a bell. I wasn't sure, so I didn't want to say too much, which is why I took them for a second opinion. My old tutor found them very interesting and asked if he could send them for an expert evaluation.' Alex flourished the letter and his eyes twinkled. 'And this is it. It says, and I quote, "We were most gratified to be given the chance to peruse the three oils attributed to Miss Harriet Moncrieff. Since she died last year, there has been a great deal of interest in the art world. Several oils of hers have fetched in excess of a one and a half thousand pounds at auction."'

'One and a half grand,' echoed Ruby incredulously.

'"And now art connoisseurs and galleries in New York and Boston are taking note of her work,"' continued Alex, grinning at them. '"Although there are no guarantees, and buyers are notoriously fickle, Mr Nolan, having seen the five sketches you sent for evaluation I would estimate their value at being somewhere between two to three hundred apiece."'

'Two to three hundred!' squealed Doris, covering her mouth with her hands.

'"And the two oils of Paris in the early nineteen-twenties,"' continued Alex, as Millie watched him, open-mouthed, '"could easily fetch up to six or seven thousand each, if not slightly more."'

Millie snatched the letter from him with her free hand and scanned down it, then looked up at his grinning face.

'This means ...' Millie's brain suddenly couldn't match the words to her mouth.

Alex put his free arm gently around her and drew her and Daniel to him. 'It means if you're happy to sell them, my love, I won't ever have to ring the police accommodation office ever again, because the Nolan family will be moving into their own nice double-fronted house with four bedrooms, an inside bathroom and a long garden somewhere posh like Forest Gate or Manor Park.' He pressed his lips on to her forehead. 'Does that meet with your approval, Mrs Nolan?'

Millie looked up at the man she'd loved for what felt like forever, as he held their daughter in one arm, and herself and their son in the other. 'Yes, Mr Nolan,' she said, smiling up into his expressive green eyes, 'that most certainly does.'

Acknowledgements

It's given me a great deal of satisfaction to bring Millie's story to a happy ending with *All Change for Nurse Millie*. Again I've tried to keep true to the strands of her and my profession as a District and Queen's Nurse in the early days of the NHS, and the change of mood as the country finally moved out of the austerity years and into the 1950s.

As always, I would like to mention a few books, authors and people, to whom I am particularly indebted.

Again, to ensure the treatments and care Millie gave her patients was authentic to the period I returned to the nursing biographies I found so helpful for *Call Nurse Millie*, including Lucilla Andrews' *No Time for Romance*, Edith Cotterill's *Nurse on Call* and *Yes, Sister, no, Sister,* by Jennifer Craig, which although set in Leeds gives much of the flavour of post-war nurse training and culture, as does *Of Sluices and Sister*, by Alison Collin. I garnered a couple of self-published gems in my travels including *My Life and Nursing Memories (from 1914–2008)* by Nurse Corbishley, and *Nurse* and *Yes, Sister* by Dorothy Gill. I, of course, read Jennifer Worth's accounts of 1950s East London in her popular books, *Call the Midwife* and *In the Shadow of the Workhouse*, although the most detailed account of a pre-NHS Nursing Association came from Irene Sankey's biography, *Thank you Miss Hunter* (unpublished manuscript). Ms Sankey became the Superintendent at the East London Nursing Society in 1946 and it's her detailed accounts of that time that most helped me bring the Munroe House nurses to life.

I've also drawn on *Learning to Care, A history of nursing and midwifery education at the Royal London Hospital, 1740–1993*, by Parker and Collins (1998) in association with the London Hospital Museum, and *The London Volume II 1840–1948*, Clark-Kennedy (1963).

For Millie's professional life I have used several text books of the period, including *Handbook of Queen's Nurses* (1943); a 1940 edition of Faber's *Nurse's Pocket Encyclopaedia and Diary and Guide*; *Parenthood, Design or Accident*, Fielding 4th edition (1943); *Psychiatry and Mental Health*, Rathbone-Oliver (1950); *Nursing and disease of Sick Children*, Moncrieff 4th edition (1943); and *A Short Text Book of Midwifery*, Gibberd (1951), which has a number of medical illustrations that are not for the faint hearted.

For Jim's political background in Atlee's post-war Labour Government I delved into Tony Benn's *Years of Hope: diaries, letters and papers, 1940–62*, which is widely acknowledged as being one of the most authoritative political records of the period.

For general background of the period I used *Our Hidden Lives*, Simon Garfield (2005); *Nella Last's Peace*, ed. P & R Malcomson (2008); *Austerity Britain 1945–51* by David Kynaston (2007); and although I can vividly remember the warmth and neighbourliness of the old streets around where I grew up, I added *The Only Way is Essex*'s very own Nanny Pat's account of her East End childhood, *Penny Sweets and Cobbled Streets* to my collection of East End memoirs this year, along with Shire Library's *British Family Cars of the 1950 and 1960s* and *Make Do and Mend*, which is a reproduction of the official second world war leaflets.

I also used several post-war photographic books including '*Couldn't afford Eels' Memories of Wapping 1900–1960*, Leigh (2010); *The Wartime Scrapbook*, Opie (2010); *The Forties, good times just around the corner*, Maloney (2005); and, although it is slightly later than the period Millie's story is set in, *London's East End, a 1960s album*, Lewis (2010), as this documented wonderfully the sights and sounds I remember as a child.

All Change for Nurse Millie also gave me the excuse for another pleasant afternoon with Doreen Bates, the Queen's Nurse who'd been an invaluable source of first-hand knowledge of what it was like to nurse in East London in the early 1950s.

My family also have been ruthlessly exploited again by having some of their stories and anecdotes included in *All Change for Nurse Millie*. You can read more about them and some of the locations used in the book on my website www.jeanfullerton.com

I would also like to thank a few more people. Firstly my very own Hero-at-Home, Kelvin, for his unwavering support, and my three daughters, Janet, Fiona and Amy, for not minding too much that they are literary orphans sometimes. My fellow author and chum Fenella Miller and my brilliant critique partners and friends Elizabeth Hawksley and Jenny Haddon. I'd also like to thank Louis Wacket who, as a practicing midwife, cast an experienced eye over William Joliffe's delivery to make sure I'd got it clinically correct.

Once again my lovely agent Laura Longrigg, whose encouragement and incisive editorial mind helped me to see the wood for the trees. Lastly, but by no means least, a big thank you once again to the editorial team at Orion, especially Jenny Parrott and Laura Gerrard, for once again turning my 400+ page manuscript into a beautiful book.